THE ECHO OF A KISS

Roderic got to his feet, then reached down to give Maryana a hand. She took it and rose, and would have held on to it longer if he hadn't released her to lead his horse into its stall. She thought that she must crave his touch as some men seemed to crave wine.

"I came to warn you," she said when he returned to her. A small silence fell between them that felt both thrilling and very dangerous.

"I think you should go away for a while," she said, forcing her thoughts away from the way he made her yearn for him. "Until after the king as come and gone. My uncle fears a rebellion if you are arrested, but Miles may yet persuade him, and when the king and his troops arrive. . . ."

"I'm not leaving my lands and my people."

"Then will you at least promise me there'll be no more provocations?"

"Of course—as long as he does nothing to provoke *me*!"

Angry now at his stubbornness, Maryana turned away and started toward the stable doors. "I think perhaps you have a death wish, Roderic!"

He caught up to her quickly and took her arm, spinning her around to face him. "That might have been true before I met *you*. But now I have something to live for."

His kiss was soft and teasing—and it ended so quickly that she had barely registered its imprint on her parted lips. And then he was gone, leaving her to the echoes of his words.

Prince Of Thieves

Saranne Dawson

LOVE SPELL BOOKS NEW YORK CITY

LOVE SPELL®

December 1998

Published by

Dorchester Publishing Co., Inc.
276 Fifth Avenue
New York, NY 10001

ISBN 0-505-52288-8

The name "Love Spell" and its logo are trademarks of Dorchester Publishing Co., Inc

Printed in the United States of America.

Prince Of Thieves

Chapter One

Maryana stared at the craggy hills and dark, impenetrable forests and still could not believe her fate. For the past several hours, despite the heaving seas, she had stood at the rail of the small sailing ship and watched the landscape grow ever more distinct. But she had continued to hope that this was merely a nightmare from which she would soon awaken to find herself back home in bed, with the meadows and gently rolling hills of Neran just beyond her windows.

She knew, of course, that it wasn't a nightmare, but her benumbed brain was as yet unwilling to face reality. How had it come to this: that she must leave her beloved home and travel across these angry seas to the forbidding land of the Sakims?

Well, she knew the answer to that, too, though she didn't much like it. She was here because her father had died and she was now to become the ward of an uncle she'd met a few times as a child, but couldn't really remember.

Ignoring the precariously tilting deck, she released her grip on the rail and instead clenched her fists in helpless anger. How unfair it all was! Here she was, a woman, not a mere child—and furthermore, she was a woman who had managed her father's huge estate quite capably since his health had begun to fail. And now she was to be reduced to this—becoming the ward of her uncle in some gloomy Sakim castle he'd gained as the spoils of war. It was enough to make her wish that she'd acted on an earlier impulse to enter a convent rather than make this journey. Only her certainty that the nuns would, in short order, discover her lack of piety had prevented her from doing just that.

Her cousin Julienne, secure in her marriage to a fool with a title and great landholdings, hadn't even spared her any sympathy, instead reminding her that if she'd only done as her father wished and married Miles Foulane, she would have remained as mistress of the chalet and lands that were her inheritance.

Maryana made a most·unladylike sound of disgust and tossed her head, sending her golden hair flying in the stiff breeze. She'd unbound it the moment she boarded the ship, having decided that if she was going to a land of savages, she might as well look like one.

Behind her, the sailors began to trim the sails as the ship moved into the small harbor, where she could now see a cluster of small houses and other buildings and men moving about. Through her mind ran all the stories she'd heard about the Sakims—none of them were pleasant.

Her people had fought these enemies across the narrow strait for centuries, sometimes winning, but more often losing. Now, however, was a period of victory for her people, the Nerans, and now her uncle, Baron DeLay, ruled this portion of the Sa-kim lands.

Maryana remained at the rail as the ship ma-neuvered up to the dock. She studied the men she could now see awaiting the ship's arrival. One look at their size and darkness told her that they were all Sakims. Where was her uncle? She knew from the captain that, thanks to favorable winds and rel-atively calm seas, they were arriving ahead of schedule.

The ship docked and the gangplank was quickly lowered. A youth sent by the captain inquired if she would prefer to wait on board until her escort arrived. Maryana shook her head. She was eager to be off the ship, even if she had to step onto Sa-kim soil. So she smoothed her tangled curls with her hands and disembarked, paying no attention at all to the stares of the men waiting to unload the vessel.

She had, however, taken note of one man, a tall Sakim who was lounging casually against a stack of crates. In truth, she'd noticed him chiefly be-cause of the handsome stallion whose reins he held. It was a seeming incongruity, since he was dressed no better than the other men. So, after one brief glance, she paid him no attention—that was, until he strode up to her and planted himself di-rectly in her path.

Maryana felt only the faintest stirring of alarm. After all, the captain and his crew were nearby. So she intended only to favor him with an annoyed look at his impertinence before turning away.

Instead, her breath caught in her throat as she met the very direct gaze that pierced her, seeming to lay bare all her secrets. He was very tall and broad-shouldered, and now she could see that his attire, while rather shabby, was definitely of better quality than that of his fellow Sakims who were unloading the ship.

But for all that, it was his eyes that caught and held hers effortlessly: the darkest, most deep-set eyes she'd ever seen, gleaming now with a wicked silver fire. He smiled at her, revealing a set of even white teeth above a strong cleft chin. Then he suddenly swept an elaborate bow in her direction, clearly mocking Neran customs.

"The lady Maryana, I presume?" he said in an accented version of the tongue they shared.

But before she could even think of responding, he had gone on, studying her with obvious amusement. "Then again, perhaps not. Surely no Neran lady would go about with her hair unbound, like a common harlot. Have you come to ply your trade here? If so, that hair would win you much gold—if we had any left, that is."

Maryana felt a flush creep across her fair skin, partly from embarrassment and partly from a rising anger at his unforgivable behavior.

"How do you know who I am?" she demanded. She could not believe that her uncle would have sent this man to fetch her.

"There is little that escapes my notice. These are, after all, *my* lands."

"I don't know who you are, but I *do* know that this is my uncle's land: Baron DeLay."

He smiled again. "Temporarily."

She was trying to formulate a suitable reply to that when she saw a carriage approaching at high speed. He turned toward the sound, and she expected him to vanish quickly. But instead, he merely stood there as the carriage came to a halt a short distance away.

"The carriage is mine, too," he said. "Though to be honest, I never used it all that much."

The carriage driver climbed down and approached her. She saw, to her very great relief, that he was Neran. But she also noticed that he seemed rather wary of the Sakim stranger.

What is happening here? Maryana wondered.
How can a victor be afraid of someone he's conquered? She was still asking herself that question
as she was helped into the carriage. And she
couldn't quite prevent herself from turning to
watch the stranger from the carriage as it clattered
away. He made another mocking bow, then swung
lightly into the saddle and rode off in the opposite
direction.

Her uncle's letter had referred to his new home
as a castle, but to Maryana's eyes, it looked more
like a fortress: cold and forbidding. She stared up
at the high stone walls and the rounded, crenellated towers visible beyond them and decided that
it was well suited to the land in which it sat, a dark,
mysterious land of thick forests and narrow valleys
and steep hills—so very unlike the rolling meadows and small wooded copses of her home.

The great wooden gates stood open and they
drove through. She stared in growing dismay at
her new home: a huge pile of dark stone with numerous towers and tall, narrow windows. She'd
never seen so ominous a place. But before she
could take it all in, the carriage came to a halt near
wide stone steps, and a set of ornately carved
wooden doors opened.

Maryana took some badly needed comfort in the
familiarity of the man who came forward to greet
her. She barely remembered her uncle from his
visits, but the family resemblance was strong. He
had the same pale golden hair and bright blue eyes
that his sister—her mother—had passed on to her.

"My dear Maryana," he said, taking her proffered hand and bending to kiss it. "I hope the journey wasn't too difficult for you. The crossing can
often be quite unpleasant."

"It wasn't difficult, Uncle," she replied, wondering if her unkempt appearance had caused him to

11

believe she'd suffered on the journey. It wasn't the journey itself, of course, that had been unbearable but rather the fact that she'd been forced to make it at all.

"Then welcome to Varley Castle—your new home. I assure you that it isn't as primitive as it might appear to you at the moment."

Maryana had her doubts about that, but as her uncle led her into the high, vaulted entryway, she began to believe that he might be right. Dark, ornately carved beams soared far above her head, and both the walls and floor were of dark stone; she quickly found herself quite intrigued by the place.

It was the contrasts, she decided, that made it fascinating: those cold walls and floors that provided a backdrop for richly colored tapestries and rugs of strange designs and furniture of dark, heavily carved woods.

"How old is this place?" she asked as he led her up the great staircase.

"About three hundred years," her uncle replied. "Or at least this portion is that old. It was actually built over a period of several centuries."

He led her to a spacious suite that was richly furnished in that same heavy, dark furniture she'd seen downstairs, together with more tapestries and thick, brightly patterned rugs.

Maryana stared at the largest of the tapestries, which covered nearly an entire wall. It depicted a hunting scene in a thick forest, and near its center was a solitary hunter with a bow, his one arm raised to aim an arrow. He was clearly a Sakim—and that reminded her of the man she'd met at the dock. She turned to her uncle.

"While I was waiting for the carriage, a man spoke to me. He didn't give me his name, but he knew mine." She described him, though she didn't

mention those deep, dark eyes that had so capti-
vated her.

"He said that these were *his* lands, and claimed
that the carriage was his as well."

"That would have been Roderic," the baron said
in a grim tone that reminded her of the driver's
wariness around the man.

"Who is he, Uncle?"

"Lord Roderic Hode, the Earl of Varley."

Maryana swept an arm around them. "Then this
is his home?"

"It was, yes. He lives now in one of the tenant
houses."

"I don't understand. Why is he still here? Why
wasn't he driven away or imprisoned—or killed?"

The baron heaved a sigh. "He wasn't here when
we captured his lands. He was away in the north,
fighting the Boravians. We knew that, of course.
That's why we invaded when we did. Normally the
strait is too dangerous to cross at that time of year,
but we were fortunate to have a spell of gentle
weather."

"Then why didn't you take him prisoner or drive
him away when he returned?"

"We would have, but at the time he returned, it
had become clear to me that his people would have
risen up against us if we had. We'd only just gotten
a foothold here. There weren't many of us here at
that time—certainly not enough to stave off the
other Sakim lords if they had decided to unite with
him."

She had taken a seat and the baron sat down
opposite her. "This is a strange land, my dear. As
you may know, various men have attempted to
unite the Sakim lords, but with no success. They
are a fiercely independent people. So I arranged a
sort of truce with him. He has promised not to
rebel and I have promised that he can remain free."

"And you trust him in this?" she asked skeptically.

"He gave me his word."

"He certainly sounded to me like a man who intends to reclaim what is his," she observed, startled at how clear her memory of him was. He might have been standing there now, staring intently at her with those devil's black eyes, his square jaw thrust forward and his black hair whipping about in the breeze.

The baron said nothing in reply, although Maryana sensed that her comment had disturbed him. Whether it was her words or simply the fact that she, a woman, had dared to venture an opinion, she didn't know.

Soon after, her uncle took his leave, and Maryana began to unpack her belongings, such as they were. She hadn't brought with her more than a small portion of her extensive wardrobe, since it was her intention to stay here only long enough to assure her uncle that she was quite capable of managing her own affairs.

Neither had she brought along a maid. Maryana, for all that she could be spoiled and willful in many ways, was very sensitive to the welfare of those who depended upon her, and she knew that all the maids were terrified at the prospect of having to cross the dangerous strait to enemy territory. Besides, she'd assumed—wrongly, it seemed—that there would be maids here who could serve her needs.

As she unpacked, she thought about her uncle. It was too soon to be sure, of course, but she sensed that he was malleable. She thought that she could recall her father's having remarked once that the baron was a good man, but not a strong one. She hoped he was right. Weak men definitely had their uses.

And that thought brought back yet another image of Lord Roderic Hode. Despite his seeming willingness to live virtually as a serf on his ancestral lands, Maryana was very certain that he was *not* weak.

She returned her attention to her uncle. Like the other nobles who now occupied Sakim lands, he had not actually fought in the battle that had won these lands. He'd been chosen by the Neran king to rule after the victory.

But had there been a true victory, as she'd been led to believe? It seemed to her that her uncle's position here—and by extension, her own—was precarious indeed, dependent upon the forbearance of a Sakim lord. It was yet another reason to convince her uncle quickly that she was capable of managing her own affairs and must return home.

"You know as well as I do that the crops were poor this year, Baron. My people cannot afford to pay your heavy taxes. If they do, they will starve this winter.

"Or perhaps that's exactly what you have in mind. Starving people can't rise up against you."

Maryana paused just outside the partially open door. She didn't need to see the speaker to know who he was. That deep, taunting voice had haunted her dreams last night. Lord Roderic Hode.

"It is the king who sets the taxes—as you surely know, Roderic. I am merely the collector."

Maryana recoiled as Roderic swore a colorful oath. "Your king is a degenerate whose coffers are already overly full. He roams about from one great palace to another while his subjects live inssqualor and go hungry!"

Maryana smiled. She was beginning to like this Sakim lord. It seemed he knew their king well. She had always detested the man and was eternally glad to see the back of him when he left his seaside palace near her estates.

"His troops, nevertheless, were victorious over *yours*, Roderic," the baron said, though Maryana noticed that he didn't otherwise attempt to defend the king.

"Only because most of us were off fighting in the north," Roderic flung back at him. "That was exactly the cowardly sort of battle he would fight."

"At least our people are united," the baron pointed out.

"United? You mean that you have all given over your sovereignty to one man and you grovel at his feet. The Sakim will never do that."

Roderic's voice grew louder as he spoke, which should have sent her running, lest she be discovered eavesdropping. But Maryana was so taken with his impassioned words that she didn't think to move away, out of sight, until it was too late.

His dark eyes were ablaze with silver fire as he strode from the room, then stopped abruptly when he saw her standing there. But before she could think of anything to say, he walked away. She stared at his broad back, fascinated by him even more than before.

Then, deciding that this might not be the best time to begin persuading her uncle that he should allow her to return home, Maryana turned and followed the hallway to a door and stepped out into the courtyard.

She was surprised to find herself in a small but lovely garden. Her expert eye saw quickly that it would soon be overgrown, but the flowers and shrubs were nonetheless quite beautiful. She began to walk among the beds, examining strange blooms as she pondered the meaning of the conversation she'd overheard.

It wasn't surprising, really. The king overtaxed his own people, so why should it be any different here, in the land of their enemies? But Lord Roderic had spoken against it with a passion she admired, since it was so lacking among her own people. Even her father, whom she'd admired in so many ways, had never spoken out against the king.

If I were a man, she thought, I would be exactly like him. And then she made a sound of surprise, born of a lifetime of wrongly believing the Sakim to be a savage people, worthy only of contempt from the Nerans.

Suddenly, out of the corner of her eye she caught movement and turned to see Roderic moving swiftly along the perimeter of the gardens. He seemed to be headed toward a plot of land devoted to a vegetable patch she could just glimpse around a corner. He obviously hadn't seen her, so she began to move in that direction herself, curious about his destination.

By the time she reached the corner of the castle wall, he had vanished. She could see only a door that apparently led to the kitchens, and as it was the only exit in sight, she assumed he must have gone through it.

She looked around for a place to hide, then, seeing none, decided to wait and see if he returned. Intriguing though he might be, Roderic Hode was still the enemy, and if he were engaged in some nefarious activity at her uncle's expense, she needed to know. Besides, it just might be a way to ingratiate herself with her uncle and prove her own capabilities.

He emerged a few moments later, with two large sacks slung over his broad shoulders: very well filled sacks, she noticed. He saw her and stopped, a challenge apparent in his stance and his dark eyes.

"Are you stealing from my uncle's kitchens, Lord Roderic?" she inquired, though it was already clear that he was.

17

"Only fools ask questions that are already answered, milady—you disappoint me. I had thought you were perhaps somewhat less a fool than your uncle."

His sharp words stung her, and she felt an unwelcome flush stealing over her fair skin.

"Enough food is wasted here to feed several widows and their children," he said, moving closer to her. "Widows of men who fought at my side."

"Do you do this regularly?" she asked, silently acknowledging the truth of what he'd said. At dinner last night, her uncle's table had been weighted down with enough food to feed at least a dozen people, though they were the only two dining.

"Every day. It's the only reason that Mary and the others continue in your uncle's employ. I persuaded them to stay when the others left."

"Does my uncle know this?"

He shrugged, the heavy sacks bobbing up and down on his back. "Perhaps. He may enjoy knowing that I am reduced to stealing from the kitchens."

"And why are you reduced to that, Lord Roderic?" she asked, knowing the question to be insulting, but too consumed by curiosity to care.

He stared at her in silence for a moment, and she thought that perhaps he believed her to be simply mocking him for having lost his lands.

"I cannot answer that, except to say that all things happen in their time."

And with that rather enigmatic response, he strode away, the sacks swinging against his back. Maryana watched him until he vanished around a corner. Then she wrapped her arms around herself and shuddered. What a strange man: so full of fire and yet so cold. She most definitely did not envy her uncle his tenuous position here—and she was even more determined to get away from this place quickly.

Roderic watched her from the deep shadows. She galloped along the narrow road that ran through the hunting grounds, her golden hair once again unbound and flying out behind her. He thought it was a safe bet that her uncle didn't know she was out riding alone—or that she was riding astride the horse, for that matter.

Yesterday he'd seen her in the town, riding side-saddle in her elegant clothing, accompanied by two of DeLay's guards. He'd thought then that she looked every inch the Neran lady. Now she looked more like a peasant girl. Which image was real—or did she somehow manage to sit astride two worlds?

Several times from the first moment he'd seen her, walking off the ship looking none the worse for wear from her difficult journey, he'd been forced to readjust his image of her. He knew she was heir to great wealth and that she was now a ward of her uncle, and he guessed that she didn't like that very much.

All in all, Lady Maryana didn't fit within the confines if the image he'd had of pale, delicate Neran nobility.

He waited until she drew near to the place where he was hiding, then urged his horse forward to meet her, far more eager than he had any right to be to see her again.

Freedom! Maryana loved the feel of the wind in her hair and the sure, powerful movements of the horse beneath her. She knew there would be trouble if her uncle found out she'd gone riding alone, but he'd left the castle earlier, and she thought it unlikely that she'd encounter anyone out here in his game preserve.

Getting the horse saddled and out of the stable hadn't proved to be as difficult as she'd anticipated.

It appeared that Lord Roderic had been right about most of the staff leaving when her uncle took over the castle. At least, there'd been no one around the stable. She assumed there must be some grooms left, for the horses were clean and fed, but they remained hidden.

Now, she didn't quite believe her eyes when she saw the man ride out of the forest toward her. Roderic? Yes, it *was* him! She recognized his handsome gray stallion even before she could determine his features.

She slowed her mount, wondering if she had any cause to fear him. Perhaps she should—but she didn't. In fact, if the sudden fluttering inside her was any indication, she was eager to see him again, danger or no.

He rode on to the narrow track and stopped. She brought her horse to a halt a short distance away. They stared at each other as their mounts whickered in greeting.

"So it's back to the peasant girl look today," he observed with a smile.

"As I recall, that isn't how you described me when we first met," she replied acerbically.

He laughed. "But yesterday I saw a Neran lady who looked much like you, riding through town in the company of two guards."

"I don't recall seeing you," she said, wondering how he could possibly have escaped her notice.

"No doubt I just looked like another half-starved peasant to you."

"You scarcely look half-starved to me, Lord Roderic."

"But now you know that I spoke the truth about my people."

"They don't look any worse than the peasants at home," she said, though the statement wasn't true. It certainly wasn't true of her own people.

"That only proves my point about your king." He

20

made the last word sound like an obscenity.

"As it happens, I agree with you—but there is nothing I can do about it."

"You agree?" he echoed in surprise, both dark brows arching.

"I'm always happy to see the back of him, but as I said, there is nothing I can do about it."

"Perhaps there *is* something you can do about it, now that you're here. You could make your uncle understand that he can't take everything from my people."

"It seems to me that you made that case quite eloquently, and it got you nowhere," she observed. "Besides, I do not intend to be here long."

"Oh? But I thought you'd been made a ward of your uncle."

"I have, but I intend to prove to him that I'm quite capable of managing my own affairs. I've been doing it for years. My father was ill for a long time before he died."

"Then why didn't he marry you off to some suitable nobleman? I understand that you would bring quite a handsome dowry—not to mention your other obvious attributes."

His gaze slid over her, not quite blatant enough to be insulting, but very close to that. She ignored it. "Oh, he tried," she said. "But I refused to accept any of the proposals."

"What you're saying is that you took advantage of his not being well to remain free."

She bit back a sharp reply. She preferred not to think about it that way, but he had a point. Her father's will had deteriorated along with his body.

"An opportunist—just like me." Roderic smiled. "Does your uncle know that you're out here alone?"

"No. He left early this morning."

"In that case, you'd better follow me." He turned his mount and started back into the woods.

"Why?"

"Because there are some men riding this way—
some of your uncle's guards, I believe. Hurry. I
don't think they've seen us yet."

She turned in the saddle and saw nothing. But
it was possible that he'd seen them cresting the last
hill. After a moment's hesitation, she plunged into
the forest behind him.

They rode down a short, steep hill, weaving their
way through the thick woods. He came to a stop
beside a small stream. "We should be safe enough
here."

"We? You mean they can't see you, either?"

"I'd prefer not to give your uncle an excuse to
bring me up on charges of poaching on my own
lands."

"Is that what you were doing?" She didn't see any
game, but he did have his bow and a quiver full of
arrows.

"It's what I was intending to do before I saw
you," he replied as he swung easily out of the saddle, then walked over to her.

She turned to peer back through the forest. "Are
you certain you saw someone?"

"Yes, but I can see that you require proof."

Before she could protest, he reached up and
lifted her out of the saddle. In that moment, when
he held her securely above him, Maryana felt
something very strange—but not so strange that
she couldn't identify it. The oddness came from a
previous certainty that she could never feel that
helpless loss of control that some foolish women
called love.

He swung her to the ground and released her,
but not before she saw that silver fire in his eyes
again, together with a knowledge she didn't want
to see. He knew perfectly well the effect he was
having on her.

"Come along," he said, starting up the hill.
"You'll be able to see them from here."

22

She scrambled up the steep hillside behind him. When he turned and saw her struggling, he reached back a hand and hauled her the rest of the way up. She very nearly recoiled at the roughness of his hand. All the men she knew had soft hands. It occurred to her that though he thought she looked both a peasant and a noble, the same could be said of him.

"Stay down!" he ordered, pulling her hand until she was crouched beside him. "They should be along any moment."

He was right. He had scarcely finished speaking when she saw three riders galloping along the track. She held her breath, hoping they would go on, then released it noisily when they vanished.

"Thank you," she said when he turned toward her questioningly.

"You're welcome, but why are you so worried? Surely you're not afraid of him?"

"No, of course not. As I told you before, I intend to persuade my uncle to let me return home, and that means staying in his good graces."

"He's far more likely to want to marry you off," Roderic observed.

"No! I won't let him do that! I'll enter a convent first!"

"You're beginning to sound like my sister. That's exactly what she did when my father attempted to marry her off to a neighbor."

"Well, why didn't you stop him?" she demanded.

"I tried. Then, after our father died, I went to get her, but she'd discovered by then that she liked it there."

"Well, I have no intention of letting some man take Chamoney. It's *mine!*"

He regarded her with a smile. "I'm beginning to think that men must be far worse than I'd thought."

"Being one yourself, I can't imagine that you'd understand."

"Perhaps not, but I *can* understand wanting what belongs to you."

"My uncle told me that you've given your word that you won't stir up a rebellion against him."

"That's true—unfortunately. I'm afraid that the only thing I value more than my land is my life. Besides, I'll get it back one day. I'm a patient man."

"You don't strike me as being the patient type, Lord Roderic."

"Ahh, but you don't know me. I'm both patient and determined."

He stood up, then extended a hand to help her to her feet. As she took it, she felt again that callused warmth, and thought for a moment that her legs might not support her. Her reaction to this Sakim lord was really quite strange.

Then she saw him staring at her skirt. "You're wearing trousers!" he cried in surprise.

"They're not trousers," she insisted. "I just found it impossible to ride sidesaddle all the time—especially after my father became ill and I had to manage the estate. So I had my seamstress make up some special skirts."

He released her hand and threw back his head and laughed. "You're an extraordinary woman, Lady Maryana. I like that."

His dark eyes glittered, and she felt her whole world being narrowed to nothing more than those eyes, as though she might, at any moment, be drawn right into them. She lowered her gaze quickly and began to brush off her skirt.

"Well, you aren't exactly what I'd expected of a Sakim lord, either."

"Friends, then?" he asked, still grinning as he once more extended his hand.

She took it, trying to ignore the tiny curls of

heat that were unfurling themselves inside her. "Friends."

"I come here often," he told her as they started back down the hillside, their hands still clasped. "This is one of my favorite spots."

"It *is* lovely," she replied. "I might find myself coming here as well."

"We will be having company, my dear. That should please you. I'm sure you must find it quite tiresome being here without any friends your own age."

Maryana looked up from her dinner, surprised. Her uncle's mention of friends brought back that moment with Roderic when he'd declared them to be friends: "Oh? Is it someone I know?" And will it mean that I cannot sneak off to meet Roderic? she asked herself.

"Yes, I believe you do know him: Sir Miles Foulane."

Maryana nearly choked on her soup and was forced to cover her dismay with a cough. "Yes, I know him. Why is he coming here?"

She did her best to conceal her rising anger, and apparently she succeeded because her uncle seemed not to notice.

"He comes as an emissary of His Majesty, to see how we're faring here. His Majesty will be arriving in a few months."

She shivered in disgust. Miles had undoubtedly persuaded the king to give him this mission. He'd long since insinuated himself into the king's good graces.

"In his letter, he said that he was looking forward to seeing you again." The baron smiled.

"No doubt he is—but I am not looking forward to seeing him. He asked my father for my hand in marriage, but my father refused." That was true enough, though certainly not the *whole* truth.

"I see. Well, of course, your father was not a well man at the time . . . though I would think that would have been all the more reason he would have wanted to see you settled into a good marriage."

"My father agreed with me that Miles was not a suitable husband." Another half-truth. Her father had agreed only after she flatly refused to consider it.

"He seems to me to be quite an agreeable young man, and His Majesty certainly thinks highly of him."

All the more reason for me to dislike him, Maryana replied silently.

"It is true that he is penniless," the baron went on. "But he comes from a fine family, and money is not a consideration for you, since you have Chamoney."

And I intend to keep it, she thought but didn't say. "Miles Foulane is the last man I would consider taking as a husband," she stated firmly, though she knew it to be unwise.

"Umm. Well, it may be that your opinion of him was colored by your concern for your father's health."

She quickly attempted to turn the conversation to other matters and was relieved when her uncle seemed unwilling to pursue the issue. But she knew that relief would be short-lived. When Miles arrived, he would immediately begin to work on her uncle, using his influence with the king to press his suit.

"You seem troubled by something," Roderic observed.

She glanced at him in surprise. She'd thought she was concealing her unhappiness quite well. It was easy enough to do when she was here with him. She hadn't been able to get away for several days, and her eagerness to see Roderic had grown with each passing minute.

She sighed. "My uncle is about to have a visitor. He says he's coming as an emissary of the king, but that's not his true intent. He's coming to try to persuade my uncle to marry me off to him."

"Oh? It's someone you know, then?"

She grimaced. "All too well. His name is Miles Foulane. He comes from a very old family, but one that has fallen upon hard times—deservedly so, from what I've heard. Instead of giving back to the land, the Foulanes for years have only taken from it—until there is almost nothing left of their estate.

"He wants Chamoney. He asked my father for my hand, but Father refused. Now I'm sure he intends to persuade my uncle."

"Was it your father who refused—or you?" Roderic asked.

She grinned. "Me. That's when I first threatened to enter a convent."

"Wasn't that rather cruel? Or was this before your father became ill?"

"No, he was already sick. And yes, perhaps it *was* cruel. But I had to use whatever weapon came to hand."

Roderic shook his head, chuckling. "What a wicked daughter you must have been."

"That's not true!" she protested. "I loved my father. Besides, he knew I'd never enter a convent—or if I had, they would soon have thrown me out."

"I don't doubt that. So what do you intend to do?"

"I intend to prove to Miles Foulane that if he were to marry me, I would make his life not worth living."

Roderic laughed. "I don't doubt you could do that, too."

"It's so unfair! Can't you see that?"

"There is much to life that is unfair," he observed. "But you are right. Being forced to marry against your will is wrong."

"Why haven't *you* married?" she asked curiously, having wondered about that in their time apart.

He turned away from her. "There was someone once. She was the daughter of a neighboring lord. We grew up together. But then she died during a bad winter when there was much sickness."

"I'm sorry, Roderic. But surely you must want to marry. You need an heir."

"To what? I have nothing now."

But I do, she replied silently. *I have more than enough for us both.* For one brief moment, she could see the two of them, riding through her beloved home. The thought shocked her. Was she falling in love with this man? Of course she couldn't marry him. A Sakim lord in Neran? Impossible.

"I don't understand why you won't fight for what is yours," she said.

"Oh? Are you encouraging me to do battle with your uncle?"

"No, I didn't mean that—exactly. I just meant that I would certainly fight to regain Chamoney if it were taken from me."

"Do you think me a coward, Maryana?"

"No," she said quickly. But she wondered if maybe she did.

"All things happen in their time," he said, repeating his earlier statement, and it annoyed her even more now than it had before. She didn't understand that kind of patience.

"I can't ask my people to fight now, when they're barely able to keep body and soul together," he went on.

"I brought something that might help," she said, reaching into the pocket of her skirt and withdrawing a small leather bag. She handed it to him.

"It is all I brought with me, but I have written to

28

my manager at Chamoney and asked him to send more on the next supply ship."

Roderic took the bag from her and opened it, then let the gold coins trickle through his fingers. "You should be stealing from your uncle, since what he has, he's stolen from me and my people."

"I thought about that, but from what I've seen, he's very careful in his record-keeping. Though perhaps he might not miss a few coins from time to time."

Roderic was seated on the mossy bank of the stream, facing her. Suddenly, he set the bag aside and leaned over to plant a quick kiss on her cheek. She recoiled before she could stop herself. It felt as though he had touched her with fire. The sensation traveled all the way through her.

"Sorry," he said, withdrawing quickly. "I merely wanted to thank you."

She couldn't resist touching the spot he'd kissed. "I was just surprised, that's all."

When she left, her husky reply echoed through her brain all the way back to Varley Castle. Surprised? That wasn't the half of it. How could one brotherly peck on the cheek have turned her inside out? And was that really only brotherly affection she'd seen in his eyes?

Chapter Two

"What a pleasure to see you once more, Lady Maryana!"

Maryana looked into the pale eyes of Miles Foulane and thought she might be sick. It didn't help at all that in her mind's eye, she was dreaming of the dark, gleaming eyes of Roderic Hode.

She belatedly proffered her hand, then had to force herself not to recoil when he took it and kissed it. How, she wondered, could the same touch of lips to skin produce such very different reactions? Even his soft hand repulsed her now, though it was something she'd never considered before she met Roderic.

Miles swept an arm around the entrance hall. "A fine place, is it not? Not at all like Chamoney, but quite handsome in its way. The spoils of war have been good, eh, Baron?"

A war you stayed as far from as possible, Maryana said silently to them both. Like most of the nobility, Miles was eager to let other men fight and die, then step in and claim their hard-earned victories. Was it any wonder that Roderic and the other Sakim lords considered their Neran counterparts to be less than men?

She studied Miles covertly as he talked to her uncle. Most women found him to be quite handsome, with his golden curls and his lean, angular face. She had once thought him handsome as well—until she'd gotten to know him. Now, however, she found him to be a pale, weak imitation of a man with his vain posing and his arrogant demeanor.

Dinner was a trial. Miles was clearly doing his very best to charm her uncle, and it was all too easy to see how he had managed to gain the good graces of the king. It appeared to be working on her uncle as well.

"I understand that you have arranged a truce of sorts with the Sakim lord who owned this place," Miles said. "Has he given you any trouble, Baron?"

"No, none to speak of. He is living in one of the tenant houses, but he comes here from time to time to harangue me about the taxes. His concern seems to be primarily directed toward his people's welfare, not his own."

It was difficult for her to be certain, but Maryana thought she actually heard a hint of admiration there, or a sort of grudging respect.

"Or so he wants you to believe," said Miles dismissively. "I think it's a mistake to allow the man to run free—unless he's a total coward, that is."

"He's no coward," the baron replied. "But he's a difficult man to read. I think perhaps he is merely biding his time, waiting for an opportunity. And given our history with the Sakims, that opportunity is quite likely to come."

"His Majesty is determined that this time, he will hold on to the Sakim lands. The taxes he's levied upon them will enable him to raise a large army, and since the truce with the Huttars, he will be able to concentrate on securing his control over Sakim."

"Unless they rebel against the taxes," the baron replied. "They lack only someone to unite them."

"This Earl of Varley—could he be such a man?" Miles inquired.

"It's possible, though he's shown no intention of doing that. As I said, he's a difficult man to read: outwardly easy going, but perhaps with a great underlying strength."

Maryana hid her surprise. She would not have expected to hear from her uncle her very own assessment of Roderic. He made her think of fires that burned deeply, hidden from view but ready to erupt at any moment. Great passion hidden behind a smiling face. Anger concealed by a casual shrug.

"Have you met this Earl of Varley?" Miles asked, directing his question and his attention to her.

"I met him very briefly when I first arrived here," she replied. "He seemed no more than one would expect of a Sakim lord."

She managed to make her tone convey contempt, which was what Miles would expect. The knight nodded, seeming to accept that, but Maryana saw surprise on her uncle's face, and recalled how she'd told him that Roderic seemed very determined to regain his lands.

Following the lengthy dinner, Miles and her uncle excused themselves and withdrew. Curious about their discussion, Maryana took herself out to the gardens in the hope of being able to eavesdrop. But the window shutters were closed and she could hear nothing.

She lingered in the gardens, trying to decide what to do about this new threat to her freedom. It was very clear to her that Miles intended to win her uncle over and then request her hand in marriage.

She had quickly become convinced that her uncle was indeed a weak and malleable man—and furthermore, all too eager to please the king. Since Miles was one of the king's favorites, she had no doubt that he would succeed.

She thought about the statement she'd made to Roderic, about how she would convince Miles that marriage to her would not be to his liking, even if it would give him the wealth he so craved. That, she thought sadly, might well be her only hope. Roderic had said he had no doubt she could do just that—but then, he didn't know just how badly Miles wanted Chamoney.

She thought about her home, about the fertile fields and the carefully tended orchards and the long rows of grapevines that marched up the hillsides, about the well-maintained tenant houses and the winery. If Miles ever gained control over them, it would all soon go to ruin, as his own family's estate had.

And she thought about her people: the children who were all being taught to read and write, and the elderly who received pensions sufficient to let them live out their final years in some comfort. He would put a stop to that immediately.

She clenched her fists and raised her face to the heavens and vowed that she would do whatever it took to prevent that from happening.

The evening grew cool, and she was about to go back inside when she saw him approaching. At first, her heart skipped a few beats as she thought it might be Roderic, but when the man emerged from the shadows into the light of a nearly full moon, she saw instead that it was Miles.

"This garden requires some attention," he said with distaste.

I'm surprised you would notice, she replied silently, given the fact that you've let your own home go to ruin.

"Your uncle should take a firm hand to these Sakims," he went on.

Ahh, so that's it, she thought. *He wants me to know that he is capable of providing that firm hand.*

"Nearly all the people who were working here left when my uncle arrived," she said. "There is no one to spare to tend to the flowers."

"Then he should conscript them."

"I think you have little understanding of these Sakims, Sir Miles. They are very independent, and as I'm sure you know, there are far more of them than there are of us."

He nodded. "And it is your duty to defend your uncle."

"I'm not aware of his requiring any defense. I was merely stating the facts."

"You have an edge to your voice, Maryana. I did not come here to argue with you."

"Oh? And just why *have* you come here, Miles?"

He thrust out his chin. "I came as the king's emissary. Surely the baron told you that."

"He did, but I had my doubts. I'm very relieved to know that you haven't come to pursue your suit."

"And if I have?"

"Then your mission is doomed to failure. I haven't changed my mind."

Perhaps he intended it to be a smile, but what Maryana saw was a sneer. "I doubt you'll be able to wrap your uncle around your lovely fingers as you did your father."

Maryana tilted her head sideways and regarded him with a level and very direct gaze. "How could you possibly want to marry someone who not only doesn't love you—but truly *loathes* you?"

He blinked and almost took a step backward before he caught himself and fixed that sneering smile to his face again. "Perhaps I like a challenge."

"A challenge?" she scoffed. "If it was a challenge

you wanted, you might have gone to war, Miles, instead of parading at court in your finery. Find yourself someone there, Miles. I'm told there are many ladies at court who find you quite charming."

"But they are not *you*, Lady Maryana," he said with a poor attempt at gallantry.

"What you mean is that none of them would bring you great wealth. You will never have Chamoney—or me. I promise you that."

Then, before he could come up with a reply, she walked away, hoping that she had at least sown some seeds of doubt.

Roderic! Maryana actually blinked several times before she could believe he was actually there. She'd been trying for days to get away to meet him in the woods, but Miles had seemed determined to force his unwanted presence on her for all her waking hours. Now, she'd only gotten away into the gardens because he was closeted with her uncle.

Roderic gestured again and she quickly followed him into a secluded corner of the garden, surrounded on three sides by walls. It was a favorite spot of hers, because the walls were covered with sweet-smelling flowering vines.

He gave her a mock bow. "If milady won't come to the woods, then I will bring the woods to her."

He held out a small bouquet of the wildflowers she'd admired in the woods. She took them with a smile and inhaled their delicate fragrance. "Thank you. It's not been for lack of trying that I've not come to the woods."

"I know. I saw you with him in town yesterday."

"Be grateful that he didn't see *you*," she said with a grimace. "I think he is rapidly becoming obsessed with you, Roderic. He's very unhappy that my uncle has allowed you to remain free. In fact, you shouldn't be here now. He's bound to come looking for me soon. He seems to believe that familiarity might breed love, rather than contempt."

"And is he succeeding?"

"No, of course not. I told you that I loathe him."

"Many women would find him attractive, I think."

"Many do—but I don't."

Their eyes met, and once again, she felt herself in danger of becoming lost in the depths of those dark eyes. Unspoken words seemed to be hovering in the fragrant air between them. She feigned interest in the bouquet again and willed her heart to slow before its rapid thudding could be heard by him.

"I'm sorry that I have nothing more to offer you," he said in a soft, sad voice that drew her attention quickly.

"I've not asked you for anything—except your friendship."

"You already have that," he replied.

Would I have more if our situations were different? she wondered. He guarded his emotions so very closely, but surely she was seeing more than friendship in those dark eyes.

"Has he asked the baron for your hand yet?"

She shook her head. "But I know he intends to, and I fear that my uncle will accept on my behalf. I don't know what more I can do, since I've already told Miles that I truly loathe him. He seems to regard that as a challenge."

"Some men are like that," Roderic said disgustedly. "Especially if the lady in question brings what they seek most: wealth."

"Yes." She sighed, then reached into her pocket. "And speaking of wealth, I have some more coins for you. I took them from my uncle's treasury. With Miles here, he isn't likely to be paying quite as much attention to his taxes."

He took the coins from her and thanked her. "Doesn't it bother you to be stealing from your uncle?"

"Not at all. It isn't his money anyway. It belongs to the king—and I have no guilt at all about stealing from *him*. Besides, it truly belongs to you and your people."

Roderic chuckled. "Stealing from those who steal *does* have a certain appeal."

She reached out to touch his sleeve. "Roderic, I think you may be in danger. I'm sure Miles is trying to convince my uncle to have you put into prison— or worse."

He took her hand and carried it to his lips, his eyes never leaving hers. "Do not worry about me, Maryana."

"But I can't help worrying," she said softly.

A fraught silence grew between them. It vibrated with a tension that seemed to draw her to him and him to her, though she wasn't conscious of either of them actually moving.

He dropped her hand with a soft exhalation, then drew her slowly into his arms, holding her as though she were very fragile, which was just how she felt at that moment. She closed her eyes, longing to feel his lips on hers, his body pressed against hers. But when his mouth did touch her, it was only to place a chaste kiss on her brow. And then he let her go.

Disappointed and almost ready to fling herself into his arms again, Maryana wasn't prepared for his quick, husky good-bye and his equally rapid disappearance.

Had she made a fool of herself? she wondered, blinking back tears of frustration. Maybe all he wanted from her was a replacement for the sister he'd lost to the church.

Or maybe he would not offer her love because he had nothing else to offer.

"Would you care to join me, Lady Maryana? As I recall, you're quite an accomplished rider, and it's a perfect day for a hunt."

Maryana hesitated at Miles's request. With her uncle off somewhere and Miles and his men about to embark on a hunting expedition, it would be a perfect time for her to steal away and meet Roderic—if he were waiting for her, that was.

But perhaps he wouldn't be. He'd made no attempt to see her since they'd met in the garden four days ago, even though she knew he must be coming still to collect food from the kitchens. Besides, it wouldn't be wise for her to be riding in the game preserve if Miles was out there somewhere.

She accepted his invitation, knowing that at least she wouldn't be alone with him, and his attention would be focused on the hunt. She went off to change into her riding clothes, feeling increasingly frustrated. Not only was she being forced to fend off Miles's suit, but now her uncle had begun to press her—so far in only a subtle fashion—to accept Miles's offer of marriage. And it was beginning to seem likely that she might never see Roderic again.

It's my own fault, she told herself. *I should never have allowed Roderic to see my feelings. I should have learned to dissemble, like other women do.*

They rode out from the castle on a lovely day, one in which she would certainly have enjoyed riding alone—and not dressed in all her finery on a sidesaddle. Miles and his two men were in high spirits, talking about the plentiful game they'd seen on a previous scouting expedition into the large preserve.

Men were like that, she'd often observed. When they weren't at war with each other, they liked to wage war on other creatures. They would often return with a glut of small, bloody corpses—far more than they could all hope to eat.

Of course, that might mean that Roderic would have even more to fill his sacks, and she actually smiled to herself, thinking it would be fitting indeed if Miles and his men procured game for the tables of Roderic's people. She knew Roderic would have enjoyed that, too. He had, she thought, a keen sense of irony, a quality she much appreciated in a man.

Ignoring the men's conversation, Maryana concentrated instead on her problem with Miles and her uncle. She was more and more convinced that if his mild hints didn't work, her uncle might well order her at some point to marry Miles. The money she'd requested that her manager send had arrived with a supply ship yesterday. It had been her intention to turn it over to Roderic for his people, but now she wondered if she should put it to use booking passage on a ship home for herself.

It was a very tempting thought. She couldn't see her uncle sending his men to drag her back here against her will, and without her uncle's backing, she doubted that Miles would have the nerve to visit Chamoney and demand that she marry him.

But none of this was certain. She couldn't be sure, for example, what role the king might play in this affair. Miles might persuade the king to order her to marry him under penalty of forfeiture of her lands. And then where would she be? She might avoid marrying Miles, but she would lose the only thing that truly mattered to her.

No, not the only thing. If she left here, she would certainly never see Roderic again.

Suddenly, a shout from one of Miles's men brought her out of her bleak thoughts. At first thinking that he'd merely spotted a stag or some other creature, she was slow to realize that the object of his attention was in fact a man.

Since she'd lagged behind, she was some distance behind them, and she couldn't see him clearly as Miles and the other two surrounded him. Could it be Roderic? Her heart thudded in fear and icy fingers skittered along her spine. They weren't far from the spot where she'd been meeting Roderic.

She urged her mount forward, praying that if it were Roderic, Miles would think him nothing more than a peasant. But she knew, even as she hoped, that it was a foolish thought. Even clad in rough clothing, Roderic was obviously not a peasant.

Then she reached the others and saw with relief that it wasn't Roderic, after all. She didn't know the man's name, but she did recognize him. He was a tall, thin man with an ugly scar that began just above his brow and ended along his nose, in the process puckering his left eye. And he was terrified.

He stood in the center of a circle formed by Miles and his men, clutching a well-filled sack to his scrawny chest as he tried to avoid the shifting movements of the horses. A poacher.

Just as she reached them, Miles urged his horse forward, knocking the man to the ground. He lost his grip on the sack and Miles reached down to grab it, grinning.

"Well," he cried triumphantly, "what have we here? Is it possible that we've caught ourselves a poacher?"

He loosened the string that held the bag shut and dumped onto the ground perhaps a half-dozen rabbits and squirrels. Then, as Maryana averted her gaze in disgust, Miles and his men set their horses to trampling on them, until there was very little left.

Miles grinned at his men. "I think perhaps we should save our host the trouble of dealing with this criminal and in the process have ourselves some sport.

"At a count of ten, begin running, poacher. We'll see if your desire to live will make your legs faster than our arrows."

"No!"

At the sound of her shout, Miles turned to her as if remembering only then that she was there.

"You will not kill him!" she stated firmly. "The poor man was only seeking to feed his family."

"But he was doing that at your uncle's expense," Miles replied coldly.

"Then let my uncle decide his punishment."

"An example needs to be made, milady," Miles said. "And with all due respect, the baron hasn't done enough of that."

Then, turning his back on her, he began to remove an arrow from his quiver as he commenced counting. Maryana was about to urge her mount forward, to protect the man, when the thud of rapid hoofbeats behind them made them all turn.

Roderic! A thrill ran through her even though she knew what danger he brought with him. He brought his handsome stallion to a halt, then moved forward to put himself between the three men and the poor, terrified poacher.

"Well," said Miles with a broad, evil smile. "Would you be the Earl of Varley?"

Roderic nodded, smiling as well. "*Not* at your service, you Neran swine."

Maryana heard the sharply indrawn breaths of Miles's two men and she cringed inwardly. It would be dangerous enough for Roderic to plead the poacher's case, but to insult Miles on top of that . . .

She sat there uneasily, staring from one man to the other as Miles glared at Roderic and Roderic continued to smile, seeming completely at ease.

"Let him go. You've already destroyed his catch.

41

Seeing the faces of a wife and six hungry children will be enough punishment for him."

"Is this how you protected these lands when they belonged to you, Hode?" Miles sneered. "If so, we did you a favor by taking them from you."

"No, this isn't how I 'protected' them," Roderic said, ignoring Miles's derisive tone. "I opened these lands to my people at regular intervals. So you see, he is accustomed to hunting here."

"But the lands are no longer yours."

"A temporary situation." Roderic shrugged. "They were in the past and will be again. At the very least, this man's punishment belongs to the baron—or, in his absence, to the lady Maryana, his niece."

Roderic turned to her for the first time and inclined his head slightly. "And how would *you* punish him, milady?"

"I already said that I would let him go, Lord Roderic."

Roderic smiled at her and turned back to Miles. "There, you see? We are of the same mind. Now take yourselves off and enjoy your hunt. The matter has been resolved."

"This is not a matter for a *woman* to resolve, Hode—and you know it!"

"Oh? Are you saying, then, that the lady Maryana is too feebleminded to be capable of meting out justice?" Roderic challenged with an arched brow.

"You try my patience, Sakim!"

Roderic chuckled. "To be honest, I doubt there was much there in the first place. Perhaps an archery contest, then? Do you see that dead twig yonder? If you succeed in knocking it down, then the man is yours to punish. If I separate it from the tree, then he goes free. I'll even give you the first try."

Maryana squinted as Miles and his men turned to see the twig in question. It was a very small tar-

get and a very great distance. In fact, the only reason she could see it at all was that several dead
leaves clung to it. Back in Chamoney, each year
during the spring planting festival, she'd given a
prize to the man among her people who displayed
the greatest talent with a bow, but she knew that
not even the best of them could do such a thing.
She wondered if Roderic could, or if it was only a
bluff.

Miles stared at it in silence for a long moment,
then turned back to Roderic. "You're in no position
to set the terms, Hode. In fact, you're guilty of tres-
passing here yourself." He made a quick gesture to
his men.

"Take him! We'll carry both of them back to the
castle."

The men hesitated just a fraction of a second,
perhaps sensing that their smiling adversary might
prove to be more formidable than he appeared.
And that gave Roderic the opportunity he needed.

He leaped off his horse and called to the poacher
to take it and be off, then drew out a wicked-
looking dagger and faced the two men who had
belatedly gotten down from their own horses.

Maryana sat, frozen with horror, as the men
drew their own knives and began to advance warily. Miles, she noted, remained on his horse and
even backed out of the way, making his own cowardice very evident to her.

But her full attention was focused on Roderic,
who was still—unbelievably—smiling! Was he a
fool—or simply incredibly brave?

The next moments passed in a blur of movement
and flashing knives. One of Miles's men cried out
and fell to the ground, clutching his arm. His knife
flew from his grasp, and Roderic picked it up almost casually, as though he were retrieving a lost
coin.

"Roderic!" she cried out as the other man moved at him from behind.

But it seemed that her warning wasn't needed. Roderic spun about and grabbed the other man's upper arm, wrenching his knife from his grasp and then flinging him to the ground as though he were no more than a lightweight sack.

Now he had all three knives: one in each hand and the third stuck in his belt. He turned to Miles, who began to back his horse away.

"Don't you find it surpassingly strange that you Nerans managed to defeat us—even temporarily?" Roderic said, flashing a brilliant smile.

Then, without awaiting a reply, Roderic leaped onto one of the men's horses. But instead of riding away, he brought the animal over to Maryana, then lifted her hand from the reins and kissed it.

"My thanks, Lady Maryana, for the warning. Give your uncle my regards and tell him that the horse will be returned to him."

Their eyes met and held for what seemed to her an eternity, but was in fact only a second. And then he was gone, thundering away down the trail.

Maryana ignored Miles and the two men who were now getting to their feet slowly. Instead, she turned in the saddle to watch Roderic until he vanished over a rise. And when she turned back, she found Miles watching her with a look of pure hatred.

"He helped the poacher to escape! Then he insulted me and attacked my men! And he stole one of your horses!"

"He promised to return it," Maryana put in, trying not to smile at Miles's red-faced harangue. "And he did not attack the men. They attacked *him*, on Miles's orders."

The baron looked distinctly uncomfortable, and Maryana almost felt sorry for him. From the moment they had reached Varley Castle, Miles had been insisting that Roderic be arrested forthwith.

"He even insulted Lady Maryana!" Miles whined.

She ignored him, instead facing her uncle. "I believe that I am quite capable of knowing when I've been insulted, Uncle. Lord Roderic merely kissed my hand and thanked me for warning him."

"Warning him of what?" the baron inquired, clearly confused.

"I warned him that one of the men was about to attack him from behind. But, as it turned out, he didn't require a warning.

"Lord Roderic acted from the noblest of motives, Uncle. He merely sought to save the life of one of his people. Miles was planning to kill the man, rather than bring him back here for you to mete out punishment."

"The miserable wretch was caught in the act of poaching, Baron. I merely sought to relieve you of the burden of judging him."

"By treating him like an animal," Maryana said in disgust. "He told the man to start running and then they were going to hunt him down. That scarcely conforms to Neran justice."

"Neran justice is for Nerans!" Miles shouted, his face redder than ever.

The baron had been staring from one to the other of them, but now he turned his attention to Miles. "It seems to me that such a punishment could well set off the rebellion I warned about, Sir Miles. I can understand your anger and I appreciate your efforts to aid me in my duties here, but I would prefer you let me decide what justice is best for the land."

"But what about Hode? He insulted me—and all Nerans. And he injured two of my men."

"He could have killed them," Maryana pointed out, sensing that she had her uncle on her side now. "Certainly *you* made no attempt to save them,

Miles, so it's a bit strange to hear you expressing such concern for them now."

Her uncle might well have been trying to conceal a smile, but it was the hatred in Miles's eyes that Maryana felt. She knew that she had made a formidable enemy.

"Baron, I insist that the Sakim be brought to justice. If you wish to excuse the poacher, that is your right. But Hode insulted me and nearly killed my men!"

"I will take your request under consideration, Sir Miles," Baron DeLay said, then left them.

"Miles, are you even more foolish than you appear?" Maryana said with a grimace. "He *can't* arrest Lord Roderic. Everyone will hear what happened—that he was only trying to save that poor man's life—and we will have a rebellion on our hands."

Then, even though she knew she'd already gone too far, she still went on. "Tell me, Miles, are *you* prepared to do battle with the Sakims?"

Miles glared at her, his pale eyes as cold as ice. "Is it possible, Lady Maryana, that you know Lord Roderic better than you suggested?"

"Now *you* insult *me*, Miles. Do you dare imply that I am sneaking off for trysts with a Sakim lord?"

"He will pay for this."

She watched Miles stalk away, her thoughts veering between contempt for him and fear for Roderic. What she'd witnessed made it plain that Miles was capable of anything. She could only hope that Roderic also understood that.

The castle was dark and quiet as Maryana let herself out through the kitchen door. Dinner had been the most disagreeable meal she'd ever eaten—even worse than the dinners she'd been forced to host for the king.

Her uncle had remained mostly silent, then had

quickly excused himself. Miles had alternately blustered and brooded, all the while consuming vast quantities of wine and complaining about its poor quality. After dinner, he'd staggered off to his rooms, taking more wine with him. By now, he would be deep in a wine-soaked sleep.

The night was cool and the moon was bright as she stepped out into the kitchen garden and breathed deeply of the aromatic herbs that grew in abundance. She wished that she might go on walking beneath the moon until she had reached Chamoney.

No, that wasn't entirely true. She *did* wish that she were back in her beloved home—but she also longed to see Roderic again. And besides that, she *needed* to see him, to warn him. The more she'd thought about it, the less convinced she was that he'd realized how dangerous Miles could be.

She smiled to herself, thinking of his treatment of Miles. Dangerous though it surely was, she'd enjoyed seeing him show Miles the contempt he deserved.

She made her way quickly to the stables. Roderic had said he would return the horse, and she was sure he would not hand over that risky task to one of his people, who might then be accused of having a stolen animal. He would bring it himself, and she would wait there for him.

When she reached the stable, she decided to wait inside, out of the cool night wind. So she walked through the big, open doors and then found a bale of straw upon which to sit and wait, well hidden in a dark corner in case anyone else should come. Several horses whickered at her presence, then settled down quickly.

She replayed the incident in her mind, marveling all over again at Roderic's behavior. It was nearly impossible to imagine a man being so calm and unconcerned in the face of death. No wonder she'd almost made the mistake of believing him to be a fool.

And she had to admit that his fighting skills were truly frightening—especially in a man who seemed so casual, even flippant. Were all Sakims like that, or was he special? She didn't know, but she was inclined to believe the latter.

She thought about Miles's continued insistence at dinner that her uncle must do something to avenge the "insult" to his guest. It was clear enough that her uncle wished to do nothing, but if Miles kept at him . . .

Whatever happened now, it was likely—even certain—that something would be done when the king arrived in a few months. He would be bringing with him enough troops to put down any rebellion that might result from Roderic's arrest. And unfortunately it sounded as though Miles intended to stay until the king arrived.

She knew that she must persuade Roderic not only to fore-swear any further provocations, but also to go away for a while—until after the king had gone. But she already doubted he would agree. She would be asking him to leave his home, after all.

She drew her cloak more tightly around her and then curled up among the bales of straw, drifting into a light doze as she waited for him to appear.

Her eyes snapped open when she heard several horses snort and stamp their feet. In the dim light, she saw someone leading a horse back to a rear stall, but she couldn't be certain it was, in fact, Roderic.

She got up from her temporary bed and moved quietly along behind the horse, trying to make out the man leading it. Then suddenly, there was a loud clatter as she knocked over a pail she hadn't seen. The horse whickered and shied—and then a dark figure descended upon her, knocking her to the floor before she could even think of escaping!

Hands that felt like iron bands pinned her arms beside her, but she still couldn't see his face. She tried to wriggle free, but her bulky cape prevented her from moving easily. Still, she struggled, her body pushing against a much larger body.

"Maryana?"

"Roderic!" She stopped struggling and instead sagged with relief.

"Did I hurt you?" he asked, levering himself off of her and sitting back on his heels.

"No," she said, sitting up and rather wishing that he hadn't identified her so quickly. Her body tingled pleasantly where his had touched her.

"I wasn't sure it was you. I fell asleep waiting."

"And now *I'm* waiting, to find out why you were hiding in the stable to begin with."

"I was waiting for you, of course. I assumed that you would do as you said, and bring back the horse."

He got to his feet, then reached down to give her a hand. She took it and rose, and would have held on to it longer if he hadn't released her to lead the horse into its stall. She thought that she must crave his touch as some men seemed to crave wine.

"I came to warn you," she said when he returned to her.

"About what?"

She told him what had transpired. "He won't let the matter rest, Roderic. If he can't persuade my uncle to arrest you, he might well come after you himself."

"Like he did today?" Roderic asked in a contemptuous tone.

"I didn't mean him; I meant his men. Just because he's a coward, don't dismiss the threat. And I think he's even angrier because he believes that you and I . . . that we're . . ." She stammered to a

49

halt, wishing she hadn't raised that particular issue.

"That we're *lovers?*" Roderic said softly, teasingly.

"Y-yes. I think he believes that."

"I wouldn't have credited him with being that observant," he said with a low chuckle.

"What do you mean? We're not . . ."

"I know. We're friends. But it's a fine distinction he isn't likely to be able to make."

A small silence fell between them that felt both thrilling and very dangerous to her. Her treacherous mind shifted to thoughts of that bed of straw.

"I think you should go away for a while," she said, forcing those untoward thoughts away. "Until after the king has come and gone. My uncle fears a rebellion if you are arrested, but Miles may yet persuade him, and when the king and his troops arrive—"

"I'm not leaving my lands and my people."

"Roderic, listen to me! You can do nothing for your people if you're in prison—and you might get many of them killed if they rise up in anger over it!"

"I'm not going to be imprisoned, either!"

"Then will you at least promise me there'll be no more provocations?"

"Of course—as long as he does nothing to provoke *me!*"

Angry now at his stubbornness, Maryana turned away and started toward the stable doors. "I think perhaps you have a death wish, Roderic!"

He caught up to her quickly and took her arm, spinning her around to face him. "That might have been true before I met *you.* But now I have something to live for."

His kiss was soft and teasing—and it ended so quickly that she had barely registered its imprint on her parted lips. And then he was gone, leaving her to the echoes of his words.

Chapter Three

"Uncle, you cannot do this!"

"I have no choice, my dear. I can't further risk the king's displeasure."

"Do you not think a rebellion will bring the king's displeasure?" Maryana demanded.

"Sir Miles assures me that he will obtain some additional men from Baron Damene, whose land abuts these lands. The baron is his cousin."

"But you know that Roderic did nothing wrong! Miles would have killed that poor man."

"If it were only that, I would agree. But Roderic insulted him as well."

"He called Miles a Neran swine—which he is. Would you punish *me* for speaking the truth about him?"

"You fail to understand the situation here, niece. It is a grave offense to insult a man's honor. Roderic finally went too far." He shrugged. "Besides, I do Roderic a favor. If this matter waits until the king arrives, the punishment will be far more severe."

"What will the punishment be?" she asked nervously, thinking that Roderic was unlikely to accept *any* punishment.

"As the injured party, Sir Miles can recommend the punishment."

"And has he done so?"

"No. He wants Roderic brought before him first. I have already sent men to fetch him."

"I wish to be there, to speak on Lord Roderic's behalf."

"That would not be proper. Besides, Sir Miles seems to believe that you have, ah, a certain fondness for Roderic."

"He's right; I do!" The words were out before she could stop them, but at least she managed to prevent herself from saying that it was more than fondness.

However, she saw at once that she had made a grave mistake. The baron's demeanor hardened.

"You have given me cause to believe that Miles may be right, niece. You are suffering from the lack of a firm hand. It wasn't your father's fault, of course. He was too ill and you had no mother to guide you."

Rage burned within Maryana, but she kept her voice ice cold. "And I suppose that his solution to this 'problem' is for him to marry me and take me in hand?"

"He did suggest that, yes." The baron's gaze slid away from hers.

"And you agreed?"

"I told him that I would give the matter my consideration."

Before Maryana could respond, they both heard the sounds of booted feet in the corridor, and a moment later, Roderic was standing there, flanked by two of the baron's guards. His expression was grimmer than she'd ever seen, but she thought that his gaze softened slightly as it fell briefly upon her.

The baron ordered one of the men to fetch Miles, then asked her to leave. She thought about refusing, but realized that it would serve no good purpose. In fact, her presence might inflame Miles even more. She turned on her heel and walked from the room. Then, as soon as she was out of sight, she hurried through the castle and out a side door into the courtyard. It was a warm day and the shutters were open. She should be able to hear well enough.

By the time she reached the window and hid herself beside it, Miles must have appeared, because her uncle was listing the charges against Roderic, which, to her dismay, included having insulted her.

Maryana clenched her fists in helpless anger. If, in that moment, she'd had a weapon in her hand, she would have cheerfully killed Miles Foulane.

Inside, the proceedings dragged on. Miles described the incident, embellishing wherever he could, claiming that his men had sought only to restrain Roderic, who then attacked them viciously and threatened him as well, desisting only when she begged him not to harm Sir Miles.

Then, according to Miles, Roderic had taken liberties with her before stealing a horse and riding away.

Maryana could barely restrain herself, and was probably able to do so only because she wanted to hear what Roderic would say. As yet, he hadn't spoken. But now, her uncle asked him what he had to say in his own defense.

"Sir Miles speaks the truth—except for a few details," Roderic said dryly. "He neglected to mention his intention to kill the man who was poaching. And the lady Maryana never requested me to desist. As to my taking liberties with her, I plead guilty—or I will if the lady herself wishes to charge me."

"The lady Maryana has asked me to speak on her behalf," Miles blustered.

"I don't know the lady well," Roderic said in that same tone of dry amusement, "but it is my strong impression that she is quite capable of speaking for herself—as you perhaps already know, sir."

Maryana, despite her anger and fear, was forced to cover a giggle. She could easily envision the expression on Miles's face right now.

"It seems to me, Lord Roderic, that you are agreeing with most of the charges brought against you," the baron said. "Therefore, it is Sir Miles's right to recommend punishment."

"Quite so!" Miles stated loudly. "I want to see this Sakim cur receive twenty lashes—in public, so that his people may learn a lesson."

"Uh, that *does* seem a bit severe, Sir Miles," the baron stated. "I was thinking of a few weeks' imprisonment."

"Imprisonment? For interfering with the arrest of a poacher, attacking two men, and insulting both me and lady Maryana? His Majesty would not see that as being sufficient punishment." Miles's voice seemed to rise with every word.

"Baron," Roderic said, "imprisonment is bad enough, but a public lashing will inflame my people, and you will have a rebellion on your hands."

"One we will put down easily enough," Miles replied in a contemptuous tone. "I have requested additional men from my cousin."

A long silence followed, and Maryana could almost hear Roderic's thoughts. More men meant that even more of his people would be killed. She held her breath, awaiting his response even as she tried not to think about him suffering the lash. What could she do? She had to do something!

"Now, in addition to everything else, he has threatened you with rebellion, Baron. He should be lashed!"

There was another silence, during which she could envision her uncle squirming uncomfortably. But then he agreed, stating that Roderic should be held in the castle's prison for the time being.

Maryana sagged against the stone wall, as angry and miserable as she'd ever been in her life. How could she help Roderic? She didn't even know where the cells were, and she knew he would be well guarded in any event.

Then suddenly, there were shouts and the sounds of a scuffle inside the room. Unable to contain herself any longer, she stepped in front of the window and peered in—just in time to see Roderic's back as he ran through the door. Miles was just picking himself up from the floor, while the two guards lay motionless.

She gathered her skirts in her hands and ran as fast as she could toward the front of the castle. By the time she rounded the corner, Roderic was on his horse and riding hard toward the gate.

Miles emerged from the entrance and shouted to the guards to lower the huge wooden gate—but it was too late. Roderic rode beneath it just as it began to lower. She wanted to cheer, but decided to content herself with some gloating. So she approached Miles, who stood there, still shouting at the guards, who, of course, could do nothing.

"It seems to me," she observed in the same dry tone Roderic had used, "that you might have made certain his horse wasn't so available. Or perhaps that the gate was lowered after he arrived."

Miles turned to her, his face dark with rage. "He'll die for this!"

She smiled. "But you will have to catch him first, won't you?"

Then she walked away, leaving him to sputter helplessly and issue meaningless orders.

* * *

For three days they hunted for Roderic, the small force from the castle augmented by the guards on loan from Miles's cousin. But no one had seen him, and no one had any idea where he might have gone. Maryana beseeched her uncle not to make his people pay for Roderic's escape, but his assurances did little to assuage her fears. Miles was like a man possessed, organizing the search and riding himself from dawn to dusk.

Maryana wasn't really worried about Roderic's safety. This was his land, and these were his people, while the guards searching for him were hated strangers. Her only fear was that she would never see him again. And there was the added benefit of Miles's having turned his attentions elsewhere, for the time being at least.

When she feigned innocence and asked her uncle what had happened, she thought that he seemed almost pleased. But having already seen how easily Miles could influence him, she took little comfort from that.

Instead, she began to think about how she could do something for Roderic's people in his absence. He would no longer be able to collect food from the castle's kitchens, and she doubted that the cook or anyone else would steal anything. And then there was the money she'd had sent from home. She'd quite forgotten to give it to Roderic that night at the stables.

So she announced to her uncle her intention of visiting the people, saying that it was a time-honored tradition for the lady of the castle to pay such visits. Just to improve her chances, she also suggested that it could be a good opportunity for her to discover the mood of the people. The guards that had been lent to them would surely be leaving soon. Then she held her breath, awaiting her uncle's reply.

But he temporized, saying that he must think

about it. He could see the wisdom of her suggestion, but he was concerned about possible danger to her.

Maryana waited impatiently for more than a day. She didn't doubt that her uncle had spoken the truth about his concern for her safety, but she also suspected that he wanted to consult with Miles—and that gave her cause for alarm because the decision should surely be her uncle's to make, as master of the castle and its lands.

In the end, he agreed, however, and she set out on a pleasant morning, accompanied by two guards. She had known that she wouldn't be permitted to go alone, but she was hopeful that she could manage to speak to some of the people privately nevertheless.

The person she most wanted to see was the poacher. If anyone would trust her enough to tell her what had become of Roderic, it would surely be him. He would remember that she'd spoken up on his behalf.

She saw that the harvest was under-way, though her expert eye told her that the crops were less than bountiful, and she recalled Roderic's having warned her uncle about that and imploring him not to exact heavy taxes for that reason.

Maryana had already known that Roderic's people were suffering, but the full extent of that suffering became clear to her as she went from one dwelling to another. The signs of malnourishment were everywhere: hungry, big-eyed children who stared at her as though she might be concealing food within the folds of her elegant clothes, and mothers whose eyes held both fear and hopelessness.

As she'd hoped, the guards didn't enter the little houses with her, but instead remained outside after ascertaining that there were no men present. Maryana had brought with her the new supply of money, and at each visit, pressed into the women's hands a gold coin or two, depending on the size and condition of the family.

"This is *my* money," she told each of them. "And you must not tell anyone where it came from."

She would leave after they promised solemnly not to tell, not even trying to hide their glee over their good fortune. Maryana thought about her own comfortable, well-fed people and wondered how much more she could do for these people. The fact that they were Sakim made no difference to her. She'd long since given up hating her people's old enemies.

But she began to despair of finding the poacher as she realized that all but the oldest or most afflicted of the men were out working. And when she happened upon a cottage where the man of the household had come home for the meager midday meal, the guards remained with her.

By the time she reached the home of the local miller, Maryana had all but given up hope of finding the man and instead was contenting herself with distributing her dwindling supply of coins. After looking around the neat little house that was well filled with noisy children, the guards withdrew as usual.

It was obvious to her that this was a home that had once been comfortable, despite the larger than usual size of the family. And the woman seemed friendlier than the others had been. She offered Maryana a cup of tea and some fresh-baked bread, though there was no butter or jam in evidence.

Maryana didn't want to further deplete their stores of food, but she accepted because to have refused would have seemed insulting. So she held the youngest child, a mere babe, on her lap while the mother made tea.

"I passed through many fields on my way here, and it looks as though the harvest will not be good," she said to the woman to make conversation. A poor harvest would mean less work for this woman's husband, whose mill was just behind the house.

"Aye," the woman responded. "The worst in many years. Too much rain and cold weather this spring, and then another cold spell just after the sprouts came up. People will go hungry this winter," she added quietly as she cast an uneasy glance at her brood, who were busy devouring their bread.

She had an attractive face, Maryana thought—or rather, she'd had one before time and too much childbearing had begun to wear her down. She was trying to think of something else to say when the back door opened and a man walked in, then paused halfway through his greeting to his wife when he saw her.

It was the poacher! Maryana couldn't believe her luck, and now she understood why she'd been received more cordially in this house.

The man took off his dusty cap and bowed to her. "My pardon, milady. I didn't know we had a visitor." Then he shifted about nervously. "I'd like to thank ye for trying to help me that day. It would have been my life for sure."

"I tried," Maryana said, "but it was Lord Roderic who saved you."

"Aye—and at great cost to himself, it seems," the man said cautiously.

"It wasn't saving you that got him into trouble," she replied. "My uncle, the baron, was prepared to let that go, but Sir Miles insisted that Lord Roderic had attacked his men and insulted him—and me." She allowed contempt to creep into her voice, which wasn't difficult.

Rather to her surprise, the man chuckled. "Lord Roderic's a fine one, when he gets his dander up. But I can't see him insulting a lady like you."

"He didn't," she assured him. "And I told my uncle that—but it did no good. I'm very sorry for what happened to Lord Roderic. I tried to help him."

She paused for a moment, then added, as casually as she could, "I can only hope that he's safe. The guards have been searching for him for days now."

The miller, who had been avoiding her gaze, as was the custom with peasants, was silent for a moment, and then looked her straight in the eyes.

"He is safe, milady. He won't let them find him."

It was, she thought, as much as she could hope to hear, though she wanted much more. She got up to leave, then remembered her bag of coins. But when she withdrew one to give them, the miller refused to take it.

"We know what you're doing," he said, "and we're grateful. But there's those who need it more than us."

Then, when her expression must have told him what she was thinking, he went on. "I wasn't hunting for myself, milady. That game he trampled beneath his fine horse's hooves was intended for two widows and their families. Lord Roderic always let me hunt on his lands for them. Their husbands died in his service, y'see."

"Lord Roderic is a good man," she replied, then added, "I wish that my uncle were as good."

Then she took out another coin to add to the one she still held. "Perhaps I've already visited them, but I'd very much appreciate it if you'd take these coins for them as well—or for anyone else you know may need more help than I gave."

This time he took them, with a solemn promise to see that they were put to good use.

"She gave out coins to nearly everyone. Some said maybe she was trying to bribe them to say where you were, but myself, I don't believe that, and I told them so."

"You're right," Roderic said. "She wouldn't do that. Besides, it was she who gave me the money I passed out before. I said it was mine because I thought it best that no one know of her involvement. But the truth is, I can't get at my own money. I wasn't smart enough to hide it outside the castle."

"Ye couldn'a known that the accursed Nerans would invade while ye were gone," one of the men said soothingly. "Hindsight's always better."

"The tax collectors'll be startin' their rounds any day now," another man said, shaking his head in disgust.

"Another mistake I made," Roderic replied. "I'd had some hopes of persuading the baron to ease up on them a bit. But Sir Miles Foulane has put an end to that. He has the baron's ear now."

"That washed-out excuse for a man should meet with an accident," one of the men growled.

"No, Tandy. That won't help at all; instead, it'll make things even worse. He's a favorite of the Neran king."

"Then what can we do?" the miller asked.

"Nothing—for now. I must think on it."

After they had gone, Roderic lingered outside the little cottage. He was taking a chance by staying so close to the castle, when he should have headed south, where he had some friends. But he refused to be driven from his own lands. Besides, no one but the men who'd been here tonight knew of the cottage. It had been built more than a century ago, deep in the hills at the edge of his lands. He'd used it as his father and grandfather and great-grandfather had: as a shelter for hunting expeditions into this game-rich forest.

When the cottage was built, there'd been no attempt to hide it, but the location they'd chosen was perfect: in a narrow ravine next to a small stream, surrounded on all sides by very dense forest and thick clumps of blackberry bushes that could shred a man's clothes. The only easy way in and out was to walk through the little stream for nearly a mile, and the cottage itself was invisible from any direction until one was nearly upon it.

It would have been a good spot to bury his money, he thought glumly—not that he had all that much to bury in any event. Like any noble worth his salt, he'd returned most of his money to his land and people in one way or another.

So what was he going to do? It was a good question that needed answering. The baron's men had apparently given up searching for him, probably believing that he was long gone. He had to do *something*.

Roderic knew that if he asked his men to revolt against the baron, they would do so. But what would it gain them in the long run? The baron might be driven out, but the Neran king would send troops, and too many of his people would lose their lives in the struggle.

There had to be another way, he thought, then found himself smiling at the thought of Maryana distributing money to his people. He didn't know if it was her own, or money she'd stolen from the baron's treasury. If it was the latter, she was taking a big risk, and that bothered him.

Maryana. Roderic lifted his head and stared at the stars. She was as far from him as they were—and as unreachable. But it seemed that fact didn't stop him from wanting her, or from imagining himself as lord of his castle once more, with her at his side.

He wondered if Miles Foulane was still pressing his suit for her hand. He'd know if the man succeeded, because the cook would pass along the word if there was to be a wedding. Weddings required a lot of preparation.

The more pressing problem was his people. Maryana couldn't possibly steal enough to provide for them for the coming winter. He frowned, thinking. And then, suddenly, he began to laugh. Yes, he liked the idea. He liked it very much.

"You seem troubled, Uncle. What is it?"

"I've just received a report that one of my tax collectors was waylaid and robbed. Fortunately he wasn't carrying much, but it's still troubling."

"And the robbers got away?"

The baron nodded glumly. "They tied up the collector and his guards and took their horses. The horses were found only a few miles away. And there's no hope of identifying them. They all wore hoods."

He slammed a fist against a table. "I can't let this happen again! His Majesty won't like it if he thinks me incapable of keeping the peace here."

"He's even less likely to be pleased at the decrease in his taxes," she observed, hoping he didn't intend to press Roderic's people for replacements.

"I'll just have to collect again."

"But Uncle, those people could ill afford to pay what they have already paid! How can you demand more?"

"I have no choice."

"Do you think it might happen again?"

"I fear that it will. I'll have to send out more guards to accompany the collectors, which will only slow down the process."

But it seemed that extra guards made no difference at all, and before many days had passed, it became clear that the thieves had gotten much smarter. The collectors were being waylaid only after they had made many collections.

Maryana was appalled when her uncle sent the tax men back to the same places, to extract still more from the impoverished peasants. Didn't the thieves know they were condemning children to starvation this winter? Such men apparently didn't care.

But she had another, more immediate problem. Miles was back to pressing his suit, ever more strongly. And worst of all, she suspected that her uncle was moving closer to demanding that she accept. She had foolishly given out all her money and now had nothing left with which to book passage home. She'd written to her manager for more money, but it might not arrive for months. At this time of year, storms prevented ships from making the already dangerous crossing. No supply ships had come in since she'd sent her message.

The only good thing she could say about the highwaymen was that they had succeeded in capturing her uncle's full attention, which left him little time to listen to Miles's demands.

Miles had switched from making demands to attempts to charm her, though he had to be a complete fool if he truly believed it would work.

Seasonal storms kept her confined to the castle for several days, and when they passed at long last and the weather became dry and sunny, she requested guards to accompany her on a ride, knowing that she wouldn't be permitted to ride alone. Besides, with the highwaymen about, it seemed risky, even though they had yet to waylay anyone but tax collectors.

Unfortunately, Miles came in as she was making her request, and he immediately insisted upon accompanying her himself. So it was with considerably less than her earlier enthusiasm that she set out.

Because the storms had made the fields all but impassable, Miles said they would have to stay on the roads. After ascertaining that she'd never ridden on the road that led north from the castle, he decided they would go that way.

"It should be safer, too," he remarked. "There's nothing in that direction for many miles, so it's unlikely that the thieves would be there."

He went on to say that it was heavily forested land—hilly with narrow, deep ravines and all but impenetrable because of the large numbers of blackberry bushes there. The game, he declared, was indeed plentiful, but not worth risking the thorns.

Maryana ignored his attempt at pleasantries, but she soon saw that he was right. It was a strange but lovely land. The narrow road felt more like a green tunnel as huge branches arched overhead and trees and shrubs pressed against the banks, as though eager to reclaim the road itself.

She began to imagine herself galloping down the road, free of everything and everyone—with Roderic awaiting her at some unknown end: a place far from Miles's plot to win her hand and equally far from her uncle's guards who sought to capture Roderic. They were foolish daydreams, but they were all she had. The likely future for both of them was unbearably bleak.

They reached a high spot in the road, where a lovely vista of seemingly endless hills lay before them, with no habitation of any kind in sight.

"A wild place," Miles remarked. "Mayhap your friend, Lord Roderic, vanished into these forests and lives now like a wild animal himself. It won't matter if we don't find him. When winter comes, he will die out here. I'm told that the winters can be quite severe."

She turned to him and saw a smile of pure evil on his face. Apparently as she had her dreams, he had his.

"Lord Roderic seems to me to be quite resourceful," she said, careful not to betray the anger he

65

clearly wanted to see. "In fact, it would not surprise me if he were hiding beneath your nose."

Failing to elicit the reaction that he'd wanted, Miles jerked his horse's head around and announced that it was time to turn back. So they reversed their direction and began to ride back through the green tunnel toward the castle.

But they had gone only a few miles when one of the men behind her shouted a warning. Maryana barely had time to turn in the saddle before they were suddenly surrounded by a group of men on horseback—all of them wearing hoods.

The masked men pushed them all into the center of a circle, and then their leader demanded that they hand over all their valuables. She immediately began to comply, removing a thick gold chain that held a crucifix—a gift from her father—as well as several rings she'd inherited from her mother. Much as she hated to part with these things, she valued her life far more than she did any objects, and she preferred to remove them herself, rather than have these thieves' hands upon her.

Miles, however, began to harangue them, promising to have them hunted down like stags and cursing them as "Sakim scum." Maryana thought that it must be some poor attempt to show bravery for her benefit, because she couldn't believe even he could be so foolish. There were eight men—all of them heavily armed with bows and knives—against three men and herself.

"Miles," she said to him quietly, "give them what you have. You risk the lives of all of us."

And yet still he resisted. When the hooded men had apparently satisfied themselves that the guards had no valuables at all, one of them took the jewelry she offered, and then they turned their attention to the angry, blustering Miles.

Their leader sat holding the jewelry she had given them, but one of the other men drew his knife and approached Miles, while the others hovered around him.

I wish they would kill him! she thought, then, shamed at such a desire, once again exhorted him to yield his valuables. This time he complied, removing a heavy ring and then handing over a small bag of coins.

The tall man who had menaced Miles carried the items to their leader, and Maryana saw him conversing briefly with him, though she could hear nothing of what was said.

"Get off your horse, Neran swine!" the leader ordered in his thick Sakim accent.

Maryana drew in a sharp breath. Would they actually kill him—or were they merely going to take the horses as well? She knew this must be the group of highwaymen who were plaguing the tax collectors, but they'd never stolen horses before.

Miles refused, and the tall man who had menaced him earlier now brought his horse up against Miles's steed and touched the nobleman's throat with the tip of his knife. A trickle of blood ran down into his fine tunic. Squealing and clutching his throat, Miles got off his horse, all of his bluster now gone. Maryana knew she should be pitying him—or worrying about her own safety—but instead, she couldn't help feeling a sort of triumph at seeing him humiliated far more effectively than she herself could do.

"Take off your finery, Neran. They should fit me quite well, and I don't wish to see them further bloodstained." The leader laughed uproariously and was quickly joined by the others, except for the tall man who had nicked Miles with his knife. He merely watched silently, still brandishing the knife as though barely able to prevent himself from using it again.

"I . . . I can't do that," Miles stammered. "There's a lady present."

Saranne Dawson

"What? Do you think she will faint dead away at the sight of your pale Neran flesh? She looks to me to be able to withstand that."

In the end, it was the tall, silent man with the knife who convinced Miles. He truly wants to kill him, Maryana thought, studying the man as Miles began to remove his clothes.

The man circled around Miles, deliberately taunting him, though still silent. And then he was standing beside her. The truth had begun to dawn on Maryana as she watched his lithe movements, but not until he raised his head and, for one brief moment, looked into her eyes, did she know for certain that she was right—and why he was remaining silent.

They took all of Miles's clothes save his under-tunic—even his fine leather boots. Then they laughed, and before leaving, the leader offered her an apology for "assaulting her gentle eyes with the sorry sight."

Maryana barely heard him as her eyes followed them until they had vanished over a rise. They'd ordered the guards off of their horses and had tied their hands, and now Miles was shouting for her to untie them.

But she ignored his whining for a moment as she stared after the thieves. How she wished he'd taken her with him! Just seeing that familiar gleam in his dark eyes had heated her all the way through.

She dismounted slowly, then feigned tremors in her hands to prevent her from untying the knots too quickly. After that, one of the guards untied Miles, who made a rather comical sight as he stood there, nearly naked, blustering once again.

She had worn a light cloak, and now she removed it and flung it at Miles. "You have only yourself to blame," she told him in disgust. "You're fortunate that they didn't kill you."

Rather to her surprise, Miles actually nodded,

then touched the small cut at his throat. "He wanted to kill me. I could see it in his eyes."

Miles remained silent as they rode back to the castle. Maryana was rather looking forward to his entrance into the courtyard. Her cloak wasn't quite long enough to cover the length of his legs, and of course, his feet were bare.

But it seemed that her pleasure was to be denied. When they were only a short distance from the castle, Miles brought them to a halt, then told his men to escort her back to safety and return with clothing for him. After that, he withdrew into the cover of the woods.

As soon as she arrived at the castle, Maryana went to see her uncle and told him what had happened—withholding one crucial piece of information.

"They took your jewelry?" the baron asked.

"Yes," she replied, then contrived to look despairing. "The crucifix my father gave me and several rings that had belonged to my mother."

"How very terrible for you, my dear," her uncle said sympathetically. "We will redouble our efforts to find them, and perhaps then we will recover your items as well."

Maryana merely nodded, trying without success to squeeze out a few tears. But the truth was that she'd stopped worrying about her jewelry the moment she'd stared into Roderic's eyes. He would see that she got them back at some point.

Her uncle had called in the captain of his guards and now began to discuss with him how they might capture the thieves. Maryana only half-listened to them. Roderic was playing it very smart. He hadn't spoken once, because his cultured voice would have given him away. Instead, he'd designated someone else to act as leader.

And of course she knew now what was *really* happening to the stolen tax money. She hid a smile, wondering if she might have inadvertently given him the idea when she'd stolen from her uncle's treasury to give the money back to the people. It amused her to think that the tax collectors were in fact collecting the same money over and over.

But how long could he continue before they captured him and his men? She sighed inwardly, thinking that at least no one but her knew that Roderic was leading the band of thieves.

Then Miles arrived, his face flushed with anger all over again as he told the baron the same story she had already given—as though she were incapable of telling it properly. Of course, he made it sound as though he'd suffered his indignities in an attempt to prevent them from taking her jewelry. She could scarcely believe that he could stand there and tell his lie with her right there.

The baron was trying to soothe him with promises to catch the thieves when Miles abruptly cut him off.

"Baron, I have been thinking about this ever since it happened, and I am very nearly certain that one of them—the man who threatened me with a knife—was Lord Roderic."

Maryana could only hope that her gasp hadn't been heard. The baron stared at Miles as though he'd lost his mind as well as his clothing.

"But you said that they wore hoods!" he protested.

"So they did—but I saw his eyes." Miles frowned. "And now that I think of it, he was the only one who didn't speak. And I also saw him speaking briefly to the so-called 'leader.' I've no doubt that he put the man up to stealing my clothes."

Maryana had forgotten about that brief discussion, but now she knew that Miles was right. Roderic would have enjoyed Miles's humiliation—especially in front of her. But she was shocked that Miles had identified him from just his eyes. Somehow, she'd thought that only she had seen that gleam that distinguished his dark eyes from those of his countrymen.

"Well," said the baron, clearly not at all convinced, "that would certainly put a different light on the matter, wouldn't it?"

Yes, she thought, *it certainly does. What it means is that Miles will spend every waking moment urging my uncle to search still more for him.*

Chapter Four

"You saw this man as well, my dear," the baron said, turning to her as Miles stormed from the room, still in high dudgeon over the grievous insults to his person—not to mention his dignity.

"Do *you* believe this thief to have been Lord Roderic?"

Rather surprised to be asked for her opinion, Maryana shook her head quickly. "I saw as much of him as Miles did, and I found no resemblance. The man seemed to me to be both taller and leaner than Lord Roderic." She affected a shrug.

"Miles is obsessed with Lord Roderic. I've no doubt he would have believed the man to be him if he were *my* size. Besides," she went on, deciding to pile lie upon lie until she'd built a formidable mountain of them, "I was closer than Miles was to the leader and I overheard some of the conversation he mentioned—between the leader and the man Miles claims was Lord Roderic.

"The man was actually suggesting that Miles

should be killed to set an example. He'd resisted giving up his things, you see. And I heard his voice. He spoke like a peasant."

As she'd already guessed, she'd woven a lie that pleased her uncle. It was clear enough to her that he didn't want a confrontation with Roderic, though she couldn't have said why. Perhaps it was merely cowardice—or perhaps, in his own way, he actually *liked* the Sakim lord.

The baron nodded. "I myself believe that Lord Roderic has gone south, to a place where he has friends who would take him in and hide him."

More fool you, then, Maryana thought, if you truly believe that Roderic would abandon his lands and his people.

"He's a strange man," the baron mused. "Unknowable, really. At times I have thought him to be a coward. But other times I find myself thinking that he is far from that, indeed, and that what I perceive to be cowardice is instead patience."

He chuckled. "Then again, he does not seem to be a patient man, either. And it's unlikely that his people would hold him in such high regard if he were, in fact, a coward."

Maryana was rather surprised at her uncle's words, which so closely mirrored her own feelings about Roderic. She still hadn't quite resolved the many contradictions she saw in him, although she suspected that those contradictions were part of her attraction to him.

"What do you intend to do about these thieves?" Maryana asked curiously.

"Ahh, there's the question. For certain, we must do something. His Majesty will brook no excuses for our failure to collect his taxes. I will simply have to send out more guards with the tax collectors, even if that means leaving the castle poorly defended."

"If you do that—and if Lord Roderic *is* still here

somewhere—he may seize the opportunity to storm the castle." She offered this theory in the hope of dissuading him from increasing the guards—and thereby putting Roderic and his men more at risk.

"That's possible, but this castle can actually be held by very few defenders. Don't worry yourself, my dear. I wouldn't put you at risk."

I'm not at risk in any event, Maryana replied silently. *But Roderic is.*

Two days later, Maryana found out quite by accident that her uncle had taken another step to prevent the theft of his precious taxes. With no supply ship having yet arrived from across the strait, she was growing desperate—both to find more money for the peasants and to have enough of her own to book passage back to Chamoney.

Although no supply ships had arrived from Neran, she had already observed that smaller ships, either fishing vessels or small coastal traders, were coming and going from the harbor. She feared that any day, Miles would succeed in persuading her uncle to give her away in marriage. If that happened, she knew that Miles would demand an immediate ceremony.

Miles knew—far more than her uncle did—the extent of her feelings for Roderic. He'd lost no opportunity to remind her that finding the Sakim lord was his only objective now, and she couldn't help seeing the hatred that blazed from his pale eyes every time he spoke Roderic's name.

No doubt he assumed that Roderic returned her feelings and that he would be driven to a mad foolishness if he found out that she was about to be wed to Miles. Therefore, she now had two reasons to prevent that union, and it might be that the only way she could prevent it would be to go home. So she needed the gold to bribe a fisherman or one of

the coastal traders to take her across the straits—
back to Neran—should that become necessary.

And the trip would have to be arranged quickly.
If her uncle agreed to the marriage, not only would
Miles insist that it happen immediately, but he
would also be watching her closely, knowing that
she might possibly try to escape.

If she were any other woman, the thought that
she might try to escape into the land of their ancient enemies wouldn't occur to Miles, but unfortunately, she'd let him see enough of her
unladylike behavior for him to guess that she
might try. There were disadvantages to flouting
convention.

So she decided to steal some money from her
uncle's coffers, even though the risk was rather
greater than before. His man was counting it more
regularly, now that the taxes were coming in.

Still, she thought that in light of the amount of
money now in the castle's vault, a small quantity
might not be missed. In all likelihood, the wizened
little keeper of the treasury would think that he
had simply miscounted.

She knew that the tax collectors returned late in
the day, and that the vault was locked and empty
until their return. All that was necessary was for
her to wait until she could be certain that her uncle
was nowhere about; then she could steal his large
ring of keys, which must surely include a key for
the treasury.

Her opportunity came one fine morning, when
her uncle announced his intention of going hunting. He'd invited her to accompany him, but she
declined, saying that she was feeling rather fever-
ish, having perhaps indulged in too many sweets
the night before.

The truth, of course, was that she was feeling
fine and had never in her life felt ill—not even
when the various ailments of winter swept through

her estate. This, she knew, would be the best opportunity she would have, since Miles was away from the castle as well, no doubt searching for Roderic.

She had no difficulty slipping into her uncle's suite to borrow his keys, which he'd left in plain sight. But having found them so easily, she paused to survey the handsome suite, knowing that it had once been Roderic's.

Her gaze locked onto the big bed—and stayed there as a soft heat stole through her. It felt strange, almost alien—as though some other being had taken temporary possession of her body. Maryana had never been one to think about marriage—except, that was, about how to avoid it. And she'd certainly never given any thought to actually lying in a marriage bed with a man.

From the whispers she'd heard, it was anything but pleasant—and yet she could not imagine it being unpleasant to be there with Roderic. No, not unpleasant at all.

Finally, she dragged her gaze from the bed and hurried from the suite. She *must* stop such foolish thoughts. There would be no marriage bed for her and Roderic—not even if he did in fact return her feelings. Instead of foolishly daydreaming about what could never be, she must concentrate on helping him and his people as long as she could, and then avoiding at all costs marriage to Miles Foulane.

After leaving her uncle's suite, she made her way through the maze of corridors to the vault, concealing the ring of keys in the deep pocket of her skirt. The room was at the end of a short hallway, and she stopped as she reached it, then peered cautiously around the corner.

To her dismay, one of the Sakim servants was there, filling the lanterns that hung on hooks set into the wall. She turned quickly and went back to her own quarters, hoping that the man wouldn't take too long at his task. She'd already noticed that the Sakim servants seemed to move at a very slow pace as they went about their duties, no doubt a small rebellion against their hated Neran overlord.

The man might well spend half the day there, she thought miserably. And if her uncle had good luck on his hunt, he could return by mid-afternoon.

She was pacing about her quarters impatiently, wondering how soon she should try again, when a servant brought her a tray. It had become her custom to take her midday meal in her quarters, since her uncle was generally busy and Miles was usually away.

Maryana turned, frowning at the interuption of her unpleasant thoughts, but when she saw the young girl's dismayed look, she smiled quickly.

"I'm not angry with you, Gisel," she told the girl. She'd been trying in various ways to gain the girl's confidence, hoping to use her as a channel to the Sakim people.

The girl gave her a small smile of relief as she set down the heavily laden tray. Maryana gestured to it.

"There is more than enough food here for three people, let alone one who has little appetite at the moment. Tell me, Gisel, what happens to all that is returned?"

The girl gave her a wary look. "I . . . I don't know what you mean, milady."

"I know that Lord Roderic was taking kitchen leftovers—and perhaps more—and giving them to his people. What I would like to know is if anyone has taken over that task, now that he appears to have gone."

"Ummm." The girl stalled, casting her eyes about as though wishing to escape.

"Gisel, if I knew this was happening and took no

77

action to stop it before, doesn't that tell you that it was being done with my blessing?"

"Ummm."

"Please tell the cook that I insist that she continue as before. Do you understand me?"

"Yes'm."

"The baron has turned over the running of the castle to me now, because he is far too busy hounding your people for their taxes. And you can assure the cook that I will not be keeping an eye on the food supplies."

The girl stared at her in silence for a moment, then finally allowed herself a smile as she bobbed her head. "Yes'm. I'll be sure to tell her that, milady."

The girl curtsied and vanished before Maryana could decide if she should inquire whether she or any of the others here knew someone with a boat. But she decided it might not be wise to press her luck at this point. She had accomplished *something* anyway.

After nibbling the food and fortifying herself with a small glass of wine, she set out for the treasury room once more. If that servant were still there, she would simply have to order the man to move on to some other task. This would be her last opportunity to get in there because she would have to return her uncle's keys before he came back from his hunt.

But before she had quite reached the corridor that led to the safekeeping room, she heard men's voices: Neran voices. She stopped, then risked peeking around the corner.

Two of the guards were there, standing just outside the room. At their feet were the bags she'd seen before: the leather pouches that contained the tax money.

She retreated a short distance down the dimly lit hallway, wondering what they were doing there in the middle of the day—and without the tax collectors. But before she could puzzle it out, she heard footsteps approaching.

Swiftly, she opened the nearest door and slipped into a musty, obviously unused room, then left the door open a crack to see who was coming.

The little counting man passed by, then vanished around the corner, heading toward the counting room. Maryana stepped out into the corridor again and moved swiftly to the intersecting corner.

"No trouble then?" she heard the counting man say.

"Not a bit," one of the guards replied. "We kept the pouches well hidden—just two guards out on patrol," he finished with a chuckle.

Then their voices trailed away as they followed the counting man into the room and closed the door behind them. Maryana reluctantly moved away, lest they find her there when they left.

It didn't take much guesswork on her part to see that her uncle had made some changes. The appearance of the two guards halfway through the day told her that her uncle had decided to split up the day's collections. Until now, the money had always remained with the collectors, who were surrounded by a large contingent of guards. Now it appeared that the money was being divided, with some of it being sent back in the care of the guards alone.

Maryana's thoughts turned abruptly from her own problem of getting at the money in the treasury to wondering how she could let Roderic know about the change. There would certainly be less risk to him and his men if they could take the bags from two guards, rather than being forced to fight a whole contingent of them.

Then, as if to lend further confirmation, she saw, coming toward her, two more guards, carrying still more pouches. Fortunately for her, she was by now in a portion of the vast castle where her presence didn't raise suspicions. Still, she couldn't help holding her breath until they had bowed to her and moved on.

She then hurried on to her uncle's quarters and returned his ring of keys, this time ignoring completely the big bed that had once been Roderic's as she tried to come up with a way of getting the word to him.

Maryana was frustrated—and that frustration was about to drive her to take a big risk. She'd already been denied what would have surely been the simplest way to contact Roderic, thanks to her uncle's concern for her welfare.

She had told him that she wished to pay visits once again to the people in the village, but this time the baron had denied her request. The time wasn't auspicious, he'd said. With the band of thieves on the loose and the people already disgruntled over the tax collections, it might not be safe for her to venture beyond the castle grounds. Besides, he'd pointed out, he couldn't spare any guards to accompany her.

It had been her hope to visit the miller again. She was certain that he had been among the "thieves," and even if he hadn't been she felt that she could trust him to pass a message on to Roderic.

Now, the only way left to her was to take a more direct—and therefore, far more risky—approach. She'd been carefully cultivating the friendship of the servant, Gisel, knowing that it could become important—even essential—to have an ally inside the castle.

Yesterday, she'd noticed that the girl's boots were badly worn. So on this day, as she waited for her to bring the noon meal, Maryana dug through the wardrobe and pulled out an old pair of her own boots, ones she wore when she was forced to be outdoors in bad weather back home. Even worn as they were, they were many times better than the ones the girl wore, and the two of them were the same size.

Gisel arrived promptly, and Maryana was heartened to see the girl give her a genuine smile. As soon as Gisel had set down the heavy tray, Maryana indicated the boots.

"I wonder if you might be able to use these boots, Gisel," she said casually. "I have no need of them here, and I think we are very close in size."

Maryana promptly felt guilty as the girl's eyes lit up with the kind of eagerness she was accustomed to seeing in women being offered a new piece of jewelry or a particularly lovely length of fabric.

"Oh, yes, milady. I do believe we're of a size— and I do need new boots."

"Well, just try them, then," Maryana said, gesturing for her to take a seat. "Can you not afford new boots yourself? Is my uncle not paying you enough?"

The girl hesitated in the act of unlacing her boots. "It isn't that so much—milady. It's that what I make must stretch so far. Mama's a widow lady, you see. M'dad was killed in Sir Roderic's service, and there're little ones to feed."

"I see. And Lord Roderic was providing for your family?"

"Yes'm. He gave me this job and he helped mama, too."

The girl turned her attention to the boots, and Maryana began to think that she might not be taking such a risk, after all. Still, she chose her words carefully.

"I would very much like to speak to Lord Roderic, but of course I have no way of reaching him. It's very important. Is it possible that you or the cook might know of some way to reach him?"

The girl stopped in the act of lacing up her new boots and cast Maryana a wary look. "But he's gone, milady."

Maryana was tempted to say that she knew perfectly well that he was still here; she'd seen him herself. But she decided to adopt a more indirect method.

"But it's possible that he might return. I cannot imagine him staying away from his people and his lands for very long. If he should return, I would be very grateful if a message could be gotten to him that I would like a meeting." She paused, then added, "He will know the place."

The girl made no response except to thank her profusely for the boots, which she claimed fit better than her present boots had ever done. She started to leave, then turned back at the door.

"Cook says to thank you, milady. I passed on your message to her."

Maryana smiled as the girl slipped through the door. Perhaps it was only her hope speaking, but she read into the girl's parting remark an agreement to pass on this message as well.

The following day, the weather turned cool and rainy—not a day when Maryana could reasonably be expected to go for a ride. The baron was prowling about the castle like a wounded bear, complaining to one and all about his losses at the hands of the highwaymen. Miles was there as well, and when he wasn't trying to force his attentions upon her, he was advising her uncle to send the tax collectors back out, to make up for the losses. To her uncle's credit, he seemed resistant to that, hoping instead that the thieves could be caught and the money recovered.

"But the people have nothing more to give," Maryana protested. "You can see for yourselves that the harvest is poor this year."

"They can give the same money they gave before," Miles pronounced ominously.

"What do you mean?" the baron asked sharply.

"One of my men heard a rumor. It's said that they're calling the leader of this band the Prince of Thieves. When he inquired just what that meant, they shut up quickly, but I think the money is being returned to them."

"What?" The baron appeared to be astonished. "You mean the thieves are robbing my collectors to give it back? That's preposterous, Miles!"

"Not so—if their leader is the scurrilous Earl of Varney."

"If he *is* their leader—and I still doubt that—he would be tucking it away to raise an army against me—not giving it back," the baron stated dismissively.

"That would be the sensible thing to do," Miles agreed, nodding. "But this man is mad. We cannot expect him to behave with good sense."

They are one and the same, Maryana thought—but of course didn't say. She was somewhat disappointed with her uncle's failure to understand that, even if it were for the best. Miles, of course, would never look ahead far enough to see that feeding one's own people meant that one would then have a strong and willing army.

But she also knew that Roderic would feed his people in any event—just as she herself would do.

After Miles had left them, the baron quickly raised the issue of his suit for her hand. "This must be settled between you soon," he told her sharply, then adopted a more reasonable tone.

"If you are not married off by the time the king arrives, he might very well decide to take Chamoney, claiming that you are unfit to manage such a large estate, thereby allowing it to fall to ruin and depriving him of his taxes."

"The king knows very well that I have been managing Chamoney for years. He was well aware of my father's declining health."

"What I am saying, my dear, is that you will be giving him an excuse to do what he could not do while your father was alive. And there is no hope of persuading him to allow *me* to take over Chamoney. He's made it clear that he wants me to remain here.

"Miles is quite fond of you, you know. I think you do him an injustice by refusing him."

"The only thing Miles Foulane is fond of is getting his hands on my money."

"Nevertheless, I fear that you will be forced to choose between accepting Miles as your husband and losing your beloved Chamoney."

And so there it was, she thought despondently: the choice that she had known she might be forced to make—and the choice she could *not* make.

After another cool, rainy day, Sunday dawned warm and bright. Maryana wondered if the message had gotten to Roderic and if he understood that she could not get away from the castle because of the weather.

Sunday, though, was surely the best day for him. The tax collectors didn't make their rounds, and therefore, there was no loot to be found. Her uncle was in much better spirits, since the last two robberies had netted the thieves very little, thanks to his scheme.

It was possible, she thought, that Roderic would soon figure out what her uncle was doing, and her information would be unnecessary. But having set into motion a plan to see him, she was very eager to do so—and for reasons that had little to do with passing on information.

Her dreams were filled with him, and being dreams, they were of the two of them safe and happy in Chamoney, far from this dark, gloomy land. She sighed; thinking that that was exactly what dreams were for: making real for a time what was, in fact, impossible. Even if Roderic were willing to leave his own lands—which he wouldn't be—the king would never permit her to take a Sakim husband. He would instead seize her lands forthwith.

After returning from the chapel service, during which the priest's dronings formed nothing more than a background for her unhappy musings, Maryana returned to her quarters. The time before the elaborate Sunday noon meal was intended for quiet contemplation of one's duties to God, but instead, Maryana was scheming—on very earthly matters. It wasn't that she didn't believe in God, but rather that He wasn't at the top of her priorities at the moment.

She was convinced that Roderic would be waiting for her at their special place in the woods—but how was she going to get there? Or rather, how was she going to get there alone? If she suggested going for a ride, surely either her uncle or Miles, or perhaps even both of them, would insist upon accompanying her.

But perhaps the Almighty was thinking about her, even if she was giving Him short shrift. When she came down to the heavily laden table, it was to discover that a guest had arrived at Varley Castle: another emissary from the king.

Conversation, thanks to her presence, was general during the long meal, but it was apparent to her that their guest had business with her uncle, and perhaps with Miles as well. She gave little thought to what that business might be because she knew that she had been handed a golden opportunity. All that remained was for her to be able to slip away unseen after the meal.

As soon as the men had closeted themselves to discuss their business, Maryana hurried upstairs and changed into her riding clothes, then wound her way through the seemingly endless hallways until she emerged at a side door close to the stables.

Unfortunately, when she reached the stables, she saw a young stable boy still attending to the horses of their guest and his men. So she was forced to hide in an unused stall and wait impatiently for the boy to finish his chores and be gone. And all the while, she feared that Roderic would come and go, believing that she'd been unable to meet him.

After what seemed to her to be just short of an eternity, the boy finally departed, and Maryana sprang from her hiding place and quickly saddled the mare she'd ridden before.

She was just reaching for the stall door when she heard footsteps and voices. She froze, her mind spinning to come up with some excuse for her being there.

Fortunately, the mare's stall was in the dimly lit rear of the stable, and the men who'd come in seemed to be staying near the doors. Still, she waited tensely, fearing that even if they didn't discover her, they might be riding in the same direction, which meant that she would be further delayed.

As soon as she heard them leading their horses from the stable, she unlatched the stall door and crept toward the entrance to see where they were going. Behind her, the mare whickered her annoyance that she'd been saddled and then left in her stall.

Her luck held! When she peered cautiously around the edge of the doorway, she saw them riding off toward the main castle gate. If they'd been headed toward the game preserve, they would have used the smaller side gate near the stables. Or so she hoped, anyway.

A short time later, Maryana was through the gate and on her way, glorying in her temporary freedom beneath a bright blue sky and praying that Roderic would be there, waiting for her in that lovely place they'd claimed for themselves. It wasn't Chamoney—but it would do.

The fields were muddy from the rain, somewhat impeding her progress, which only increased her impatience, which . . .

The closer she drew to their place, the more uncertain she became: unsure that he would be there, even if he had gotten her message, uncertain that he would trust her enough now, when her uncle was trying to find him—and finally, of course, uncertain that anything at all existed between them, let alone the love she'd been so busy imagining.

It had never been in Maryana's nature to doubt herself, which only served to increase still further her impatience at her slow progress, impatience that she, nonetheless, did not take out on the mare.

She almost missed the turnoff to the place, and in fact would have missed it if she hadn't suddenly recognized it by spotting the huge old oak tree nearby, with one torn and dead limb. And that provoked still greater uncertainty. How could she have nearly forgotten this place that had been the scene of so many dreams?

She brought the mare to a halt, then dismounted and led her into the thicket, following the barely discernible path over a small rise and then down again, into the narrow ravine where she could already hear the happy gurglings of the small stream.

The woods were so dense that she was upon the spot before she could see it clearly. When she did, she exhaled the breath she'd been holding, letting it out on a soft moan of regret. Roderic wasn't there.

He might yet come, said her hope. If he were

coming, he'd be here already, said her reason. Maryana hovered precariously between the two voices.

She tethered her mare loosely to a nearby tree, then sank down on the bank of the little stream, which was deeper and faster than it had been before, thanks to the rains. She breathed deeply, inhaling the odors of moss and rich, damp earth and the faint sweetness of the wildflowers that grew nearby: the same flowers he'd brought to her at the castle.

Remembering that—and the kiss that had followed, she smiled, more certain now even though he wasn't here. Perhaps he hadn't yet gotten her message—or perhaps he was unavoidably detained. That last gave her some pause, but she doubted that Miles had sent his men out after Roderic on this day. Always before he'd led them himself he obviously wanted to be there when Roderic was captured.

How long could she wait? It seemed likely that her uncle and Miles would be closeted with the king's messenger for some time, but still, the longer she stayed away, the greater the risk that she would be missed.

It was the mare who warned her of his approach, perhaps scenting one of her own kind. She turned sharply, then rose to her feet as first the familiar gray stallion, and then its master, appeared from amidst the leafy thicket.

Instead of tethering the stallion, Roderic merely tugged once on its reins and said, "Stay!" Then he turned to her. She smiled, feeling the movement of each of a myriad of tiny muscles—just as she felt the quiver of thousands more in her loins.

He looked different: harsher, leaner, older. But his dark eyes were the same—eyes she had easily recognized even beneath the hood that day. Even in the deep shade of the small clearing, they glittered with fire.

She stretched out both hands to him: not what she wanted to do, but a barely acceptable substitute for flinging herself into his arms. He took both hands in his and she was struck all over again by how very different he felt: hard and strong, not soft and weak like the other noblemen.

"I've missed you," he said in a low, almost begrudging tone. "Much more than I'd expected."

"And I've missed you as well," she replied huskily, then smiled. "But then I expected to miss you."

He threw back his head and laughed, still holding her hands in his. "Ah, Maryana—Maryana the Unexpected. You make a lie of everything I'd ever heard about Neran women."

"My father once said that he feared he'd gotten a boy in a woman's form."

His dark eyes swept appraisingly over her. "Definitely a woman's form."

For one brief, heart-stopping moment, she was sure that he intended to kiss her. He even moved slightly, bending toward her. But then he straightened up again and released her hands, leaving only the ghost of a kiss on her willing lips.

"I was afraid that you hadn't gotten my message," she said finally, into a silence that had become unbearable—at least for her.

"You took a risk," he admonished mildly.

"Not really." She shrugged. "I couldn't imagine Gisel running to my uncle—but I wasn't certain that she would pass on the message, either."

"And coming here today—that isn't taking a risk?" he queried, arching a dark brow.

"Perhaps a bit, but fortune smiled upon me. An emissary from the king arrived just this morning, and my uncle and Miles are occupied with him."

He nodded solemnly. "Yes, I knew someone had come. Do you know why?"

"No. They wouldn't discuss business in the presence of a mere woman."

"Rather wise of them, under the circumstances," he observed with a wry smile. "But since men tend to be excessively loose-tongued around 'mere women,' you can probably find out."

"I will, but it's likely that he has come only to see if the tax collections are going well. His Majesty has an all-consuming interest in such things."

He grinned. "Then I feel sorry for your uncle—unless, of course, he's a good liar."

"He might request more troops from the king," she said thoughtfully. "And the king just might send them, given his self-interest."

"I doubt that." Roderic shrugged. "The king is having some problems of his own. Two boatloads of Neran soldiers were lost in a storm in the straits, so I doubt he has any to spare—even for tax collecting."

He gave her a wicked grin. "I'm told that some Sakim witches cast a spell that brought that storm."

She shivered. She'd heard tales of witchcraft among the Sakim. "Surely you don't believe that."

Roderic shrugged. "I am happy to believe anything that suits my purposes." Then the corners of his wide mouth were tugged down. "That's a sad comment on my present state, isn't it?"

She was touched by this brief glimpse into the inner thoughts of the man, this sudden dropping of his normally devil-may-care attitude. Someone who'd had experience with the Sakims had once remarked that they were a dark people—and not only in their coloring. There lived within them a deep melancholy, the man had said—and she thought she was seeing that now.

"But you've been doing what you can," she protested. "What is possible."

The brief darkness was gone as he smiled. "And

I have you to thank for that, because it was from you that I got the idea to rob the tax collectors."

"From *me?*" she asked in surprise.

He nodded. "You told me that you would steal from the baron's treasury—and that's just what I'm doing, in a different manner, of course."

She smiled, recalling that she'd wondered if he might have gotten his idea from her. "That's what I came to talk to you about. My uncle has revised his methods, thanks to you."

"I know. He's now dividing up the spoils and sending small quantities back with a pair of guards."

"Then my trip here was wasted. I should have known that you—"

He seized her hands, startling her. "No! It was not wasted! Seeing you is the only pleasure in my life now—except for stealing money back for my people, of course."

Then he dropped her hands quickly, leaving her feeling bereft, almost as though he'd taken away a part of her as well.

"Is your uncle still trying to force you to marry that idiot, Miles Foulane?" he asked harshly.

"Yes." She told him what her uncle had said about the choice she might be forced to make, and as she spoke, she saw his expression darken.

"Go home, Maryana. The baron and the king will be too well occupied to follow you and force you into marriage. I can arrange safe passage across the straits for you."

She said nothing as she tried not to see his words as being a rejection of her. He must have seen it in her face, for he continued.

"It is you I am thinking of—not myself. I don't want you to leave, even if I can see you only occasionally like this."

"If I have no choice left, I will go," she promised him.

"Just let Gisel know. Her cousin is a fisherman, and I will arrange for him to take you safely back to Neran."

"Miles is still searching for you, you know," she told him. "He truly hates you, you see. And he also suspects that you are the leader of the band of thieves. I think, though, that I have convinced my uncle that he's wrong about that."

"That sniveling coward had better hope that he *doesn't* find me, because if he does, it will be his last day on this earth."

She was startled at the vehemence in his voice. "You can't kill him, Roderic. He is a favorite of the king, and—"

"All the more reason to kill him then—as if I didn't already have reason enough."

She put out a hand to touch his sleeve. "Please, Roderic. Not for me. Terrible as he is, I don't want Miles to die because of me."

He took her hand gently and brought it to his lips. "Do you see how bad it is—that I am reduced to thinking of killing a man because I cannot be a worthy rival?"

"Stop it!" she cried. "How dare you say that? I'd heard tales of Sakim melancholy—and now you are proving it! Miles Foulane is not your rival! You have no rivals, Roderic!"

And then she stopped, astonished at her outburst. As he stared at her, her face grew warm and she lowered it so he couldn't see it. But he hooked a finger beneath her chin and drew it up again.

"How has this happened so quickly, Maryana? We barely know each other."

"I know," she whispered.

His kiss was soft and sweet—and far too fleeting. She had only begun to lean into him, let her lips meld with his, when he straightened up again.

"You must get back before they miss you," he said huskily. "If you can get away, meet me here again—on the first night of the full moon. That's a week and a day. Can you do that, do you think?"

"I'll be here," she promised, the words barely audible over the rapid thudding of her heart.

Chapter Five

"It is His Majesty's wish that you marry Sir Miles Foulane."

"Perhaps that is indeed his wish—but it is not mine!"

Maryana's words and tone were intended to shock the king's emissary, and they accomplished that, although she thought that he was somewhat less taken aback than she might have expected. She didn't know the man, but perhaps he knew of her. She had acquired a certain reputation at court for her sharp tongue and her "unwomanly" ways.

"Mayhap I do not make myself clear, milady," the odious man said smoothly. "His Majesty has deemed this union to be important enough to send me here."

"I've no doubt that he deems it important, since he intends, through Miles, to lay claim to even more of my wealth. But I have no intention of marrying Miles Foulane—or anyone else, for that matter." At least not any Neran, she said to herself.

"It grieves me to think that you could be disloyal to our king," the man said, rearranging his narrow face into a semblance of sadness.

"Disloyal?" she echoed archly. "Perhaps you can tell me just how I can be disloyal, when it is Chamoney that provides more taxes for the king than any other estate?"

"Loyalty may be measured in other ways." He sniffed.

"Not for *this* king," she replied. "Furthermore, he knows quite well that I have been managing Chamoney for years on my own."

"But your father—"

"Don't play tiresome games with me, Sir Claude. Everyone at court—the king certainly included—knows that my father was too ill to tend to his own needs, let alone the needs of Chamoney. It is I who have been filling the king's coffers for the past three years—and even before that as well."

"Sir Miles is a fine man, much favored by the king."

"But not favored by me." She cocked her head and stared at him. "Tell me, does the king not fear that Miles Foulane will do to Chamoney exactly what he did to his own estates? How many taxes has *he* provided for the king?"

She had him there, and he knew that. The emissary's face grew even redder, until Maryana feared that he might have some sort of attack on the spot. But he finally managed to pull himself together.

"His Majesty has sent me to witness the nuptials, which are to be held immediately."

"Then it will be a wedding without a bride," she stated—and walked out of the room.

But her bravado vanished as soon as she slammed the door to her quarters behind her. She clenched her fists in helpless rage. It would do no good to talk to her uncle again. He was already fearful of incurring the king's wrath over his failure to provide sufficient tax monies. He sympathized with her—or claimed to do so—but he could not go against the king.

Through an act of sheer will, she calmed herself, knowing that she could not afford the luxury of anger right now. Instead, she had to make plans.

She was still weighing the choices she had when there was a knock at the door. Half-expecting it to be her uncle, come to remonstrate with her over her treatment of the king's emissary, she flung open the door. But instead of her uncle, it was one of the scullery maids, carrying her meal tray.

"Where is Gisel?" she demanded sharply as a sliver of uneasiness pierced her. Had her uncle or Miles found out about her budding friendship with the girl?

"Her ma is feeling poorly, milady. She sent word this mornin' that she couldn'a come for a few days. But she'll be back," the girl finished, clearly fearing that Maryana might dismiss Gisel.

Swallowing her fear that Gisel might return too late, Maryana softened her tone and told the maid to leave the tray. But after the door had closed behind her, she ignored the food and instead paced about the room.

What could she do if Gisel didn't return in time? Whatever she decided to do, she would need her assistance. Could she get word to her through the cook? That might be difficult, since the woman was never alone. The castle's kitchens were always filled with scurrying servants.

Never mind that for now, she told herself firmly. *First you must decide what it is that you need her for. Then you can worry about getting word to her.*

Only one thing was certain now: she would *not* marry Miles Foulane. Most women might sit idly, waiting for their true love to rescue them from such a fate. But Maryana was most decidedly not that kind of woman, and she could not put Roderic to such a great risk, even if he were so inclined.

And that produced yet another worry. What if Roderic heard about the wedding and decided to rescue her? She suspected that Miles might just be hoping for that. If she didn't already know how badly he wanted to get his weak, soft hands on her money, she'd suspect him of forcing this marriage just to get those hands on Roderic.

Then—perhaps as a way of avoiding the decision she had to make—Maryana began to wonder if Roderic *did* truly love her. He'd made no declaration, though he'd certainly shown affection. Or maybe he *did* love her, but would see the loss of her as just one more. That would fit with that dark Sakim frame of mind she'd glimpsed in him.

No—she shook herself—it was up to her to take action. She would either have to find a way to return to Chamoney, or . . .

She was just considering that other possibility when there was another knock at her door. Hoping against hope that the cook might have sneaked up from the kitchens, she opened the door eagerly this time.

But the woman who stood there was Neran: the wife, she thought, of the captain of her uncle's guard. She knew that the guards who were married had brought their families over after the fighting had ended, but she'd paid scant attention to them. They were all quartered in a distant part of the castle, and she rarely even saw them.

Behind her stood two of the castle's Sakim servants, each of them carrying lengths of white fabric. Even before the woman spoke, Maryana understood why she was here.

"Baron DeLay asked me to come to you, milady, to see to your wedding gown." The woman smiled, even in the face of Maryana's obvious lack of pleasure.

"Sakim fabrics are not as fine as ours, of course, milady, but I have done my best to find some nice things. And I was lately dressmaker to the lady Tisane."

Maryana, who hadn't yet moved from the doorway to admit them, supposed that her words were a high recommendation indeed. Marie-Claire Tisane was the most fashionable—if empty-headed—of the ladies at court.

"Very well," she said ungraciously, stepping back to allow them to enter.

By now, it was apparently becoming obvious to the seamstress that Maryana was unlike any bride she'd ever encountered, but she immediately began to sing the praises of the various fabrics the servant girls spread out for her inspection.

At least she has one thing correct, Maryana thought as she pretended to inspect the fabrics closely. *Neran fabrics are indeed superior.*

"This one will do," she said, choosing one at random since she had no intention of being present to wear it.

"A lovely choice," the seamstress chirped happily, though Maryana knew she would have said the same no matter which cloth she'd selected.

She allowed herself to be measured and agreed with the woman's suggestions as to style, then got rid of them as quickly as possible, closing the door firmly behind the clearly puzzled seamstress.

Then she nibbled a piece of fruit from the tray as she resumed her thoughts. Somehow, during that unwanted interruption, she had reached a decision.

If she were to flee across the straits to Chamoney, she would only be postponing the inevitable. Sooner or later, the king would return to Neran himself—and quite possibly sooner rather than later. Miles would undoubtedly come with him—

and she'd be in the same fix she was now in. And have nowhere to run.

She permitted herself only a small sigh as she thought about her lovely home and wondered when she would see it again. Then she turned her attention to formulating an escape plan. The gold she'd requested from her estate manager had arrived, finally, so she had no need to plunder her uncle's treasury.

Instead, she would take both the gold and her jewelry—and herself—to Roderic. He might actually prefer to see her safe in Chamoney, but she knew that she wouldn't be safe there for long, and she'd make him understand that. Instead, she would stay here—somewhere—and help him regain his lands.

Whether he likes it or not, she told herself. The only thing she could be certain of was that he wouldn't try to send her back to the castle.

But to effect her escape, she needed Gisel's assistance. Not that she couldn't escape on her own, but she needed to know where to find Roderic. She couldn't just wander around his lands, asking for him.

Maryana was desperate. The wedding was scheduled for the next day, and still Gisel had not returned to the castle. Her inquiries about the girl had produced little in the way of information. No one knew when she would return.

Several times, she'd tried to find a way to see the cook, but with wedding preparations under way, it had proven to be impossible. Maryana was now convinced that she would have to leave on her own, and then try to find her way to Gisel's home, which surely couldn't be far.

In the meantime, she'd had to fend off Miles's smarmy attentions and her uncle's pleas to accept this marriage with good grace. She ignored them both. If only she could postpone the wedding for a few more days, she could meet Roderic at their private place. But it was too late for that. She knew she couldn't even feign a sudden illness, because neither her uncle nor Miles would believe her.

For a time yesterday, Maryana had believed that the wedding would be postponed—and with no intervention on her part. The Neran priest who was to marry her had fallen victim to a hunting accident, and although he would probably survive, the man certainly wouldn't be able to perform the ceremony.

But after consulting with Miles and the king's emissary, the baron had determined that a Sakim abbot could officiate in his place. She was now on her way to meet the man, though decidedly without any enthusiasm—or piety, for that matter. She wondered if she might be able to shock the abbot sufficiently so that he would refuse to perform the ceremony. Being a man of the cloth, he had little need to fear reprisals from his Neran overlords.

A servant admitted her to a small anteroom of the chapel, then departed. Maryana quickly took the measure of the short and rather rotund abbot who she found was watching her with his bright, dark eyes.

He came forward and grasped both her hands. She was startled—not by the gesture, but rather by his strong, callused grip. Did all Sakims have such hands? Was it something inbred to their natures? How, otherwise, could an abbot have acquired such calluses?

"My dear lady, it is a pleasure to meet you," the man said in his heavy Sakim accent. "I am certain that you must be quite busy with your preparations, but I thought that we should at least meet before the ceremony."

The ceremony that won't be happening, Maryana said silently. "I thank you for your thoughtfulness, Brother."

He then launched into an explanation of the ceremony itself, saying that he didn't believe it varied from the Neran ceremonies she must have witnessed.

Maryana's thoughts drifted. His touch had reminded her of Roderic. How she longed to see him again! How late should she wait before leaving tonight? At least she didn't have to worry about either her uncle or Miles keeping an eye on her. Both of them would be drunk at the bachelor's feast— and so, too, would be the guards and the king's emissary. It was a perfect time to escape—if only she knew where to go.

There might be one last chance to speak to the cook. She could say that she wanted to check on the preparations and perhaps get the woman away from her staff.

Unfortunately, by the time it had occurred to her to use that excuse, she had discovered that her uncle himself had already taken charge of the preparations. And then she feared that her involvement would only cast suspicion on the cook after she vanished. But if she were to wait until night, when the men would all be too drunk to notice . . . But wouldn't that be too late for the cook to get word to Gisel? Perhaps the chef could just tell her how to find Gisel.

"Milady?"

Maryana snapped her attention back to the abbot, who was frowning at her.

"I am sorry to seem so inattentive," she apologized, trying to determine what words could shock him into refusing to perform the ceremony.

"Ah, but that is understandable, under the circumstances," the abbot said, nodding.

"The circumstances are not what you think, Brother," Maryana said. "I am being forced into this marriage by a man I detest, who wishes to marry me only to gain control of my wealth."

The abbot looked shocked—but somewhat reserved as well. Perhaps her uncle had spoken to him—warned him that she might try to get out of the marriage.

"Umm, I see. So you, ah, have no feelings for this man, Sir Miles Foulane?"

"Oh, I have feelings for him," she replied. "I despise him. In fact, it's quite likely that I'll stab him to death in our marriage bed."

Well, she thought, pleased with herself, *that* should do it, if anything will. At the last minute, she'd remembered Roderic's suggestion that he kill Miles. And worst of all, she was wondering if she might actually be able to do that herself.

"My dear young lady, I am shocked!"

"Are you?" she asked, peering at him closely. "I thought that perhaps my uncle would have warned you that I might say something to prevent the ceremony. I assure you that I mean just what I say. So you see, if you do perform this ceremony, you will be sending a man to his death. Surely you can't countenance that—even if he is a Neran."

To her utter amazement, his dark eyes twinkled merrily. "On the contrary, ridding this land of even one Neran would please me greatly."

Maryana stared at him, aghast. Did he think she was mad, and he was trying to humor her? What had her uncle told him about her?

"However," he went on with a smile, "Since our Lord does frown upon murder, it seems to me that the best thing to do is to prevent the marriage from taking place."

Maryana gasped. "You would do that?" She couldn't believe her luck, but she was already beginning to realize that, like running back to Chamoney, this would be only a temporary reprieve. Either her uncle's priest would recover from his wound, or they would find another Sakim.

"I could, of course, refuse to perform the ceremony, but I'm afraid that would only postpone it for a brief time. On the other hand, if you were to vanish . . ."

By now, Maryana's astonishment was beginning to edge toward suspicion—a suspicion that delighted her and brought a smile to her face.

"That is exactly what I plan to do, but unfortunately, the person I'd counted on to help me isn't available."

"Ah, yes, the girl Gisel. Her mother has need of her at the moment, but I'm quite sure she'll return after the wedding. In the meantime, will I do?"

Maryana peered at him closely. "Are you really an abbot?"

"Of course. Among my duties is that of being confessor to Lord Roderic Hode, lately of this very castle."

"Lately, yes. But do you happen to know where he is now?"

"At this very moment—no. But it is of no consequence. Now let us—"

"He sent you, didn't he?" Maryana demanded, unable to quell the joy rising within her.

"Let us just say that the Lord sometimes moves in mysterious ways," the abbot intoned, leaving her to wonder which "lord" he was referring to. "Now let us make our plans."

Maryana's expression hovered somewhere between a smile and a frown as she hid in the shadows of the gallery. Sounds of revelry reached all the way up to the high, vaulted ceiling. She wished that she could go to the railing and seek out her would-be husband—see his face red with wine and boasting and pleasure at having achieved his goal. It would be a wonderful image to carry with her into an uncertain future.

But she did not dare tempt her luck. She could not get this far and then risk it all for such a frivolous notion. And in any event, she already had the image of Miles as he'd appeared at dinner, smirking and making clumsy jokes.

She would carry with her, too, the memory of her uncle and his refusal to meet her eyes. A weak man, just as she'd suspected from the beginning. Not a bad one, necessarily—but weak, and to her mind, weakness was just another form of evil.

She slipped from the shadows and hurried along the deserted corridors, laden with a sack containing a single change of clothing and her jewelry. In her pocket was the pouch of gold coins sent by her estate manager.

For a time, she'd considered the possibility of another raid on the treasury. Accomplishing it now would not be difficult, with her uncle downstairs and his ring of keys no doubt hanging in his suite. The thought was still tempting, but she knew that if she took the tax money, her uncle would surely send his collectors out to harass the people again.

But it would have been a lovely good-bye: robbing the treasury and at the same time letting him know just where she had gone. He'd have understood her purpose immediately, since he'd know that she couldn't have wanted the money for herself.

She made her way down a rear staircase, then out through a small door into the courtyard. Ever since she had decided that she must escape, Maryana had tried to determine how many guards were posted at night, and their positions. Rather to her surprise, it seemed that her uncle felt quite secure within the castle, since it seemed that there were no guards anywhere, except for those posted on the battlements above the main gate.

Can you really trust him? The question, which she'd pushed aside earlier, came back to torment her now. Could she really be sure that the merry abbot was on her side and had been sent by Roderic? Maryana knew of too many corrupt men of the cloth to trust him solely because of his position.

But he was also Sakim, and that made it easier. Her uncle had complained once that he'd not been able to find a single one of them to trust—except perhaps for Roderic, whose word he'd claimed to accept. What an irony then, she thought, that the one Sakim he might have been inclined to trust was the very one who was betraying him now. But Roderic had only given his word that he would not stir up his people against the baron. He'd never mentioned stealing a niece.

Her hand went unconsciously to the pocket where she carried her small but very sharp dagger in its leather pouch. The dagger had belonged to her father, and he'd kept it beneath his pillows even after he'd become so weak that he couldn't possibly have wielded it.

Trust him—but be wary, she told herself as her gaze skittered around the courtyard, pausing briefly at each and every shadow. Just as she'd expected: no guards in sight.

She hurried into the deep shadows alongside the stable. The abbot had told her he would bring a horse for her and meet her at the small rear gate, the only other exit from the castle. If she were going to be challenged, it would be there. There had been no guard posted at that gate when she'd checked a few nights ago, but if either her uncle or Miles thought she might try to escape, that was surely the place they would post one.

Her biggest worry as she walked swiftly along the length of the stable was that she'd be unable to open the gate. By day it was left on the latch, since there were frequent comings and goings—but at night it was heavily barred. She was certainly stronger than many pampered Neran noble-women, but was she strong enough to be able to move the heavy wooden bar?

She paused at the rear of the stable, set down her burden, then peered cautiously around the corner. A small gasp escaped from her as she drew her head back quickly. Then she risked another look.

Yes. That was definitely a body lying there, just to one side of the gate. Even in the dim light of the single lantern hung beside the gate, she could see she was right. And the bar had been removed!

But that body! Could it possibly be the abbot? She couldn't be sure, but the cloak that covered the man looked as though it might be the dark green of a Neran guard, not the gray of the abbot's frock. Besides, if he'd been found there, he certainly wouldn't have been killed or injured.

Or would he? If he'd been killed, they might well have left his body there for her to discover, with others concealed nearby to capture her. Miles was capable of such a thing, she decided. And he would want to be there himself to capture her, to see her expression at that moment. She wished now that she *had* risked going to the railing to ascertain that Miles was indeed down there among the revelers.

Still clinging as best she could to the shadows alongside the stable, Maryana rounded the corner, her eyes searching every shadow, every possible place of concealment. Then, with her heart thudding in her throat, she ran across the open space between the stable and the gate, her eyes now fixed on the unmoving body in the shadows.

Closer now, she could see that the man wore a Neran guard's uniform. He was lying facedown, and as she drew still closer, she could also see the darker stain against the deep green. She averted her eyes as guilt swept over her. She now had the blood of one of her own people on her hands.

Then suddenly, something detached itself from

the deep shadows to one side of the gate. Maryana made a small sound—a cutoff scream—then dropped her bundle and reached for her dagger.

"It is I," said the abbot, now stepping deliberately into the lantern light. "Come. I have horses outside."

Relief flooded through her, but she turned to the unmoving guard. "Is he dead?"

"Quite," came the satisfied reply. " 'Tis a good thing he guessed that a guard might be posted here this night—in case you tried to escape. Myself, I would never have thought of it, given what we've always heard of Neran ladies."

" 'He?' You mean Roderic? Is he here?" Her heart began to thud again, though for a very different reason.

"No. Come quickly now. I want to be well away from here as swiftly as possible."

Two horses were tied up in the woods that grew close to the rear of the castle, where the land dropped off sharply. The abbot offered to help her mount, but Maryana was on the horse before he could reach her. He chuckled.

"So you do indeed ride astride like a man. I'm sure our Lord would be offended by that, but perhaps his attention is elsewhere tonight, and if not, I shall beg his forgiveness on your behalf in the morning."

"Are you sure you're really an abbot?" Maryana asked as he climbed ponderously onto his own mount. She'd never met a man of the cloth who had a sense of humor, let alone one who treated his master in such a light manner.

"I am," he replied, leading the two of them off into the woods. "But after twenty-three years in His service, I feel that I can take a few liberties. Most of the time we get along well enough."

"Where are we going?" she asked. She'd never been back there before, and it was so dark that she couldn't see if he was following a path, or merely winding his way through the woods.

"To a small cove that's not far."

"A cove? You mean to a boat?" Maryana brought her horse to a halt. Alerted by her incredulous tone, the abbot turned in his saddle, and when he saw that she had stopped, he reined in his horse as well.

"Yes, milady—to a boat. You need not fear. The owner is a skilled sailor and he will get you safely to Neran. He even has friends there who will assist you in reaching your home."

"I'm not leaving!"

She couldn't see the abbot's face in the dim moonlight, but she heard his heavy sigh. "Milady," he said with a trace of exasperation, "there is no other place for you to go."

"There must be! If I go home, it will be only a matter of time before Miles follows me and the king orders me to marry him or forfeit my lands."

"But your lands will surely be forfeit if you simply vanish," the abbot pointed out in a gentle tone.

Maryana hadn't considered that—though she knew she should have. But when all one's choices were bad ones, she realized, one didn't go looking for reasons for them to be even worse.

"But I can help your people defeat mine," she protested, then added quickly, "I have gold to help."

"Gold is always helpful," the abbot agreed. "But we Sakims need more help than that. We need a leader."

"Surely Roderic—"

"Sadly, no—at least not yet. He could be a great leader, but the others are not good followers. That has always been our problem, you see.

"Strange, isn't it?" he mused. "Both Sakims and Nerans share a language and a god—but little else. And when a dissolute, greedy man like your present king appears, it only serves to remind us that we have chosen well."

"I don't deny what you say about him—but he *did* defeat you."

"True. I've said as much myself—many times. But it falls on deaf ears. Still, we cannot sit here debating the deficiencies of the Sakims or the greed of the Nerans."

"Take me to Roderic," she ordered.

"I can't do that, milady. The way he lives now is not fit for you. And he would have my hide if I were to bring you to him. He wants you safely back in Chamoney."

"But I *won't* be safe there—not unless he plans to rescue me by defeating the king."

"Aye, I take your point, but—"

"You *must* help me, Abbot!"

The abbot sighed heavily. "So it seems. Lord Roderic has always accused me of being too soft-hearted for my own good."

Softhearted? When he'd just moments ago killed a man? But Maryana kept that thought to herself. He would undoubtedly reply that it was only a Neran. It seemed that she would have to adjust her thinking a bit if she were going to join them. And could she really do that: help to make war against her own people, however abominable their king might be?

But there was no time to ponder such matters now. They had to be far from the castle before the guard's death was discovered and her quarters were searched. One would follow the other in short order.

"What if I were to join Roderic without his knowing it?" she asked suddenly as an idea began to take form.

To her very great surprise, the abbot didn't immediately reject that possibility. "And how would you do that?" he inquired.

"Just get me some peasant boy's clothing. I could pass for a youth if I cut my hair and dye it and darken my skin." She was thinking as she spoke.

"And what about your voice, with its lovely Neran accent?" he challenged.

"I'll . . . be a mute. You can tell them that. If you take me there, no one will question my identity." The idea had come to her because two children on her estate suffered from that particular affliction.

"That will last only until you are no longer able to keep your mouth shut," the abbot said, but she could hear a smile in his voice.

"By that time I will have been accepted—and Roderic will not be able to do anything about it."

"I am surely a fool to go along with this," he replied, but he turned his horse's head in a different direction as he spoke.

"Well, Abbot, what do you think?"

"I think that this must surely be blasphemy. If I were as pious as my bishop would like, I could surely quote scripture on the matter."

"You said yourself that the Lord moves in mysterious ways," she reminded him.

"And so he does. But there is a difference between mysterious and outrageous."

"But tell me: will I pass?" Maryana had been unable to see her new self, except in a cloudy piece of mirror that had been one of Gisel's few treasures.

"I suppose you will—as long as you remain quiet and I vouch for you," he admitted grudgingly.

The abbot had taken her, under cover of darkness, to Gisel's home, which lay close to the edge of the forest and somewhat isolated, since her father had once been Roderic's gamesman, before dying in battle.

From Gisel, she had learned what she'd already guessed: that the young woman's mother had not needed her, after all. She had been ordered by Roderic to stay away from the castle as soon as he'd heard of her developing friendship with Maryana. Gisel needed to keep her job, and he needed a spy within the walls of Varley Castle—especially one whose tasks allowed her to roam freely.

And her uncle's priest had not suffered a hunting accident—which she'd also suspected. Roderic had decided to get the man out of the way upon learning of the impending nuptials, knowing it was likely that Baron DeLay would then turn to Abbot Locke. The "poacher" who'd brought the priest down had been none other than Roderic himself, whom Gisel had said was the best bowman of all. He'd managed to wing the priest without doing too much harm.

Gisel and her mother had cut Maryana's hair, then darkened it to a sort of muddy brown. Then they'd applied an ointment that had darkened her skin, giving her the remainder of it to take along. Nothing could be done about her eyes, but Gisel said that blue eyes weren't entirely unheard of among her people. After all, for centuries, and despite their innumerable conflicts, there had always been some intermarriage between Nerans and Sakims, particularly within the coastal villages, which continued to trade freely even during times of war.

After all of that, it had been a simple matter to outfit her in the garb of a peasant boy, using clothing borrowed from Gisel's brother.

Gisel had returned to work this morning, chiefly to find out what she could about the situation there. She'd returned just before the abbot put in an appearance.

"It would appear that I'm not under any suspicion," the abbot said after studying her closely. "Fortunately, I'm blessed with an honest, open face."

111

"No one I heard said anything about you," Gisel confirmed. "Sir Miles is beside himself: shouting meaningless orders and cursing the dead guard for his failure to prevent your escape."

"What about my uncle?" Maryana asked.

"I saw him only once—but I truly thought that I saw him trying to conceal a smirk as Sir Miles raved on."

"But they *have* mounted a search for Lady Maryana?" the abbot inquired. "I myself was told only that the wedding must be postponed, and I couldn't risk asking questions."

"Oh, yes, they've been searching for her since the dead guard was discovered. I heard the baron say that she must have bribed a fisherman or trader to take her back to Neran, so I imagine they're making inquiries among the coastal villages."

"Did Sir Miles seem to believe that?" Maryana asked.

"That's hard to say, milady. He was ranting and raging so much that he appeared not to be doing much thinking at all."

Maryana smiled at that image. "But what about the people in the coastal villages? Will they be harmed, do you think?"

"In all likelihood, no. The weather is fine, and they'd all been told to get as many boats out as possible, to help cover for the man who was supposed to take you back to Neran." The abbot smiled. "I think they will soon see that you might have been aboard any one of dozens of boats. That will spread the blame. Besides, I think we can count on your uncle to restrain Sir Miles's more murderous impulses, if only because he fears an uprising."

Maryana nodded. Her uncle's fear of an uprising was very great—and certainly would work to their benefit now. "When do we leave?" she asked the abbot.

"After full dark," he replied. "It is perhaps a two-hour ride."

Maryana had feared that the abbot might change his mind and refuse to take her to Roderic's camp. But that fear was quickly disspelled as soon as they set out. The fat little man chortled merrily as he bounced in the saddle, and it was clear that he was delighted at the thought of putting one over on "Roddy." Nor did he appear to be at all concerned about the possibility of his sham being discovered.

"Oh, he would darken with rage and engage in much shouting—but that is all. He'd never harm me, nor even send me away. Truth be told, milady, I think it would please him to have you there—though of course he'd never admit that."

"What do you mean?" Maryana asked, hoping, of course, that she knew exactly what the abbot meant.

"The earl is sweet on you, milady—but I think you knew that already."

"But he would have sent me back to Neran," she protested mildly, though her heart warmed at his words.

"Aye, but only to protect you and to prevent that idiot Foulane from marrying you. He was thinking only of your safety—and perhaps of his own future."

"His future?" Maryana echoed.

"Aye. I think his lordship is beginning to lose patience and may be ready to have a go at uniting the Sakims against your people. He's the only one can do it—if anyone can, that is.

"Y'see, it's this way. We Sakim are a highly suspicious lot—not to mention independent. So if anyone could unite us, it would have to be someone with no hidden plans to set himself up as our king afterward. And the Earl of Varley is known to

113

be the most independent of all. He's spoken loud and long against uniting under a king—as did his father before him, God rest his soul."

Maryana heard the abbot's words, but she was still thinking about his earlier statement that Roderic was sweet on her. "He told me that he'd loved only once—and that she died."

"Ahh, the lovely Lady Claire. 'Tis true that he loved her, but it was a boy's love—not a man's. He'd known her all his life, and their fathers pushed them together.

"There is a dark side to us Sakims." The abbot sighed. "Perhaps you have already noticed this. Oftimes, it seems to me that we wallow in our losses and our grief—and Roddy is no exception."

"But he seems to me to be so . . . carefree," she protested, even though she herself had seen evidence of the darkness of which the abbot spoke.

"So he does—but it's no more than a cover, milady." He paused, then seemed to contradict himself. "Or mayhap it's his true nature, trying to break free from all that Sakim gloom."

They rode on, skirting the village on a well-worn path, headed she knew not where. Thus far, they'd not encountered anyone, but suddenly the abbot made a sound, then brought his horse to a halt.

Maryana saw what he must have seen only a moment later: tiny pinpoints of firelight bobbing among the trees at the top of a rise ahead of them. Torches.

"It's likely some of the baron's men, still out looking for you," the abbot whispered. "Come quickly!"

They dismounted and led their horses off into the thick woods that grew close to the path. The abbot didn't stop until they had descended into a ravine. Then he told her to quietly soothe her horse, to prevent it from trying to make contact with its relatives. She did so, then all but held her breath as the men drew even with them. Surely she could not have come this far only to be hauled back to the castle!

On the other hand, would they even recognize her? It wasn't likely, since she'd barely recognized herself from what little she'd seen.

It seemed to take forever until the clip-clop of the horses' hooves was swallowed up in the silence of the night. But finally, the abbot heaved a sigh of relief and gestured for them to climb back up to the path.

"We could have braved it out," he told her. "They'd never recognize you. People see what they expect to see. But I thought it best not to be seen out here at night myself. If they'd found us, I would have said that I heard men coming and feared the highwaymen, who are probably godless creatures who'd not have any respect for a man of the cloth."

"And who would *I* have been?" Maryana asked as they regained the path and set off again, both of them casting looks over their shoulders.

"I was about to get to that when we were interrupted. Your name is Clieve: Clieve Tenerly. You grew up in Webley. That's one of the fishing villages not far from here. You were struck mute at the age of ten, following a terrible accident at sea— a storm that took the lives of all others on board. When you were found by other fishermen, you'd lost the ability to speak.

"Your ma managed, through her sister, who's the cook at Varley Castle, to get you a job there— replacing one of the kitchen boys who'd fled after the Nerans captured it.

"One of your brothers was killed by the Nerans, so you took your revenge the only way you could. That is to say, you stole what you could get your hands on in the castle. Most people think you're an idiot, so no one paid much attention to you. And that gave you the opportunity to steal the jewelry from the lady Maryana and even some gold from time to time.

"But the cook thought that you were coming under suspicion, so she asked me to get you to Lord Roderic, and you want to give your stolen jewelry and gold to him to help the people."

Maryana laughed. "You're a wondrous storyteller, Abbot."

"Aye, I am that—but it's not all a story. Y'see, the best lies always contain a kernel of truth, and I'm sure that Lord Roderic knows the story about the boy who survived that storm at sea."

"You mean there actually is a Clieve Tenerly?" she asked. "But—"

"There is, and as far as I know, he's alive and well and staying with some relatives on the other side of the strait—in Neran. His ma sent him there just before the war broke out. There's supposed to be a woman there who's had some success getting those like him to start talking again. The boy even has blue eyes, so they say. Lots of intermarriage in that clan."

Chapter Six

Maryana was growing less and less certain that she'd ever reach Roderic's camp. The abbot had finally admitted that the journey was taking much longer than he'd anticipated, owing to the fact that he'd never before made it in darkness. And still later, he admitted that he'd gotten them lost, and they would have to wait for daylight before he could find the way again.

So they waited along the banks of a small stream that he thought was the one they should be following. He apologized profusely, and Maryana accepted it with good grace. After all, this man had already done her a very great favor.

Unconcerned that they might be found by the baron's men—the abbot said that if they themselves didn't know where they were, how could her would-be captors possibly know—they slept on the mossy bank of the little stream.

Maryana dreamed: wonderful dreams of Roderic welcoming her to his forest home with open arms and telling her how much he loved her. And dreams of the two of them, making love on a mossy bed beside a gurgling stream.

The birds woke them, chattering noisily in the trees overhead, no doubt protesting their presence in a place they'd thought to be theirs alone. The abbot hauled himself to his feet and stated that he needed to explore a bit, to see the lay of the land.

Maryana got up and ran a hand through her hair, startled to rediscover its shortness. Then she peered at her hands and lower arms, half-fearing that the stain might have worn off. Gisel and her mother had said that not even water would wash it away, so she decided to put that to the test.

First she scrubbed her hands in the waters of the stream, and then, when the dye remained, she splashed water on her face as well. By the time the abbot returned, she had finished her morning ablutions and was trying to convince herself that she didn't miss the comforts of her old life at the castle.

"I was right!" he proclaimed happily. "This is the proper stream. We should reach the camp in an hour—or perhaps less."

This time the abbot spoke the truth. But before they had reached the camp itself, they encountered a guard: one of several posted at all times in the huge trees. He recognized the abbot, of course, and welcomed him, paying scant attention to her as he inquired about the success of his mission.

"The lady Maryana is at this moment on her way to Neran," the abbot told him. "The groom has men searching the countryside for her, but Baron DeLay believes that she has gone home."

"That is good news, then," the guard said. "Best you hurry to camp and tell Lord Roderic your tidings. He's been beside himself with worry. Strange thing, that—our earl smitten by a Neran lady."

"Love can often be blind to such things," the abbot intoned as he turned to Maryana with a twinkle in his eyes. "I've brought this youth with me for safekeeping. Seems he got himself into a bit of trouble at the castle."

"Oh? And what trouble might that be?" the guard asked, staring at Maryana for the first time.

The abbot began to spin his tale about her supposed thefts from the castle, and the man broke out into raucous laughter. "Bringing a dowry, is he? I reckon Lord Roderic'll be happy to see him."

Maryana had all she could do not to laugh at the man's mention of a dowry. She hadn't thought about it before, but it did seem like that.

The abbot went on to give him the boy's name, then added, "He's a mute. You might have heard about the boy found at sea after his comrades perished."

"Aye. I did hear about that some years back." He winked broadly at Maryana. "Well, a boy who can't talk can't tell secrets. He'll do just fine."

Maryana breathed a quiet sigh of relief as they took their leave of the guard and rode on toward the camp. But they'd gone only a short distance when they encountered a group of men riding toward them—and one of them was the miller whose life she'd spoken for when Miles would have killed him.

Her mouth went dry and her heart leaped into her throat. Would he recognize her? She'd never seen the guard before, so that incident hadn't proven much.

They stopped and the abbot repeated both his stories: how she'd left for Neran and how he happened to be bringing this youth to them. But the miller just studied her for a moment, then nodded. He too had heard the sad tale of the boy's misadventure at sea.

Maryana thought—hoped—that even if he did recognize her, he might keep quiet out of gratitude, but she was quite sure now that he saw only a mute youth, running from trouble at the castle.

The abbot turned to her. "From now on, milady, you must not speak. The boy, Clieve, does make sounds: grunts and cries and such, if he's hurt or if he's trying to get someone's attention. But not words.

"We can say that I've learned to communicate with you, more or less—like your family does. You use gestures to convey what you mean. Practice when you get the chance."

Already, it was beginning to sink in to her that living without speaking at all was going to be very difficult indeed. "How long will I have to stay silent?" she asked a trifle impatiently.

The abbot chuckled. "That is surely up to you— and to how you judge his mood. But in another month, the strait will be too dangerous to cross, so then he can't send you back."

One month! How could she stand it—being around Roderic day after day—not to mention night after night—and unable to speak to him or to reveal her true identity? Or would he see through her disguise, as the others hadn't? Then at least she'd be given the opportunity to plead her case.

But she had little opportunity to dwell on the matter now. The abbot dismounted and gestured for her to do the same. They made their way along a faint path at the edge of the stream, pushing low, overhanging branches out of their way as they went.

Maryana had never seen such a place. Huge old trees towered over thick underbrush, letting in very little sunlight. The stream wound its way through a narrow ravine barely wide enough to accommodate it, with steep green walls on both sides.

And then the way became even more difficult.

They were now forced to walk through the stream itself, and the old boots she wore were soon leaking. But she didn't dare remove them because she hadn't used the dye on her feet—an oversight she would correct as soon as possible.

Just when she was beginning to wonder if the abbot had gotten them lost again, her nose picked up the smell of smoke and food cooking. Her stomach growled in response, reminding her that she hadn't eaten for more than twelve hours now—and little before that, since she'd been reluctant to take much food from Gisel and her family.

"Any last words?" the abbot whispered, turning to her.

"Thank you for all your help," she whispered back. And then they came to the camp.

There were more men than she'd expected: perhaps twenty of them, from what she could see. She scanned the faces that turned toward them, but saw no sign of Roderic.

The camp sat in a small clearing in the bottom of the ravine, which widened out a bit at this spot. She could see that the land had only recently been cleared; raw stumps were scattered about, creating seats for the men who were eating breakfast.

Crude lean-tos had been fashioned from limbs and branches, but there was also a small cabin, set somewhat apart from the rest. And as her gaze fixed upon it, a man emerged from the open doorway.

Maryana drew in a sharp breath at the sight of him, which in turn drew an admonishing glance from the abbot. How handsome he looked, despite his rough clothing! She fought down a nearly overwhelming urge to run into his arms, and managed it only by reminding herself that he would not be happy to see her and would, in all likelihood, send her back to the coast.

By now, he'd spotted them and was making his

way quickly toward them, his brow furrowed with concern. Seeing the way he moved, with an almost catlike grace, Maryana was struck all over again with the wonder of him. Surely no one could ever mistake this man for a peasant, no matter what he wore.

"Is she safe?" Roderic asked the moment he was within speaking distance of the abbot.

"Aye. By now, she should be halfway across the strait, on her way home."

Roderic's handsome face relaxed, then crinkled into a smile. "And she gave you no problems? I'd feared she would refuse to go home."

"She did protest a bit, but I made her see that it was the only way."

Roderic's brow furrowed once more. "Hmmpphh! I rather expected her to refuse to leave."

Maryana, watching him closely, thought that what he really meant was that he'd *hoped* she would refuse to leave. Or was that merely wishful thinking on her part?

After glancing around them, but continuing to ignore her, Roderic asked in a low voice, "Did she give you a message for me?"

Maryana's gaze went to the abbot. They hadn't talked about that. She wondered what the abbot would say.

"She knew even before I told her that you were behind the scheme, and she told me to tell you that she thanks you—and that she will see you again one day."

Well, it wasn't exactly the message that she might have passed on, but there was no help for that. She silently thanked the abbot for yet another kindness.

Roderic merely nodded, then finally turned to her. "And who is this?"

Maryana held her breath. If he were going to see

122

through her disguise, it would surely be now, when she was on his mind. But she saw no light of recognition.

The abbot spun his tale once again, then handed Roderic the two pouches he'd taken from her earlier: the gold and her jewelry. Roderic weighed the gold in his hand, then opened the jewelry pouch and removed some of the contents.

"I'm grateful for the gold, but I wish the lad hadn't stolen her jewelry." Then, abruptly, he smiled—a smile that nearly broke her heart.

"But I will keep it for her—and return it to her one day."

Then he turned to her. "You're welcome here, boy—and thank you for the gold."

The abbot cleared his throat. "I'd thought that perhaps the boy might serve as page to you, milord. I fear that he could become an object of sport to some of the men, because of his affliction."

Roderic glanced at her again, then returned his attention to the abbot, seeming rather distracted. But he nodded. "Yes, you're right. He can stay with me."

Then he turned away, still clutching in his hand one of her necklaces. The others scattered out of hearing as well. The abbot leaned toward her.

"I spoke the truth, milady. Some of these men are not to be trusted completely, though they all share the same goal."

Maryana somehow managed to keep her mouth shut. So she was now to become a page to Roderic? With him day and night? This was definitely not what she'd expected. She had envisioned herself moving along the fringes of his band, largely invisible because of her "affliction."

She silently cursed the abbot's concern for her welfare, even as she also admitted that a part of her was intrigued—even pleased—at the thought of deceiving Roderic while gaining the opportunity to study him closely.

In Maryana's experience, men tended to behave in an unnatural manner around women, so now she would see the true man. After all, who would know a man better than his ever-present page?

Maryana soon discovered that she *was* nearly invisible in this group of men. Apparently, the word about her affliction had spread quickly, and the abbot had been correct in his belief that she would be viewed as an idiot. When the men did find it necessary to converse with her, they tended to speak very slowly and very loudly—but for the most part, they simply ignored her.

Roderic ignored her as well, except to issue orders. But at least he spoke in a normal tone when he did so. At first, when she found him staring at her with a slightly puzzled look, Maryana feared— and perhaps hoped—that he might be about to see beneath her disguise. But then she realized that his puzzlement probably arose from the direct looks she gave him. And thereafter, she made certain to keep her head down and avoid staring directly at him, in the manner of a peasant youth dealing with his betters.

By midmorning, the camp was all but empty. The abbot had left to tend to his religious duties— and to pick up such gossip as he could from their spies within the castle. The rest of the band, save for two men to act as camp guards, had split themselves into two groups to "collect" from the tax collectors, which was how Roderic wryly put it.

Maryana had hoped to be invited to join them, but she wasn't.

Boredom overtook her quickly. The two guards were some distance away, patrolling the boundaries of the encampment and spending their time fitting arrowheads to shafts.

She decided to explore the little cabin that Roderic now called home, and was surprised to find it snug and quite comfortable. The furnishings were old and crude, yet pleasant enough. There was only one room, with several chairs placed in front of the fireplace, a table and chairs occupying the central space, and a narrow cot in one corner, with a well-stuffed straw pallet in the opposite corner.

Her gaze traveled from the bed to the pallet and back again, unconsciously measuring the space between them, since she assumed that the pallet would soon be her bed. The thought of even such intimacy as provided by this arrangement was enough to set tiny curls of heat unfolding within her.

How many nights would she be forced to lie there—so close and yet so far from him, while he dreamed of her—or perhaps of his lost love? The abbot's statements about Roderic's childhood sweetheart had been reassuring, as was Roderic's keen interest in her own fate. But still she had the strange thought that Roderic might prefer to pine for lost loves than to face a real one.

His bed was untidy, the covers left in a heap and the pillow crushed. In her new and unaccustomed role of page, which she supposed in this case also meant acting as his maid, Maryana set about tidying up the bed.

When she picked up the pillow to fluff it, she gasped as the sunlight streaming through a window set fire to what lay beneath it. With suddenly trembling fingers, she picked up the ring: a thick band of gold encrusted with diamonds and rubies.

It was clearly a woman's ring—and just as clearly not hers. A sharp stab of pain knifed through her, followed quickly by the icy chill of betrayal. Had it belonged to his dead love—or was there some other woman?

She put it back and then covered it again with

the pillow, almost dizzy now with the implications of this discovery. Her mind was already busy revising every encounter with Roderic, infusing every word he'd spoken with new and different meanings.

Not even the memory of the abbot's words—that Roderic was sweet on her—could dispel these bleak thoughts. Perhaps he'd merely been saying what she wanted to hear—or perhaps he too had misinterpreted Roderic's interest.

Such doubts were a new and unwelcome addition to Maryana's life. Her mirror had long told her that if she wasn't quite the fairest of them all, she was certainly close to being that. She hadn't required the attentions of men to learn that—especially since her wealth had always made her suspect the motives of any man who paid court to her.

So now she wondered why it had never occurred to her that Roderic might be just like all those others—including the repellant Miles Foulane. Wouldn't he, too, be covetous of her wealth—all the more so, in fact, since he'd been dispossessed of his own?

And yet . . . She sighed, remembering their brief times together and all she'd felt and believed that he'd felt, too. Was it all a lie?

The men returned to camp late in the day: first one group and then the other. It was impossible for her to make out, at first, what was happening, since the voices overlapped so that it seemed to her that everyone was talking and no one but her was attempting to listen.

She moved among them, completely ignored, until she had pieced together enough words and phrases to learn that they'd had a very good day. The abbot had returned with Roderic's group and he took charge of the pouches containing the gold, then went off to Roderic's cabin, presumably to count it.

126

The miller came back with a huge sack containing loaves of bread and other foodstuffs, and several men appeared with fresh-killed game. Maryana steered clear of the area where the food was being prepared for the evening meal, lest she be pressed into service and forced to demonstrate her ignorance where such matters were concerned. Skinning rabbits and plucking fowl were not among her talents—and neither were they skills she wished to learn.

With all the tumult, it was some time before she learned the big news of the day. Roderic had, it seemed, been unmasked—quite literally.

As she pieced it together, one of the guards who'd been entrusted with the tax collections had lunged at him and ripped the hood from his head, even though Roderic, as usual, was hanging back and not showing himself to be the leader.

Apparently the man hadn't seemed to be surprised to make this discovery, though Maryana suspected that her uncle would indeed be shocked, since he'd brushed off Miles's suggestion that Roderic might be the leader of the band of thieves.

She learned, too, that the others had then wanted to kill the two guards to keep their secret, but Roderic had decided instead that the men should return to Varley Castle and let the baron know that as long as he continued to collect exorbitant taxes, he—Roderic—would continue to take them away.

Then, as though that were not enough, Roderic also sent a message by way of the guards to Miles, saying that he was the one responsible for ruining Miles's wedding plans.

Upon learning this, Maryana made her way back to the cabin to speak to the abbot. Roderic's recklessness was breathtaking—and to what purpose? Perhaps the abbot could provide her with some answers.

She found the rotund cleric at the table, with piles of gold coins stacked all around him. When she appeared, he looked up at her and grinned— the smile of a pleased little boy.

"A good haul, milady. The best yet."

"Never mind that," Maryana said impatiently. "Do you know what Roderic did today?"

"Of course. I met up with him on the way back."

"He's *mad*, Abbot! He is deliberately goading Miles—not to mention my uncle! But of the two, I am more concerned about Miles."

The abbot shrugged. "What can Sir Miles do that he has not already been doing? Besides, Gisel tells me that he has accepted that you have returned to Neran."

"But will he continue to believe that when he learns that Roderic aided in my escape?" she demanded.

The abbot now frowned. "Aye, I take your point. I hadn't considered that."

"And neither, apparently, did—"

She broke off her angry outburst abruptly as the abbot made a quick, furtive motion, all the while gazing toward the door. A moment later, Roderic's voice broke the sudden silence.

"Well, Abbot, how did we do?"

"Very well, Roddy—very well indeed."

Roderic strode past her as though she weren't there and slapped the cleric on the back. "A truly good day, then ! A good haul and the cat out of the bag—and that fop Foulane about to be spitting nails."

"Mmm," the abbot said, sliding a quick glance her way. "But I've been thinking, Roddy. The girl Gisel tells me that Foulane has finally accepted that the lady Maryana returned to Neran. But when he learns that it was you who arranged her escape, he might begin to think otherwise."

Roderic frowned. "What are you talking about?"

"He might just take it into his head that you stole his bride for your own reasons. A man who never does anything out of pure goodness is unlikely to ascribe that trait to others."

Roderic threw back his head and laughed uproariously, then slapped the abbot on the back again. "I hope you're right, my friend! Let him think that I have spirited her off to my own bed, humble though that may be at the moment."

He swept an extravagant gesture toward his narrow cot in the corner, then continued to laugh. And when his laughter had finally subsided to mere chuckles, he spoke again.

"Perhaps I should have done just that."

The abbot, now pointedly ignoring her, arched a brow. "And what makes you think the lady would have been willing to share your bed?"

"A man knows these things," Roderic stated smugly.

Maryana's face was growing warm with the effort required to keep her lips sealed. *What arrogance! What insufferable arrogance!* So she *was* getting to see a side of him that he would never have shown to her!

Then Roderic heaved a sigh. "But perhaps she would have refused me, after all. I fear that perhaps I do not know her as well as I'd thought. I would never have guessed that she'd go peaceably back to Neran, for example."

He stood there for a moment, staring at the gold coins stacked on the table, then abruptly turned to her. She started nervously, irrationally certain that he knew who she was. But instead, he merely asked her to fetch him a tankard of ale, and one for the abbot as well.

Maryana's deception nearly came to an abrupt end a few hours later. She'd brought him his ale.

She'd fetched his dinner, then cleared away the table. And all the while, she was secretly seething. Roderic's statement that perhaps she *would* have refused him had not lessened her anger with him over his original arrogant remark. To her mind, a person was more likely to have uttered the truth first, then covered it with a lie later.

Then there was the matter of that ring, now hidden again beneath his pillow, but still very much on her mind.

The end of her deception nearly came when they had returned to the cabin after the evening meal. The night was cool and he told her to build a fire. She'd never built one before, but she'd seen it done often enough, so she managed, all the while wondering if fighting Miles and the king might not be better than taking orders from this arrogant Sakim lord.

Then he wanted a mug of the strong tea brewed by the old man who served as cook. So she went to get that—and one for herself as well.

When she returned to the cabin, she found him seated in one of the chairs that faced the fireplace, where, she was pleased to see, the fire was burning well. After she'd handed over his mug, he stretched his long legs toward her.

Maryana frowned, certain that he was expecting something, but not at all sure just what it was. By the time he spoke, she had just worked it out herself.

"Take off my boots, lad," he ordered, but not unkindly.

And that was when she came closest to losing her careful disguise. For what seemed to her to be a very long time, but must in fact have been no more than a second or two, she hesitated, the words bubbling up in her throat.

Then, finally, she knelt before him and pulled off one boot and then the other. The second boot resisted her attempts to pull it off. She tugged harder—and it came loose suddenly, sending her tumbling backward toward the fire.

She scrambled to her feet, feeling the heat against her backside, then smelling scorched fabric. And Roderic, damn him, chuckled as she felt around to see if there might be flames.

"It seems that you have a few things to learn about being a page, lad. But never mind. You'll pick it up quickly enough."

What Maryana wanted to pick up was her mug of hot tea and fling it in his handsome face. She had a very clear image of that face dripping with brown liquid and filled with astonishment, as she told him who she was. And if he hadn't spoken in that moment, she might very well have done that.

"It occurs to me that I could put you to good use while I'm gone—making arrows. Do you, perhaps, already have that skill?"

She managed to shake her head, while at the same time choking back her little speech.

"Then go fetch the makings and I will show you. You can practice tomorrow while I'm gone."

She'd already seen the piles of shafts and arrowheads and leather thongs, so she left hurriedly, then slowed to a walk the moment she was outside.

How could she withstand a month of this? Why had she been so addlebrained as to believe that she might actually enjoy her deception? If this was what love did to the brain, she wanted none of it.

But she'd come this far and she was unwilling to give up now. No doubt the abbot could still find her passage across the straits, but sooner or later Miles would follow her, with the king's order that she marry him forthwith.

She drew in a deep draft of the night air and released it with a sigh. She'd stay for the month—and then she'd tell him the truth and watch his reaction. And in the meantime, surely she could find out who that ring belonged to. But if she had to listen to him sighing over some woman . . .

She carried the arrow-making supplies back to the cabin and dumped them at his feet. He glanced at her curiously, but said nothing. Instead, he picked them up and carried them over to the table, then sat down and gestured for her to take a seat across from him.

They sat there for more than an hour in the lamplight. He was a patient instructor, she a fumbling but increasingly determined student. When he learned that she didn't have a knife—which wasn't quite true, since she still had her dagger— he dug one out of a small chest and gave it to her.

Finally, he leaned back in his chair with a smile. "You've got the right of it now, lad. Just be patient and take your time. You remind me of myself— impatient but quick to learn.

"You'll be happy to know that the gold you brought has been put to good use—as all of it is."

She wondered about her jewelry but, of course, couldn't ask. In truth, she didn't mind about the gold. She'd intended to give some of it to him in any event. But she hated losing the jewelry, most of which had been her mother's, or gifts from her father.

So when she saw that he was watching her, she made a motion of circling her neck and then her fingers. He'd said earlier to the abbot that he would return it to her one day, but she was no longer certain that she believed that.

"The jewelry?" he asked.

When she nodded, he went on. "I don't fault you for taking it, but I intend to return it to the lady Maryana."

He lapsed into silence then, leaving her to wish that she could read his thoughts. Surely he must feel something for her, or he would put the jewelry to use in his cause.

Stop it, she told herself. *You're pitiful—just like all the whining, sighing women you've detested all these years who leap with joy at the merest suggestion that a man favors them.*

He returned to his chair in front of the fire and she went off to her pallet in the corner, turning her back on him—but unfortunately not able to turn off her thoughts so easily.

Sometime later, he left the cabin, then returned and added a few more logs to the fire. After that, she heard him cross the room to his bed.

Moving quietly, she rolled over to face him. He was sitting on the edge of the bed, his face lowered to examine something he held in his hands. At first she didn't know what it was, but then it caught the firelight and she saw that it was the ring.

Tears spilled over onto her cheeks as she watched him, not wanting to see this but unable to turn away. She didn't need to see his face to feel the pain and sadness in him. It was in the dejected way he sat, staring at the ring.

She wondered if the ring might have belonged to his dead love—or might have been intended for her. Did he intend to spend the rest of his days mourning her loss? Or was there someone else: perhaps a woman for waiting him in the south, where he had friends?

Finally, just when she thought she could stand it no longer, he replaced the ring beneath his pillow, then stood up and began to undress.

Maryana waited only until he had stripped off his shirt, revealing a lean, muscled chest—and then she turned over again and fell asleep as the tears dried on her cheeks.

By midday, a substantial pile of arrows lay next to her. When Maryana compared them to the ones Roderic had made the night before, she could find no difference.

Her fingers had been rubbed: raw from the un-accustomed work, so she left it for now and went to the stream to bathe. As before, all the men had left camp early, save for the two guards, who were some distance away, settled into their guard posts in the trees.

Still, she chose her spot carefully, a place where a thick screen of bramble bushes would easily conceal her. Then she stripped off her dirty clothing and washed them in the stream, hurrying in her self-consciousness over her nakedness.

After she'd spread out the clothing to dry on some rocks, she waded into the stream, shivering in the cold, rushing water. She looked down at herself with amusement: brown arms and feet and hands and pale skin elsewhere, except for her face and neck, which she couldn't see.

When she had scrubbed herself thoroughly, she bent down into the water to wash her hair. Gisel had said that the hair dye wouldn't come off, either, but she saw now that a small quantity was in fact dripping from her head. Still, it certainly wasn't enough to cause her any alarm.

Gisel had said that she must worry about the roots as her hair grew out, but since there wasn't a mirror anywhere in the camp that she could find, there was nothing to do about that except to hope that her hair grew slowly. Besides, she wore a cap most of the time anyway.

Clean now and wearing fresh clothing, Maryana felt much better as she walked back to the camp. When she came into sight of the clearing, she saw a horse tethered that hadn't been there when she left, and she recognized it as belonging to the abbot.

She found the cleric himself seated near the cooking fire, eating some bread and cheese. He started to get laboriously to his feet, but she waved him down again. "An abbot doesn't rise to meet a page," she told him with a smile.

134

"Right you are, milady page. And how are things going for you?"

"As well as possible," she lied, then gestured to the pile of arrows she'd made. "That has been my morning's work. Roderic showed me last night how to make them."

The abbot picked one up and examined it closely. "Then you must be a quick student."

"Roderic said that as well, although he also said that I'm inclined to impatience."

The abbot laughed. "The pot calls the kettle black."

"He admitted as much." She smiled, thinking how much pleasure she was finding in the simple act of speaking with someone.

"He would. Among his many good qualities is the ability to be honest with himself."

Then his round face abruptly grew solemn. "There is bad news, which I've already given to one of the men on guard to pass along to Roderic when he returns. But I need you to make certain that the information reaches him, since I must leave in a few moments and will be unable to return tonight."

"Why would you worry that the message won't reach him?" Maryana asked in confusion.

"Because of the message itself. Now that Baron DeLay knows Roderic is the leader of the 'band of thieves,' he has set a handsome price on his head.

"Of course, to your uncle's credit, the price is to be paid only if Roderic is brought to him alive. I am certain that Sir Miles tried to persuade him otherwise."

"But surely none of his own people would—"

The abbot waved a pudgy hand dismissively. "Roderic is much loved by his people, but there is always someone who would place gold above love and loyalty—perhaps even among the men here. That is why it is important that you make certain he knows. Most of the men here I would trust with my life—or Lord Roderic's—but that does not include the guard with whom I spoke. He is the only one here, I'm afraid."

"But what can Roderic do? If he can't trust anyone—"

"He will have to take care to surround himself at all times with men he believes he can trust—and hope for the best. The only other thing he could do is to go away, to the south—and he won't do that.

"Also, the baron is starting to squeeze the people for even more taxes, to replace what we've stolen. I think that he still fears above all an uprising, so he isn't likely to try to gain back all that he has lost. But he will try that at some point."

Maryana nodded her agreement. "Goaded, no doubt, by Miles, who will be constantly reminding him of the king's displeasure."

"Aye. Double displeasure, since the baron also allowed you to escape."

"What of that? Are they still searching for me?"

The abbot shook his head. "Many of the villagers along the coast were questioned, but not treated too harshly. One of them even risked saying that he believed he'd seen you late on the night you disappeared from the castle. But he didn't point a finger at anyone, of course.

"So they seem to have given up, assuming that you are now back in Neran, at your beloved Chamoney." He smiled at her. "And perhaps you wish that were the truth."

It was, she thought, an opening for her to give voice to her fear that Roderic had no feelings for her. But much as she liked and trusted the abbot, she said nothing. This was a private matter—between Roderic and her.

"No, I do not regret coming here instead," she told him—and it was probably the truth. Nothing seemed certain to her anymore.

Chapter Seven

"Now that the truth is out, some of the people are calling you the Prince of Thieves. I heard it myself several times this day."

Roderic chuckled. "How very kind of them to elevate me to the title of prince."

The miller chuckled, too, at the same time holding up his mug for Maryana to refill. "I'll admit that it trips pleasantly off the tongue."

But then he sobered quickly. "Still, it has grown more dangerous now, with Baron DeLay having put a price on your head."

"A very handsome price at that." Roderic smiled. "I wonder if Sir Miles has contributed to it."

"That poor excuse for a man—even a Neran—hasn't got any money, from what I've heard. And now that the lady Maryana has escaped his clutches, he isn't likely to, either. But that doesn't mean he isn't dangerous." The miller grimaced. "Lady Maryana is well rid of him, but from what I've heard, she hasn't seen the last of him. He has their king's ear, so they say."

"Like to like," Roderic replied, glancing at her as she refilled his mug, too. "I'm not worried about him, Tom."

"It isn't him I'm worried about, either," the miller agreed, nodding. "It's that accursed reward. 'Tis enough to turn someone's head and make him take leave of his senses."

"You're saying that one of my own people could betray me?" Roderic asked, his tone clearly incredulous.

" 'Tis exactly what I'm saying, milord. It takes only one, and you're for the dungeons at Varley Castle. I even have my doubts about one or two of the men here."

Roderic frowned thoughtfully. From her position in a dim corner of the cabin, Maryana could see that he was having difficulty believing that he could be betrayed by one of his own people. She sympathized with him. If their positions were reversed, she, too, would find it nearly impossible to accept that one of her people could betray her. And yet, she believed that the abbot and Tom Small, the miller, spoke the truth.

"I'm planning to keep an eye on the ones I can't trust," the miller went on. "I'll see to it that they're never left alone to get word to anyone."

Roderic nodded, but reluctantly.

"Mayhap you should disappear for a time," Small suggested, but Maryana thought without any real hope of the earl complying. "We can handle things here. The collections will be finished soon. And you could speak to your friends in the south."

"Don't start on that again, Tom. I know you want me to lead a rebellion, but I'm not about to set myself up as king of the Sakims."

"Couldn't be a better man," the miller persisted. "And we can't rid ourselves of the Nerans if we don't come together."

138

"We kept them out before—and would have this time if it hadn't been for the Boravians and the weather."

From her corner, totally ignored by the two men, Maryana listened and watched with interest—and with frustration as well. She just didn't understand Roderic's reluctance to lead his people. What was it with these Sakims? Of course, she'd prefer to be free of the present Neran king, but she understood the necessity of having a king—even if it meant getting a bad one occasionally.

Maryana was aware of her disloyalty in wanting the Sakims to defeat her king and his army. But she also knew her history, and so took the long view of things. When the Sakims *had* managed in the past to defeat the Nerans, they hadn't followed up their victory by trying to lay claim to Neran territory. Instead, they'd simply driven out the Nerans and then stayed in their own lands.

"You might even be able to get the Innish behind us," Tom Small went on. "Since you're part Innish yourself."

This was news to Maryana. The Innish were the people who controlled the southern part of the large island, while the Sakims ruled the northern and central portions. There'd been wars between them from time to time, but not in recent years.

"I doubt that," Roderic replied. "They don't trust us any more than we trust them, and anyway, I haven't seen my Innish kin since I was a child."

"But the blood is there, milord. They might at least give you a fair hearing."

"And then toss me out on my ear," Roderic scoffed. "Why should they fight the Nerans, when we're the ones having trouble with them?"

"Because once the Nerans get a firm enough grip on us, they'll make war on the Innish."

"Perhaps. But I intend to see that they never get that grip on us."

"Beggin' your pardon, milord, but all we are now is fleas on a dog."

Roderic smiled. "But when there are enough fleas, the dog takes notice."

Maryana wanted to scream with frustration, and from the look on the miller's face, he shared her feelings. It was enough to make her wonder if she'd been correct, after all, when she'd thought that Roderic might be a coward at heart.

The miller gave up his pleas, and the two men began to talk about further thefts from the tax collectors. Maryana retreated to her pallet and watched them, but with less interest than before.

Had she invested Roderic with qualities that he did not, in fact, possess? She was still reluctant to admit to that, just as she couldn't yet accept that he had nothing more than brotherly feelings toward her because his true love was elsewhere.

What irony, she thought, that she had disguised herself and come here believing that she would learn to love him even more—and instead, she found herself questioning that passion.

After a time, the miller left, and Roderic moved over to the fire she had lit earlier. She stared at him in the flickering firelight. His expression was pensive—even sad. If only she could be privy to his thoughts—or if only she could share her own thoughts with him!

She didn't move from her pallet, and if he knew she was there, he gave no indication. After a time, he even removed his boots himself, and later still, got up to fetch himself more ale. Then he walked over to his bed and slid a hand beneath the pillow. The ring glittered in his hand as he carried it back to the fire, where he sat, turning it over and over in his hands.

Tears welled up in her eyes and she brushed them away angrily. But the movement must have caught his attention, because he turned to her.

140

"Come share the fire's warmth, lad. It's a cold night."

Reluctantly, she got up and walked to his side, then sat cross-legged before the fire near his chair. But she kept her billed cap low on her head, obscuring her face as best she could.

Roderic continued to stare at the ring, and much as she tried not to watch, she couldn't take her own eyes from it. Apparently he took note of that.

"A lovely thing, isn't it—but not as lovely as the one who should be wearing it."

She merely nodded, her throat too constricted to allow a response even if she'd been able to come up with one.

Then abruptly, he closed the ring within his fist and looked at her. "You did a good job with the arrows, lad. Very fine work. You heard Tom saying that one of my own people could betray me. Do you agree with him? What do you hear among the men?"

Maryana was startled. Thus far, he hadn't really asked her anything, simply issuing orders. Keeping her head down, she nodded.

"So you think the same as Tom? But what of the men here?"

Maryana struggled to find a way to express herself. This situation she found herself in reminded her of a childhood game called silence, in which players had to communicate with only gestures. She'd always been good at that, she recalled.

She shrugged, then raised her face to his and passed her hand over it several times before lowering it again. Roderic was silent for a moment, then grunted.

"The men treat you as though you were invisible to them—is that it?"

Without raising her head, she nodded vigorously.

"Hmm. Well, that could have its advantages.

141

Keep an ear out, lad, and let me know if you hear anything or see anything."

She nodded again, realizing that he was right. She could move easily among the men, even though she'd largely stayed away from them up till now.

"Do you know the two men Tom the miller suspects?" he asked.

She nodded. In truth, she wasn't certain about the identity of one of them, but she did know who the other one was. His name was Harry, and she'd caught him staring hard at her a few times, though he'd done nothing more. There was a shifty look to him, she thought, and she'd noted that the other men often seemed to avoid him.

"Then you can keep an eye on them as well—perhaps even better than Tom can."

Once more, she nodded, still keeping her head down.

"Look at me, lad! How can you hope to do as I say when you do nothing but stare at your feet?"

Roderic's tone was that of an exasperated parent chastising a recalcitrant child. Maryana raised her face, hoping that the fire-light would prevent his seeing it too well.

"Blue eyes," he said, staring hard at her as though really seeing her for the first time. "There's Neran blood there somewhere, isn't there?"

With her heart pounding in her throat, she nodded, then made a gesture meant to indicate that it was far back in her ancestry.

"No need to be ashamed of it, boy. They are not all bad."

Then his gaze fell upon her mouth, and Maryana had all she could do not to rise up and flee. When she'd stared at her transformed self in the small mirror at Gisel's, it was her mouth that she feared might give her away: those accursed soft, full lips that kept her from being called truly beautiful, but

142

at the same time made her too obviously girlish.

It now seemed that her heart was pounding as loud as a drum and that he must surely hear it. But she forced herself to look at him. His gaze seemed to be trained on her mouth still, but there was something in his eyes that seemed very far away, as though he had fixed on her, but was actually seeing something else.

Then, just when she thought she could bear it no longer, he got to his feet and stretched, then crossed the room to his bed and began to undress. She hastened to her pallet, keeping her eyes averted.

"Fetch me some of that, lad," said a rough voice behind her as Maryana ladled some of the stew into a bowl for herself.

She knew the voice even before she turned to face the man, Harry. His voice was as unpleasant as the man himself. He shoved a bowl at her, and when she hesitated, he emitted what might have been a laugh.

"His lordship ain't here just now, so ye can play page to *me.*"

Maryana took the bowl and filled it with the stew, then handed it to him. He gave her a snaggletoothed grin that was an ugly parody of a real smile.

"Pretty little boy, ain't you? Almost girlish, with that mouth."

Maryana lowered her face and started to back away, but he suddenly reached out and grabbed her chin roughly, jerking her face up to meet his, scant inches away.

"What are ye afraid of, boy? Mebbe ye think that some o' us might take ye for a girl?"

His taunt terrified her. She'd heard whispered tales of young boys and older men. But she forced herself to relax. There were too many others around, and a few of them—the miller included—were watching them.

"His lordship's eyes and ears, are ye? But then, there ain't much you can tell 'im, is there?" He laughed at his own joke. "Page to the Prince of Thieves, eh?"

Several other men approached the stew pot then, and Harry turned away. Clutching her bowl, Maryana made her way to the cabin and sagged with relief when she reached its safety.

So much for her ability to move unseen through the men. She didn't know Harry, but she thought she knew his type. Having now discovered her, he wasn't likely to let her alone. She would be useless to Roderic now—at least as far as watching Harry was concerned.

She ate her dinner, expecting Roderic to arrive at any time. But by the time she finished, he was still nowhere to be seen. Nor were the men with him.

Fear clutched at her. Already dusk was falling, and they'd always been back well before dark before. Could he have been captured—with or without the help of Harry or the other man Roderic and Tom didn't trust? From her vantage point at the door of the cabin, she scanned the group of men clustered about the fire. She didn't see the man she thought was Steffen, the other man under suspicion, and her fear grew still more.

But then she did spot the man, on the edge of the group. Of course, that didn't mean that either he or Harry might not have told her uncle's men where to find Roderic. In fact, if they had, they would undoubtedly want to be here, to protect themselves from suspicion.

Still, she thought that Roderic and Tom had taken as much care as possible to prevent either man from knowing where Roderic would be going when he left the camp. They'd discussed it this morning, and Tom had taken both men with him this day. The destination of both groups had been kept secret, so neither Harry nor Steffen could have known where Roderic would be, except that they would be intercepting one or another group of tax collectors or guards en route back to the castle.

But what if they gave away the location of the camp? That thought sent a chill through her, at least until she recalled just how difficult it was to find this place. Tom had remarked this morning that it was a good thing that only the three of them—that is, Roderic, Tom, and the abbot—could find it.

"Anyone else could spend his life following some little stream without coming on this place," Tom had said with satisfaction. "You were right to see to it that we take different routes here each time."

But still . . . Maryana stared into the gathering darkness and worried. Finally, when she saw that Tom was alone, she approached him, not certain how to ask her question, but determined to find a way. As it happened, there was no need.

"Worried about him, are you, lad?" the miller said. "Well, so am I, to tell the truth. But he might just have taken a longer way back this time. He knows these woods better than anyone, so he'll find his way here sooner or later."

Unconsciously, her gaze turned to the two men, Harry and Steffen, now sitting together some distance away. She saw the miller turn to see what she was looking at.

"They weren't out of my sight all day," he said with satisfaction. "But I'm thinking that Harry is up to no good just the same."

She wondered what he meant, but she had no opportunity to find out as several of the other men came up and began to express their concern about Roderic and his group.

Maryana returned to the cabin and sat down in the doorway. Dusk turned quickly to night: a very dark night since there was no moon. She wished that the abbot were here, but he'd not put in an appearance this day and was unlikely to arrive now.

What if Roderic had been captured by her uncle's men? There was no way they could hope to save him once he'd been taken to Varley Castle.

Her thoughts drifted. What if she were to get a message to her uncle, offering herself in return for Roderic's release? Would he accept that?

She thought he might. She remained convinced that her uncle bore Roderic no ill will—or very little, in any event. And he might be able to mollify the king if he had her back again and married to Miles.

She shuddered. How could she possibly give herself up to marry Miles Foulane—even to save Roderic?

"You'll catch your death, lad. Come on in."

Maryana struggled up from the dark of sleep, where she'd been following Roderic through a misty woods. She recognized his voice immediately, but the words seemed strange—at least until she felt the cold. Shivering, she opened her eyes to find him standing there.

He reached down and hauled her somewhat roughly to her feet, then draped an arm casually across her shoulders. Vaguely confused, she was caught between her dreams and reality—her real self and her disguise.

Finally, her head cleared at last, she looked at him questioningly. Where had he been? The night was still very dark, with no hint of dawn. She'd fallen asleep there in the doorway, waiting for him, worrying that he'd been captured.

She started toward the fireplace, knowing that

she should have built a fire hours ago, but he had gotten there before her and laid the fire himself, then turned to her.

"We were followed, but we lost them in the woods." He gave her a grim smile of satisfaction. "They're probably still out there, wandering around and lost."

Then he stretched and yawned. "Right now, I'd like something to eat, if there's anything left."

She nodded and hurried from the cabin. The stew pot was still on the fire, and several of the men who'd been with Roderic were busy filling their bowls and congratulating themselves on their safe return. Drawn by their voices, a few men sleeping close by were getting up to hear the news.

She returned to the cabin with a well-filled bowl for Roderic. He was already seated at the table, his boots off, drinking a mug of ale. She set the bowl before him, and he looked up to smile at her. It was a tired smile, and somehow all the sweeter for that. A rush of warmth flowed through her and she turned away quickly, hastening to her pallet in the corner.

From the safety of the dimly lit corner, she watched him as he ate. The firelight flickered over him, casting deep shadows into the hollows of his cheeks. And for the first time, she thought about how kind he was to her.

It was strange that she'd given no thought before to his behavior toward the mute youth he believed her to be. Perhaps she was thinking of it now because of Harry's behavior toward her earlier.

The earl would be a good father, she thought: kind and patient and affectionate. And then she was startled anew at that thought. Most women longed to get married and have children, but *she'd* never felt that way. With no younger brothers or sisters, she'd had no experience with children and tended to regard them rather warily.

Saranne Dawson

This time, when he got up from the table and moved toward his bed, stripping off his clothes as he went, she didn't turn away. Instead, she watched with fascination and an increasing heat as his body was revealed to her.

And for the first time she allowed her thoughts to move beyond kisses and caresses—to that most intimate act of love. How would it feel? What would it be like to have him inside of her?

He had climbed into bed, and now she saw the gleam of the ring in his hand as he held it up to the firelight. She turned away, banishing her foolish thoughts. It would never happen.

The abbot still did not put in an appearance the next day. Maryana missed him and hoped that nothing had happened to him. She spent the day making more arrows and washing Roderic's clothes and tidying up the cabin. Despite having come in so late, Roderic and his men had gone back out with the others early in the morning.

When both groups returned, somewhat earlier than on previous days, there seemed to be less gold. Apparently the tax collections were coming to an end—for now, at least.

Tom appeared in the doorway of the cabin only moments after Roderic had returned. He and his group had arrived only a short time before Roderic's. One look at his long, homely face told Maryana that something was amiss.

He greeted Roderic, then with seeming reluctance handed him a small, folded piece of paper. Maryana stared at it, frowning. She was too far away to see it well, but the delicate parchment looked familiar.

Then, as Roderic turned it over in his hand, she had to stifle a gasp. No wonder it looked familiar. It was *her* paper, and the blue-and-gold seal was hers.

She tore her gaze away from it to see Roderic's reaction. His face wore a frown—but something else as well. She waited, holding her breath as he opened it and read it.

" 'Tis from her, then?" said Tom, who was also watching Roderic closely.

Roderic nodded. "She's come back. The baron sent men to bring her back. She's asked me to meet her at the old abbey tonight."

"It's a trick!" the miller proclaimed. "Don't go, milord!"

"How did this come to you?" Roderic asked, still holding the letter.

"A lad who works at the castle brought it—gave it to my wife just before I got there. I found him and questioned him. He said the lady Maryana gave it to him herself—but I don't believe it.

"No one knows I'm here with you. I've been making certain that I'm seen regular in the village."

"But *she* would know—or guess, anyway. At the very least, you're someone she'd trust, Tom."

"Aye, that's true enough, but—"

"It's her paper and her seal—and a woman's handwriting."

"I still don't trust it," Tom persisted.

"Are you saying that you don't trust *her?*" Roderic asked in a dangerously quiet tone.

"No, I dinna mean that. I trust the lady Maryana—but I don't think she sent this. Someone else has got hold of her paper and seal."

"If she's back, then she must need my help, because her uncle will surely try to marry her off to Miles Foulane quickly."

"Wait a day," Tom implored. "Let me get in touch with someone from the castle that we can trust—and find out if she's really back."

Yes! cried Maryana silently.

"A day might be too late," Roderic said, shaking his head.

149

"But how would she even know about the old abbey?" Tom persisted. "It's not likely that she's ever seen it."

Maryana saw doubt cloud Roderic's features for the first time. *Think,* she implored him silently. *If it were really me, I'd ask you to meet at our place.*

"She's gone out riding enough," he replied. "She's probably seen it."

Suddenly an image popped into Maryana's mind. She *had* seen the abbey. She just hadn't paid it much attention. It lay north of the castle—not far, as she recalled, and deep in the woods. But because it was on a hilltop, she'd seen a crumbling wall from the road. That must be the place.

The miller had apparently given up trying to dissuade Roderic. "Then let me come with you—and bring some men we can trust. If it *is* the Lady Maryana, we'll leave."

Roderic set down the note. "Let me think on it, Tom. I'll let you know."

The other man left, and Roderic left soon after him. Maryana picked up the note. He was right. The handwriting was definitely that of a woman. She thought about the seamstress wife of the guard commander. That woman would have been all too happy to be part of such a plot, in order to curry favor with the baron for her husband's sake. And a few coins would have sufficed to bribe the boy to lie.

How they'd thought to give the note to the miller she didn't know, but perhaps that had been Miles's idea. He no doubt recalled how she'd spoken up on the man's behalf that day, and how Roderic had risked his own life to save him.

Would Roderic go? Or would he think it over and agree with Tom that it could be a trap? If so, then she had no choice but to break her silence and reveal herself.

Still, even in the midst of her fears, Maryana

couldn't help feeling pleased that Roderic would even consider taking such a risk for her sake. Perhaps he loved someone else—but he still cared for her, too.

She waited nervously through the evening meal, watching Roderic for some sign that he had reached a decision. Surely if he did decide to go, he would take Tom and some men with him.

But dusk arrived, and nothing had happened. Roderic remained in the cabin, sitting in front of the fire, his expression unreadable. She decided that he must not be going, after all. She wasn't sure how long it would take to get to the old abbey, but surely he would be leaving by now if he were going.

Then he asked her to go fetch him a mug of tea, and she roused herself from her thoughts and hurried down to the campfire. She felt both relieved and yet vaguely disappointed as well. He wasn't going, after all. Did that mean he'd decided the message wasn't from her—or had he decided that she wasn't worth the risk?

But when she returned, the cabin was empty. She paused in the doorway, her thoughts whirling. He hadn't followed her to the campfire, where the men lounged about in small groups. And she'd seen Tom, so she knew that Roderic hadn't taken him.

Dropping the mug of tea, she ran around the side of the cabin toward the crudely constructed horse pen—just in time to see a shadowy figure leading a horse through the gate, then swinging into the saddle and riding off into the dark forest.

Maryana was running toward the pen herself before she could even think about it. He'd decided to go alone—probably because he hadn't wanted to put anyone else at risk. And if she took the time to get Tom and then still more time to explain with gestures what had happened, it would be too late.

The abbot had said that no one knew these woods as well as Roderic.

Fortunately, the pen was far away from the campfire, and none of the men heard or saw her as she hurriedly saddled the little mare the abbot had provided for her.

The forest had swallowed him up in minutes, but Maryana plunged into it at the point where she'd last seen him. At first, she could see no trail at all, but after a short time, she did see a faint trail in the gathering dark.

She hesitated only a moment before setting off to the right. She didn't entirely trust her sense of direction, but she was guessing that he would have gone this way. Then, seeing that the trail, though quite narrow, was well worn, she hurried the horse as much as she dared.

The moon rose, nearly full, and once as she urged the little mare on, she saw a figure on horseback crest a hill some distance ahead. Relieved that she'd chosen correctly, she kicked the mare to speed her up still more. But no matter how fast she rode, the occasionally glimpsed figure remained well ahead of her. He, too, must be riding hard, and he had the twin advantages of a bigger and stronger horse and knowledge of the way.

Filtered through the high-arching trees, the moonlight was a mixed blessing. It cast patterns on the path, making her nearly dizzy as she strained to see the way, with the result that she had to trust the mare's instincts.

And then the path ended in a small clearing. Maryana reined in her mount—but did not quite curb the colorful oath she'd picked up from some of her peasants. There were times when a lady's language just wouldn't suffice—and this was definitely one of those times.

Surely she hadn't come this far just to lose him— and in more ways than one. The miller—and perhaps Roderic as well—might have suspected a trap, but she was the only one who knew it for certain.

She urged the mare in a circle, studying the forest surrounding it for a continuation of the path. In the end, it was the mare that found it, perhaps scenting one of her brethren.

Off she went again, and when, a short time later, she came to an intersecting path, she let the mare have her head, and the animal unhesitatingly chose to turn right.

On they flew through the night, with Maryana now shivering from the cold. She hadn't taken the time to dress more warmly, certain that each moment lost would bring Roderic closer to imprisonment—or worse. It had occurred to her that while most men would be tempted to bring Roderic to her uncle alive, a reward would not tempt Miles, who, though virtually penniless, would forgo a reward for the satisfaction of seeing Roderic dead.

Another clearing! This time she merely swore under her breath as she brought the mare to a halt once more. Then, just as she was about to repeat what she'd done before, she was suddenly knocked from the saddle.

She'd had only a scant second to see something rushing at her from the shadows—and no time at all to react. Suddenly, she was on the ground, struggling to breathe after the wind had been knocked out of her. A dark figure loomed over her, now bending down to examine the results of his work.

She fumbled for her dagger, and somehow her hand closed around its hilt. But no sooner had she begun to raise it when her wrist was caught in an iron grip and the weapon was shaken away.

"Roderic! Stop it!"

Her startled cry of recognition hung there in the

night. While she was still gasping for breath and trying to face the end of her deception, he sat down hard beside her, as though his legs had suddenly given way.

The moon, which had hidden itself behind a cloud just as she entered the clearing, now blazed forth once more, bathing both their faces in bright silver.

"Maryana?" he said, hesitating over each syllable.

"Yes. You're riding into a trap." she spoke slowly, too, since she was still trying to regain her breath.

"But . . ."

"Why would you think I'd meet you at the old abbey, instead of our place?" she demanded. "How could you be such a fool?"

The uncertainty that had settled over his face now instead became a grin. "It's definitely you," he said, nodding.

"Where are we? How far is it to the abbey?"

"Another twenty minutes' ride." He shrugged, still staring at her as though he were seeing a ghost.

She scrambled to her feet. "Then let's go—before they find us."

He got up, too. "You wait here. I'm going to see what they had planned for me."

"Are you daft? You know what they have planned. They're going to take you captive. And if it's Miles behind this, rather than my uncle, he's going to kill you."

"He can try. Wait here."

Before she could speak again, he was off on foot, presumably to the horse he'd left tethered somewhere nearby. She wanted to shout after him, but held her tongue. Sounds could travel far in a silent forest.

Instead, she looked around for the mare, who'd been spooked by Roderic's sudden assault. Then, when she found her at the far edge of the clearing, she swung into the saddle again and set off in the direction he'd taken. She was finished taking orders from him!

The mare found the path again, and a few moments later they had climbed to the top of a hill. Now, at last, Maryana knew where she was—more or less. Clearly etched against the heavens in the bright moonlight, the towers of Varley Castle stood out against the distant horizon. And then, as she let her gaze travel slowly around the moonlit scene, she thought she caught a glimpse of the ruins of the old abbey on a nearby hill.

She set off again, down into a deep, narrow ravine. And at its bottom, she found Roderic's horse tethered loosely to some branches. So she left her mare there as well, and began to climb up the hill, moving as quietly as possible through the thicket. Halfway up, she paused and peered at the top of the hill. Yes, those were definitely the abbey ruins up there. But she couldn't see anyone—neither Roderic nor his would-be captors.

The crest of the hill, where the ruins stood, was bare of trees, so she stopped near the edge of the forest and peered through the screen of blackberry shrubs.

Near one of the crumbling walls, a woman sat on horseback—on the same white-stockinged mare she herself had ridden at the castle. Although Maryana assumed that it must be the wife of the guards' commander, she had to admit that the woman had disguised herself well. She wore one of the cloaks Maryana had left behind at the castle, and her blond hair was unbound and tumbling about her shoulders. It was of a somewhat darker shade than Maryana's, but in the moonlight it was close enough.

Maryana gritted her teeth in barely controlled anger. How she would have loved to walk up there and confront the woman. But although she appeared to be alone, Maryana knew that would not be the case. And there would be hiding places aplenty among the ruins, or in the forest at the edge of the clearing.

She was convinced that this must be Miles's doing. Her uncle was incapable of such deviousness. Did that mean that Miles himself was here—or would he have simply sent men to do his dirty work? She guessed that he was here. He would take that risk in order to be the one who killed Roderic.

She wondered where Roderic was now. He could be anywhere, hiding in the shadows just as she was. She rose from her crouched position and began to peer into the darkness around her.

Then suddenly a hand clamped itself over her mouth and she was hauled back against her captor, who used his other hand to point a long, ugly knife at her chest.

Maryana struggled, but she had delayed for a vital second, believing that it was Roderic. And then it was too late. The man knocked her to the ground. She saw his arm begin to swing in a wide arc, the knife aimed squarely at her chest.

She had just begun to scream when the man suddenly toppled to the ground, knocked sideways by something that had launched itself from a nearby tree, then moved on.

No, it hadn't moved on! In the next instant, the swinging figure returned and she was swept up into Roderic's arms, her legs dangling well above the ground.

Their landing was abrupt and hard. Roderic slammed into a thick trunk, then managed to let go of the heavy vine and at the same time steady both of them against the trunk and a thick limb.

As soon as he let go of her and of the vine, he

clamped a hand over her mouth. "Quiet! They won't be looking for us up here."

Maryana didn't doubt that at all. The ground was a dizzying distance away. And just as she forced herself to look down, a group of men burst into view, going quickly to their fallen comrade, who wasn't moving.

Balancing himself against the trunk, Roderic removed the longbow from his shoulder, then reached behind him to pluck an arrow from his quiver. Maryana stared at him, aghast. Had he gotten them up here to safety of a sorts, only to give away their location by loosing arrows upon the soldiers? He couldn't hope to get them all, and then they'd be trapped in a tree—easy targets for those who remained.

But his face was turned up, and he climbed nimbly to a higher branch—and then one higher still, until he was near the top of the tree. Once more bracing himself against the trunk, he fitted an arrow to the bow and sent it upward in a high arc. Then he climbed back down to her as quickly and silently as he'd ascended.

Maryana heard the arrow strike at the same moment the men on the ground below them heard it—and then they were all rushing off in that direction, leaving behind their dead or unconscious comrade.

"Come on, let's go."

Go? She stared down and felt the dizziness come over her again. But he was already moving, and she had no recourse but to follow.

It wasn't as difficult as she'd thought—especially once she learned not to look down but to concentrate, instead, on each step toward firm ground. And Roderic was there with strong arms to guide her in the last part of the descent. Frightened as she was, she did not fail to react to his touch—and that reminded her that her game was over. No more deceptions—but was she as good as on her way across the straits?

"Is your horse with mine?" he asked in a low voice as he grabbed her hand and dragged her after him down the hill.

"Yes."

"There's that to be grateful for, then."

She wondered what he meant by that, but since he was setting a fast pace, she had all she could do to keep up, let alone carry on a conversation. But she was certain that she'd heard the clear implication that he found much *not* to be grateful for.

They reached the horses and set off through the woods, her mare following his stallion on the narrow path. The moon had slipped behind a thickening cloud bank, and she could just barely make him out in the darkness.

He is not *going to send me back to Neran!* she told herself. *He can't* order me to go there—or anywhere, for that matter. On the other hand, however, if her true identity became known in camp . . .

They rode hard for a time, and then, when they had reached the first clearing Maryana had encountered on her journey, he brought them both to a halt and dismounted.

"Why are we stopping here?" she asked. "We're not lost. I—"

"I know we're not lost," he said with a trace of a smile in his voice. "But we're safe now. They don't know these woods well enough to follow us."

"Did you see if Miles was among them?" she asked. She'd not been able to identify the men from her perch in the tree.

"He was. Who was the woman?"

She told him whom she suspected. "I guessed that this was Miles's doing. My uncle just isn't that devious."

"Oh? It seems to me that being devious must run in the family."

She remained mounted, while he stood beside her mare, his arms now folded across his chest.

"You left me no choice, Roderic. I couldn't go back to Chamoney. Miles would simply have followed me—with an order from the king that I marry him."

"The abbot has a lot to answer for."

"It was my idea—not his."

"But he went along with it."

"He's a good and kind man."

"If he weren't, I'd be tempted to forget that he's a man of the cloth."

"Well, what's done is done. What do we do now?"

"Oh? Are you saying that I've lost a page?"

Maryana decided that he seemed to be taking this better than she'd anticipated—which made her very suspicious. " 'Fetch me some ale, boy.' 'Take off my boots.' 'Here are my clothes that need washing.' " She'd lowered her voice to mimic his.

"I think I liked it much better when you were mute."

"Do you have any idea how hard it is not to talk?"

"I have a feeling that I'm going to find out."

"It's horrible! And so it is to be all but invisible— as though I were a pet dog."

"Perhaps it will make you kinder toward servants in the future."

"I've *never* been unkind to servants!" She bristled angrily.

"Are you saying that I am—or was?"

"No, not really. But I can't believe you were so blind as to fail to recognize me."

"We see what we expect to see, I guess." He shrugged, unconsciously repeating the abbot's words. "Though there was one time when you did come to mind."

A rush of heat swept up to her face—which he very fortunately could not see in the darkness. She knew exactly when that was: when he had stared for so long at her mouth. Remembering the time he'd kissed that mouth, she touched her fingers to her lips.

He chuckled, then turned and swung into the saddle again. "Back to camp, boy."

" 'Boy?' Then I will—"

"You'll continue to be my page, though I'll take care when I ask you to remove my boots now that I know whose lovely bottom is likely to be singed."

"I think you're liking this entirely too much, Roderic."

Chapter Eight

At the sound of their approach, a shadowy figure pulled itself to its feet and stood in the doorway to the cabin. Maryana drew in a sharp breath and came to a halt, but Roderic continued toward the cabin, and after a moment, she trailed along behind him.

"So you went to the meeting," Tom said, then glanced at her and added in a dry tone, "But I see that you didn't go alone, at least."

"I didn't take the boy. He followed me."

"A good lad—if a bit foolhardy. What happened?"

Roderic gave him an abbreviated version of the events—a very much abbreviated version.

"So it was Foulane," the miller said, nodding. "Methinks we should rid the world of him—and the sooner the better."

"I'll admit that it's a tempting thought," Roderic acknowledged. "But cold-blooded murder isn't my way, Tom."

"It's *his* way," Tom protested. "If it hadn't been for the lady Maryana and then you, I would have been done for."

"Are you saying that I should be no better than him?" Roderic challenged.

Tom hesitated, then shook his head. "No, you're right, milord. So what happens now?"

"We continue as we have been—until the collections are over. After that, we'll see."

Once again, Maryana found herself sharing the miller's frustration with Roderic. What a strange man was Roderic Hode, Earl of Varley! That he was brave, she no longer doubted, and though she certainly shared the miller's anger with Miles, she respected Roderic's belief that cold-blooded murder was not the way to be rid of him.

But when was he going to *do* something—to take some action beyond stealing? Yes, she certainly understood the miller's frustration.

"There is another matter I didn't speak of earlier," Tom said. "Harry managed to slip away for a short time today—or yesterday, as it were. When I found him, he was having a drink at the tavern and claimed that he was merely trying to gain some information for us. But I didn't like the looks of his drinking companions. They're not men I trust."

Roderic thought about that in silence for a moment before speaking. "But what could he have said—assuming that he said anything?"

The miller shrugged. "Not much that I can see. He'd have the devil's own trouble telling anyone where our camp is, since I don't think he could find it himself."

"Well then, perhaps he was doing nothing more than he said."

"Perhaps," the miller echoed, but without conviction.

* * *

"I'd give you my bed, but the men are accustomed to coming and going from here at will, and it'd be difficult to explain how my page came to be sleeping in my bed."

With or without you in it? she thought, but of course didn't say. Instead, she turned her face toward the pallet to prevent his seeing the flush that stole over her pale skin.

"I'm comfortable enough on the pallet," she told him.

"Now I'm going to lie awake mulling over everything I've said and done since you came here," he went on.

And when will you get to that ring? she wondered silently. *Or doesn't it matter?* None of this was going as she'd thought it would. She'd conjured up fantasies of what would happen when he discovered that his page was really her—but the reality fell far short of that. *Very* far short.

"Did I do or say anything that offended you?" he asked with a hint of exasperation in his voice. No doubt he'd expected her to speak up on the subject.

"Not that I can think of," she replied, stealing a glance at the pillow that hid the ring. "Thank you for not selling my jewelry. But exactly when did you think you'd be able to return it to me?"

He shrugged. "One day. The future is a dark mirror."

Indeed, she thought. "Good night, then."

She went over to her pallet and lay down, immediately turning her face to the wall. Behind her, she heard him move to his bed, then sit down to remove his boots. But she didn't hear the sound of his clothing being shed.

"I suppose you're wanting me to say that I'm glad you're here."

She was very nearly asleep when his words floated across the darkened room. "Are you?"

"Yes and no. Despite that fool, Miles Foulane,

you'd be better off in Chamoney—safer, anyway."

She waited for a second part to his statement, since he'd said yes *and* no. But it never came.

I'm like a little sister to him, she thought. *His feelings are not so very much different even now that he knows the truth. Before, I was like a little brother, and now I'm a sister.*

And with those bleak thoughts, she fell asleep, even though she'd been certain that she couldn't sleep in the same room with him.

"So you found this spot, too."

Maryana couldn't see him well because of the sun's glare on the water, but she'd known—even before he spoke—that it was Roderic. It had shown in his agile grace as he climbed over the rocks lining the small pool.

She'd found this little pool only yesterday, when for lack of anything better to do, she'd gone exploring, using the stream as a way of preventing herself from getting lost.

It was, in fact, the origin of the stream: a waterfall that tumbled down from a high, rocky crevass into the pool, then overflowed to become the stream. The water was still cold, but with the sun on it since early morning, it was somewhat warmer than the stream itself.

He sat down beside the blanket she'd brought to wrap herself in while her clothes dried on the surrounding rocks. She'd been in the pool for some time and was growing chilled. Now what was she to do? He gave no indication of knowing her discomfort or her predicament. Or was he playing a game: waiting for her to give voice to that problem?

She quickly decided that was it. Roderic had more than a touch of deviltry to him, and it was undoubtedly payback time for her deception.

"I thought you'd gone off tax collecting," she

said, referring to it in the same way she'd heard him do.

"No, it seems that they're finished—for now, at least. So far, your uncle seems to be resisting Foulane's demands that he go back again. Is he a wealthy man himself?"

"Yes. He inherited his wife's estates when she died. I see what you mean. You think he might make up for the losses by using his own money?"

"Would he do that?"

"I'm not sure. I really don't know him well enough to guess at that."

"Mmm. Well, for sure Foulane will be pushing him to take from the people again. The baron isn't a bad man, as Nerans go, but he *is* weak."

By now, Maryana's teeth were beginning to chatter and her legs were cramping from the effort required to remain in a crouch beneath the water, which was what she'd been doing when he appeared. But the pool was only about three feet or so deep, so she had no choice.

"Why hasn't the abbot been here the past few days?" she asked, determined to show him that she could remain where she was indefinitely.

"He's had religious duties to attend to. His affiliation with me is well known, so he must protect himself. His superiors are very much against men of the cloth becoming involved in temporal matters.

"I saw him earlier, however, at our meeting place not far from his abbey. He'd known nothing of the plan to snare me. Apparently Miles Foulane has become quite circumspect around the castle servants."

"Does that mean that Gisel and the cook could be in danger?"

"No, I don't think so. They work for your uncle, after all, not for Foulane. And I doubt that he'd go so far as to try to get rid of them on his own even if he does suspect them."

"Did you tell the abbot about me?" she asked, trying not to let her voice betray the icy chill she was feeling.

"That subject did arise, now that you mention it," he responded dryly.

"And?"

"I'd think that the water—even in the pool—would be too cold for you by now. At least it is for me."

"Then what do you propose I do about it?" she demanded.

"Get out." He shrugged. "Why should a page become modest in front of his lord?"

That did it. It had already been in her mind simply to walk out of the water as though showing her body to a man were something she did regularly. But his insolent words and tone put action to thought before she could allow herself to consider it further.

So she stood up, then walked through the water to the rocky ledge, where she hoisted herself up onto the rock near him. The whole thing was accomplished so quickly that she was there before she quite realized what a brazen thing she'd done. And then she was shivering so violently that she couldn't carry it through by adopting a defiant stance.

Roderic got to his feet and picked up the blanket. "Once at a fair, I saw a freak with mottled skin—some light and some dark. But the patterns were more artistic."

Maryana glared at him—or tried to. Between the exterior cold and the heat that was suffusing her from the inside, she was paralyzed. And then there was that wicked gleam in his dark eyes.

"Ah, so now we have pink as well. A veritable artist's palette."

"Give me the blanket, Roderic," she said between clenched and still-chattering teeth.

"Of course." He unfolded it and held it open.

She hesitated for one brief moment, then stepped toward him and turned her back so he could wrap it around her. His strong fingers caressed her shoulders through the thick wool, and she felt her legs grow weak.

"I think I can see a hint of gold beneath those black hairs," he said with a smile in his voice.

Clutching the blanket with one hand, she raised the other to touch the top of her head. "I didn't think that would happen so soon."

"It's not really noticeable yet, but perhaps I'd better get some more dye from Gisel."

"I have more," she replied, her voice husky as she attempted to dry herself without bumping against him.

"And the stain on your skin—will that come off?"

"At some point. I have more of it, too."

She stepped away from him, still holding the blanket close, then turned to face him. "Well, Roderic, are you satisfied now that you've made me pay for my game?"

He laughed. "I don't think you found the price too high. I saw no cringing or trying to hide yourself from me."

"What are you suggesting—that I—"

"I'm not suggesting anything, Lady Maryana. It is you who have chosen to interpret what I said."

Then, perhaps seeing the anger in her eyes, he stepped away and began to strip off his own clothing. After he had removed his shirt, he reached for his pants, then stopped and grinned at her.

"I'd say that turnabout's fair play, but since you've already seen me . . ." He shrugged and resumed stripping off his clothes.

"I didn't watch you," she said huffily—though she was doing exactly that now.

"Not even once?" he asked, casting a look back over his naked back just before he stepped off the ledge into the pool. "I'm disappointed."

So I *did* look—once, she thought. But there was a big difference between a quick glimpse in the darkness and a bold stare in bright sunlight.

And there was also considerable satisfaction. One could not spend one's time on a large estate filled with animals and not recognize the sign of male arousal. So his feelings toward her weren't brotherly—but what, exactly, were they? Men, she suspected, could probably be aroused as easily as animals were.

She checked her clothing and found that it hadn't quite dried, so she sat down, with the blanket still wrapped securely around her, and watched him in the pool. Unlike her, he made no effort to hide himself beneath the water—which she now saw was poor covering at best, since it was so clear.

The question she most wanted to ask—about the ring beneath his pillow—hovered just behind her lips. Had she become so practiced at deception that she could no longer speak her mind?

No, she decided. It was just that some questions were so important that they *could not* be asked, lest everything after that be changed.

The day was warm, owing to the bright sunshine—but Maryana could nonetheless detect a chill in the wind that swept down from the cliff that overhung the pool. And that made her think of all she'd heard about the winters in Sakim.

Winter in Neran, though it was not that far away, was much milder and brought far less snow. Or were the stories about the weather as false as the stories she'd heard of Sakim savages?

"I've heard stories about winter here," she said as he waded over to the ledge near her. "Are they true?"

"That depends on what you've heard."

"That it is very cold and there's much snow—deeper than a man is tall, I was told."

He nodded. "Sometimes it *is* that bad. That cold and the snow have saved my people several times from the warm-blooded Nerans."

"Then what will we do? There is no shelter for the men."

"I haven't decided yet."

"It seems to me that you take a very long time to decide *everything*, Roderic," she said disgustedly.

"Oh?" He regarded her with a slight smile, one that suggested he might be thinking along very different lines from her.

"I wonder that your people follow you at all, when you take so long to decide anything."

He levered himself out of the pool. "They follow me because they know that when I do make up my mind, the decision will be the right one."

She averted her eyes as he picked up a blanket and began to dry himself.

"Am I not what you want me to be, Maryana?" he asked softly.

She brought her gaze around sharply, to find him busy getting dressed again. The question was seemingly a casual, teasing one, but she sensed an underlying seriousness. So she answered honestly.

"In some ways, yes—in other ways, no."

"And you've had some opportunity to get to know me in ways you might otherwise not have had."

He was echoing a thought she'd herself had when she'd set out to deceive him, so she nodded.

"I believe you heard Tom make reference to my Innish blood, and you undoubtedly know the ways of the Sakims by now. We—the Sakims, that is—can be a dark and fatalistic people. The Innish, on the other hand, are of a very practical turn of mind, not inclined to mull things over for very long. I think that I combine both natures—which may

169

make me difficult to understand at times."

"There is Innish blood in me as well," she told him. "My grandmother was Innish, though I never knew her. My father used to say, from time to time, that I was much like her."

"And so you are, I think—but with a dash of Neran arrogance thrown in for good measure."

"Arrogance?" She bristled. "How can you call me arrogant when I've been playing page to you?"

"Ah, but that was your Innish side—your practical side."

He laughed at her frown, then extended his hands to help her to her feet. She took them, but after she'd stood up, he dropped her hands and circled her waist instead. His dark eyes roved slowly over her face and her short, dark hair—not to mention her rough boy's clothing.

"If I kiss you now, I'm undoubtedly going to have to beg forgiveness for my sin from the abbot. Kissing one's page would be a very grievous sin indeed."

His wide mouth was curved in a lazy smile, but there was nothing lazy in the look he gave her.

"I believe the abbot would find it in his heart to forgive such a sin."

It began as the other kiss had: soft and tentative. But this time, she grasped his head between her hands and kept him there.

Lips and tongues explored, melting one into the other, it seemed to her. She was so lost in new sensations that she very nearly forgot to breathe, and when she did, she exhaled with a soft sigh and arched against him, her body fitting its curves to his hard planes and angles.

But once again, it was Roderic who ended it, taking her hands gently from his face and holding them for one moment as he stepped away.

"Time to be going back to camp."

She followed him, both disappointed and yet

perhaps a bit relieved as well. She wanted him—but she wanted a declaration more. And she thought about what he'd said earlier about taking his time but then making the right decision.

And she thought about that ring, too.

Maryana watched the abbot ride away, regretting his absence even before he was out of sight. Roderic was away from camp as well, and she hadn't seen Tom, either.

Now that Roderic knew the truth, she was finding it very difficult to maintain the fiction of her disguise. For a time, she'd actually *felt* like the youth she was pretending to be, but now she felt herself again, and chafed at the necessity of maintaining the disguise—especially the silence.

The purpose of the abbot's visit, he'd told her, was to be certain she wasn't worrying herself over Roderic's reaction. According to him, Roderic had done little more than complain that a "proper" man of the cloth wouldn't practice or countenance such lies. And even that, the abbot said, had been said with a definite twinkle in his eyes.

She'd told the abbot the truth: that she hadn't concerned herself overmuch with the his welfare, since she knew that Roderic was not a cruel man. And that was true enough, but cruelty could take many forms.

Roderic might not have been cruel toward the abbot, but he was certainly being cruel toward her. In fact, he had her spinning around for fair: one moment treating her like a sister, and the next moment fanning the flames of her desire with his own.

Where is the truth? she asked herself. *Does he feel about me the same way I feel toward him—or has he not yet made up his mind completely?*

She scanned the camp, searching for Tom. Roderic had not said that Tom could know the truth, but she knew he trusted the miller completely—and so, too, did she. When she couldn't find him, she started back to the cabin, then changed her mind and went instead to the horse pen. The day was lovely and warm and the forest was ablaze with the glorious colors of autumn. It would be a perfect day for a ride.

She saddled the mare and set off into the woods, skirting the camp and then following the little stream so she couldn't get lost. Her thoughts plunged into bleakness, then soared to the heavens as she thought about Roderic's kiss. She almost convinced herself that that accursed ring wasn't important.

She had no idea how far she'd gone when she heard sounds behind her, and turned to see two figures approaching her from the direction of the camp. Because of the trees and the heavy undergrowth, she couldn't make out who they were, but she felt no real fear. They had obviously come from the camp, so she ignored them and rode on.

Then they were directly behind her on the narrow path next to the stream, and just as she turned again, they both crowded against her, one on either side.

At first Maryana thought that they were simply being rude in an attempt to pass her—but that was before she realized that one of the men was Harry.

"Good of ye to help us out by comin' this way, milady," Harry said, showing his ugly yellowed teeth in a wolfish grin.

She simply stared at him, willing her face into a frown of incomprehension. Surely he'd meant the "milady" as a joke of some sort!

"The way I see it, ye're goin' to fetch us a fair price at Varley Castle," he continued. "Even if ye don't have a price on yer head like his lordship."

She continued to frown at him while at the same time trying to maneuver the mare past both of them by urging her up the steep bank. But the other man reached out and grabbed the reins, tearing them from her hands before she realized what he was doing.

Then Harry crowded against her on the other side and reached out as well—but to grab at her chest. She tried to push him away, but he laughed triumphantly.

"Too much there for a boy," he said, grinning, then grabbed at her head and lowered it for his inspection. "And ain't that gold I see 'neath all that black hair? Seems his lordship has got the best o' both: a page and a woman to warm his bed."

With the other man continuing to hold her mare's reins, Maryana did the only thing she could do: she leaped off the horse and started to run up the bank. But Harry, who had seemed to be as slow on his feet as he was slow-witted, was after her with surprising speed. She didn't even make it to the top of the bank before he'd grabbed her and flung her roughly to the ground.

Propping himself above her and trapping her beneath his hard, smelly body, he began to fumble with her clothes. She heard something tear and began to struggle even more desperately.

"Well, milady," he said, still grinning, "I think I'll just take a sample of what his lordship's been gettin'."

Terror coursed through her, roaring in her ears so loudly that she didn't hear the words of the other man as he joined them. But then, with obvious reluctance, Harry moved off her.

"Aye, ye're right, Timmy. But ye can't blame a man for wantin', can ye?"

She struggled to her feet and immediately began to run again, but before she'd gotten very far, something crashed against her skull—and her world went black.

* * *

The voices were close by, but strangely muffled. Even as she struggled up from the darkness, Maryana winced at the pain in the back of her head. She tried to reach up to touch the spot, only to discover that she couldn't move her arms.

It was only when she finally recognized one of the voices as belonging to the man, Harry, that it all came back to her: his filthy hands touching her, his foul breath against her face—and his knowledge of who she was.

She had no idea where she was. It was very dark, and she lay bound hand and foot and wrapped in a smelly blanket just loose enough around her head to permit her to breathe. It was the blanket that was muffling the voices of the men, who must have been somewhere nearby.

She doubted, despite Harry's words, that she was back at Varley Castle. The floor beneath her felt like dirt, not stone. Perhaps there was yet a chance to escape. She began to struggle with the ropes that bound her. They didn't seem all that tight. And as she struggled with them, she also tried to hear what was being said. Then suddenly, one voice became louder than the rest—and Maryana knew that there would be no escape.

"Let me see her!" Miles ordered.

"O' course, milord. She's wearin' a disguise and pretendin' to be a mute—but it's her." Harry's voice was loud and hearty, eager to be rewarded.

She was unwrapped from the blanket. The ropes securing her arms were cut. She sat up, blinking in the light of a lantern—and the first face she saw, bending over to peer at her, was that of Miles Foulane.

"Jes' hold the lantern to her head, milord, and you can see the gold at the roots of her hair." Then he cackled. "Or undress her, if you like. That way ye'll know fer sure."

"Wait outside!" Miles ordered curtly. Then, after

Harry and the other man had gone, he squatted down beside her. "It *is* you, isn't it? Have they harmed you?"

Maryana blinked at him. There was, at least for Miles, a tender note in his voice. She thought fast. If she didn't speak, he might do as Harry had suggested—or he might go away and leave her to them.

"Yes, it's me. Untie my feet, Miles."

He drew out a knife and did as she requested. Then he stared at her again. "What have they done to you? Your hair? Your skin?"

"I did that myself."

She struggled to her feet, but a wave of dizziness overcame her, and she would have fallen again if Miles hadn't reached out to seize her and hold her tight in his arms. She raised a hand to the back of her head and winced as she touched a lump.

"They knocked me on the head," she told him. "That's why I'm dizzy."

"I brought the carriage. It's right outside. Let me get you into it, and then I'll deal with them."

Even through her pain and dizziness, Maryana noticed the hard way he spoke those last words. But as far as she was concerned at that moment, if Miles wanted to kill Harry and his companion, that was perfectly all right with her.

She came to some time later in the carriage: the same carriage she'd ridden in the day she'd come to Sakim. The day she'd met Roderic. When she opened her eyes, she saw Miles sitting across from her, his pale eyes studying her with satisfaction.

Never had she thought a day could come when she would be happy to see Miles Foulane, but when she thought about Harry . . .

"What did you do to them?" she asked, though merely forming the words was difficult, and her speech sounded slurred to herself.

175

"They've been taken care of," Miles said shortly, now sounding much more like his usual self.

Maryana sighed and let her head fall back against the cushioned seat. Then she closed her eyes as a wave of nausea threatened.

When she awoke again, she was in her bed in her old suite at the castle. Her head still ached, especially when she tried to move it. And when she attempted to focus on the figure seated in a chair next to the bed, she saw not one but two women there, their outlines blurring into each other. But before she lapsed once again into unconsciousness, she was fairly certain that it was the guard commander's wife—the woman who she believed had impersonated her to trap Roderic.

Maryana drifted through an unknown number of hours or perhaps days, floating from a near-awake state back to oblivion, then back again to a semiawareness of her surroundings. During these latter times, someone was always there. Mostly it was her impersonator, but on a few occasions her uncle was there as well, and once it was Miles who stared down at her.

The look of triumph on his long, narrow face would stir her to anger—and then, briefly, to full consciousness. But with that came a realization of her situation, and she would relinquish her grip on reality and fall back into the darkness.

Finally, it was the concern evident in her uncle's voice that drew her back—not Miles's smirk or the disapproving silence of the woman. For all his weakness and his willingness to marry her off to a man she hated, the baron was obviously worried about her.

She opened her eyes to find him bent over her, his round face creased with worry, then smiling as he saw her fix her gaze on him.

"You're awake!" he exulted.

"Yes," she replied in a voice rusty with disuse, to which she added silently, But not happily. Her head still ached and she felt weak as a newborn kitten, but at least she could see him clearly.

"Dear child," he said, taking her hand. "I thought never to see you again."

Maryana frowned at him. She had no doubt of his sincerity, but she also knew that nothing would have changed. He would marry her off to Miles as soon as she could leave her bed.

"See that Sir Miles is summoned," the baron ordered the woman who sat near the window.

Maryana turned her head and watched the woman leave, her dark gold hair once more bound up tightly. "Was it you who ordered her to impersonate me, Uncle?"

His smile turned to confusion and then to fear, as though he feared she might have returned as an idiot. "What do you mean?"

"I thought it must have been Miles," she said with bitter satisfaction before explaining what had happened.

"I knew nothing of that," he said when she had finished. "But are you saying that you were with Lord Roderic all this time?"

It was now clear to her that her uncle knew very little about what had happened. She weighed the consequences of telling him the truth, and decided that they were nonexistent. Roderic was already being sought—with a price on his head.

So she told him the truth—including her betrayal by two of Roderic's men. "But it was my fault," she finished. "I already knew that one of them wasn't to be trusted."

"Did they, um, harm you? That is to say . . ."

Seeing his discomfort, Maryana saved him from having to give further voice to it. "Other than hitting me on the head, no. But the one called Harry would have done so had his partner not stopped him." She wondered if that meant she owed the other man a debt of sorts.

And that thought gave birth to yet another. What had happened to the two men? Had Miles managed to gain from them the location of Roderic's camp? She recalled the miller's doubts that Harry could find it on his own, let alone give that information to anyone else.

"What happened to those men?" she asked, though her real question concerned Roderic. She suddenly feared that he'd been caught and was even now in the castle's dungeon—or worse, if Miles had had his way.

"It is my understanding that they were questioned concerning the location of Roderic's hideout, then killed when they attempted to escape."

Maryana recalled Miles's cruel sport with the miller and suspected that much the same had happened to Harry and his partner. Though she did, perhaps, owe the other man a debt of gratitude, she could not rouse herself to sympathy for them.

"Then Roderic has not been captured," she said, not even bothering to hide her relief.

"No, he has not." The baron met her eyes for a moment, then shifted his gaze to the window. "I should have imprisoned him when I had the chance. A very deceptive man, the Earl of Varley."

Maryana wasn't sure, but she thought she heard a sort of grudging admiration there. She kept her silence, waiting for her uncle to continue.

"The king has sent word that he expects to arrive at Varley Castle before winter's onset," the baron went on. "Though Sir Miles calls me a fool and will undoubtedly tell His Majesty, I have decided to make up the tax losses out of my own money."

"I will help, Uncle—as soon as I can get word to Chamoney."

"I fear that decision will not be yours to make,

my dear. The king also sent an order that you are to be married to Miles Foulane forthwith—and I doubt that he will see fit to part with any money when it becomes his."

"Uncle, you can't do this! I detest Miles Foulane—and so do you, though you haven't yet admitted it."

"My feelings on the subject have no more weight than your own, Maryana. Miles has the ear of the king—and my own situation, thanks to Roderic, is shaky at best."

She wondered if she could kill Miles in their marriage bed. It seemed the only way out. She could not hope to escape again. But she recalled the conversation between Roderic and Tom about cold-blooded murder. Did what she was contemplating fit into that category? And how could she think that she could do such a thing? Was she really capable of murder?

Miles put in an appearance some hours later, after she had been helped from the bed and given a proper bath by a maid she'd never seen before. She wondered where Gisel was. Had her part in this been found out?

She was seated in a chair near the windows when he arrived, though she was already beginning to regret her decision to stay out of bed longer. And she felt hot, angry bile rise to her throat when he strode in, his smirk firmly in place.

"I can't think why you're looking so happy with yourself, Miles," she stated coldly, having decided to go on the offensive. "You are about to marry a woman who may well decide to murder you in your sleep—and you haven't managed to kill Lord Roderic."

Then she smiled with satisfaction at the effect of her words. He clearly hadn't expected her to remain defiant. Perhaps he thought she would be

Saranne Dawson

grateful for his having saved her. Seeing that she had gained some sort of victory, however small, she sought even more.

"And you will also be marrying a woman who will be forever comparing you to the man you hate—and finding you wanting in every way."

She placed a none-too-subtle emphasis on her final words, to let him interpret them as he chose—because she knew exactly how he would interpret them. And even if she had no intimate knowledge of men, she knew of their vanity in such matters.

Miles's expression went quickly from incredulity to a dark rage. Maryana's hand went instinctively to her pocket—or to where the pocket would have been, had she been dressed as usual. But she wore only a heavy robe over her shift, and the dagger wasn't there.

"I will ignore those words, since you are not yet well," he stated finally, still struggling to control his anger.

"That is your choice, of course," she acknowledged in the same cold tone he'd used. "But they will not change even when I am well. I hated you even before I met Roderic Hode. He has only given me someone to compare you to."

Miles sneered. He was very good at *that*, at least, she thought. "Your lover can't rescue you again, milady. In fact, he'll be hard-pressed to keep his own skin whole."

Then, before she could respond, he strode out of her room with all the dignity he could muster.

Maryana shivered and wrapped her arms around herself. What had he meant by that last remark? Had he gotten some information from Harry and the other man? Perhaps they didn't know exactly where the camp was, but they would have known the general area.

She closed her eyes, conjuring up an image of Roderic, trying to send her thoughts to him—to warn him. But he must know he is in danger, she consoled herself. Her ill-considered words to Miles would have little effect, except to stoke those fires of hatred still higher.

"They were less than an hour's ride from here when they finally turned back at day's end. They were following the wrong branch of the stream, but they'll get it right sooner or later."

Roderic nodded. "Yes, you're right. We will have to leave here soon. But at least they won't be searching for the next three days. The harvest festival begins tonight."

"Aye—such as it is. Not much to celebrate this year," Tom said, shaking his head. "But at least Baron DeLay doesn't seem inclined to collect the stolen tax money again."

"Then there *is* something to celebrate," Roderic said with a smile. "Not that there's any need for a reason. Tradition alone is enough. And speaking of tradition . . ."

Tom betrayed no surprise as Roderic told him of his plan. He'd already been thinking along the same lines himself. The only question was whether, under the circumstances, Baron DeLay would follow that tradition. But Roderic seemed to believe he would.

"This is personal, Tom," Roderic said in a low voice. "I cannot ask the men to help me."

"They will help," Tom assured him. "Many of their families benefited from her generosity. And they are already feeling bad about not protecting her—though of course they had no idea that it *was* her."

"How could they have—when I didn't even know myself until the end? If there is blame to be laid, it is on me, because I failed to take action when you said that Harry couldn't be trusted."

Tom made no response to that. In truth, he blamed himself for what had happened. He knew that his lord was inclined to be too trusting, and he should have taken matters into his own hands.

"Does the abbot have any news from the castle?" he asked instead, knowing that Roderic had met with him earlier.

"Only that she is on the mend, and that the wedding will be scheduled as soon as possible. But the abbot won't be needed to perform the ceremony. The baron's priest has recovered."

"A pity, that. Perhaps your arrow should have found a truer mark."

"It *did* find its true mark. I will not have on my conscience the murder of a priest—even a Neran." Roderic swept a hand in dismissal of the subject. "We have plans to make."

Chapter Nine

It was cruel that the day should be so glorious. Maryana stood at the windows, staring out beyond the castle's walls to the reds, golds, and greens of the hilly land, smoldering brightly beneath a brilliant blue sky. She wondered why autumn seemed so much more beautiful in Sakim. Perhaps it was the presence of so many pines and firs to provide contrast.

She remained at the window, resolutely keeping her gaze away from the bed, though it did no good. She could see her wedding gown in her mind's eye, spread across the coverlet.

Her hand went unconsciously to the dagger in her pocket. She'd been surprised to find it, tucked into one of her dresses. Certainly it hadn't gotten there by itself. She knew that Gisel was still in the castle, though she herself now had a different maid. She could only assume that the boy's clothing she'd been wearing when Miles had brought her back here had somehow found its way to Gisel, who had then discovered the dagger and returned it.

She let go of the dagger with a sigh. She couldn't kill Miles, however satisfactory a fantasy that might be. To murder a man just because he was unpleasant and greedy would be a mortal sin not even the abbot could forgive—though she'd no doubt that he would search to find a way.

Besides, her practical Innish nature told her, killing him would solve only one problem—and not the greatest one. Chamoney would still be taken from her and she would be sent off for the remainder of her days to repent in a convent.

She continued to stare out the window as she thought of her beloved Chamoney. In a few days, the weather willing, she would be going home— with a new husband who was eager to begin reaping the rewards of his marriage. How long would it take him, she wondered, to destroy all that she and her ancestors had built there?

Maryana lived now in a strange sort of daze that had nothing to do with her injury. Rather, she had simply withdrawn a part of herself from her surroundings—always aware of those around her, but not allowing herself to be affected by them.

Roderic had become a distant dream, or memory—or perhaps both. She assumed that he was safe, since she would surely have heard otherwise. In all likelihood he'd gone south, perhaps to his Innish kin. Perhaps even to the woman for whom that ring was intended or to whom it belonged. She'd only lately realized that the workmanship looked Innish, much like some pieces she'd inherited from her grandmother.

In any event, Roderic was gone from her life. How she wished that he hadn't let her go that day at the pool. Then at least she would have a memory of love to sustain her—or something like love, in any event.

184

Through the open windows, she heard a clamor far below and out of her view. So the gates had been opened to the revelers. Her uncle had ignored Miles's protests. That, at least, pleased her.

The Sakims, she learned, celebrated the harvest much as her own people did: with three days of dancing and drinking and merriment. It all culminated with a celebration of All Saints' Eve, at which time people went about costumed and masked in horrible guises, celebrating in the old pagan style to ward off the demons that were believed to wander the land through the coming winter. The Church frowned upon it, of course, but even they were powerless to stop an ancient tradition.

It was traditional—both here and in Neran—to open the great houses and castles to the people, but Miles had argued vehemently against her uncle's continuing that custom. He said that he feared Roderic and his men might use it as cover to enter the castle and carry her off.

But her uncle, rather to her surprise, had held fast, pointing out to Miles that the knight had only hours before been proclaiming that he'd chased Roderic and his band of thieves from the land.

For a brief moment, Maryana had let herself hope that Roderic might come to rescue her. But then reason had prevailed. Miles had stated smugly that they were closing in on his hidden camp, that they already knew the general area. And if that were the case, then she knew Roderic would know it as well—and be gone.

She turned away from the window, still pointedly ignoring the gown spread out on the bed, and opened the door into the hallway. A guard had been posted there—one of Miles's men, naturally— but she swept past him, ignoring his stammered warning.

She stopped only when she had reached the upper gallery that overlooked the main hall. The guard had followed her, but she ignored him as she scanned the garishly costumed and masked crowd below, milling about in the great hall, helping themselves to the barrels of wine and ale that her uncle had set out for them.

We truly are one people, she thought as she studied the various costumes and elaborate masks. She might have been home at Chamoney, watching her own people. There were wolves and bears and weasels and varying attempts to create leering devils' masks.

If only we didn't insist upon making war on ourselves, I could be marrying Roderic. Certainly he would be considered a suitable match, were it not for the enmity that exists between our peoples. And we could divide our time between here and Chamoney. She wouldn't mind that. She'd come to love this darker, wilder place.

Foolish dreams, she told herself angrily, turning abruptly away from the railing and nearly colliding with the hovering guard.

The chapel was detached from the castle itself, occupying one far corner of the great courtyard. The revelers had been kept out of this area by the guards, though Maryana could hear them as she walked slowly across the paving stones, accompanied by two maids, her uncle, and two guards.

She slanted a glance at the baron and took some small comfort in the knowledge that he was unhappy. His expression might be more appropriate to a funeral service than to the wedding of his niece.

In her mind, Maryana had moved beyond this time—back to Chamoney. She was working out how she could prevent her new husband from destroying it as he'd destroyed his own estate.

So when she came at last to the chapel and

walked through the open doors, it took her a few seconds to comprehend what she was seeing.

Miles stood at the altar, together with the priest. That was as it should be. But standing next to him, with a knife pressed against his throat almost casually, was Roderic. And next to the priest, also holding a knife, was the miller.

Between the doorway and the altar lay some bodies. A few were bloodied, but most were merely tied up, including the women. For some reason, Maryana chose to focus on the guard commander's wife, Aleta, the woman who had made her gown. She'd obviously been pushed roughly to the floor before being bound, because her hair was spilling out of her beaded cap.

"Tell the guards to lay down their weapons," Roderic ordered, his voice echoing in the vaulted chapel as he stared at her uncle.

"Do as he says," the baron told them quickly—and perhaps even eagerly.

Maryana could do no more than stare. She was still trying to let her mind catch up with what she was seeing. Roderic was here! Could it be real?

But the guards owed their allegiance to Miles, and one of them started to rush forward. Then men she hadn't seen before, still wearing their costumes and masks, appeared and subdued the man quickly, then produced lengths of rope and tied the soldiers to pillars.

"Lady Maryana," Roderic called. "Do you wish to marry this poor excuse for a man?"

She very nearly began to laugh. His words—consciously or not—seemed to be mocking the ceremony that was to have taken place there and then.

"No, I do not!" she cried, her voice joining his to echo through the chapel.

"Then by the powers of decency vested in me, I pronounce this wedding to be canceled."

Now she did laugh—and at the same time, she

picked up her long train and ran toward him. But instead of taking her in his arms, he wrapped one arm around Miles's throat and continued to press the knife against him. When she came to an uncertain stop at the altar, Maryana could see a thin trickle of blood running down Miles's throat to stain his elegant, embroidered tunic.

"Has he harmed you in any way?" Roderic demanded harshly.

Maryana let her eyes meet those of Miles Foulane. She knew that if she said yes, Roderic would kill him right there and then. It was surprisingly tempting to lie. But in the end, she decided that Miles's being forced to let her see his fear was enough. She shook her head.

Roderic removed the knife, then released Miles, only to switch the knife to his other hand and strike Miles with his fist so hard that he flew backward and crashed through the altar railing.

Then Roderic turned to the baron, who had followed her to the altar. "I would like to think that you were an unwilling participant in this, Baron DeLay. And besides, I owe you a debt for not hounding my people for more money and for opening the castle to them—and to us."

When the baron said nothing, Roderic gestured for the men to join him. Then he smiled at the baron. "I've also helped myself to some of the tax money in the treasury room, though not all of it. You may tell your king that it will be put to good use, raising an army to defeat him. And if either you or he tries to tax my people again, I will return and make each and every one of you pay dearly."

Then, finally, he turned to Maryana and extended his hand. "It's time we're going, milady. We have a long journey ahead of us."

It didn't occur to her to ask where they were going. Instead, she gave him her hand. He carried it to his mouth briefly, then smiled at Miles Foulane, who had managed to sit up and was holding his head in his hands.

"And don't start dreaming of Chamoney, either, Sir Miles, because it will never be yours."

There were questions aplenty that she wanted to ask, but Maryana held her tongue as they raced through the chapel rooms, downstairs, and then through what appeared to be a tunnel. In a very short time, she had lost all sense of direction. But this was Roderic's home and he knew it well.

They emerged in what she took to be the guards' barracks, to judge from the furnishings. The place was empty, since all the guards were on duty to control the crowds she could now hear again out in the courtyard. They seemed to her to be making an extraordinary amount of noise, though the sounds didn't have the urgency of fighting.

"There will be many without voices tomorrow," Tom said, chuckling.

"They *are* a rowdy lot, aren't they?" Roderic responded with a grin.

Too breathless from running to ask the question, Maryana nonetheless thought she knew the answer. Roderic's people had been told to make as much noise as possible, to keep the guards distracted.

Then they were outside again, in a narrow passageway that wove around several buildings and ended near the stables. They ran through the stables, where a young stable boy gaped at them, then grinned when he caught sight of Roderic, who clutched the boy's shoulder briefly before hurrying on.

She knew their destination now: the rear gate. But she also knew—even before she saw them— that there would be guards there. The two men were armed with both knives and sharp pikes, but they simply stood there, one on either side of the

189

gate, as the strange group approached them.

Had they been struck dumb at the sight of a bride and two roughly dressed men being trailed by five revelers in various costumes? And then, as they drew closer, she understood. The guards were Sakims, not Nerans. Roderic had indeed planned this well. The "guards" had even stolen Neran uniforms, which she now saw didn't fit very well.

They hurried through the gate, followed by the two men in guards' uniforms. Another man she recognized from camp was waiting with the horses. Roderic led her to a chestnut mare fitted with a sidesaddle. She was about to protest at that, but then realized that he truly had thought of everything. She couldn't possibly have ridden astride a horse in her wedding gown.

He helped her onto the horse, then gave her a grin. "I have other clothes waiting for you, but right now, we must put as much distance as possible between us and the castle."

All the questions she hadn't yet asked started to make their way to her lips, but Roderic had already leaped onto his stallion, and a moment later they were deep into the woods.

He'd said they had a "long journey" ahead of them, and she had assumed he'd meant south—to the land of the Innish. But they were traveling north instead.

"Where are we going?" she asked as she clung to the saddle.

"To Gisel's family's cabin—by a roundabout route that will keep us away from the roads. There you can change clothes and have the pleasure of burning that gown."

Maryana threw back her head and laughed: the first time she'd laughed in days. Freedom! Freedom and Roderic! And now she was seeing the man she longed to see—the courageous man of action she'd believed him to be.

Her laughter proved to be infectious. All the others joined in, until the woods were filled with their mirth. Even the horses seemed to be joining in, though they were probably snorting in surprise at their riders' behavior.

Roderic was in the lead, and he turned to look back over his shoulder at her. The laughter was in his eyes as well as on his lips—but she saw something else there as well, and her breath caught in her throat. Only her memory of that accursed ring kept her from being swept away by the desire in his eyes.

The flames embraced the white fabric, devouring it in mere seconds. Maryana smiled as the gown was reduced to nothing. She was quite sure that no other woman had ever been so happy to exchange a lovely wedding gown for the rough clothing of a peasant youth.

Then Gisel handed her the headdress, from which she'd already removed the sparkling gems, and Maryana tossed it into the fire as well.

"For a moment there, I thought you wanted me to kill him," Roderic said quietly as he came up behind her.

She nodded. "I'd even thought of doing it myself. But it would have been wrong."

"I don't know about that, but it seems to me that leaving him alive to face humiliation is an even worse fate."

"My uncle," she said, not certain just what she was thinking about him.

"The baron must lie in the bed he made, but I think he was not unhappy to see you rescued. He'll pay a heavy price, though, when the king gets word of this."

"He's a good man, but weak," she replied.

"Good but weak men are often responsible for

bad things, which makes them little better than those who are evil to begin with."

"Where are we going?" she asked.

"South, to visit my Innish kin."

"You said that you took the gold from the treasury to raise an army. Did you mean that?"

"Yes."

She turned to face him. There was no smile in his eyes or on his lips now. "You've made up your mind?"

He nodded. "I have decided that I am willing to lead—if others are willing to follow. I've sent messages to the other Sakim lord, and perhaps I can persuade my Innish kin to join us as well. But with or without them, I intend to drive the Nerans from this land."

Why? she wondered. *What happened to make you decide upon this course of action?* But before she could ask the question, he took her arm.

"Come. We must be off, so that we can put as much distance between us and the castle as we can before dark."

By the time Roderic called a halt for the night, Maryana had long since lost any sense of where they might be. To judge from the sun before it set, they were riding west, not south. Several times they crossed roads, but for the most part they followed trails that wound through the deep forest.

Late in the afternoon, they had come upon the ruins of an old castle deep in the woods—and there, the rest of Roderic's men awaited them. There was much cheering when the men saw her, riding just behind Roderic. Maryana was touched by their reactions—and amused by their stares as they tried to see her now, not as a mute page, but as a Neran lady.

"The men remember the help you gave to them and their families, milady," Tom said, leaning toward her as he came alongside. "Looking back now, I think it would have been better if you hadn't disguised yourself. Then the men would have protected you from the likes of Harry and Tim."

No, they wouldn't have, she replied silently, because Roderic would have sent me away. Despite that brief moment of pure desire she'd seen in his eyes, she still doubted that he wanted her along on this journey. He'd said nothing of the sort, but she still felt it. Never mind the fact that she could pass for a youth—she was still a woman in the company of men bent on making war. But at least the fact that she was also Neran didn't seem to trouble them.

"And mayhap you can help us even more," Tom went on. "Lord Roderic says that you have Innish kin, too."

"I do—although I met them only once." Ah, she thought, so he *does* need me, after all. That settled her mind somewhat. She'd been half-fearing that he might be planning to drop her somewhere along the way—perhaps in a convent. He'd told her that his sister had joined one somewhere to the south.

"Still," Tom said, "the blood ties are there, and we have to persuade the Innish to join us."

"But you've defeated my people before without the Innish," she pointed out.

"True enough—but we didn't have the Boravians waiting for a chance at us then. We can't ask the northernmost lords to join us or the Boravians will see their opportunity."

"Even in winter?" she asked. "How could they fight in all that snow?"

Tom chuckled. "The Boravians live in snow half the year. That won't stop them. It'll only slow them down a bit. No, we need the Innish if we're to have a chance."

"What made him change his mind, Tom?" she

asked as she watched Roderic talking to the men who had just joined them.

The miller shrugged. "That's hard to say, milady. Lord Roderic can be a hard man to read sometimes." He gave her a bashful sort of grin.

"But I think *you* might have had something to do with it."

"Me?" She was surprised and confused—but also pleased.

"Aye. He was like a bear with a sore paw while you were gone."

Roderic came back to them then and said that they should be on their way, so Maryana was left staring at his back and wondering why *she* should be the reason he'd decided to make war against her people.

She was still pondering that as they set up camp in a clearing near a stream. She could understand why Roderic had rescued her. After all, it had been two of his men who had betrayed her, and he would have felt a sense of obligation. But how did that then turn into a sudden willingness to lead his people to war?

There was no shelter and the night was cold, but they had blankets and food aplenty, since the men had brought along all they could from the camp. Roderic made a bed of sorts for her with blankets, screened from the others by some bushes, then left her there for a moment before returning with blankets for himself, which he put on the ground a small but all-important distance from her.

"Two more nights like this, and then you can sleep in a real bed for a night or so," he told her as he stretched out.

"Where?" Despite what Tom had said, she immediately thought that he intended to leave her somewhere.

"Drumm Castle. Lord Henry is an old friend of mine and he's expecting us."

Drumm Castle was a welcome sight, even seen through the cold, fine mist that had been falling for more than a day. By now, she had become accustomed to the great, forbidding fortress-castles built by the Sakim lords.

The group kept well clear of the village, then circled around to the rear of the castle under cover of darkness and rain. Maryana was soaked through and shivering, but she was also wondering how they could hope to stay there, since surely there must be a Neran overlord like her uncle in residence.

She waited tensely while Roderic approached a rear gate, then spoke with two dark figures she could barely make out. After a moment, he beckoned to them and they all rode up to the gate.

"Leave the horses here," Roderic ordered. "They'll be taken to another stable."

Maryana now saw that the two men who met them were clearly Sakim: an older, white-haired man and another about Roderic's age, though smaller than him.

When she had dismounted, Roderic took her hand and led her over to the two men. "Milords, may I present the lady Maryana, lately of Varley Castle, where her uncle is in temporary residence. Lady Maryana, this is Lord William Drumm and his son, Lord Henry."

Both the men stared at her in shock—but then the younger one broke out into laughter, drawing a puzzled smile from his father as well.

"It's a pleasure to meet you, milady. I'll never again believe the tales I've heard of Neran ladies."

Maryana smiled. She liked Lord Henry instantly.

They were led into the rear courtyard. Then another man appeared and took all the men except for Roderic with him. After they had vanished into the darkness, the two Drumms led Roderic and Maryana into the castle itself by a back door that took them through the kitchen and up narrow stairs.

"My apologies, milady, that I must welcome you to my home in such a manner. But we have a problem, as you might have guessed." Lord Henry's dark eyes twinkled with amusement.

"What is your problem's name? Perhaps I know him."

He chuckled. "Baron Devane."

"Oh." She did indeed know him, but mostly by reputation. The baron was reputed to be far too fond of his drink, and Lord Henry's next words confirmed that.

"He passed out some hours ago, which is his usual pattern—and most of his men take their cue from him. The castle's cellars are emptying fast— but it's a small price to pay to be rid of him for a time."

They hurried along dimly lit corridors, and then Lord Henry opened a heavy door and they climbed still more narrow, winding stairs—into one of the towers, she thought. And that proved to be the case. After a long climb, they emerged in a round room that had clearly been furnished as a lady's sewing room.

A fire was already burning in the small fireplace, and Maryana started to feel warm for the first time in two days. "This is lovely," she said to her hosts.

"My mother and my sister used this room often, but it's been empty for years now—and it's well away from the baron and his men. Roderic and I will be just below. A maid will come soon. Rest well, milady."

Thus saying, he gave her a slight bow and backed out of the room, his arm draping itself across Roderic's shoulders. Roderic merely turned briefly to nod at her before engaging in an animated conversation with his friend.

An hour later, bathed and fed, Maryana sat before the fire in the pretty little room, listening to the low hum of men's voices in the room below. Unfortunately, she couldn't make out any words, thanks to the thick floors and the incessant pounding of the rain against the tower windows.

She could still hear the voices below when there was a knock at her door, so she was reasonably certain that it couldn't be Roderic. But still, as she opened it, she hoped to be proved wrong.

The woman who stood there smiling was lovely, aglow with the special light that seemed to characterize all women who were with child. From her swollen belly, Maryana guessed that she was soon due to deliver.

"I'm Daria, Henry's wife," she said, staring with undisguised interest at Maryana. "Henry forbade me to come all the way up here, but this won't be the first or last time I have disobeyed him."

Maryana laughed. "Come in, please. I'm Maryana, and you must forgive my appearance, but—"

"Oh, I've already been told all about you. That's why I had to meet you. You sound like a woman after my own heart."

Maryana smiled, only now realizing how much she'd missed the company of women—even though she frequently became angry with most of them. But Daria was clearly different. This woman, she knew, could easily become a friend and confidant.

Daria looked around the room with a sad smile. "This is the first time this room has been used since Henry's mother died—and even she used it little after his sister's death. Henry said once that she used to come up here to commune with her daughter's spirit."

"How long ago did they die?" Maryana asked as they both seated themselves before the fire.

"Henry's mother died only a little more than a year ago—just before our wedding. But his sister died years before that—in a plague that struck us one winter. I lost my sister to it as well."

It struck Maryana then that Henry's dead sister might be the woman Roderic had intended to marry. He'd said that she was the daughter of a family friend and neighbor, and that she'd died in a plague. But he'd never said her name.

"Was she . . . the one Roderic intended to marry?" she asked hesitantly.

Daria nodded. "That's right. So he told you about her. It was very sad. They'd known each other since childhood, you see—and neither of them ever had eyes for any other."

"Claire was my friend, too: the only friend I had, really. My home is not far from here."

"What was she like?" Maryana asked, unable to stifle her curiosity even though she didn't want to hear the virtues of Roderic's dead love being extolled.

"I remember her as being full of life and full of laughter. When I think of her, I still hear that bell-like laughter. But she was always delicate, and when the plague struck that winter, she didn't have the strength to resist it."

She went on to describe a girl whose type Maryana knew well—and disliked just as much: empty-headed and quite probably very vain, though Daria never actually said that of her.

As the other woman spoke, Maryana became more than ever aware of herself—and of the contrasts. Despite her delicate features, no one who knew her would ever have called her delicate. The proof of that was there now. She'd just spent two days riding through drenching rains with a group of men, and she'd complained far less than they had. Neither would anyone have dared to call her empty-headed.

Maryana was so lost in her thoughts that she had to pull herself back to the present when Daria heaved a sigh.

"Sometimes, though, it does seem to me that she might not have been a good wife for Roderic, after all. Perhaps he loved her because she was so different from his mother and his sister."

"What do you mean?" Maryana asked.

"They were very strong women—or I should say that Ammy still is. I visit her from time to time. She's in a convent two days' ride from here."

"Ammy?" Maryana echoed, thinking it a very strange name.

"It's Amelia—actually Sister Mary Rose now. We always called her Ammy. Hasn't Roderic told you about her?"

Maryana confirmed that he had. "She joined the convent rather than marry a man she didn't love."

"That's what I meant when I said that she is strong. I would never have had the courage to refuse the man my father chose." Then she smiled radiantly. "Fortunately, I didn't want to refuse Henry."

"I considered killing the man I was ordered to marry," Maryana told her. "Of course, I don't think I could have done such a thing, but I'm not sure."

She was surprised to note that Daria didn't look quite as shocked as she'd expected. Well, why not? She still looked more like a boy than a woman, even in the borrowed gown. Furthermore, she was beginning to realize that her days of masquerading as a boy and living among men had made it difficult for her to return to the behaviors of a woman.

They talked of other things: Daria's wish for a daughter, even though, of course, Henry wanted a son; the unpleasantness of her life now, under the drunken baron's rule; their mutual longing for a day when their two peoples could live in harmony.

"Henry says that Roderic's finally come to his senses and realized that he is the only one who can hope to unite our people and the Innish to drive the Nerans from this land." Then Daria colored slightly.

"Forgive me. I forgot that you are Neran."

Maryana waved away her embarrassment. "Obviously I'm not being a very loyal Neran at the moment. I, too, want to see my people driven out—especially since I know that history teaches us that the Sakim will not try to rule *us*."

"That's true. Our people have always wanted nothing more than to be left in peace. We've never invaded Neran."

Then a sharp rapping at the door drew their attention. Maryana started nervously, fearing that their presence had been discovered, after all, by the baron or his men. But Daria merely laughed softly and got up to answer the summons.

"I fear that my husband has heard our voices and knows I'm here."

She was right. When she opened the door, a frowning Lord Henry stood there. But Daria merely smiled at him.

"Surely you didn't think I would stay away from our guest, did you?"

He arched a dark brow. "Let's just say that I sometimes credit you with more sense than you appear to have. Do you wish to see our child born on the steps of the tower?"

"She will be born when it's time—and that isn't quite yet," Daria replied.

Henry rolled his eyes expressively and looked at Maryana. "I suppose she's told you that if she has a girl, I intend to throw them both from the top of the tower."

Maryana laughed. "She did happen to mention that you're hoping for a son."

"What I am hoping for," he said, with a mock-stern look at his wife, "is a healthy child—and a healthy mother."

He took her hand. "Come along now, and say good night to our other guest, who's been eager to see you."

They both said good night to Maryana and went down the steps to Roderic's room. Maryana returned to her seat before the fire, and heard the talk and laughter from the room below. Envy caught her in its evil clutches. Henry and Daria were that rarity that she had always hoped she could find for herself: a truly happy couple—and all the more surprisingly so, given their present circumstances.

Before long, she heard them leaving Roderic's room, and then she found herself holding her breath, awaiting another knock at her door. But it didn't come, and all was silence below.

Finally she went to bed, certain now after Daria's revelations about Roderic's mother and sister—not to mention the dead Claire—that Roderic saw her as another sister. Not even the memory of his kisses could change that. If he felt anything else for her, it was surely nothing more than ordinary male lust for an available woman.

And as she drifted into her dreams, Maryana was telling herself that it was time she stopped dreaming about a future with Roderic and instead concentrated on her own very murky future.

The rains continued the following day, and Roderic decided to remain at Drumm Castle for another day. He came to her room to tell her this early in the morning, then vanished for the remainder of the day. But soon after that, Daria sent a maid to show her to the suite she shared with Henry.

Saranne Dawson

Maryana was surprised to learn that the baron
hadn't put them out of the castle—and hadn't even
taken over their quarters. Instead, he'd installed
himself in a suite reserved for guests in another
wing of the huge castle.

"Henry explained that I was with child and
shouldn't be forced to move in such condition,"
Daria explained. "So the baron decided to be generous."

"Do you not find such things to be strange?"
Maryana asked. "My uncle sent Roderic away from
his castle, but allowed him to roam freely, instead
of keeping him prisoner. My people are never so
generous when they make war on other people."

"Nor are mine," Daria agreed.

"I think it is because, when all is said and done,
we both recognize that we are one people, however
often we kill each other."

After spending the day pleasantly with Daria,
Maryana returned to her tower room to see the sun
break through the clouds just before it set. No
doubt that meant they would be leaving in the
morning. She was not looking forward to any
more long days on the road—or on forest tracks,
more likely, since they still had to concern themselves with Neran troops.

In fact, though she didn't know exactly where
the king and his troops were now, Maryana was
fairly certain that their route south would take
them close to her countrymen.

On the other hand, there were her Innish relatives to meet, and she was looking forward to that.

But all in all, she felt that she was doing nothing
more than putting one foot in front of the other,
with no clear plan beyond the next step. And that
rankled, because she'd never lived her life this way.
Always, until she was forcibly uprooted from

Chamoney, she'd awakened each day to the knowledge that she had more to do than could possibly be done in that time—and more still to anticipate beyond that.

Chapter Ten

Although the sun shone once again, deep in the forest the water dripped from the trees that over-hung their narrow path, making Maryana very grateful for the heavily oiled woolen cape that Daria had given her.

Her former hostess had also given her other clothing, including some full skirts that Maryana had managed to turn into the wide-legged pants she preferred for riding, with the assistance of one of Daria's maids.

The dye that had darkened her skin was wearing off, thanks to some vigorous scrubbing in the baths she'd taken at the castle, and her hair was growing out as well, though only about an inch of gold was visible at the roots.

Ahead of her, Roderic led the way, though even he was less certain of their route now, except to say that they must remain deep in the forest and avoid the roads and villages.

She had seen Roderic only briefly the previous

evening, when he had come to tell her that they would be leaving Drumm Castle just before dawn. She'd asked him about the king and his army, and Roderic said that they would be passing them on their way south. Lord Henry's people had kept an eye on their whereabouts, and the king was expected at Drumm Castle within the week on his way north.

She wondered aloud to Roderic if the king could have heard of her escape by now, and he told her he was sure of it, but he doubted that the king would risk getting his troops lost in the Sakim hills to pursue her. Instead, he was likely to make his way quickly north to Varley Castle, and thence across the straits before winter made the journey impossible.

"His Majesty isn't likely to want to spend a winter in Sakim, although he won't be so considerate of his troops," Roderic had said.

"He will likely issue an order confiscating Chamoney as soon as he returns to Neran," Maryana said, trying to hide her pain at that thought.

"Perhaps, but before long he'll have other things on his mind," Roderic replied.

"You intend to attack during the winter?" she'd asked, surprised.

"If at all possible."

She stared now at Roderic's broad back, wondering what he saw in his future. Somehow, she didn't doubt that he would succeed in uniting his people and gaining the support of the Innish as well, then defeating her people—but what did he see beyond that?

She wanted to ask, but she didn't. A wall seemed to have gone up between them. The wry and amusing man she'd met upon her arrival in Sakim was still occasionally in evidence, but for the most part, he'd been replaced by a grim and determined man she didn't know.

She missed the abbot, and wished that he were making this journey with them. Tom seemed to have taken on his lord's countenance, as had the other men.

They rode on through the forest. From time to time, Roderic would send one or more men to a nearby hilltop, she assumed to check for the presence of Neran troops, or perhaps to look for some sign that they were on the right path.

Then, when there were still several hours of daylight left, Roderic called a halt and left them in a clearing near a stream. As he rode away, Maryana turned to Tom. She was becoming annoyed at Roderic's failure to tell her anything.

"Where is he going?" she demanded of the miller.

"To see if we will be welcome for the night, milady."

"Welcome where? He tells me nothing."

"He has much on his mind, milady. But he is going now to a monastery nearby. We may be able to spend the night there."

"A monastery? But how can I go there?"

"That is why he goes there now, to see if arrangements can be made for you."

"Well, I could always become a boy again if necessary," she pointed out.

"I think he hopes to be able to avoid that," the miller said with a touch of dryness in his voice.

"If *I* don't find that offensive, why should he?" she demanded, growing more irritated by the moment.

"I can't say, milady. That is only my guess."

Roderic returned to say that they would be welcome at the monastery after evensong. Maryana managed to contain her annoyance until she could speak to Roderic alone while the men were preparing the evening meal, cooking game they'd caught along the way and adding to it victuals brought back from the monastery.

"Have you made arrangements for me?" she demanded.

Roderic stared at her in silence for a moment, then grinned. "No, I thought I'd leave you to your own devices for the night."

"I could go with you disguised as a boy again."

"That won't be necessary. Arrangements have been made."

"Is it too much to ask just what those arrangements are?"

"We will be accorded accommodations as husband and wife," he said with a shrug.

"What? But—"

"If we lived as page and lord, we can surely manage as husband and wife for a night."

"You might have asked me first." But she was already wondering just what those "accommodations" might be, and that treacherous heat she'd tried to banish was stealing through her again.

He bowed deeply. "Would milady care to be my wife for a night?"

Her face flushed warmly and she turned away very quickly. "I just meant that maybe I would have preferred to be your page again."

"Oh, I see. You've grown fond of being a boy, have you?"

"Fonder than you were, apparently," she replied as anger replaced the telltale heat.

"That may be true. The image I carry of you is that of the Neran lady stepping off the boat."

"As I recall, at the time you accused me of being a Neran *harlot*."

"Only to see if it were possible to break through that Neran iciness. Besides, ladies shouldn't even know that word."

Maryana folded her arms across her chest and regarded him levelly. "For your information, Roderic, I know that word and many others that would undoubtedly burn your ears. And you may very well hear all of them before this journey is ended."

He smiled. "Why are you so angry with me? Where is the gratitude for my having saved you from Miles Foulane's bed?"

"You saved me because you felt responsible, since it was *your* men who kidnapped me."

"Even so."

She was crushed at his admission, but she didn't let it show. "I thought we had become friends, but it seems I was wrong."

"We *are* friends. It's almost like having Ammy back again, though you may not understand that when you meet her."

"Your sister, you mean? Are we stopping there as well?" she was just barely able to withstand this latest crushing blow. So he *did* think of her as a sister.

He nodded. "We will stop to see her tomorrow, if possible. It depends on whether there are any enemy troops in the vicinity."

He paused, then went on in a softer tone. "It is difficult for me to visit Ammy now that she has taken her vows. Sometimes she lets me see the sister I knew, but most of the time now, she is Sister Mary Rose—a stranger to me."

And so you have decided to "adopt" a new sister, she thought bitterly. *And those kisses meant nothing, except that you are like other men: taking pleasure where you find it.*

Dusk had given way to darkness by the time they approached the monastery, which sat at the end of a narrow, isolated valley, surrounded by high stone walls. In a tall tower visible beyond the walls, bells were ringing, their melodious sound drifting out over the valley.

Maryana had just noticed the small cottage outside the walls, nearly buried within the verdant for-

Thrill to the most sensual, adventure-filled Romances on the market today...

FROM 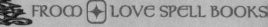 LOVE SPELL BOOKS

As a home subscriber to the Love Spell Romance Book Club, you'll enjoy the best in today's BRAND-NEW Time Travel, Futuristic, Legendary Lovers, Perfect Heroes and other genre romance fiction. For five years, Love Spell has brought you the award-winning, high-quality authors you know and love to read. Each Love Spell romance will sweep you away to a world of high adventure...and intimate romance. Discover for yourself all the passion and excitement millions of readers thrill to each and every month.

Save $5.00 Each Time You Buy!

Every other month, the Love Spell Romance Book Club brings you four brand-new titles from Love Spell Books. EACH PACKAGE WILL SAVE YOU AT LEAST $5.00 FROM THE BOOK-STORE PRICE! And you'll never miss a new title with our convenient home delivery service.

Here's how we do it: Each package will carry a FREE 10-DAY EXAMINATION privilege. At the end of that time, if you decide to keep your books, simply pay the low invoice price of $17.96, no shipping or handling charges added. HOME DELIVERY IS ALWAYS FREE. With today's top romance novels selling for $5.99 and higher, our price SAVES YOU AT LEAST $5.00 with each shipment.

AND YOUR FIRST TWO-BOOK SHIP-MENT IS TOTALLY FREE!

IT'S A BARGAIN YOU CAN'T BEAT! A SUPER $11.48 Value!

Love Spell 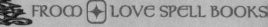 A Division of Dorchester Publishing Co., Inc.

Get Two Books Totally
FREE —
An $11.48 Value!

▼ Tear Here and Mail Your FREE Book Card Today! ▼

PLEASE RUSH
MY TWO FREE
BOOKS TO ME
RIGHT AWAY!

Love Spell Romance Book Club
P.O. Box 6613
Edison, NJ 08818-6613

est, when Roderic turned to her and then pointed
to it.

"That's where we'll stay. It is a guest house for
visiting nuns and the occasional husband and wife.
Wait there. I'll return soon."

So she turned her horse in that direction as the
men approached the gate and rang the big bell that
hung beside it. She was still angry with Roderic,
but by now she had at least recognized that anger
as being irrational. He had never proclaimed his
love for her, and he'd never made her any promises. The fault, quite clearly, was hers, for having
fallen in love with him.

Maryana had never been in love before, and neither had she ever encountered a man who had
nothing more than brotherly feelings toward her.
Mostly she had represented a challenge to men—
and men liked challenges. With Roderic, she had
gone from fighting off such attentions to fighting
her own feelings.

The little cottage was furnished in what she took
to be the same austere manner as the monastery
itself: a simple set of tables and chairs, crude but
sturdy, and sleeping cots scattered along three of
the walls. Despite the fact that a fire had been laid,
the place smelled musty from a combination of
disuse and its location beneath large, overhanging
trees.

Just outside the back door was a well, and she
was struggling to draw a pail of water when she
heard a sound and turned to find the abbot approaching her.

"We meet again, milady," he said with a pleased
smile, then drew the water for her.

She smiled, too, happy to see him again. Until
she'd met the abbot, she'd never liked clerics; they
were invariably cold and self-righteous and all too
concerned with her spiritual well-being.

"I didn't know you would be here," she told him

as he carried the water into the cottage for her.

"As it happens, I suddenly found it necessary to visit my superiors not far from here. And on the way, I stopped to visit my brethren here and beg their assistance to hide a certain group of thieves—and a fleeing bride."

She laughed. "But what do you mean by 'hiding'? We haven't been pursued, as far as I know."

"Oh, but you have been—and are. The baron—or more likely, Sir Miles—has obviously informed the king of your disappearance. Unfortunately, his version is somewhat at odds with the truth. The king believes you were kidnapped—against your will—by a thieving madman. And he was told that you would be coming this way."

"Does Roderic know this?"

"He will when I tell him. I've just returned from a nearby town, where I was able to learn all this. The area is swarming with Neran uniforms. They have a description of Roderic and of you as well—including the fact that Roderic might have forced you to disguise yourself as his page."

"What can we do?" she asked in alarm.

"That is Roderic's decision to make. My function is simply to look properly pious and gather what information I can." He chuckled. "I'm quite good at that, you know. It's this honest face of mine, combined with my clerical garb, of course. Even enemy soldiers are willing to talk freely in my presence."

He studied her for a moment. "It seems that the soldiers are inclined to discount the story that a grand Neran lady could be disguised as a Sakim page. It wouldn't surprise me if you could walk among them and go unrecognized, despite the warning."

"I don't think it would be wise to put that to the test," she replied, though she found herself tempted to do just that.

"Sir Miles himself is said to be on his way here, to try to find his bride."

"Roderic should have killed him when he had the chance," she stated.

"Now, now, milady. As a man of the cloth, I can't countenance murder. If being cruel and greedy and stupid were reasons enough to kill, the bodies would be piled high in the streets."

"Will we have to turn back?" she asked.

"Why would we do that?"

Both of them turned to find Roderic in the open doorway. He greeted the abbot and thanked him for making the arrangements, then listened quietly as the abbot told his tale once again.

"We can't turn back," Roderic said when the abbot had finished. "It is no safer for us back home than it is here. And if we can get past the king's men, we'll reach safety soon enough. They won't dare pursue us into Innish territory."

"That's true enough." The abbot nodded. "I also heard that the Innish have put troops along the border to prevent any incursions."

Roderic poured himself a mug of ale and stared into the fire. "Could you travel into the Innish lands?" he asked the abbot.

"Of course. Who would suspect me of anything?" He opened his arms wide, presenting the perfect picture of innocence.

Roderic laughed. "One day, my friend, that cherubic face of yours is going to get you into trouble. But not this time, I hope. I'd like you to get a message to my Innish kin, to apprise them of our situation.

"I don't expect them to come here, but as soon as I have studied the maps at the monastery, I can tell you where to have them meet us near the border."

"I will leave at first light," the abbot assured him.

*　　*　　*

Maryana was tired, and as soon as the two men had gone, she selected a cot and fell into it, after drinking a mug of the strong ale herself. Another bad habit she was picking up from the men, she supposed.

She was dreaming of Chamoney when she was awakened by a sound. The fire had burned down and the cottage was dark. From the tranquillity of her old life, she'd been thrust into the danger of her present existence—with no time to think. Her hand went automatically to the dagger beneath the thin pillow, and it was raised to defend herself before she could make out the features of the dark figure standing there.

His strong fingers closed around her wrist even as he spoke her name. Then he pried the dagger from her hand.

"What have I done to you that you awake prepared to fight?" he asked as he set the dagger aside, then lowered himself to set on the edge of her cot. His weight sent her tumbling against him, and she quickly scooted back against the wall.

"It is not you who have done anything, Roderic," she said in a voice made husky by sleep and by that brief contact with him. "I chose my own way."

"Perhaps. But if it weren't for me, you would have resigned yourself to marrying Foulane and making the best of it."

She wasn't quite certain what he meant by that, so she remained cautiously silent.

"You could still do that, you know," he said softly. "We could arrange for you to 'escape,' and the abbot could lead you to the king."

She gathered her feet beneath her and sat up on the cot, her back against the wall. "Is that what you want me to do?"

"No, of course not. I was merely offering you a way out of this if you want."

"I don't."

"You may come to wish that you'd chosen differently," he said quietly. "I've been studying the maps, and the only way we can be sure of slipping past the Neran troops will take us into the mountains and then to the seacoast. It's a long and difficult journey that may take us more than a week, while the route I'd intended to follow would have had us in Innish territory within two more days."

"And if I weren't with you, you could take that route."

She could barely see him shaking his head. "No. They want me as much as they want you, I think. Someone—perhaps Baron DeLay—has told the king that I intend to lead a rebellion against him."

"Miles must have been responsible for that, too. Telling the king that would only stir him up to find you. He may have feared that my being 'kidnapped' wouldn't make the king sufficiently angry, since I know he will want to go north and then home to Neran before winter."

"But surely finding you would be a matter of honor for him?" Roderic protested.

"It might be—if he had any honor, which he doesn't. In fact, my disappearance removes a thorn from his side and would allow him to confiscate my lands. The result would be the same as if he'd forced me to marry Miles—and he wouldn't have to waste any time or expend any troops in the process."

Roderic nodded slowly. "So you will lose Chamoney either way."

"Yes." Images from her dream floated through her mind, and she turned her head as tears welled up in her eyes, even though she knew he could barely see her in the darkness.

Then she started in surprise as Roderic's callused hand captured and covered both of hers.

"I will get your lands back for you—just as I will reclaim my own," he said in a low but determined voice. "I will make the return of Chamoney the price he will have to pay for peace."

"Thank you," she murmured, even though she doubted that it would ever happen. She no longer doubted that Roderic was brave, but he was one man, with only a ragtag band of twenty, and no guarantee as yet that he could raise an army big enough to fight the king and his troops.

"You doubt me," he said, and she could hear the amusement in his voice.

"I don't doubt that you will try your best," she replied.

"Then take this as a sacred oath, Lady Maryana. I will get Chamoney restored to you."

For a long moment, they stared at each other in the darkness. Her mind filled in what she could not see of him—including the light in his dark eyes. And she believed him. For all that he could so often seem to be anything but a warrior, she knew, suddenly, that it was in him as well. A laughing warrior. A most unique man.

She leaned forward and kissed him lightly on the cheek. But then, just as she started to withdraw, he turned his mouth against hers and wrapped a hand around her head.

She didn't want this to happen again—didn't want to be reminded that in this, at least, he was an ordinary man wanting pleasure wherever he could find it.

But it was her mind that didn't want it. Her heart—and all the rest of her, right down to her hidden female core—wanted this, and more.

With her head now imprisoned between both his hands, his lips and tongue explored hers, firm against her softness. The heat rose within her, threatening to burn away all reason. And yet he also seemed to be holding back, so that when he released her after caressing her head gently, she was, at least, prepared for the loss.

He got up from her cot. "We will leave at dawn. I don't want to put the brothers at any greater risk than they've already taken. The others will go the route we'd planned, because they can blend in easily enough. They will meet up with the abbot at the border and join my kinfolk."

They were going alone? She said nothing as she sat there, staring at his shadow as he crossed the room and put more wood on the fire. It made sense, of course. There was no reason to make the journey longer and more difficult for the others, but . . .

Maryana lay down and drew the covers over her. Yes, of course he was doing this for purely practical reasons. And perhaps his men could even pick up some useful information along the way.

She saw the mountains late the following day. They had traveled over ever more rugged terrain, but the dark smudges she now saw against the horizon looked truly frightening to one who was accustomed to gentle, rolling hills and wide valleys.

"How can we get across them?" she asked, unable to imagine such a journey.

"We won't cross them," he replied with a smile. "We'll be going *through* them. There is a pass, a narrow track that winds through them. That's the dangerous part, since it's possible that there could be some Neran troops there. But if so, it isn't likely to be more than a small outpost, sent there to guard the pass itself."

"From what? Are there people there?" She tried to envision people actually living in such a place, but couldn't.

"No. No one lives there, but in the last war we defeated the Nerans by putting troops onto boats, carrying them to a cove on the far side of the mountains, and then sending them through the pass. The Nerans weren't expecting an attack from

215

that quarter and they were badly beaten."

"Yes, I remember that now. My father was a student of military history. It never interested me, but I remember his talking about that battle." She frowned. "What is the name of the cove? I'm sure he knew that."

"It's called Lost Souls in Innish, though it's actually Sakim territory. You'll see why when we reach it."

"That was the name." She nodded. "Is that where we're going?"

"Yes. With luck, my Innish relatives will be meeting us there."

"Tell me now why it's called such a terrible name."

"No. That would ruin it."

"You've already ruined it by telling me that name."

Roderic chuckled and cast a glance at her over his shoulder as they rode single-file along a narrow track through the wooded hills. "I thought you Nerans were above believing in ancient superstitions," he said mockingly. "Unlike us savage Sakims."

"That may be true, but I'm in Sakim now."

"Nevertheless, you will have to wait," he replied smugly.

She complained a bit more, then gave up, certain that he must be teasing her. And yet, hadn't there been more to her father's story: tales of huge, dark birds that would attack men?

"If there are Neran troops in the pass, do you know where they're likely to be?" she asked as she continued to peer at the dark mountains.

"They'd be on this side of the pass—not in the pass itself."

"Why?"

"Because they're superstitious, too," he replied without turning, but with a smile in his voice.

"It's the birds, isn't it? My father said something about huge birds."

"Wait and see."

Now she knew it must be the birds. But how big could they be? She'd seen crows and pheasants, and they weren't frightening at all.

That night, Maryana caught him again—but once more, she said nothing. Where, she wondered, had her forthrightness gone? It wasn't a trait much admired in women, so the description had never been intended to be a compliment, though she chose to take it that way. But now it seemed to have vanished.

She had drifted off to sleep, wrapped in blankets near the small campfire. And once again, she awoke to find Roderic lying on his side nearby, propped up by an elbow as he stared at her. Or at least she assumed he must be staring at her. The same darkness that prevented him from seeing that she'd opened her eyes also kept her from knowing for certain that his eyes were on her. But what else would he be staring at?

She decided it must be that stare she couldn't see that awakened her. As before, the night was quiet, the only sound being that of the fire slowly burning itself out.

It's his thoughts, she told herself as she stared back as blindly as he must be staring at her. His thoughts that she couldn't read—and couldn't even guess.

They spent long hours on the trail without speaking, in a silence that was, for her at least, alternately annoying and comforting. Once, he'd remarked that she had a gift for silence and that it was rare in a woman. She assumed the statement had been a compliment, but it wasn't exactly the kind of compliment to warm a woman's heart. Or so she'd thought at the time. There didn't seem to be much she was certain of at the moment.

Who are you, Roderic Hode? she asked silently.
*And why have I allowed you to steal my heart as
easily as you stole my uncle's taxes? Have I become
as big a fool as other women: reading things into
glances and smiles and words, as though nothing
could really be as it appears?*

She closed her eyes again—but she could still
see *his* eyes, dark and brooding and alight with
something that she wanted to believe was more
than mere desire for a nearby warm body.

The mountains were no longer a smudge on the
horizon. Maryana was astonished at how quickly
they seemed to be reaching them. They had paused
at the crest of a hill, and beyond them lay a narrow,
forested valley, ending in another hill. Beyond that
were the mountains.

"We'll have to be careful from now on," Roderic
said as he stared down into the valley. "I'd prefer
to leave you here for a time while I check to see if
there are any troops there, but it's too risky. They
could be out hunting and stumble upon you—or
something else might be out hunting."

"What do you mean?" she asked as she quickly
glanced around. She was unaccustomed to such
huge, deep forests and had already been imagining
all sorts of creatures lying in wait.

"Bears, wolves—or giant birds," he added,
chuckling. "So you'll have to come with me."

Maryana tilted her head to stare up at the sky.
She'd almost forgotten about the fabled birds. But
the sky was empty.

They rode down the hillside and through the valley. When they neared the top of the next hill,
which was in the shadow of the mountains, Roderic came to a halt and dismounted, then helped
her from her horse.

"We'll leave the horses and go on foot. If there

are troops, they should be in the next valley somewhere."

"What will we do if we find them there?" she
asked, not failing to notice that he continued to
hold her hand after she'd dismounted.

"Try to figure a way around them. And if that
isn't possible, then I'll just have to get rid of them."

She stared at him. "How many will there be?"

He shrugged, still holding her hand, almost as
though he'd simply forgotten to release it. "Probably no more than a dozen—maybe less. They
would only be here to keep watch, not to fight. And
they won't be watching for anyone to come from
this direction. Their eyes should be on the pass."

"Still, how can you hope to get rid of a dozen
men?" How could he kill them was what she
meant, but she couldn't bring herself to say it. Only
now was she starting to face up to the reality of
war.

He shrugged again. "One Sakim against a dozen
Nerans. That sounds reasonable to me."

She was sure that he must be joking—but
equally certain that she didn't want to find out.
Courage, she thought, often went hand in glove
with recklessness—and she'd seen both in Roderic
already.

He did release her hand then—only to take it
again as they reached a steep part of the hill. Maryana, who wasn't one inclined to pray, since she was
somewhat less than devout, still prayed that the
soldiers wouldn't be there. Roderic stopped just
short of the hilltop, then told her to wait while he
crawled to the top.

She didn't, of course. She'd never been good at
taking orders, since she was far more accustomed
to issuing them—but also because she was still annoyed at the subservient role she'd been forced to
adopt throughout much of her time with Roderic.

Crouching at first, and then crawling as he was,

219

she followed him, fully expecting him to turn around and see her. But he didn't, at least not until they were both lying on their stomachs and peering into the valley beyond. Then he merely glanced at her before turning his attention back to the valley. She noted that he didn't seem at all surprised to find her there.

At first she saw no sign of any soldiers, but she realized that they could be difficult to spot in their dark green uniforms. They would blend in well with the surrounding forest. Instead, she scanned for their horses or for signs of a camp, but since she couldn't guess exactly where the pass was, she didn't know where to look.

"Over there," he said in a low voice, pointing.

And then she saw them: not the horses, but the men themselves, a few of them moving about, but most sitting quietly beneath the trees.

"I count only five of them," Roderic whispered.

"Then it should require only half of a Sakim," she replied acerbically.

He grinned at her, that devil-may-care smile that could make him seem so harmless. Then he pointed back the way they had come, and they both went down the hill.

"They probably have a guard or two posted closer to the pass," he muttered when they had once more reached their horses.

"What are we going to do?" she asked nervously.

"If they have guards at the entrance to the pass, then we don't have much choice. But it's some distance away from their camp, so if I work fast and quietly, we can make it."

They climbed onto their horses and rode along the base of the hill for a distance before starting to climb it. The route Roderic had chosen should keep them well clear of the camp, but he pointed out that there was always the risk of encountering one or more of them out hunting.

Once they had climbed the hill and begun their descent into the valley where the camp was located, they were both completely silent, their heads swiveling constantly to watch their surroundings. Maryana's throat had gone dry and her heart had leaped into it. She wondered how men could stand this—and why they were willing to do so.

Once, something moved in the shadowy underbrush, and they both froze. Roderic was already taking his bow from its resting place on his shoulder when the stag stepped into plain view, and she sighed with relief. Seeing them, the creature made quite a lot of noise as it plunged back into the thick brush. And then all was silent again, except for the occasional birdsong.

"We're past the camp now," Roderic told her after a while, "and the entrance to the pass should be just ahead. We'll leave the horses here for the time being."

So once again, they moved stealthily through the forest, but on level ground this time. Roderic took a zigzag approach that kept them in the thickest cover.

The two men were right where Roderic had expected them to be. Maryana could see, just beyond them, a narrow trail that led into the mountains at a point where two of the peaks plunged downward, forming a narrow ravine. And it was obvious to her that there was no way around them.

From behind the leafy cover, she studied the two men—or boys, actually. Neither of them appeared to be more than eighteen or so. She could easily guess how they'd come to be here in uniform in a strange land. Except for the career officers, the Neran army was made up of peasant boys with no futures, young men seduced not by the supposed glories of battle but by hunger. They could be from estates like Miles's, with greedy lords who failed to

221

take care of their people. She turned to Roderic.

"Let me go to them. You can find a hiding place nearby. I'll tell them to lay down their weapons and let us pass. It will at least give them a chance. They're only boys, Roderic. They're not killers."

He said nothing as he stared at her, and she could guess the direction of his thoughts. He thought she was unwilling to fight her own people. It wasn't true—but it was.

"I want to give them a chance," she repeated.

Finally, he nodded. "All right, but put on your cloak and put up the hood as well. Otherwise they might not let you get close enough to be sure that you're female. And if either of them so much as raises a bow, they're dead."

She nodded. It was as much as she could ask, and she knew that it was a concession he didn't want to make. It would have been easy enough for him to move quietly into place and pick them off before they knew what was happening.

He drew a small hourglass from his saddlebag and handed it to her. "Wait until the sand drops, then ride toward them, calling out as soon as you know you can be heard."

Then, before she could even thank him, he rode off, vanishing into the forest within seconds. She knew he'd moved fast in order to prevent second thoughts, and her gratitude—and love—grew still more. He was doing this for her, because he certainly had no compunction against killing enemy soldiers.

She watched the grains of sand fall, wondering now if she'd been foolish. Roderic was right that the cloak would help to identify her as a lady—and one of some distinction, considering that it had come from Daria. Without it, she might well have looked like a Sakim youth. Even with it . . .

She donned the cloak as soon as the glass was empty and urged her horse forward. Besides her dry mouth and the pounding of her heart in her throat, she was also now trembling all over. What if they refused to believe she was Neran—or didn't care even if they knew? If their lords were like Miles—and there were many like him—the fact that she herself was of the nobility could be reason enough to kill her.

But she had committed herself, and she had to trust that Roderic was quick enough and skillful enough to save her from her own folly. So she rode toward them, trying to keep them in view between the trees. And then, when she judged that she was close enough, she opened her mouth.

Nothing came out except for a tiny squeak. She swallowed and tried again. "You, there! It is Maryana, Countess of Chamoney. I must speak with you!"

Her shouted words hung there, suspended in the still air. The men got quickly to their feet and began to look around for the source of the voice, but at least neither of them had drawn his bow as yet.

Then they saw her as she emerged from the thickest part of the forest. They were still standing there, no doubt dumbstruck to be hearing the voice of a Neran lady deep in the Sakim woods. Or perhaps they already knew of her, but could not believe she could be there.

As she rode up to them, one man fingered his bow nervously, but didn't remove it. The other had no bow at his shoulder, but he did have a long knife in hand. She stopped some yards from them and repeated her name.

"I am not alone," she told them. "Right now, the best bowman of the Sakims has his weapon trained on you. If you will let us pass, you will not be harmed."

"Uh, would that be this Lord Roderic, then—the one they call the Prince of Thieves?" one of the youths asked.

She saw no reason to lie, so she nodded.

"But he kidnapped you, didn't he?" the other one asked in obvious confusion. "And how can you be her with that black hair?"

"My hair has been dyed," she replied, pushing the hood away and lowering her head so they could see the golden roots. Roderic had said that they were becoming more and more noticeable. "And he did not kidnap me. I went with him willingly. Please let us pass. He is taking me to my Innish kinfolk."

The two men approached her cautiously, both of them swiveling their heads to search for Roderic. She held her breath, knowing that Roderic would soon become impatient.

"Don't come any closer," she implored them. "If he believes I am being threatened, he will kill you."

They stopped in their tracks, still turning to study the forest on all sides. "Is't true that he stole the tax money and gave it back to the people?" one youth asked.

"Yes, he did." She found it surprising that Roderic's exploits had reached their ears.

The two men exchanged glances; then one of them spoke. "We have no quarrel with him, milady—nor with you, either."

Maryana finally allowed herself to relax. But in the same moment, she realized that if this worked, it might be more because of Roderic than because of her.

"Don't move!"

All three of them suddenly saw Roderic—much closer than she'd expected. He was on foot, and his bow was stretched, the arrow pointed at one of the men.

"They've agreed to let us pass!" she cried, fearing that he would kill them anyway.

"A very wise decision," Roderic said, now moving quickly to lower his bow and draw his long-bladed knife.

"Over there," he ordered, gesturing to a nearby tree. "Sit down against that thick oak."

The two men did as told, and Maryana saw that they were less frightened than curious. But still, she didn't let go of her own fear for them completely until Roderic went to their horses and cut off the reins with his knife, then approached the two men.

"When are you to be relieved?" he asked as he tied them both to the tree.

"Before nightfall," one youth said, then, after a pause: "Is't really true, then, what you did?"

Roderic frowned at them and at her. "What do you mean?"

"We heard a story that you stole the taxes and gave them back to your people."

Roderic laughed. "You heard right. My people need it more than your greedy king."

Both men shook their heads, apparently at the wonder of it.

"When they come for you, tell them not to try to go into the pass after us. If the Innish don't get them, the ghosts will."

Both youths gaped at him. "That's true, too?" one of them asked. "I heard about that, but I dinna believe it."

"Believe it!" Roderic replied sternly. "I've seen them myself."

Chapter Eleven

"Do you think they'll try to follow us?"

Roderic shook his head. "No. There aren't enough of them to take on the Innish army I conjured up—and besides, they don't want trouble with the Innish now, anyway."

"If they believe you about the Innish army, that is."

He gave her a look of mock surprise. "Why wouldn't they believe me? I'm obviously a candidate for sainthood—and everybody knows that saints don't lie. I'd bet they even believe in the ghosts at this point."

"I didn't tell them about you. They guessed that you were the one with me, then asked if the story was true."

His laughter rang out in the narrow pass. "So I've become a legend. Perhaps that will become useful at some point."

"I didn't have a chance to thank you for letting them live," she said when his laughter had died away.

"I very nearly didn't—despite what I promised."
Then after a brief silence, he went on. "Strange,
isn't it, that that kind of courage in a man would
be praiseworthy even if the cause wasn't. But in a
woman . . ."

"I was terrified," she admitted.

"Courage and fear should always go together."
He turned in the saddle to look back at her briefly
as they rode single-file. "You frighten me, Lady
Maryana."

"I frighten you?" she echoed incredulously.
"Why?"

"Because you are unlike any woman I've ever
known."

She knew that she should leave it at that: take
his statement as a compliment and store it away
in her heart. But she didn't. "Is that intended to be
a compliment, Roderic?"

"I'm not sure," was his reply—which certainly
proved to her that she *should* have left it alone.

"When can I expect to see the ghosts?" she asked,
mostly to change the subject.

"Probably not for a time yet. And you're likely to
hear them before you see them."

"Roderic, you might have convinced those boys
that there are ghosts—but you haven't convinced
me—quite possibly because *I* don't expect to hear
of a Saint Roderic anytime soon."

He chuckled, shaking his head. "So the lady requires proof—of both the ghosts and of my fitness
for sainthood."

She didn't believe in the ghosts—but still, she
kept peering at the rocky cliffs that hugged the narrow trail, and constantly scanned the huge old
trees that grew in the narrow ravine. And she decided that if ghosts did indeed exist, this was exactly the kind of place they might favor. She'd
never seen its like before.

The trail wound around and around, barely wide

enough for one man—or woman—on horseback. At times it climbed steeply, then turned again and again, so that she could look back and see behind them more easily than she could see ahead. And the dark mountains made her very uncomfortable, as they seemed to be leaning toward them, as though threatening to engulf them at any moment.

Here and there, water gushed down toward them from unimaginable heights, and several times they rode through a fine spray as the water poured into small pools at the base of the rock. The trees were taller and their trunks thicker than any she'd ever seen, even though by now she'd grown used to the forests of Sakim.

Altogether, it was an eerie place, one that her mind whispered was not truly of this world.

If Roderic felt any of her uneasiness, he gave no indication. Neither did he seem concerned about ghosts or huge birds. Every time she lowered her head from gazing at the mountains, she found him seemingly staring straight ahead, and he rode relaxed, like a man unafraid and unconcerned.

I don't believe in ghosts, she told herself, but if I did, this would be their home. Not a ruined abbey or castle or the great stone megaliths she'd seen on her way here.

Darkness came early down in the pass, where daylight was never bright to begin with. She'd assumed that they'd stop when it became dark, but Roderic said he wanted to go on for a time, to put as much space between them and the Neran soldiers as possible, even though he continued to doubt that they'd come into the pass.

Soon it was so dark that she couldn't even see Roderic and his horse, though she rode close behind him. The only concession he'd made to the darkness was to travel more slowly.

His voice floated back to her. "I was here once

before, some years ago, with Henry. We decided to come to see the pass—and the sea."

She was confused. "Why would you come here to see the sea, when it is at your doorstep?"

"This is different. You'll see."

She was growing very tired of that phrase: ghosts, huge birds, and now a sea that was "different." And she began to suspect that it was all a joke—a game he was playing with her, perhaps to test that "unnatural" courage he believed she possessed.

Finally they stopped for the night, choosing a spot near one of the pools formed by the gushing waterfalls. Roderic didn't make a fire, since he continued to insist upon caution. So they were forced to make their evening meal from the dried meat and fruits and bread they carried with them. He promised to find some game tomorrow, and perhaps some berries and nuts as well.

Wrapped in her cloak and the blankets, Maryana fell asleep while she worried that she might not sleep at all. Not even Roderic's presence close by could keep her awake.

For two days, time seemed to be standing still. The trail alternately climbed steeply, then descended precipitously, and was never straight for more than a few hundred feet. Maryana was beginning to believe that she would spend the remainder of her life in this strange, wild place.

Their long silences were interrupted by periods of lazy conversation. She talked of Chamoney and he spoke of his childhood and of his own lands. It was the talk of two people who know each other, but have not yet had the time to learn all the details that make up a life.

Then, late in the afternoon of the second day, they were climbing yet again, this time less steeply but for a much longer time. And then she could see ahead of them something she hadn't seen for three days: an expanse of blue sky.

A few minutes later, they rode into a clearing at the top of a mountain—one of the lesser peaks, she saw quickly, since they were still surrounded on all sides by much taller, craggy mountains that looked as though they pierced the heavens themselves.

The feeling of being weighted down that had plagued her since they entered the pass lifted, and she smiled as she breathed in the cold air that was fragrant with the scent of pine. And then she saw the stone circle.

It stood some distance away on the broad mountaintop, but Roderic was riding straight for it. Although she'd earlier seen a few of the strange standing stones, this was clearly different because they formed a circle.

Roderic rode to the edge of the circle, then dismounted and came over to assist her. When she was on the ground, she stared up at the nearest stone. It was nearly twice as tall as she was, as were all the others. And now she saw that in the center was a wide, flat stone that bore traces of dark stains.

"What is this place?" she asked, her voice unconsciously dropping to a near whisper.

"An ancient place of worship. There are supposed to be others, but this is the only one I've seen. The stone didn't come from here, you know."

"It didn't?" She studied the stone, then looked at other rocks nearby. It seemed that he was right. The great stones were a reddish brown, and bore traces of some sparkling material within them.

"Our ancestors must have brought them here."

"What ancestors? And how could they possibly have dragged them up here?"

"The Seltas. They were the common ancestor of the Sakims and the Nerans and the Innish as well— or so some believe. And as to how they got them here, who knows?" He shrugged. "There are those who believe they used magic."

He pointed to the flat stone in the center of the circle. "It is said that they made sacrifices here: human sacrifices. Those stains could be blood."

"Roderic!" She had started toward the flat stone, but now she stopped and turned to stare at him.

He chuckled. "I'm merely passing on what was told to me years ago. There are other legends of this place and the others like it farther south."

"I'm not sure I want to hear them," she replied as she stared at the dark patches on the stone—but from a safe distance.

"It is said that these are places of great power, and that if a man passes the night within the circle, the spirits of the ancestors might choose to favor him with some of that power."

"You don't believe that—do you?"

He shrugged. "It's as good a place as any to spend the night. By this time tomorrow, we will have reached the sea."

She was certainly eager to stop for the day, but not here. Not after hearing his tales. "Did you and Henry spend the night here?"

He nodded.

"And?"

"We both had strange dreams, but neither of us felt more powerful in the morning."

"What sort of dreams?"

He smiled. "That would be putting them into your head. We'll just wait to see what you remember in the morning."

It was twilight. A breeze blew through the stone circle, whipping her long hair about her face. She was alone—but not alone. Although she couldn't see anyone else, she sensed a presence somewhere nearby.

The wind was murmuring through the trees beyond the circle, but as she listened, it seemed to her that she could hear voices chanting.

Suddenly the great stones began to glow! It was as though they were lit from within by some unearthly light. She found herself turning in a slow circle, facing each great monolith in turn. And now she was certain that she heard chanting, even though the sound was no louder.

I should be afraid, she told herself—and yet she wasn't, not even as she began to feel something begin to change within her.

It began as a sort of hum, a deep, vibrating feeling that extended from the top of her head to the tips of her toes. The sound that escaped from her lips was a sigh of pleasure—a pleasure she had never before known.

Then it grew deeper and more powerful—and now she could hear the pace of the strange chanting increase, though the words were not intelligible to her.

She swayed slightly as this strange thing coursed through her, leaving her both weak and energized at the same time. Inchoate longings filled her, as though she knew that all this was leading to something, though, in fact, she knew nothing beyond the moment.

As she swayed, she took a few steps backward, and then her foot struck something. She turned and saw the flat stone at the center of the circle. But it was different. She remembered it and remembered what Roderic had told her about it, but that was only a vague memory. The reality was very different.

Four corner posts surrounded the stone, and lengths of pale fabric were draped from them and between them, creating a canopy that all but obscured the stone itself. And when she parted the soft fabric, she saw that it had been turned into a flower-strewn bed.

Puzzled, she turned away from the altar that had become a bed—and Roderic was there, dressed in a white robe like the one she wore. A garland of flowers sat atop his dark hair. She put up a hand and felt a crown of vines and flowers upon her own head.

He smiled at her, and love shone from his dark eyes as he extended a hand to her, then led her back to the canopied bed. Beyond the circle somewhere, the chanting continued, but began almost imperceptibly to fade away. The stones glowed, but the eerie light within them was fading as well.

"Maryana."

The voice was soft and husky and it drew out her name, turning each syllable into a whisper of desire. It was of the dream—and not of the dream, and somehow she knew that. Her eyes fluttered open.

Roderic lay beside her, propped up on one elbow as he stared down at her. The moon had risen and she could see him clearly in the silvery light. Had he actually spoken her name that way—or was it only the dream, after all? The moonlight danced in his eyes, but she didn't trust what she saw, because it might only be what she wanted to see.

She tried to find her voice, to ask him if she'd awakened him somehow—if perhaps she'd cried out in her dream. When they'd gone to sleep, he'd been farther away, wrapped in his own blankets, preserving that all-important space between them.

Then she saw something pale in his thick, dark hair, and without giving any thought to her action, she reached up and plucked it from his hair. When she saw what it was, she was too astonished to speak. The dream and reality began to merge. It was a pale, delicate petal from a flower—exactly like the flowers in the crown he'd worn in the dream.

She dragged her gaze away from it and found

233

him staring at it, too, and she knew that the wonder in his own eyes mirrored hers. And then his hand went slowly to her hair, and came away with a small, shiny green leaf, which he then held next to the petal.

"What . . . ?" She stopped because she didn't want to ask. There were no flowers or small leaves where they'd lain down to sleep. The ground inside the circle was bare of all vegetation. She remembered that because she'd thought it odd.

She hadn't wanted to sleep within the stone circle, but Roderic had insisted upon it and had teased her about it—fair enough, since she'd scorned his Sakim superstitions.

They both stared at what they held—and then at each other. The silence dragged on, as though neither of them wished to be the first to give voice to their astonishment. Then, finally, Roderic took the petal from her hand and tossed it aside, together with the leaf he'd held.

"Tell me what you dreamed."

She wanted to hear it first from him, but she found her voice and described the dream: the glowing stones, the chanting, the altar that had turned into a bed—and the garlands in their hair.

He nodded. "Exactly the same."

She turned and studied each of the great stones in turn, and he did the same. In the moonlight, they still seemed to be glowing slightly, but she knew that it was only light reflecting off the glittering particles in the stone. It wasn't the same.

Roderic followed her gaze, then listened with her to the sound of the wind in the trees. It was no more than that.

Then he threw back his head and laughed, and the sound seemed to rise into the dark heavens. After a moment she joined him, though with somewhat less enthusiasm. In the space of a few moments, she had gone from being a disbeliever to being, at the very least, uneasy.

Then his laughter died away, and suddenly there was something in his hand. She blinked in shock. The ring he'd hidden beneath his pillow—the same ring he'd held so many times, just staring at it—was now in his hand.

"It was my mother's ring, passed down from her mother. She gave it to me before she died. It would have gone to Ammy, but she'd already entered the convent by then.

"She told me to keep it and cherish it, and someday to give it to a woman 'worthy of it.' Those were her very words."

He held it up to the moonlight and watched it sparkle. "I think she would find you to be worthy of it."

Maryana's breath caught in her throat with a strangling sound as she stared from him to the ring and back again. She felt as though a huge, deep abyss had suddenly opened up before her—but instead of falling into it, she was floating up above it: up and up into the very stars themselves.

He hauled himself up into a sitting position, still cradling the ring in his hands. "I have nothing to offer you now, save for this ring. But I swear to you that if you take it, I will get back both my own lands and yours."

Then he cocked his head and gave her that boyish grin that never failed to delight her. "Are you willing to take me on faith, milady?"

"There is more than the ring that you have to give me," she replied huskily. "What about your heart, Roderic? Is that mine as well?"

He stared at her intently. "My heart, my soul— and all the rest of me, too. I think you had them the moment you stepped ashore onto my land."

"Then it is a gift I can accept," she said, smiling.

He took her hand and carried it first to his lips,

then slipped the ring slowly onto her finger. His dark eyes met hers.

"There is another legend about this place. It is said that a man and a woman who consummate their love within this circle will live a long and joyous life together."

Maryana searched his face for any hint that he might be teasing her, but she found none. He was very still, and seemed to be holding his breath. For one brief moment, she thought that she heard the chanting again, but when she tried to concentrate on it, she could hear only the wind rustling the pine needles.

It was a moment to savor—and to treasure. A moment when her innocence—and her whole life—seemed to hang in the balance. Maryana was too forthright not to consider honestly what she was about to do. Roderic's future was clouded at best—but then, so was hers. And without him she saw no future at all.

The aching need to know his love warred with her lifelong independence. But hadn't she already made that decision when she allowed him to give her the ring? Her gaze fell on it and she nodded, then raised her eyes to his and said, "Yes."

The night was cool—perhaps even cold. The wind swirled around the tall stones, creating eddies that buffeted them both. And overhead, the moon emerged from behind a wispy cloud, dimming the light from a million stars. The stones glittered once more with reflected light, as though they'd somehow managed to capture within their depths some of those myriad stars.

Time slowed as Roderic gathered up his blankets and rearranged them with hers into a bed for them both. Then he knelt beside her and lowered his face to hers.

His kiss was a promise, a gentle harbinger of things to come. At first both eager and yet still afraid, Maryana let go of her fear and found desire surging forth to take its place.

For what seemed a time as long as the stones had stood, they held each other and kissed each other and stroked and caressed and whispered things meaningful only to them. She could feel his hunger now, his need to possess her, and it filled her with a unique kind of power that fed her own desire.

Their clothing came off slowly, too, with sometimes awkward movements as they tried to keep themselves covered against the chill of the night. But when flesh at last met flesh, unencumbered by fabric, their bodies were heated by their mutual passion, and the cold was driven away.

His body was long and lean and hard and felt so very strange—but also so very right. And his hard, callused hands traced lines of fire along her soft curves, seeking out all the places where a touch ignited tiny bonfires whose heat spread to the very core of her being.

His mouth trailed slow, fiery pathways down across her throat and onto the gentle swell of a breast, where he teased a nipple with teeth and tongue until it had become hard and almost unbearably sensitive, drawing from her a sound she barely recognized as coming from her own lips.

Maryana was lost. The body that had anchored her to the earth seemed to be floating on a cloud of pure sensation, totally disconnected from the past. She clung to him, arched to him, explored his hard planes and angles and learned, through these blind explorations, what pleased him and what drew forth shudders that matched her own.

Had she been capable of thought, she would have been surprised—and perhaps even a bit embarrassed—at her eagerness to learn him, at the boldness that grew out of desire.

And when at last he parted her and entered her,

she was hot and moist and eager to receive him and hold him and move with him in the ancient rhythms of love. What had been slow, lazy explorations of each other now became a union of two heated bodies, pounding and throbbing and pushing for the ultimate fulfillment.

The tension built within her, as she could feel it gripping him—and then it exploded, showering them both with molten fire that left them weak and gasping for breath and still clinging to each other.

"Maryana," he whispered, drawing out each syllable in a hoarse whisper. "How I love you."

He dropped a featherlight kiss on her parted lips, and a bead of sweat fell onto her cheek and cooled there, the sensation pleasant against her heated skin. Then he stared at her with frightening intensity.

"Whatever happens, you must remember that: that I love you and will never let you go from my heart."

His words provoked both a warmth and a chill in her, but she pushed the chill aside and let the warmth enfold her. "And I love you, Roderic. Nothing bad can happen to us now."

Roderic turned in the saddle yet another time to smile at her—a smile that drove away the morning chill and conjured up instead memories of their lovemaking. Her body ached, though whether from past lovemaking or a renewed longing, she couldn't have said.

Even the harshness of their surroundings seemed softened this morning, though perhaps the mist had something to do with that. They had ridden away from the stone circle and down into a deep ravine, where fog lay heavily on everything, slowing their progress toward the sea.

It was a world of ever-shifting mists and dark shadows of steep cliffs and tall trees. From time to time they could hear the cries of birds or the scrabbling of tiny forest creatures, but their sounds were muffled, as were their horses' hoofbeats, even when they struck rock.

Maryana felt as though she were wrapped in gauze, and the feeling was strangely pleasant, despite their near-blindness. After the magic of last night and then this morning, she welcomed this muted, alien world.

Roderic had said they would reach the sea before day's end, and Maryana had all but forgotten the strange name of the place and the tales of huge birds. Nearly forgotten, too, was her dream—and the evidence that it had not been all a dream. What had come after had obliterated what had gone before.

She heard the sounds just as the path began to ascend once more, carrying them up through the mists toward a sun she could just barely make out. And even then, lost in her memories, she was slow to respond.

The cries, like every other sound, were muffled by the fog, but as they rode up the steep path, they became clearer. Her breath caught in her throat as those stories came rushing back—made all the more real now by the dream-that-wasn't-a-dream.

Lost souls. The phrase could not have been more accurate. No one hearing those terrible cries could think otherwise. They were repeated over and over, coming from a variety of directions, seeming to surround them from above. Low, long, mournful sounds of torment, ending in a terrible dry rattle of death.

Roderic had turned once again in his saddle and was watching her as she tried to see through the mists. She met his eyes only briefly before trying again to find their source.

And then she saw something! As she peered into the mists above them, one huge gray shape and then another seemed to materialize out of the mists, circling and fluttering, dipping and soaring. There was so much mist that it was impossible for her to be sure of their size, though she didn't doubt their existence.

Roderic reined in his horse and moved to the side of the narrow path to let her join him. "The Innish have always called them taladins. The word is believed to have come from the language of the Seltas. As far as I know, they exist nowhere else."

"Are they really as big as they seem?" she asked nervously.

"I once saw several with wingspans longer than a man is tall. They nest in the cliffs near the shore, which can sometimes make getting down there a bit tricky."

"Do you mean that they might attack us?" She tried to envision being attacked by birds, but simply couldn't imagine it. She'd seen falcons and owls, of course, and knew that they attacked small animals, but birds big enough to attack *people?* It was beyond her imagining.

"They might try. But there's a way to ward them off."

He climbed out of the saddle, then began to search along the path for rocks, picking up several and rejecting them. Maryana remained on her horse, hoping that horse and rider would present too large a target and wondering if he could be teasing her again.

But those cries! She'd never heard their like. Even for someone as impious as she was, they sounded like the noises of hell itself, and conjured up horrible images of writhing, lost souls begging for release.

Then the cries died away, without her ever getting a good look at the creatures. She breathed a sigh of relief and turned her attention to Roderic.

He had selected two fairly large stones and was

busy wrapping them with long leather strips she hadn't seen before that he must have been carrying in his saddle packs. When he had finished, he set one of them on the ground and demonstrated their use.

"You swing it over your head in a circle to keep them away if they threaten to attack." He swung the strap with its stone at the end for a few seconds, then handed it to her.

"It's supposed to be very bad luck to shoot them, though Henry and I were tempted to do just that. He still has a scar from when one attacked him. Then we thought of this way of fighting them off, and later, I found out that others have done it as well."

Maryana looked dubiously at the thing he handed her, trying to imagine keeping her horse under control while swinging the stone above her head. Roderic smiled and wrapped a hand around her head, then drew her down for a kiss.

"Don't worry. I'll keep us both safe."

They rode on, up and out of the fog and into bright sunshine. Maryana searched the blue sky carefully, but didn't see any of the birds. Nevertheless, her hand went from time to time to the leather thong with its stone. She was still somewhat nervous, but Roderic's kiss had succeeded in turning her thoughts in more pleasant directions.

Before them lay a broad, mostly open space that stretched for several miles before ending in the cliffs that fell to the shore. Strangely, she found this wide-open space, which was not unlike the broad plains of home, as scary as she'd once found the tall mountains and deep, dark ravines now behind them. Perhaps it was only a lingering concern about the great birds, but she felt very vulnerable beneath that broad canopy of blue sky.

As they rode along a barely discernible path through waist-high grasses, Maryana caught glimpses of the birds, but they were so high as to be nothing more than soft gray dots against the deep blue. Once, she thought she heard their cries, but she couldn't be sure.

Then, after several hours, they reached the edge of the cliffs: a very daunting sight indeed. Maryana gasped in shock at the scene below, where angry, churning gray-green water seemed to heave and boil all the way to the horizon, and hurl itself incessantly against dark rocks.

Roderic had been right: this *was* different from the straits that separated their two lands. Those waters were often calm and placid, bestirring themselves only during storms. But here the waters were ever restless, constantly in angry motion.

The Cove of Lost Souls lay directly beneath them—many hundreds of feet down, created by a wide curve of the cliffs that sloped gently at each end to meet the water.

The way down looked impossible to her, and she wondered aloud if the Innish boat would come for them. It was nowhere in sight.

"It will come," Roderic said with certainty. "We made better time than I'd expected, so it may not arrive before tomorrow."

Maryana suppressed a shiver. There seemed nothing for it then, but to go down there. But how she wished she could simply close her eyes and open them again to find herself standing on the creamy sands of the cove.

The track they'd been following led them directly to a trail that wound down the cliffs, curving about to take advantage of small flat spaces and deep clefts in the rocks. She followed Roderic, one eye on the path and the other on the heavens.

Before they had gone more than a few hundred feet, the great birds reappeared! There were three of them, and they seemed to come out of thin air, shrieking now, not like lost souls, but more like a woman undergoing unimaginable torture.

Maryana wanted to cover her ears, but between having to keep one hand on the reins and the other busy swinging the thong, there was no way to do it.

Only a few feet above her head, two of the birds wheeled and turned, their huge talons aimed at her, their bright black eyes studying her. Roderic's stallion seemed nearly impervious to their attacks, but her own horse whinnied in fear and tried to bolt, until she was forced to drop the thong and concentrate on preventing the animal from making a misstep that could send them both to their deaths.

Roderic managed to edge closer to her, still swinging the thong at the birds. "Get over here— onto my horse. Let yours go!"

She quickly saw the wisdom in that move, and managed to fling herself from her own saddle onto the back of his horse. But as she did so, she felt something rip at her heavy cloak, and she felt the giant wings brush against her. Roderic had suggested they wear the cloaks even though the day had become warm once they were in the sun, and in that terrifying instant when she was helpless to defend herself, she silently thanked him for his foresight.

"Take this and swing it," he ordered as she wrapped her arms around him from behind and fitted herself against him as best she could.

With trembling fingers, she took the thong and, holding on to him with one arm, raised the other to swing the stone again and again. In the meantime, she saw her mare stumble past them and flee down the trail. One of the three birds went after it, and both bird and horse were quickly lost to view.

But the other two persisted. Maryana was certain that her arm would soon drop off, and wished that there were some way they could change places, so that she could hold the reins while he swung the stone.

On and on it went: the slow, careful movements of the horse and the shrieking attacks by their aerial assailants. Then she felt the stone strike one of the birds. It quickly wheeled away, but the other one raked at Roderic with its talons, and she saw his hood shredded before her eyes. She screamed even before she knew she'd formed the sound.

"I'm all right," he shouted. "It didn't get me. Keep swinging the stone!"

She didn't even dare to take a few seconds to switch arms, and the one that was swinging the stone now felt as heavy as stone itself. She couldn't see what progress they had made, but the horse's slow pace suggested that it wasn't much. There was no way she could keep the stone in motion for the remainder of the journey to the seashore.

Tears welled up in her eyes, nearly blinding her. They were going to die here—and it would be her fault. She kept on swinging the stone as she tried to find the words to tell him that she couldn't do it—and then suddenly the thong was pulled from her grasp.

She blinked away the tears and saw that Roderic had taken the thong from her and was winding it around his wrist. She braced for the attack she was sure must be coming even as she wondered why he wasn't trying to defend them. And then she realized that the birds were gone.

"Where are they?" She gasped, certain they were merely regrouping for another attack. She held on to him with one arm, while the other dangled uselessly at her side.

"They're gone and they probably won't be back. We must be far enough now from their nests that they don't feel threatened."

Slowly, she turned around and looked behind them. Two of the birds were circling above a ledge, and on it, she could see dried grasses that must be nests. They had passed very close to that ledge, she could now see, and she actually felt a moment's sympathy for the birds.

"My horse," she said, remembering that the third bird had been pursuing it. "Would they attack it?"

"They might," he said grimly.

Then they both watched as more birds appeared some distance away and slightly farther along the trail. They dipped out of sight quickly and didn't reappear. When they had reached a spot near where they'd seen the birds, Roderic brought his horse to a halt.

"Wait here while I go have a look," he said as he swung out of the saddle, handing over the reins to her.

"The taladins," she cried, not wanting to be left alone even for a few moments.

"I think they'll be too busy to bother us," he replied as he began to climb over the cliff face.

Maryana swallowed hard. She knew what he meant. The presence of all those birds meant that they'd found food. But the fact that she heard no sounds must mean that her horse was already dead. She could only hope that it had died quickly.

Tears stung her eyes as she sat there with her useless arm, wriggling her fingers to see if she could coax some feeling back into them. Presently it seemed to work, but the pain was worse than the numbness, if not as frightening.

She thought about that soft, sandy beach and wondered how much farther they had to go. It was impossible to tell from where she sat, because the rocks jutted out and obscured everything below them. So she closed her eyes and imagined herself there as she continued to try to coax her arm back to life.

"How bad is it?"

Her eyes snapped open and she realized that

she'd fallen into some sort of trance while she waited for him. "It was numb, but the feeling has returned now."

"And pain with it." He nodded in understanding as he took her arm in both his hands and began to massage it gently.

"My horse?" she asked, already beginning to feel the pain lessen beneath his warm, strong fingers.

"It's dead. I think it fell and then they got it. I'll come back up in the morning and get your things."

She felt sorry for the poor animal, but she knew that she could very easily have been with it. Unconsciously, she reached out with her free arm to stroke Roderic's stallion.

"What a wonderful animal," she said.

"As his father was before him," Roderic added, stroking the stallion himself as he let go of her arm. "It's partly in the breeding, but also partly in the training. Too many people pay more attention to the former than to the latter."

She nodded, thinking of her wonderful mare at home and of the time she'd invested in training her. So they shared a love of horses, too. That pleased her—especially now, when she needed something to take away the lingering terror.

Roderic swung up into the saddle, settling behind her this time. He drew her back against him and kissed her cheek, then ran a tongue playfully along the rim of her ear.

"My brave Neran lady," he murmured. "I said that I would keep you safe, but it seems you're able to manage that for yourself."

She decided not to tell him that she could not have lasted another minute. Even a woman in love had the right to some secrets.

Chapter Twelve

Seen from where she was, the sea was somehow even more frightening. In her mind's eye, Maryana could still see it stretching out forever, while from where she stood in the soft sand, she could feel its power, its hunger as it hurled itself against the big boulders that littered the shoreline of the cove.

She'd never seen the straits in a storm, but she guessed that it must be something like this display of unimaginable, raw power.

"Beautiful, isn't it?" Roderic said, coming up behind her and wrapping his arms around her.

"No." She couldn't imagine why he would think so. "How big is the boat that will be coming for us?" Surely it must be far larger than the fishing boats or the supply boat that had brought her to Sakim. Otherwise how would it dare venture out onto that sea?

"About the size of the boat that brought you here, I would think. You looked to me as though that journey hadn't caused you any problems."

247

"It didn't, but the strait was calm."

"So is this. When Henry and I were down here, we saw a storm while we were still up on the cliffs. There were waves that could have swallowed a boat larger than the supply boats."

Somehow she didn't doubt that, but she still turned within the circle of his arms to see if he might be joking. Unfortunately, it appeared that he wasn't.

"Surely the woman who fought off the taladins couldn't be frightened by a few waves," he murmured close to her ear—and now she knew he was teasing.

"I'm not brave," she protested. "If I've learned nothing else since I came here, I've learned that much."

And she thought about the hours before Roderic had rescued her in the chapel, and how she'd given up hope and accepted her lot. No, she wasn't brave—except, perhaps, in brief spurts.

"Before you rescued me, I had even accepted that I was going to marry Miles," she told him. "And I was already busy trying to figure out how I could prevent him from destroying Chamoney."

His arms tightened around her again and he kissed the top of her head. "None of us is brave *all* the time. I was quaking in my boots when you walked into the chapel. I feared that you'd decided you wanted to marry him, after all."

"How could you even think such a thing?" she asked, astonished at his words.

He kissed her again. "Remember that we didn't know each other very well then—or at least I didn't know you that well. You, on the other hand, had been observing me from beneath your disguise for some time."

"Still, you'd seen enough of Miles Foulane to know what he is."

"I've seen enough of Miles Foulane to last a life-

248

time—but I doubt that I've seen the last of him."

His words sent a chill through her that had little to do with the cool wind blowing off the water. The future remained uncharted territory—a place to which they must go, but about which they had yet to speak.

Roderic seemed to be reading her mind. "If the abbot and the other men reached my Innish kin, we will know just what we face. I don't suppose that either your uncle or Miles told you how many troops the king has with him now?"

She shook her head. "They never spoke of such things in my presence." Then she frowned, remembering something.

"But I do recall Miles saying something about the king wanting to send some of the troops home soon, so that he wouldn't have to pay them through the winter." She made a face.

"His Majesty is known to be so greedy as to keep as much of his tax money for himself as he can manage, so that he can build more palaces and furnish them lavishly."

Roderic smiled. "His greed may well prove to be his undoing. I've been hoping that he might be foolish enough to believe we would never stage an attack in the winter—that he might not realize that we're accustomed to the winters here, as he and his men are not."

Maryana didn't want to think about the coming battle, but it seemed that her brain was ignoring her wishes. "He might not. Anyone as arrogant as he is isn't likely to believe that others might not share his views. Besides, the troops aren't all that loyal to him—other than the officers, that is."

"That's good news—and accurate, if those two men we met at the pass are any indication. It takes great loyalty—or great fear—to fight under bad conditions."

"Well, they aren't loyal, and I doubt that they

fear him all that much—or his officers, either. Each man alone might have that kind of fear, but together, I think they'd overcome it."

He gave her an admiring look. "You're a very wise woman, Lady Maryana."

"I've been in charge of Chamoney for more than five years, and I've learned a lot about people. I also learned much from my father, until his illness took away his mind."

He drew her close again. "I'm looking forward to seeing your beautiful Chamoney."

She stretched up and kissed him. "I've dreamed of being there with you, you know."

Bodies pressed together as tightly as their heavy cloaks would allow, they held each other and kissed, remaining there until the incoming tide began to lap at their boots. Then Roderic released her with a sigh.

"Would that it were summer and we could make love here in the water."

She smiled at him as the image began to form in her mind: their naked bodies entwined in a shallow pool, cool water pouring over heated flesh. She stopped them both and seized his hands.

"Promise me that we will come back here one day—in the summer."

He chuckled. "Even if we have to brave the taladins to get here?"

"Even so."

"Then I swear to you that we will return, milady." He lifted one of her hands to his lips.

They retreated to the bottom of the cliffs, where Roderic spread the remaining blankets. Already the evening was growing cold, but she knew they could keep each other warm.

Lovemaking was more difficult this time, because they dared not shed all their clothing. But there was an excitement to that, too, she soon discovered: a flavor of the forbidden as they sought out the flesh hidden beneath layers of fabric. Long before his shaft invaded her and made her whole, she was throbbing with need and lost in the wonder of him.

Afterward, he propped himself above her and smiled. "I wonder what it will feel like to make love in a proper bed, after sharing the pleasures of a bath."

"I wouldn't know," she replied, "though I imagine that you do."

He arched a dark brow. "Ah, so jealousy rears its head. I'd begun to think that you were free of that particular affliction."

"I'm not jealous," she protested—and she wasn't, except possibly of his dead love.

"There haven't been that many women," he said after a moment. "For a long time after Claire died, I had no desire for any woman."

"Did you . . . ?" She hesitated, not certain she could or should ask the question.

"No. She was still only a child when she died— barely fifteen."

He moved away from her and lowered himself to the blanket. "I've found myself thinking a lot about her since I met you. And what I've come to realize is that it was only a boy's infatuation. Claire was lovely and she laughed a lot—but my mother was right: there wasn't much more there." Maryana's pleasure at his words was such that she thought she might just bubble up and rise into the red-tinted heavens. "I think I would have liked your mother very much."

He reached over and lifted her hand that wore his mother's ring. "And she would have liked you, as I told you before."

He got up then and whistled for his horse, who had wandered off somewhere in search of food. There were coarse grasses and some low shrubs growing at the base of the cliffs. Maryana's stomach growled, and she envied a creature that could always find food. Their own food supply, such as it was, was on the rocks above with her dead horse—that was, if the taladins hadn't eaten it, too.

She shuddered, horrified anew at just how close she'd come to death. If she hadn't followed Roderic's instructions and climbed onto his horse, she would soon have lost control of her own unfortunate animal, and they both might have fallen to their deaths, to become a meal for the taladins.

But despite that, she still wanted to come back to this place one day. Did that make her brave, as Roderic had suggested—or did it merely mean that she was as foolhardy as she'd sometimes thought he was?

The picture he'd painted for her was irresistible. She stared at the foam that continued to lather the beach as the tide came in and could almost see them there: naked and free and wild in this strange place. She was surprised, and even faintly embarrassed, to think about it.

But she was still thinking about it when the stallion came galloping back through the sand just as the sun was sinking below the horizon. Roderic beckoned to her, and a few moments later the two of them were seated on the stallion's bare back, galloping through the foamy water in the last of the day's light.

Maryana clung to him, ignoring the icy spray kicked up by the animal. Their delighted laughter rang out—and for a time, at least, they were two lovers alone and free and happy.

Maryana stood at the landward end of the old wood-and-stone pier and watched the small boat riding the waves, bobbing up and down as it plowed steadily toward them. At the other end of the pier, Roderic was already waving, and now, as the boat drew closer to the pier, she could see a figure on the boat, waving back.

Their brief idyll was over. Now they must begin persuading their Innish kin to take up arms against her people. And then . . .

She shook her head, as though by doing so she could dislodge all thoughts of war—and of her betrayal of her own people. *But it's not my people whom I betray*, she reminded herself. *Rather, it is the king.* None of her people, save for those who could benefit from it, wanted war with the Sakim.

The boat was now in calmer waters, coming ever closer to the old pier. Beside her, Roderic's stallion stamped and whickered, and she wondered if it somehow knew what was in store. Roderic was certain that he could persuade the animal to get into the boat, and she hoped he was right, since she knew he would never leave the stallion.

The boat nudged up against the pier with a surprising delicacy that nonetheless sent vibrations through the old wood. Immediately, the man who had been waving to Roderic leaped from the deck onto the pier and the two men embraced. That would be Brien, Roderic's cousin, she decided, the Earl of Axton. Roderic had explained to her that the two men shared a birth date and had always been as close as the distance between them permitted.

Both men started back toward her, laughing and talking, as though neither had a care in the world. And yet surely Brien knew why they had sent for him—and what they would be wanting.

Is there something different about men, she wondered, *that they can face war so easily, as though it is nothing more than a great adventure? Why is it left to women to worry and fear for all of them?*

The introductions were made, and Brien, to his credit, treated her like the lady she supposedly was, and not the urchin with two-colored hair that she appeared to be.

"Lady Maryana, it is a pleasure!" he cried. "I have been listening to the abbot singing your praises ever since his arrival. And I am instructed to tell you that the duke and duchess eagerly await your arrival. I took the liberty of informing them."

"Thank you," she replied, "but they might not be so eager when they see me."

Both men laughed. Then Brien said that she could remake herself when they reached Axton Hall.

"How far is it from Axton Hall to Wamick?" she asked. Wamick was the grand palace of the duke, who was her great-uncle. She'd visited it once when she was a child, and her mother had wanted her to meet her Innish relatives.

"Less than a day's ride," Brien told her. "His Grace suggested sending his son-in-law, Baron Lessing, to meet you, but I persuaded him that it wasn't necessary. Do you know the baron?"

"No, we've never met. I barely know his wife, my cousin."

"Ah, well then, I'll say nothing. You'll meet him soon enough." Then he turned briefly to Roderic. "The baron will be our problem, I'm afraid. He has the duke's ear, although His Grace is still quite capable of speaking for himself."

"I don't understand," Maryana said, although from Roderic's expression, he did.

"The baron will never agree to fight the Nerans. And if he can persuade the duke to stay out of it, we have a problem. I can raise a small army on my own, of course, but without the duke's blessing, not to mention his gold, it will be small indeed."

"Oh. Then you have already agreed to fight?"

Brien draped a long arm across Roderic's shoulders. "Of course. I don't even have to be asked—

especially now that Roderic has decided he's willing to lead the Sakim."

"I don't know yet that any of them will follow me," Roderic protested.

"Ah, but they will. The abbot has good news for you. Six of the most powerful lords are willing to throw their lots in with you."

He turned back to Maryana. "It would seem that this time, your king has gone too far in his greed. Between taxes on the people and carrying off everything they can, his overlords have finally lit a fire beneath your people."

"But what about the Innish king?" Maryana asked.

"If His Grace decides we will fight the Nerans, it will happen. The king follows his holy lead in such matters. But even acting alone, the duke could raise enough troops to send the Nerans home—which I suspect all but the officers would like, anyway—especially once winter sets in."

Maryana was feeling increasingly uneasy. She hadn't realized just how much depended on her being able to persuade her great-uncle to fight.

"Well," said Brien, turning his attention now to the stallion, "let's see if we can persuade our friend here to come onto the boat."

He pulled a length of cloth from his coat and handed it to Roderic, who began to lead the stallion along the pier, talking to him quietly and stroking him gently. Brien and Maryana picked up their belongings and followed some distance behind.

"I hope he can get Basra onto the boat, because he'll never leave him," Brien said.

Maryana could see that the animal was already nervous, but he continued to walk toward the end of the pier. The men on the boat had lowered a gangplank and were waiting at the rail to assist.

When they reached the end of the pier, Roderic

took the length of cloth and tied it around the stallion's eyes. Maryana could hear the stallion whicker, but he didn't resist. She and Brien stopped some distance away to watch.

Maryana couldn't hear Roderic's words, but she could see that he was talking to the horse as he began to lead him up the short gangplank. She held her breath, waiting. If the horse bolted now, both of them could end up in the water. She didn't even know if Roderic could swim, and she was afraid to ask Brien.

The stallion offered brief resistance, then allowed himself to be led up onto the deck. Maryana sighed with relief.

Brien laughed. "Did you doubt my cousin's powers of persuasion, milady?"

The hills and mountains and forests of Sakim gave way quickly to the broad, flat plains of the Innish lands, and Maryana felt a pang of homesickness because it reminded her of Neran.

Fortunately, the journey had been uneventful, no more difficult than her crossing of the straits, which now seemed so far in the past. But once again, a boat was carrying her to an uncertain future.

She turned away from the rail to watch Roderic as he stood beside his stallion. The animal was behaving far better than she would have expected, and she smiled, recalling Brien's teasing remark about Roderic's charms.

This journey was far better than the previous one, she thought, regardless of its outcome. Now she had Roderic, though no sooner did she think that than she began to ache with loneliness over their coming separation.

Roderic would, of course, be staying with his cousin—but she would have to go to the ducal palace. The Innish were much like the Nerans in their rigid social rules, and it would be unseemly, to say the least, for her to be living with Roderic.

Neither could she marry him until her uncle gave permission, and so they would be forced to separate for a time. Frustration boiled up in her, and then she shook her head and laughed. She, who had once believed the Sakims to be primitive savages, was now wishing that her own people could be more like them.

The requirement that her uncle give his permission lent still more urgency to her need to persuade the duke to fight her people. Her uncle would never permit her to marry Roderic unless the king were defeated and in no position to give the baron any trouble over it.

She joined Roderic and Basra and stroked the animal's gleaming gray withers. "I wish we didn't have to be separated," she said, already fighting back tears.

"Oh? Have you grown that fond of Basra, then?"

She managed a smile, but Roderic saw the tears leaking from her eyes and wiped them away gently. "We won't have to be apart for long—and perhaps not at all."

"What do you mean?" she asked, daring to let her hopes rise.

"I will say nothing more until I know for certain, but there may be a place where we can meet."

"But how will I get away? The duke will never—"

"The baron didn't, either—but that didn't stop you."

"I wasn't trying to persuade my uncle to do anything."

"You were trying to persuade him to let you manage your own estate," he reminded her.

"That's true—but this is even more important."

"We could always marry, you know—without the baron's permission. The abbot would be delighted to perform the ceremony."

"The duke would not like that," she pointed out. "The Innish are much like my own people."

"Unfortunately." His dark eyes gleamed with love. "I feel as though we are already wed, my love—married within that stone circle."

They hadn't spoken of that night, but his words brought back the memory, flooding her mind with the low chants and the glowing stones.

She nodded. They were married by a power far older and greater than Neran laws—or even the rules of the Church.

"Well, my dear niece, what am I to think?" The duke paused briefly to favor Maryana with raised white brows, then went on, obviously not yet ready to hear her response.

"As I understand it, you have refused to marry the man selected for you by your uncle and guardian, and then you cooperated in your kidnapping by a Sakim lord who seems to have acquired the title of Prince of Thieves. Very noble-sounding, that."

He paused again, nodding to himself. But Maryana had seen the twinkle in his eyes that belied his gruff tones, and she began to relax a bit.

"Now you have deposited yourselves on the doorsteps of your Innish relations, while your king has mounted a search for the two of you. Does that bring me up-to-date?"

Maryana smiled. Seeing him again had brought back a flood of memories. She was delighted to find him much as she remembered him from childhood. In fact, other than his hair having become white, he seemed little changed from the man she remembered.

"Yes, it does, Uncle, except for one thing. I intend to marry Lord Roderic."

"Ahh, I see. You wish to become the Princess of Thieves, then?"

"That may be more appropriate than you know, Uncle. I *did* help Lord Roderic steal from my uncle."

"Well, then, I look forward to meeting this Sakim lord—all the more so since it appears that he has somehow managed to unite his fellow Sakims: a prodigious feat indeed, and one that gives me some pause."

"What do you mean?"

"The Sakims, as you know, have never united behind a single leader, which for us has meant a degree of safety."

"But the Sakims would never fight the Innish," she protested.

"Never is a very strong word, my dear—and not one to be used lightly."

"Roderic wants only to drive the Nerans from his lands. He has no desire to become king."

The duke nodded. "That is a wise decision on his part, then, since the nature of the Sakims is such that he would surely have to wage war incessantly to keep his kingdom together." Then he shook his head. "The Sakims are a strange people—admirable in many ways, but strange, nonetheless. Tell me about this Roderic Hode."

For a moment Maryana was tongue-tied. No one had asked her to put into words what she felt and saw in him, and she sensed that her answer could be very important.

"He *is* a strange man in many ways, Uncle. For a time I believed him to be something of a coward, and perhaps lazy as well. And there were times when I despaired of ever seeing him be serious. But now I know different.

"He can take a very long time to make up his mind, but when he does, he will not stop until he has achieved his goal. And I no longer doubt his bravery. He is also as committed to his people as I am—which is why I couldn't marry that sycophantic Miles Foulane."

"How so?"

"Miles has virtually destroyed his family's estates, by taking from them and returning nothing. I could not let that happen to Chamoney."

Then, suddenly dredging up from her memory the fact that the duke was a great lover of horses, she told him about Roderic's determination not to abandon his stallion. "If he hadn't been able to coax Basra onto the boat, he would have risked his life to go back through the pass and make his way here through the Neran army."

"I must see this noble beast, then," the duke said. "The Sakims have always had fine horses. I've bought from them in the past.

"So what are your plans now, my dear? You are, of course, welcome to stay here as long as you like, but I suspect that isn't your plan."

Maryana took a deep breath. "No, Uncle. My plan is to persuade you to help Roderic drive the Nerans out of Sakim."

He arched a brow. "You would turn against your own people?"

"No. I have not turned against the people. It is the king I renounce. He is an evil, greedy man, and when he has taken everything from the Sakims, you may be sure he will cast his eyes south, since there is far more to take *here*."

"I see. So you believe that we will have to fight him sooner or later?"

"Yes, and if it's later, you might not have the Sakims to help, since they will have nothing left.

"The Sakims would fight even then—but I take your point. I will confess that neither His Majesty nor I are much pleased with your king, but as you must know, we Innish are inclined to avoid war at nearly any cost. War is very bad for trade."

Maryana had known all along that that was the

biggest problem. The Innish were a wealthy people—far richer than either her own people or the Sakims. And their wealth derived from trade. Almost the entire population of the kingdom lived along the coast—unlike the Sakims who preferred their hills and valleys—and they traded with all their neighbors, enriching themselves greatly in the process.

"Well, I will keep an open mind on the matter for now," the duke said finally. "Lord Brien and Lord Roderic will be coming to dinner on the morrow, and we will discuss it further."

Maryana thanked him and curtsied—rather clumsily, since she'd been long out of practice. Then she left the duke's salon, trying to feel hopeful. At least he hadn't said no outright, although that could simply have been to spare her feelings.

The duke's palace rivaled even that of her spendthrift king in both size and splendor, but there the comparisons ended. Her uncle had not gained all this at the expense of his people, because they, too, lived well.

It was good, she thought, that both her uncle and apparently the Innish king shared her feelings about her own king. She hadn't been certain that would be the case.

Then, as she reviewed what she had said, she wondered if she'd been *too* honest about Roderic. She had no idea how he would behave toward her uncle, and she'd wanted to let him know that Roderic was not as frivolous as he could seem at times.

How she missed him, frivolous or not. They'd been apart for only a day and a half, but it seemed an eternity—and yet another eternity until tomorrow night.

Hoping that Roderic would make good on his promise to find a place where they could meet, she'd already undertaken to figure out how she could sneak out of the palace. But it seemed impossible. She could scarcely take a step without one servant or another inquiring if she required some sort of assistance. She could scarcely move without stumbling over them, and getting to the stable seemed an impossible task. Besides, even if she could manage that, the stable would undoubtedly be filled with even more of them.

She sighed, then set off to the duchess's quarters. Her great-aunt was in failing health, but still eager to spend time with her grandniece, whose gold and black hair would surely not fail to bring laughter to her lips.

Fortunately, though, the current fashion among Innish noblewomen was to cover the head with beaded and jeweled caps that were tied beneath the chin, so she wouldn't have to embarrass her relatives at dinner tomorrow night.

Maryana supposed that she should have guessed that dinner here meant far more than the mere taking of a meal together, and that the guest list would include every Innish noble within a day's travel—not to mention the crown prince and his wife, the princess.

Her gaze traveled over the glittering assemblage, stopping only when it fell on Roderic, who was seated near one end of the very long table, next to the crown prince. Maryana was irritated to be so far from him, but she suspected that her uncle might have decided to put the two men together without the distraction of her presence.

She glanced down at the gorgeous gown that her cousin had lent her and smiled, thinking about the transformation. It was enough to make her wonder just who she was: Neran noblewoman or Sakim peasant boy?

But Roderic had been transformed as well, thanks, no doubt, to Brien's wardrobe. The splendid clothes might be Innish, but the dark good looks were all Sakim—and being noticed by several of the women present.

But Maryana had no jealousy within her. She had to do no more than meet Roderic's eyes to know that he didn't even see them. In fact, along with the love she saw there, she also saw his amusement. His thoughts were undoubtedly the same as hers: comparing the two ragged, dirty people they'd been only days ago to the elegant man and woman they were now.

The dinner progressed with stifling slowness as course after course was brought in and taken away. After weeks of little to eat—and simple food at that—Maryana was unaccustomed to such a surfeit and could eat only a small portion of what she was served, however delicious it might be.

Her uncle's cook was undoubtedly Neran, since the dishes being served were very familiar to her. Just as the Innish were known for their boats and their trading, the Nerans were celebrated for their food and wines. In fact, it was quite likely that the wines being served this night had come from the vineyards at Chamoney. They regularly shipped wines to the duke and to the king and other members of the Innish nobility.

Even as she carried on a meaningless conversation with her cousin, who was seated across from her, Maryana watched Roderic and the crown prince. She couldn't hear their conversation, of course, but it seemed quite spirited.

Then she glanced toward the other end of the table, where her uncle was talking to the princess, while her cousin's husband, the baron, seemed to be watching Roderic and the crown prince—and not happily, either.

"You must visit us, Maryana," her cousin was saying. "It's not far, and you can meet the children. Perhaps you could bring Lord Roderic as well. My husband is quite curious about him. Is it true that he's being called the Prince of Thieves?"

Maryana noticed that everyone within hearing distance had suddenly become silent. It amused her that the silly name had reached so many ears.

"Yes, it is," she replied. "He stole from my uncle, who was collecting the king's taxes, and returned the money to his people—who certainly have more need of it than the king did."

She ignored the shocked looks on the faces turned to her. "The harvest was very poor this year, and Roderic's people would have starved if he hadn't helped them."

"Very admirable," pronounced an older man whose name she couldn't recall: the Earl of something. "And with all due respect to you as a Neran yourself, my dear, you're quite right about your king. A very different man from his father."

As night is from day, she thought. She could not remember the previous king, who'd died when she was but a baby, but she'd heard her father speak of him often enough.

"I take no offense, milord," she responded. "As it happens, I agree with you."

"Still," intoned the nobleman next to him, "one cannot encourage such behavior—even when it may be justified."

But the elderly earl shot him a withering look. "You know as well as I do, milord, that the Sakim are a law unto themselves—and always have been. They measure a man by his deeds—not his birthright."

Properly chastened—and no doubt outranked— the other man nodded quickly. "Of course, milord. The Sakims are indeed an admirable people."

Maryana was beginning to suspect that Roderic wasn't the only one whose seating at the table was quite deliberate. She sensed an ally in this Innish earl—and perhaps a powerful one at that. She wished that she'd paid more attention when she'd been introduced to him.

"It is my considered belief that the Neran king will not stop at subjugating the Sakims—which he isn't likely to do for long anyway, if history is any guide. I believe that he will soon turn his attention to *us*."

Total silence greeted the earl's statement, broken only by gasps from the women present. Then a younger man seated to her left spoke.

"But we've never had trouble with the Nerans. Surely you can't mean they would attack us?"

"That is exactly what I mean," the earl stated succinctly, then leveled his pale gaze on Maryana. "Tell me, milady, do *you* think your king is capable of making war on us?"

Maryana was flattered by his interest in her opinion. No Neran lord would have made such an inquiry of a woman, but she knew that the Innish were different. Not long ago—within her lifetime—they'd been ruled by a powerful queen, the mother of the present king—and it was said that the present queen exerted great power over affairs of state as well.

"I believe you are right, milord. The king's greed knows no bounds, and the Innish are a wealthy people—far richer than the Sakims."

What followed was a discussion between several of the men about what should be done to prevent this from happening. Maryana glanced down the table at her uncle, the duke, and saw him watching her with interest. In fact, she would have sworn that she saw him actually wink at her. So he *had* planned this seating.

At the other end of the table, the crown prince and Roderic were deep in conversation, heads bent close, as the others within hearing remained silent and listened.

Finally, the long dinner ended. The duchess,

who had joined them at the table, retired to her quarters, leaving Maryana's cousin to assume the role of hostess to the ladies as they withdrew to the elegant ladies' drawing room. The men remained in the dining room, clustering together over Neran brandy. Maryana caught Roderic's eye, but nothing more, as she left with her cousin and the other women.

She found it difficult to take part in the conversation as the women talked of fashions and children and court gossip. Only a fear of embarrassing her cousin prevented her from describing in detail just what fashions *she'd* been wearing of late.

There were many questions for her and comments about the handsome Sakim lord with whom she seemed to have some sort of connection. Being highborn ladies all, they were very discreet, but it became apparent to Maryana that some stories were circulating about how it was that she had come to be here.

Her responses were guarded, but carefully calculated to titillate and provide grist for more conversation later. Part of this was pure deviltry on her part, but it was also intended to present Roderic in the best possible light. She had no way of knowing which of these women might have some influence over their husbands' decisions.

But she longed to be back in the dining room, pleading Roderic's cause—which, of course, was her cause as well. It seemed possible—even likely—that if the Innish allied themselves with Roderic and the Sakims, her king might give up without a battle and withdraw to Neran soil with such booty as he'd already claimed.

Never very womanly in the sense it was usually meant, Maryana now found herself even less so. She had nothing at all in common with these women, as she'd had little in common with other Neran ladies.

When she knew that she could stand no more of their chatter, she rose and excused herself, saying that she needed to partake of the night air and would go for a stroll in the gardens. Lurking within was the hope that Roderic might join her, but she knew that was unlikely at best.

Once outside, she could hear the murmur of men's voices coming from the great dining room, where doors were open to the soft evening air. For a moment, she considered stealing closer to hear what was being said, but she quickly discarded that notion. Much light was spilling out from the room, and some men were standing quite close to the doors.

Instead, she walked deeper into the gardens, drawing about her the fine wool shawl that her cousin had lent her. The voices faded behind her, replaced by the tinkling and gurgling of the water in the many fountains scattered about the acres of gardens.

She felt a sharp pang of longing for Chamoney as she listened to the musical sounds. There was a great stone fountain and pool in front of her home there. Each night she'd fallen asleep listening to it, then awakened to hear it again.

Tears spilled onto her cheeks as she thought about her lovely home and what would become of it if the king had his way with it. Every time he'd visited Chamoney, she'd seen the greed in his eyes, though it was certainly less lavish than his own palaces. Once, he'd even remarked what a perfect country home it would make. And now she'd given him more than enough reason to seize it.

She stopped before one of the fountains, where water spouted from urns held aloft by stone cherubs. But her mind was on different stones: the great megaliths on the hill at the Sakim—Innish border where she and Roderic had been touched by magic. Where they'd made love for the first time. Where a dream and reality had merged.

It was hard for her to believe in that magic now, though she couldn't quite let go of it, either. Still, magic could not keep them together, despite the old legends. They had to make their own magic—which right now consisted of persuading the Innish to help them.

"On the whole, I think I prefer the dark-skinned, black-haired page, though the fine lady here now is a pleasant substitute."

Maryana whirled around so fast that she stumbled, and would have fallen into the pool had not Roderic reached out to save her. And having caught her in his arms, he didn't let go.

"I didn't think you'd come," she said rather breathlessly, still not quite able to accept his having materialized before her.

"I thought it wise to withdraw for a time, to let our host plead my case in his own way. And, of course, I was also hoping that you might have tired of the company of the ladies."

She laughed. "I grew tired of that within minutes. Do you think me a misfit, Roderic?"

"Of course—and so am I. We are both playacting in our finery."

"You look very handsome," she said. "All the ladies are quite taken with you: the savage Sakim lord who is called the Prince of Thieves."

Roderic laughed, his breath fanning warmly against her as he continued to hold her close. "If I ever find out who started using that name, he's going to be sorry."

"On the contrary, it gives you a certain distinction. There was an elderly earl seated across from me who quite liked what you did."

Roderic arched a dark brow. "Do you know who that elderly earl is?"

"No, but I gathered that he might be important."

"He is the father of the queen, and still, even in

his dotage, a trusted adviser to the king."

"Well, you seem to have learned quite a lot about the Innish court in a very brief time."

"Necessity is a great goad to learning. With him and your uncle on my side, I'm daring to hope that we'll succeed."

"It seems that you're playing this game very well, Roderic," she stated, drawing back in the circle of his arms to give him an appreciative look.

"I've spent enough time with the Innish to have rubbed off a bit of my Sakim savagery," he replied with a wicked smile. "My mother insisted upon my coming here regularly."

"Still, I think I prefer the Sakim savage."

"Do you, now?" he asked with an arched brow. "Were I the savage you apparently believe me to be, I would ravish you right here and now."

But instead, he apparently decided to content himself with nothing more than a kiss—though with Roderic, any kiss was more than a kiss. Mary-ana felt herself melting into him—and yearning to be joined by more than two eager sets of lips and two questing tongues.

"Neran brandy is said to muddle a man's mind—but you do more than that for me," he murmured when he'd lifted his mouth from hers. "With you, I forget everything—because I *have* everything."

"I love you, Roderic—as I thought I could love no man." She raised her hand to his face and traced the strong outline of his jaw. "But how are we to be together?"

"Ah," he said, taking her hand and kissing each fingertip in turn. "I have solved that problem—for the present, anyway. I've found a place, and in a few days you will receive an invitation to spend a day—and a night—at the home of Brien's sister and her husband. Since Brien isn't married and there's no lady in the household, we had to find another place for the sake of propriety."

He shook his head. "These Innish and their rules. I think I prefer being a savage."

Maryana laughed. "My people are the same as the Innish, and I think I prefer being a 'savage' as well."

"So you are," he said, kissing her again. "My beautiful savage lady."

Chapter Thirteen

"This man your uncle chose as a husband for you—did you say that his name was Foulane?"

"Yes." Maryana wondered why the duke had summoned her to ask her about Miles. She'd feared that he might intend to question her about the invitation to visit with Brien's sister and her husband, the invitation undoubtedly having been passed along to him through the duchess.

"Well, then it would seem that he intends to press his suit," the duke said, clasping his hands behind his back as he paced about the room. "He has requested a meeting with me at my earliest convenience."

"What? Miles is *here?*" In her shock, Maryana lost all sense of decorum, drawing an arched brow from her uncle, who, up to this point, at least, had been kinder to her than she'd expected.

"So it would seem. I understand that he is staying with family friends in the area. Possibly he has decided that *I* am your guardian now."

271

"But you're *not!*" she cried, having decided that it was too late to adopt a new manner now.

"And so I will tell him," the duke acknowledged. "But your invitation to visit the Townshens for a few days is very convenient. I will put him off until after you have gone, and then I can say in all honesty that you are not under my roof."

"Thank you," Maryana said with considerable relief.

"It is possible that he comes also as an unofficial emissary of your king, to try to find out if we Innish have any intention of allying ourselves with the Sakims."

"Yes, that's quite likely. The king is very fond of Miles, who expends much effort cultivating that affection."

She wanted desperately to ask if the duke had reached any decision, but she knew he wouldn't tell her until he had discussed the matter with the king and his other advisers.

"Hmmpphh!" the duke responded before resuming his pacing. "It seems that the cold wind that blows down from the Sakim mountains is blowing up quite a storm this time. Since I assume that, during your visit, you will have occasion to see Lord Roderic, you may tell him for me that His Royal Highness, the crown prince, was much impressed with him—as was the Earl of Cosenry, who just happens to be the father of Her Majesty, the queen.

"The earl found you to be quite interesting as well," the duke finished with a twinkle in his pale eyes. "But I am finding myself beset with questions about your relationship with Lord Roderic."

"I am sorry to be causing you such trouble, Uncle," Maryana said sincerely.

He waved a hand in dismissal. "Your arrival has served to make me realize just how dull my life has been of late." He chuckled, then grew serious once again.

"You must also warn Lord Roderic that there could be problems if this Miles Foulane has arrived with a request to the king from his king that Lord Roderic be turned over to him as an escaped criminal."

Maryana gasped. "Is that likely? Would the king honor such a request?"

"He may feel that he has no choice. Such requests have always been honored in the past, and I've no doubt that Miles Foulane has found out where Lord Roderic is."

Maryana sat in the carriage that had been sent by her unknown hosts to fetch her, thinking about what her uncle had said. It was true that, regardless of his feelings, the Innish king would be unable to disregard a request to turn Roderic over. By law, he was a criminal, and the Innish were very big on obeying laws, as were her own people.

She also knew that it was likely that Miles had found out where Roderic was staying, and that he would find him soon enough at the home of Brien's sister and her husband.

They would have to flee—go into hiding somewhere. But that would prevent Roderic from being able to make his case to the Innish king, should he be given an opportunity to do so.

She clenched her fists in frustration, recalling that day in the chapel, when Roderic might well have killed Miles if she'd responded differently to his question. She should have lied then, and Miles wouldn't be causing them problems now.

But if it wasn't Miles, it would probably be someone else, making the same demand that Roderic be sent back to Sakim in chains. The king had obviously guessed Roderic's plan and was trying to thwart it. And he might well succeed.

Baron Townshen's home was far less grand than her uncle's palace, but still quite a handsome home, nestled as it was at the edge of what appeared to be a great forest. She was received by her hosts with much friendliness and shown to a pleasant room to refresh herself. But the bag she had brought with her borrowed clothing—and also her less reputable wardrobe—was not sent up. She'd packed those other things herself, on the chance that she and Roderic might be forced to flee.

When she returned to the drawing room, hoping to find Roderic there, she found Brien instead, visiting with his sister and her husband. He greeted her with a rather rakish bow and grin.

"Your escort awaits, milady," he said.

Confused, Maryana looked around, thinking he was referring to Roderic. But Brien only laughed.

"I meant me. I have it on good authority that you possess suitable clothing for riding into the mountains. Did you by chance bring them with you?"

"Yes, but . . ." Now she was *really* confused. Had the Innish king ordered that Roderic be turned over to Brien? Could such a thing have happened so quickly? And where *was* Roderic?

It was Brien's sister who took pity on her confusion. "Cousin Roderic has told us that you wish to be married, but cannot do so without your guardian's approval. So we agreed to act as your hosts while you spend some time together."

"My wife is an incurable romantic," the baron said affectionately. "And I am as porridge in her hands. There is an old stone cottage high in the mountains at the edge of my father's lands that we use for hunting expeditions, and I have been persuaded to turn it over temporarily to Lord Roderic."

Maryana by now had tears in her eyes as she stared from one to the other of those strangers.

How kind they were. "Thank you," she murmured. "I only hope that I can repay you one day."

The baron smiled. "A case of the wonderful wines of Chamoney will be payment enough— once you have reclaimed your estate."

"It's a good thing, then, that we found such a secluded place," Brien said, after listening to her repeat what her uncle had said about Roderic.

"Yes—if it can be kept secret."

"Don't worry. I'll tell them no one must know where he is. But this will make it difficult for Roderic to press his case before the king—which may be just what this Miles Foulane intends.

"Still," he went on as they rode through the forest, deeper into the mountains, "At least he had the opportunity to speak to the duke and the crown prince and the others. I think in the end, the king will decide that an alliance with the Sakims now will prevent trouble with the Nerans later."

A short time later, Brien stopped in a clearing and looked around. "This is where we're to meet Roderic. I thought he'd be here, eagerly awaiting your arrival."

Maryana had only a few seconds to worry that somehow he'd been captured, when suddenly he *was* there, landing with a flourish at her feet, then releasing the vine that had brought him there.

Maryana was too busy stifling a scream that had welled up before she saw who it was, but Brien was laughing uproariously.

"Still the Sakim savage, I see—despite my attempt to dress you up properly."

"The Prince of Thieves, at your disposal, milady," Roderic said, ignoring his friend's jibes and sweeping her an elaborate bow.

Maryana looked at the thick, ropy vine that trailed behind him. "I think I might like to try that myself sometime."

Saranne Dawson

Brien groaned loudly. "*Two* savages—well suited to each other. 'Tis a good thing the duke isn't here to see this—not to mention the crown prince and all the others you so impressed."

Then he turned serious, asking Maryana to repeat to Roderic what she'd told him. Giddy with happiness at seeing him again and already eager to get to their temporary refuge, she did so reluctantly.

The laughter left Roderic's face as she told him about Miles and the request he might make to allow him to be taken back to Sakim in chains.

"I should have killed him when I had the chance," Roderic said, his hand going unconsciously to his long knife.

Maryana, who had seen so many quick changes in this man she loved, now saw yet another. In the space of a few seconds, he'd gone from carefree lover to would-be killer.

"If he makes the request, I will find out and come to tell you," Brien said. "But in the meantime, you should be safe enough here."

"It's lovely," she said as the stone cottage came into view. In truth, it was larger than a mere cottage, and was set against a backdrop of thick forest with a small stream flowing near its door. Smoke curled from the chimney. Roderic had told her that he'd come out earlier to bring supplies and to prepare the place for them.

He helped her dismount, then held her close. "All I could think of since I arrived here is making love to you in a proper bed. And from now on, not one word about that accursed Miles Foulane and his damnable requests. This is *our* time—and I mean to take it."

And so they did. A day and a night and another day and night passed in the kind of bliss that allows one moment to melt into another. They

276

talked, they ate, they made love—often at odd hours and not always in bed.

Maryana let go of the few remaining inhibitions she had clung to, and Roderic seized the opportunity to teach her the many ways a man and woman can please each other.

She came to a new awareness of her body and took delight in it—and in the power she had over him. From a woman who had been uncertain about his love for her, she became instead one who was supremely confident of being loved and cherished. Naked, with his dark eyes feasting on her, Maryana would feel voluptuous, with every fiber of her being filled with a sensuality that was ripe and overflowing.

They would lie for hours, simply stroking each other, sometimes talking, but other times silent except for the small sounds that each of them understood implicitly. It seemed to Maryana that they had passed beyond the need for words—or that they'd found a language all their own.

Thoughts of the future intruded only occasionally—and then it was of a distant future, beyond their present problems, when they traveled back and forth from his lands to hers, trading the dark forests and narrow ravines of Sakim for the wide pastures and rolling hills of Neran.

So completely had they shut out the present beyond their forest refuge that when it suddenly intruded upon them, Maryana could not quite believe it at first.

Roderic was inside the cottage, sleeping after a long lovemaking session. But Maryana was restless, filled with joy and a surfeit of pleasure. So she dressed and went outside to enjoy what surely must be nearly the last of the warm days. Even here in the Innish hills, winter could not be very far away, though Roderic had said that it was much gentler here than in Sakim—perhaps more like the winters of Neran.

Still half-lost in the beauty of their lovemaking, she was at first stunned when she saw the riders approaching. The narrow road that led up to the cottage climbed steeply for some distance before leveling off a few hundred yards from the cottage door.

She saw the first two riders appear over the crest and froze, not frightened at first because her mind hadn't yet grasped the import of their appearance. Neither did she immediately recognize either of the two men. But then, in one terrible instant, she saw who one of them was—and at the same time, saw the others who were following them.

She was at a point halfway between them and the cottage, and she started to run, her heart suddenly pounding in her throat. But before she could reach the cottage, they had surrounded her, drawing their mounts in tightly to prevent her escape.

"Are you not pleased to see me, milady?" Miles said with a sneer in his voice and on his face. "I would think that a kidnapped bride would be pleased to be rescued by her groom."

"I'm not your bride, Miles!" Unable to move, Maryana stood her ground and glared at him. "And I wasn't kidnapped."

She had the presence of mind to raise her voice as much as possible, even though Miles was leaning down from his saddle and was only a few feet away. But would Roderic hear her—or was he too deep in a sated sleep?

"Of course you were. You were kidnapped by a Sakim savage who is a criminal wanted by Baron DeLay. Where is he?"

"He's not here. He's out hunting. This is Innish land, Miles, and you cannot capture him here."

He gave her an evil smile. "But that is exactly

what we will do. It would be most unfortunate if he tries to resist arrest."

Miles dismounted and seized both her arms. "Look inside for him. She may be lying."

"Roderic!" she screamed, trying to free herself from Miles's grasp.

But the men were already running toward the cottage, and there was nothing she could do but wait in agony, certain they would find him there, helpless in bed, his knife and bow discarded.

"He's unarmed, Miles. If they kill him, I will see to it that you pay dearly."

Miles merely laughed. "And how will you do that? The king has already issued a decree of forfeit for your beloved Chamoney, and when he learns of your treachery, you will be sent off to spend the remainder of your days in a convent."

"What treachery? How could running away from the likes of you be treachery?"

But her question went unanswered as the men reappeared. "He's not here, milord," one of them called. "And we found no weapons, either. He must have heard us and escaped."

Miles's face darkened briefly, but then he smiled again. "There is no need to look for him. If we take her, he will find us."

Then one of the other men appeared from behind the cottage and announced that there was only one horse in the small stable. Miles ordered him to bring it around, then pushed her before him into the cottage.

He stepped inside the door and looked around, his gaze stopping as it fell on the rumpled bed in the corner. He whirled around and struck her hard across the face.

"Whore! You have disgraced Neran womanhood!"

Maryana staggered back under the blow, then put up a hand to touch her injured cheek. She hated Miles, but until this moment she would not have guessed that he could hate her.

He grabbed her hand and peered at the ring Roderic had given her. "What is this? *He* gave it to you, didn't he?"

And before she could respond, he wrenched the ring from her finger, then examined it before slipping it into a pocket. "Very nice. It should fetch a pretty price when I return to Neran. It seems that your uncle wasn't very diligent in collecting valuables, either."

Maryana said nothing. She saw the dangerous light in his eyes, a gleam of pure hatred, and she knew he was close to madness.

"Pack your things. Then we can bait the trap that will yield us your Sakim savage."

She did as she'd been told, while he paced around the cottage, stopping several times near the bed. It made her sick to see him staring at the scene of their lovemaking, but she kept quiet. Instead, she found her dagger and slipped it into the pocket of the dress she wore. It couldn't offer her protection against a whole group of men, but it afforded her some protection against Miles.

Then he led her back outside again, where he handed over her bag to one of the men. "Bring her horse along, but I'll keep her with me."

She was hauled awkwardly up into the saddle, seated crosswise in front of him, and they set off. Any hope she might have had of escaping on her own horse was now gone.

"Keep a sharp eye out for the Sakim!" Miles ordered as they started down the narrow road. "He won't have gone far."

Maryana knew he was right. Roderic had awakened in time to get away—but he would never abandon her. Still, she took little comfort in that because despite his remark about one Sakim being worth many Nerans, she didn't see how he could hope to rescue her from a band of six armed men.

Her helplessness made her angry, and she thought about the dagger in her pocket. How satisfying it would be to kill Miles—but could she do it? In any event, it was a question that didn't require an answer now, since they were surrounded by his men, Neran guards who were not wearing their uniforms.

Miles clearly hadn't gotten the Innish king's permission to seize Roderic and her. Instead, he'd acted on his own, which was why Brien hadn't been able to warn them. Now, he undoubtedly was planning to take her back to her uncle—and to kill Roderic if he tried to prevent that.

A part of her wanted Roderic to stay away—for his own safety. Her life, at least, was not at risk. But another part of her wanted him to rescue her, regardless of the danger. Love, she thought, can make one selfish even as it also makes one selfless and giving.

On they rode through the forest, down out of the mountains. For a time, Maryana expected Roderic to appear at any moment. But when he didn't, she didn't give up hope. Instead, she tried to put herself into his position. What would she do? When would she strike out?

After dark seemed to be the obvious time—but it would also be obvious to Miles, and he would take care to post guards. Would Roderic wait, then, until Miles was certain he wouldn't appear?

Yes, she thought, that is exactly what *I* would do in his place. Sooner or later, Miles and his men would assume that Roderic had chosen to save himself and had left her behind. Then they would be less watchful, less careful.

She smiled to herself, thinking about the advantage their love gave her. Miles, selfish, greedy man that he was, would easily believe that Roderic had abandoned her.

They reached the main road and turned north, toward the Sakim lands. Miles had remained so silent that she found it disconcerting. In the past, he'd always been overly fond of his own voice. Still, though she did truly fear this new Miles, she remained certain that he wouldn't try to harm her—and certainly not in the presence of his men. They couldn't like him much more than she did, and in any event, it was Miles's nature not to trust anyone. Besides, she was, whatever he might choose to call her, still a Neran noblewoman.

"Don't try to cry for help," Miles said now, his voice close to her ear. "If you do, we'll kill anyone who tries to help you."

Maryana had seen a family approaching in a large, heavily laden wagon. But she'd already decided against seeking their help. It would be pointless. They had no weapons that she could see, and all of Miles's men were heavily armed.

During the next hour, they passed several other travelers, but she made no attempt to gain their assistance. Then Miles called a halt, and when they had stopped, told her that she could ride her own horse, so they could make better time.

"Your Sakim scum has abandoned you," he said with the sneer that now seemed to be permanently in place. "He has used you and abandoned you."

Maryana said nothing. She even contrived to look dispirited, as though agreeing with his words.

They rode faster now, with Maryana safely in their midst, so that escape was impossible. And they continued this way until darkness forced them to stop at a well-used campsite that was empty this night.

Once again, any thoughts she might have had of bringing about her own escape were ended by Miles's action. When they settled down for the night, he bound her feet together with ropes. She guessed that he didn't quite believe her passive, dispirited behavior. He did, after all, know her rather well.

At least, she thought as she lay in the darkness listening to the men around her snore, he no longer wants my body—if in fact he ever did. Miles, she thought, was a passionate man—but his passion was for power and gold, not for a woman.

When morning came and they set off again, Miles was exuberant. "We've seen the last of that Sakim scum," he declared to his men. "No doubt he's returned to the Innish to try to persuade them to take up his cause."

"And they will do that, Miles," she said before she could stop herself. "You have won a battle— but you will lose the war."

Anger turned his fair skin to a dark and ugly purple. He raised his hand to her, then let it drop, and she knew that if the others hadn't been there, he would have struck her again.

"Quiet!" he shouted. "You're a traitor—and you will pay for that. His Majesty will be told of your attempts to foment trouble between the Innish and us. But it won't work. The Innish would never take up arms against us."

This time she kept quiet, fearing that he was again close to the edge of madness.

The day wore on. They passed through several villages and small towns, separated by long stretches of open fields and forests. Then they began to pass by sheep farms: the source of celebrated Innish wool.

It was late in the day and Maryana was growing weary. Miles and his men rode carelessly, obviously tired themselves from a long day in the saddle.

Suddenly the road ahead of them was blocked by milling sheep, and as Miles cursed their bad luck, she saw that a fence had broken, allowing the animals to escape into the road. The farmer was just running toward the animals as they came to a halt, unable to proceed because of the blocked road and the fences on either side.

"Get these accursed animals out of the road, man!" Miles shouted.

"Sorry, milord. They broke the fence."

Maryana wondered where his sheepdogs were. She'd never seen a farmer without them, since they were intelligent creatures, far better able than a man himself was to control sheep.

It quickly began to seem that the more the farmer tried to move the flock, the more disorderly it became, until they were surrounded by a veritable sea of the woolly animals, all of them milling about and bleating nervously. Between Miles's cursing and the sheep, the horses became nervous, and they had all they could do to control their mounts. And then the first guard tumbled from his saddle!

At first, Maryana thought as the others apparently did that the man had simply lost control of his horse. She couldn't see him in the midst of all the sheep—but one of the men did.

"Ambush!" The guard cried—just before he too fell from his horse. And this time, Maryana saw the arrow protruding from his back.

"Roderic!" she murmured, holding tight to her horse's reins as she tried to find him.

The remaining men were shouting, the horses were whinnying in fear, and the sheep were bleating loudly, but in all that chaos, Maryana held on to the reins and searched for Roderic, knowing he was here and that all this had been staged.

They were all trapped in the midst of the animals, unable to escape the arrows that rained down upon them. Another man fell, mortally wounded, then another and another, none of them able to retaliate since they were too busy trying to control their horses to reach for their bows. And the farmer seemed to have vanished.

The other men had been seeking out the source of the arrows, but Miles was pushing his horse through the sheep toward her. Too late, she realized that he meant to save himself by using her as a sort of shield.

So she lost her chance to try to move away from him, and he reached her side and grabbed for her reins just as the last of his guards went down.

"Tell him to let me go!" Miles ordered, his face pale with fear. "Tell him he can't kill a Neran lord!"

Maryana stared at him, beyond loathing him now. He was pitiful in his cowardice as he huddled as close to her as he could get.

Then Roderic was coming toward her, riding his stallion across the field. As she watched, the animal leaped gracefully over the fence just beyond the flock of sheep, and Roderic came to a halt in the middle of the road. The farmer reappeared a moment later, this time with his dogs, who immediately began to round up the sheep.

A knife flashed in Miles's hand. "Let me go or I'll kill her!" he shouted, his voice high and thin.

Roderic didn't move. His longbow was once again slung across his shoulders and his knife was sheathed at his belt. As the dogs moved the sheep off the road, he urged his stallion closer until she could see the look of pure contempt on his handsome face.

"If she is harmed, you will die—slowly and painfully," Roderic said in a low, almost conversational tone that was all the more threatening for being completely lacking in menace. He even smiled.

Despite her pleasure at seeing him again, Maryana knew that what she would never forget about this moment was that smile and that calm, pleasant voice threatening a slow, painful death. It was a side of Roderic she didn't want to see.

Miles held the knife to her throat with one hand, while in the other, he continued to hold her horse's reins. For a long moment, none of them moved. Even the farmer was standing stock-still at the edge of his field.

Then Maryana decided that it was time she did something to aid her rescue. With one quick motion, she flung herself sideways and off the horse, leaving her mount to block any attempt by Miles to lunge at her with his knife.

She landed harder than she'd expected in the grassy ditch at the side of the road. When she struggled to her feet, she saw Miles riding off the way they had come. But instead of pursuing him, Roderic rode swiftly to her, dismounted, and pulled her into his arms.

"Are you all right?" he asked, his eyes searching her face carefully. Then, before she could respond, he touched her bruised cheek gently. "Did he do this?"

She nodded. "He slapped me—but that was all."

Roderic turned to stare down the road, where nothing remained of Miles Foulane except for a settling cloud of dust. "So once again, I have let him go."

Then the anger drained from his face and he smiled at her. "Tell me the truth now. Did you doubt that I would come?"

She laughed and shook her head. "Never! I even guessed that you would wait until they believed you to be long gone and became careless. But I didn't expect you to employ a flock of sheep!"

He chuckled. "Sheep love gold as much as anyone. A few coins and they thought it was a splendid idea."

Maryana laughed and he joined her, and they both saw the farmer watching them with an expression that suggested he considered them both to be mad.

But then her laughter died away as she stared at the bodies littering the road. "Are they all dead?" she asked.

Roderic nodded.

"You've killed six men, Roderic."

He studied her in silence for a moment. "I'm likely to be killing many more before this is over. It can't be helped, my love."

She nodded, trying to accept that. "But we can't just leave them here."

"I'll give the farmer some more gold and ask him to bury them. That's all I will do."

"Where are we going?" she asked as they mounted their horses.

"Back to the cottage for my things—and then back to Brien's. I don't want to leave until I have an answer from the Innish king."

"But what about Miles?"

"If I lay eyes on him again, I'll kill him."

Maryana said nothing, but a chill passed through her. No one hated Miles Foulane as much as she did, but his calm statement seemed to go beyond hatred. And she could not rid herself of the image of all those dead men, whose only mistake was to be led by Miles.

Tired, dirty, and hungry, they rode up the hillside to the cottage. They had stayed away from the road, just in case Miles had somehow managed to find replacements for his dead soldiers. Maryana had thought that Roderic would welcome the opportunity to confront Miles again, regardless of the odds. But rather to her surprise, he said that he had no desire to press his luck. She didn't know whether that signaled a change of heart in a man who seemed to relish having the odds against him—or, perhaps more likely, a desire to protect her.

As they approached the cottage, Maryana saw it in her mind's eye—and saw as well the cherished time they'd had there. She knew she had never been so happy as she had been those few days, and she wondered sadly if she would ever know such happiness again.

The brief warmth of her memories was shattered abruptly as they crested the hill and saw all the horses tied up in front of the cottage. There seemed to be at least twenty of them, and she reined in her horse sharply as icy terror crawled through her. Miles had found reinforcements—and plenty of them!

Roderic, however, continued on, then turned to beckon to her. She thought he must be mad! How else to explain the smile on his face as he rode toward what must be certain death?

But then, before he could speak, she understood. Unlike her, he must have recognized some of the horses. From the open door of the cottage, the abbot and Brien emerged, followed soon after by the rest of Roderic's men. She rode forward eagerly, now smiling herself. The sight of the rotund abbot alone was enough to make her temporarily forget her weariness and aches and pains.

Brien had his long knife drawn as he came out of the cottage, but now he put it away and ran to greet Roderic as he leaped off his stallion. The two men embraced with whoops of pleasure, and then Roderic hugged the abbot as well.

Maryana smiled, but remained on her horse, not at all certain that she could dismount without assistance. The abbot came over to her, his cherubic face filled with concern.

"Allow me to assist you, milady," he said, and proceeded to do so.

Roderic was already explaining what had happened, and when he had finished, Brien turned to her. "Are you unharmed, milady?"

She nodded, but her hand went unconsciously to the cheek that Miles had slapped, and when she raised her hand, more pain shot through the shoulder she'd injured when she fell into the ditch. She winced, but insisted that she was just fine. Roderic stared at her, frowning, but said nothing.

"Word reached me—too late, as it turned out—that Foulane might try something like this," Brien said disgustedly. "So we came here to help you—only to learn that we were too late."

"Did he go to the king?" Roderic asked, still watching her with an unreadable expression.

Brien nodded. "He did—and the king temporized. The duke had already spoken with him and apprised him of the situation. But if Foulane had been more patient, I think the king might have felt compelled to give in—at least as far as you're concerned, Roderic.

"Maryana would have been safe, of course, because she's under the duke's protection. The king would never have allowed him to take her."

"I must have an audience with the king as soon as possible," Roderic stated.

"I doubt that's possible, cousin," Brien replied. "Foulane will undoubtedly seek that himself, and press the king for a response now that his scheme failed. Don't forget that he *is* an official emissary of the Neran king, however contemptible he may be. The king will not want the embarrassment of granting you an audience under the circumstances."

He paused and his gaze encompassed both Roderic and Maryana. "You must go to the duke, and rely on him to press your suit with the king. He is on your side."

"Are you certain of that?" Roderic asked.

"He had not actually said so, but yes, that is my impression. The abbot and your men can stay here, out of sight, and the two of you can return with me to refresh yourselves before visiting the duke."

"No!" Maryana said firmly, drawing all eyes to her. "We will go directly to my uncle!"

"But milady, if you'll pardon my saying so, your present state—"

Maryana cut him off. "That's exactly why we'll go as we are. My uncle needs to see how desperate we are. I am tired of wearing finery and speaking in careful words. I want my uncle to see the truth of it!"

Roderic began to grin, and after looking from her to him, Brien laughed. "By God, Roderic, you've turned her into a Sakim!"

The others all began to laugh as well, and Maryana finally joined in. There was some truth to Brien's teasing words. While she'd never exactly been a shining example of Neran womanhood, she had generally tried to act the part, saving her true nature for the running of Chamoney.

"I think that I cannot claim that credit," Roderic said after the laughter had died away. "Maryana is Maryana—unique in the world."

"I will second that," said the abbot with a smile, "since I played some small part in setting her upon this journey. She may be Neran by birth—but she is a Sakim at heart."

There were smiles and nods from all the men, and for the first time Maryana truly felt herself to be one of them. "And I am proud of that," she said to one and all.

"Have you found it necessary to be more manly than a man, my love?"

Maryana stopped in the act of feeding herself and frowned at him. "What do you mean?" she asked after she had swallowed.

"You told me that you weren't injured when you threw yourself off the horse. But you were, weren't you?"

"It wasn't bad—and I didn't really feel the pain until later."

"Nevertheless, you *were* injured—and you didn't tell me."

"What good would that have done?"

"Perhaps it might have served to remind me that I should not take you for granted—your welfare, that is."

"Why? So you can leave me somewhere? That isn't going to happen, Roderic!"

"A growing part of me wishes that you were safely back at Chamoney."

"But I'm not! And anyway, if I'd gone back to Chamoney, we would never have—"

"Yes, we would have. Do you think I would have forgotten you? Who do you think was on my mind when I sat in that cabin, staring at the ring you now wear? You must have noticed. . . ."

He stopped as his gaze followed hers. "Where is it?"

"Miles tore it from my finger," she said sadly.

Roderic clenched his fists. "Now I have even more reason to kill him. But never mind, love, I will get you another. When this is over, I will have an Innish craftsman make one just like it."

Chapter Fourteen

"My dear niece!" the duke exclaimed, his expression as shocked as his tone. "Are you well?"

"I am unharmed, if that is what you mean, uncle. But I am *not* well—nor will I be, unless you persuade your king to help us. Miles Foulane attempted to kidnap both me and Lord Roderic—and he was acting on the orders of *my* king. He would no doubt have returned me to Baron DeLay after slapping me about a bit—but he would have killed Roderic!"

"Slapping you about? But surely—"

"I assure you that that is exactly what he did, uncle—and he also said that the king has already declared Chamoney to be forfeit and me to be a traitor."

The duke dragged his gaze from her and turned to Roderic, who nodded. "She speaks the truth, your grace. Sir Miles was acting on orders from his king."

Maryana didn't look at Roderic. They both knew

that they were shading the truth a bit—but only a bit.

The duke sank into a chair and gestured for them both to be seated. And that allowed his son-in-law, the baron, to assume center stage.

"With all due respect, your grace, I cannot believe that the Neran king would countenance such behavior. They are, after all, a people of laws."

"Laws that, by their own admission, they do not apply to the Sakims," Roderic stated succinctly.

"Why should they?" the duke's son-in-law, the baron, demanded. "They defeated you."

"Think about your history, Baron," Roderic said with thinly veiled contempt. "The Nerans and the Sakims have fought each other for centuries, with neither side winning for very long. And because we have always known that, both sides have, until now, been rather generous following a victory. Though it is certainly true that my people have been far more generous than the Nerans. We have never attacked them first, nor have we ever tried to take over their lands."

"More fool you, then," the baron said with a sneer.

"No. You are wrong. We seek only to live in peace in our own land. Perhaps you find that foolish—but we find it proper. If we had any designs on other lands, we would have seized *your* lands long ago. Can you deny that we could do that?"

"You live like savages," the baron sputtered. "You—"

"That may be—but that has nothing to do with conquest. Or rather, it has everything to do with it. You Innish are soft. Your army, such as it is, couldn't defend your country against even a small force of Sakim. And you certainly won't be able to defend yourselves against the Nerans, if they have beaten us down."

Roderic leaned forward, staring hard at the

baron. "Do you think we do not know how weak you are? My guess is that the only reason the Nerans haven't turned their attention to you is that they've mistakenly believed that your wealth means that you're well prepared for battle."

Maryana, listening to this exchange, cast a covert glance at her uncle, who remained silent. The duke's expression gave nothing away, but he was watching Roderic intently.

Was Roderic right about the Innish army not being as powerful as they'd believed? Certainly *her* people had always believed that—and for the reason Roderic had given: their great wealth.

"You insult us, Sakim!" the baron cried angrily.

"Perhaps," the duke said, lifting a hand to silence his son-in-law. "But he also speaks the truth."

His gaze shifted to Roderic. "But tell me, Lord Roderic, if our army is of such little consequence, then why do you seek our assistance in your fight with the Nerans?"

Maryana caught her breath sharply, certain that Roderic had been hoisted on his own petard.

"Because, your grace, the Nerans do not know what I know. They believe you have a mighty army, and if you ally yourselves with us, they will almost certainly concede victory to us quickly.

"Your army will not have to fight much—and perhaps not at all. It will be enough that they begin to move north in a show of force."

"That would be foolhardy, your grace! We have no quarrel with the Nerans." The baron was all but shouting again, his face crimson.

"That is correct—as far as it goes." The duke nodded. "But Lord Roderic has spoken of what will happen if we do not make this alliance—and I think he has the right of it. Their king is not to be trusted, and I've no doubt that he will soon be sending his agents here to determine our strength—or weakness."

Then he turned his attention back to Roderic. "We are not as weak as you may believe, Lord Roderic. I have managed to persuade His Majesty to provide for better arms and more training in recent years. Still, you are essentially correct: we do not have the fighting force that the Nerans believe we have."

He paused and sighed. "Nor will we ever have such a force. We have grown too comfortable through years of peace, while you Sakims have only increased your natural talents.

"Unlike many of my people, I have long admired the Sakims—and I have also known that we live free on your sufferance. Or because of your failure to unite yourselves behind one leader. But now it would appear that is about to change?"

"Your Grace, I swear to you that I have no intention of becoming king of the Sakims! I seek only to rid my land of the Nerans and then return to a life that I found quite agreeable."

"And one that I assume you would find even more agreeable with the lady Maryana at your side."

"Yes, Your Grace. And I will fight to regain her beloved Chamoney as well. We will divide our time between our two lands."

"That will never happen!" the baron stated hotly. "No Neran king, let alone this one, would ever permit a Sakim to control the largest and wealthiest estate in Neran!"

Roderic turned to him. "I said nothing about my controlling any land in Neran, baron."

"But as her husband . . ." he sputtered.

"The lady Maryana has managed her own affairs for some time, due to her father's long illness, and there is no reason why she should not continue to do that. I am prepared to sign a document upon our marriage, renouncing any claim to Chamoney."

His dark eyes met hers and she thanked him silently. She would never have asked for such a thing, but she was grateful, nonetheless. There could be no greater proof of his love for her.

"Though I am not her protector, Lord Roderic, I *am* concerned for my niece's future welfare, and your words put me at ease. Does this satisfy you as well, niece?"

Maryana smiled. "I would never have asked him to sign such a document, Uncle, because I know what is in his heart. And I know, too, that he means what he says about not wanting to become king of the Sakims."

"Better a Prince of Thieves, eh?" The duke teased, smiling at them both.

"Very well. I will leave tomorrow to make your case to our king. But in the meantime, I'm afraid that I have some bad news for you. Word has reached me that the Neran army is advancing northward, and that the king is seizing everything he can along the way. If he is not stopped quickly, Lord Roderic, many of your people will starve this winter."

Roderic glanced briefly at her as he nodded. "I know that, Your Grace. Messages were sent by several of the Sakim lords to my cousin's home in my absence. My men and I must leave tomorrow—and trust that you will be successful in your efforts to persuade your king."

"I will do my best." The duke nodded, sending a withering glance toward his son-in-law, who had seemed about to protest. "And the lady Maryana will be safe here."

"No! I'm going with you, Roderic!" She glared at him, angry that he'd kept this news from her, no doubt hoping to enlist her uncle's support in keeping her there.

"But my dear, he will be going to war! You cannot—"

"I'm going with him, Uncle. I may be able to help. I think I can persuade my uncle, Baron DeLay, to stay out of this."

"Is that important?" the duke asked Roderic.

"The baron himself is not so important," Roderic stated, avoiding her gaze. "But his location is. He controls Varley Castle, and there is no stronger fortress in all Sakim."

"So I go with you!" she cried triumphantly.

"I didn't say that. I can deal with the baron myself."

"I'm coming with you, Roderic!"

The duke stood up, signaling an end to their discussion. "It seems that this must be settled between the two of you, but I would say only that I cannot keep my niece under lock and key, and from what I've observed thus far, that would be the only way to keep her here."

The moment the duke and the baron had left the room, Maryana turned and glared at him. "You thought you could enlist his aid in keeping us apart—but it didn't work! You heard him: he can't stop me."

"My love, you can't—"

"Oh, yes, I can—and I will! If persuasion doesn't work, then I will buy off my uncle. I can do that—but you couldn't!"

Roderic's wide mouth twisted wryly and he shook his head. "Most men in my position seek a rich wife, while I find myself wishing that I had a *poor* one."

"You don't have *any* wife at the moment," she pointed out. "And if you don't let me help you, you may *never* have one."

There had been times in the past week when Maryana had almost regretted her insistence upon coming with him. She saw little of him in any event, always being relegated to the rear of the ever-increasing number of Sakim fighters who were steadily making their way north.

Now she saw before her once again the terrible results of the Neran army's passage. People lined the streets as they rode through still another Sakim town that had been stripped of everything the Neran king had deemed worthy of taking. And worst of all, what they couldn't take or didn't want, they had destroyed. Granaries and mills had been burned to the ground. Cattle and sheep had been slaughtered. And winter was riding hard on their heels. Snow had fallen the night before, leaving a blanket of white to cover the devastation.

Any recriminations she might have had about betraying her people were gone. Her king's behavior shocked even her. Roderic had told her that his strategy had by now become obvious. Not wanting to be forced to leave troops in Sakim over the winter, he had decided instead to let winter itself become his army of conquest. By spring, those who hadn't starved would be too weak to fight.

The only hope for these people, according to Roderic, was for him and his growing army to take back what the Nerans had stolen, so that these people could then buy what they required from the Innish, whose fertile lands held a surplus.

She could help as well, she told him—if she could get word to her manager at Chamoney. The excess from the vast estate could certainly feed at least several towns, and she could buy more from her neighbors.

But for the time being, she could do no more than set down in writing what she was seeing, then hire a Sakim youth to carry her report back to the duke. Perhaps it would help. They had no word yet on whether the Innish would join them.

There had been skirmishes already with the Neran forces, though Maryana had been kept well away from them. But the main army had continued to move north, and it now appeared that Roderic was right when he said that they would make for the well-fortified Varley Castle.

On this particular evening, Roderic and his troops stopped for the night in a village that had somehow managed to escape the worst of the Neran army's depradations—possibly because they had sated themselves with the sacking of a larger town nearby.

After a scant evening meal that had only served to remind her that she was always hungry now, Maryana settled down for the night in a hayloft, while Roderic's men took over the rest of the large barn and several other outbuildings. No sooner had she settled in when she heard the ladder creaking, and Roderic's head appeared at the top. Tired and hungry though she was, she felt a soft heat steal through her, dispelling the ever-present chill. More often than not this past week, she'd slept alone while Roderic rode off to meet his fellow lords, or planned strategy with his own men, who now numbered in the hundreds.

Like her, he'd lost weight, and his handsome face had acquired a lean, angular appearance, but even in the lantern light, she could see his dark eyes glowing with love.

He dropped heavily down beside her, then reached out to touch her hair. "You are becoming once more my golden lady," he said with a smile.

It was true. Her hair was growing out rapidly now, so that only the tips remained dark. Most of the time she kept her hood up, so that few ever saw the golden hair that marked her as being either Neran or Innish.

"What news is there?" she asked, though she didn't want to spend these precious moments together talking about the battles.

"From the Innish—nothing." He shrugged. "They are a practical people above all else. I think they have chosen to wait and see how we fare alone against the Nerans before committing themselves. I cannot blame them for that."

But *she* could—and did. She was furious with her uncle, even though, as Roderic had pointed out on more than one occasion, the decision was not entirely his to make.

"We have them on the run, though," he continued as he began to pull off his boots. "According to the reports I've received, the Neran army isn't doing much fighting now. Instead, they continue to make their way north—toward Varley Castle."

He tossed his boots aside and sighed heavily. "My people will bear the brunt of this, because the final battle will be fought there."

She nodded, having understood for some days now that such would be the case. It was all a matter of location. Varley Castle commanded the land on this side of the strait at its narrowest point. With winter now nearly upon them and the straits growing ever more stormy, the Neran king would be seeking to cross there, if he still hoped to return to Neran before the worst of the winter.

"Can we not get there before them?" she asked.

But Roderic shook his head as he began to strip off his clothing. "For a time I had hoped we could do that, since I doubt that the baron has many troops there. But if we took to the mountains to get around them, it would take even longer. Besides, even if we did somehow manage to get there ahead of the main army, the castle can be held with very few men. It was built for that purpose by one of my ancestors."

"But surely they cannot remain there for long: the Neran army, I mean. They would need both food and water."

"I've no doubt that Baron DeLay has already laid in a winter's supply of food, and the castle has a water supply: an underground stream that feeds the wells. My ancestor chose that location for that very purpose."

He paused for a moment, frowning thoughtfully, then resumed undressing until he stood naked before her, his lean, hard body limned by the lamplight.

Maryana let the covers fall away from her own nakedness, and was rewarded by the leaping of flames in his eyes as he sank to his knees beside her.

Then, finally, all talk of war ceased as their hands and lips relearned each other's secrets—all the many places where a touch set off an explosion of passion.

They were both tired, but their fatigue merely lent a certain unique subtlety to their lovemaking, blurring the hard edges of desire, but not dampening its fires.

He entered her and she welcomed him and they both spun away into a world of their own creation, a world that needed neither soft beds nor fine linens. Instead, they clung to the moment, trying to prolong it, wanting only to stay joined body and soul forever.

But the flesh was weak, and at last they reluctantly let go of that unique moment, and thrilled instead to the tiny aftershocks that trembled through them both.

"Milord!"

Tom's voice rang out from somewhere nearby and they both heard the ladder creaking. Roderic moved swiftly, to shield her from view, then called out to the man to wait.

"No!" she cried softly, not wanting him to be taken from her yet again. Her body might be sated, but her soul needed him, needed his warmth and closeness, his restless hands stroking her to sleep.

But he silenced her with a kiss. "He wouldn't be

bothering me if it weren't important. I'll be back as soon as possible."

He trailed a finger slowly down from her lips, all the way down to the golden tangle between her thighs, then bent to kiss her there as well.

"We're never really apart, you know. I carry you with me always."

But despite his promise to return as quickly as possible, she fell asleep in a lonely bed of straw.

"Where are we going?" Maryana asked as she watched the men begin to mount up and ride off.

"To visit Ammy, my sister. We'll catch up with them tomorrow."

When she turned to him questioningly, he went on. "There are no Neran troops within a day's ride, so I thought we would visit her at the convent. If you recall, I'd planned to visit her before, when we were on our way south.

"I want the two of you to meet, and I also want to tell her what is happening now. She is cut off from the world, but even so, rumors must have reached her ears."

So it was that they rode west, while Roderic's men continued to push north, toward Varley Castle. Maryana didn't question this sudden urge to see his sister—though later, she would wonder *why* she hadn't questioned it.

But for now she was content to be with him, riding through the cold morning, where a layer of frost glistened in the bright sun.

Roderic talked of his sister fondly. They were a scant two years apart in age and had therefore been playmates as well as brother and sister. Amelia, whom he had always called Ammy, and who was now Sister Mary Rose, had always been more devout than he was, and although it was the threat of a forced marriage that had driven her to the convent, Roderic was of the opinion that the idea had always been there.

"Trying to force her to marry Edward Planten was the only wrong thing my father ever did," he went on. "At least from my point of view. Edward's father was his friend, and they both wanted a marriage to unite the families. If there'd been a daughter, I suppose that *I* would have been the one to be forced into marriage. But Edward was the only surviving child—and much the worse for that. I can't blame Ammy for not wanting to marry him.

"Still, if she'd only waited, she would have been safe. Edward died in a fall from his horse only a year later—before the wedding would have taken place."

"But what about your mother?" Maryana asked, recalling that Daria, the wife of Roderic's friend Henry, had told her that Roderic's mother was a very strong woman. "Didn't she try to prevent it?"

"She was ill by that time, and I think she wanted to see Ammy settled down. Or perhaps she knew that Ammy was already considering giving herself to the Church.

"In any event, I was the only one who spoke up on her behalf, and all it did was to cause a breach between my father and myself that lasted for some time—nearly to his death.

"Then, after he died, I tried to get Ammy to come home, but by then she'd taken her final vows."

He was silent for a moment, then gave her a sad smile. "She has become so quiet, but there are still times when I can see the old Ammy in her eyes, if not in her talk or her actions. I confess that it is difficult for me to see her now, but it helps when I can see that smallest bit of the laughing girl she once was.

"She will be worried about me. I've no doubt that she's heard some rumors, even locked away as she is. And she is safe there. The convent is out of the path of the Nerans, and at least so far, they haven't bothered the monasteries or convents."

"Has the abbot returned?" she asked. She hadn't seen him since he had left two days ago to visit his bishop.

Roderic shook his head. "I suspect that he's having a difficult time of it with his superiors. He is no doubt being reminded that he is a man of God first and a Sakim second—a lesson he's never managed to learn."

"He seems to me an unlikely man of God to begin with," she remarked with a smile.

"Oh, he believes in his own fashion." Roderic chuckled. "But he, too, was set on a path that he might not have chosen for himself. He's a second son of a lord with small holdings. His older brother inherited everything, of course, and they didn't get along. So he had little choice."

"Yes, that happens among my people as well. Have you had any news from Varley Castle?"

"Only that the baron has made no further attempt to collect taxes, which I feared he might do once he knew I was gone."

"It was Miles who was urging him to do that," she said, then asked if there'd been any word on him.

"Nothing. Either he is still in the land of the Innish, trying to persuade them to remain neutral, or he has joined the king. There's been no sighting of him in my lands."

"If I know Miles, he'll be staying well away from the fighting."

"He could do that and be with the king," Roderic replied in obvious disgust. "His Majesty is not so much *leading* his army as *following* them. A fine example for a king."

They stopped at midday to eat the small quantity of food they'd carried with them. The day had been growing steadily warmer beneath a bright blue sky. Roderic said that the weather was always a tease at this time of year, changing greatly from day to day.

After they'd eaten, they were both reluctant to move on, and so instead lay in each other's arms, arguing over the shapes of the small, puffy clouds that dotted the sky and laughing together at various tales from the lives they'd had before they found each other. In the midst of war, they carved out a tiny peace for themselves, then clung to it for as long as they could.

The sun was setting by the time they reached the convent, deep in the woods in a narrow valley sheltered by tall, dark hills. As they approached it, Maryana squinted at the low structure she could just barely glimpse through the trees. Was it merely the result of the setting sun, or was it truly built of a very familiar reddish stone that seemed to be glittering in the waning light?

She turned to Roderic, but he had already noted her puzzlement and he nodded with a smile. "Yes, it is the same. Remember, I told you that those stones had not come from that area? This is where such stone is found—only in this valley, at its far end, not far from the convent."

"But . . ." Maryana fell silent.

"There are some things we are not meant to understand," Roderic said after a moment. "According to Ammy, the convent was built on a much older structure—many centuries older. She, of course, won't discuss pagan religions, but the abbot told me once that it was common practice for early Christians to tear down pagan structures, then build upon the ruins, as though that would drive out the old gods."

"So this must have been a holy place as well?"

"Perhaps so. When he was being trained, the abbot once came across a very ancient map that had come into the church's possession. He told me that it showed strange lines running the length and breadth of the Sakim lands—and those of the Innish as well.

"He could discern no reason for the lines. They didn't seem to mark old roads or streams, instead running quite straight. And they were marked at certain places with a strange sign. One of those places was where the convent now stands." He paused.

"Another was the place of the standing stones—and yet another was where Varley Castle now stands. When he told me about the line at the castle, we decided to go exploring, and in the deepest cellars, where no one had gone for years, we discovered several walls made of that same stone."

"So Varley Castle must also have been a holy place?"

"Perhaps so, though I've never felt there what I felt among the standing stones."

Roderic's gaze caught hers and held it, and the memory of that night seemed, for one brief moment, to have acquired reality again.

"We will go back there one day," he said softly.

Maryana would have known that the woman approaching them was Roderic's sister even if she hadn't known ahead of time. The resemblance was quite remarkable, though Roderic's strong features were softened somewhat in his sister. But her dark eyes gleamed with pleasure, and Maryana understood what Roderic had meant about the girl's manner shining forth from the woman's eyes.

In the small reception room of the convent, under the watchful eyes of an older sister, Roderic embraced his sibling, then introduced her to Maryana. Sister Mary Rose extended both hands to her, smiling.

"I had heard rumors that there was a Neran lady

with my brother—and for once, the stories were correct. Welcome, Maryana."

They were shown to a small, separate cottage within the high walls of the convent, a place reserved for visiting families or for men of the church. The older nun went with them, but she removed herself to a chair in the corner and soon fell asleep, affording them some privacy, at least.

A young girl brought them food, which was plain but plentiful. Maryana thought wryly that she had reached a sorry state indeed when she could think of such fare as being a great feast.

Roderic explained to his sister what was happening in the world beyond the convent's walls, and she asked many questions, then sighed unhappily when he told her that Varley Castle was likely to be the scene of the decisive battle.

"It's strange," she said softly. "The castle has appeared in my dreams for several nights now. Or at least, I sense that I am there, even though it is unfamiliar to me."

"What could possibly be unfamiliar about Varley Castle to one who spent her childhood exploring it?" Roderic teased.

"Well, one sight was familiar: the well room in the cellars. I can't imagine why I pictured myself there. But the rest of it . . ." She paused, frowning. "The walls were what made it seem strange. Instead of being the dark stone of the castle, they were the same reddish stone with the little lights that the convent is built of. Perhaps I was merely merging the two places."

"You weren't," Roderic said as Maryana stared at them both in shock. Then he told her about the deepest cellars that he and the abbot had found.

"This was after you were gone. The abbot had told me about an old map that had shown strange lines, one of which crossed the place where the castle now stands. Another crossed this place and was marked with a strange symbol, as was the location of the castle—and of some standing stones we visited recently."

Ammy shot a quick glance at the sleeping nun. "I, too, have heard of such maps in the church's possession, though I've never seen one. An old sister once told me that the maps were said to mark places of great power—an unholy power."

"Do you think of Varley Castle as being an unholy place?" Roderic challenged.

"No, of course not."

"Well, there you are, then."

They hadn't quite finished the meal when the convent's bells began to chime. Ammy rose quickly, then gently shook the still-sleeping nun and departed for evening prayers.

"I like her very much," Maryana said as soon as the two women had departed. "And you're right. It *is* possible to see the girl she must have been. It's almost as though one is inside the other."

"Exactly. I think she likes you as well."

Another young girl came a while later to clear away the remains of their dinner. Maryana was so lost in her thoughts about the turn Ammy's life had taken that she paid her scant attention. But as the girl was about to leave, Maryana glanced her way, then frowned at her departing figure. Surely she was mistaken!

But Roderic, who rarely failed to notice anything where she was concerned, nodded as she turned to him. "Yes, she is with child."

"But . . ." She had been about to protest that such a thing could not be, when she suddenly realized that the girl's dark clothing was not a nun's habit, though it had a like appearance.

"You might say that the baby is one of the 'spoils of war.' The father is a Neran soldier.

"There are many of them, unfortunately, and most of them have been shunned by their families.

They began to show up here, begging for food and shelter. The good sisters turned them away—until Ammy spoke up loudly on their behalf. She pointed out that the children are innocent and deserved to be cared for. Then she pledged her brother's gold to care for them." His mouth twisted wryly.

"Unfortunately, her brother doesn't have much gold, but he gave them some of what he'd managed to spirit away from the castle. And not just for the innocent babes. The girls are innocent, too—or they were, until the Nerans got hold of them. Is it any wonder that I lack piety, when God's representatives would condemn a girl for something she could not control?"

"But are they all here?" Maryana asked, knowing she shouldn't be feeling guilt herself, but feeling it nonetheless.

"Some are here and others are in other convents. I persuaded several other lords to part with what little they had left to help them."

"You're a good man, Roderic Hode," she said, stretching up on tiptoe to plant a kiss on his cheek.

"Did you ever think otherwise?" he asked, arching a brow in mock surprise.

"I confess that I thought you rather . . . shallow, at one point."

"My fault, I suppose," he replied, drawing her close. "There are times when I try to cover that natural Sakim darkness with too much light."

Maryana smiled and nodded, wondering why that had never before occurred to her. And she wondered, too, if she would ever truly know this man.

Then her thoughts turned back to the plight of the girls. "As soon as I can, I will send money to help them as well. It is only fitting that Neran gold should help to pay for the consequences of Neran savagery."

"Tell Ammy that. She'll be delighted to hear it."

"Will she be back tonight—or will we not see her until morning?"

"If I know my sister, she'll be back tonight."

And a few minutes later, Sister Mary Rose reappeared—alone this time and carrying a jug of wine, which she handed over to Roderic with a grin.

"A wedding present. It is all I can offer, but it's quite good—Neran, I think," she added with a grin for Maryana. "Mother Superior keeps it for special occasions, but I don't think she keeps a close eye on the supply."

"But we're not . . ." Maryana stopped abruptly, suddenly realizing that the very fact that they'd been given this cottage together must mean that Ammy believed them to be married.

"But you will be, I'm sure." Ammy smiled.

"As soon as possible—with or without her guardian's permission," Roderic assured his sister.

Ammy shook her head sadly. "You have set yourselves upon a very difficult path." She turned to Maryana. "I already know that my brother stops at nothing for what he truly believes, and I think you may be like that as well, Maryana. Otherwise you would not be here now."

"Roderic is right. We will marry with or without my uncle's permission." Then she told Ammy of her intention to help the unfortunate girls, and Ammy smiled at the irony.

"Thank you. The Lord does indeed move in strange ways ofttimes."

"But what will happen to them—afterward?" Maryana asked.

"It is my hope that we can place them in service with their babes. Of course, that depends on whether we Sakims can reclaim our lands. In the meantime, they must remain here—unless their families relent. And that isn't likely when relenting means two more mouths to feed at a time when there's scarcely enough for those already laying claim."

"At times like this, I am ashamed to be Neran," Maryana said with genuine disgust.

"But you are not to blame, Maryana," Ammy protested gently. "It is your king who bears most of the blame. Is it any wonder that we Sakims would never have a king ourselves?"

Maryana nodded. "When I first came here, I thought that your people were strange indeed not to have a king—even though I detest ours. Now I am beginning to understand."

After Ammy had gone, Maryana's thoughts were still on the matter of kings. "What will you do if your people decide they want *you* to be their king?" she asked Roderic.

"They won't—and even if they should, it cannot happen. When I asked the other lords to unite behind me, I gave them all my solemn word that I would never become king. Otherwise we wouldn't be united now."

His back was to her as he poured them both some wine, and she stared at him, wondering if the feelings of the others—and the people as well—might not change when Roderic had defeated her people and sent them fleeing back across the straits.

She did not doubt that victory would be his, despite the odds. It was, she realized, the mark of a true leader that he could so convince his followers, and she'd already seen how he'd convinced them. It was in their eyes when they listened to him.

He turned and handed her a mug of wine. "It has always been a tradition among my people that the Earl of Varley would be the one to call his people to war. It has nothing to do with family or divine right, but rather, location. Our chief enemies over the years have been the Nerans, and Varley Castle and its lands sit closest to the narrowest point of the straits, where the Nerans have generally invaded.

"But everyone recognizes it as being just that: a matter of location and nothing more. And the Earls of Varley have always known that."

"Hasn't there ever been one of them who aspired to be king?"

He shook his head. "Not one. It is always passed down from father and son to recognize both our responsibility—and our limits."

"You Sakims are indeed a strange lot," she said, then stifled a yawn.

Roderic chuckled. "I hope that doesn't mean that you are aspiring to marry the first of the Sakim kings."

"Not at all." She yawned again. It rather surprised her that she felt so very tired so quickly.

"Come," Roderic said. "Finish your wine and come to bed with me, since it is rare enough that we even have a bed."

She drank off the remaining wine, which was an excellent Neran vintage, as Ammy had said. It might even have been from her own vineyards. And perhaps it was responsible for her sudden tiredness. She'd become unaccustomed to drinking wine at all lately, except for during her stay with the duke.

"I am angry with my uncle," she told him as he undressed quickly, then began to undress her as well.

"Which uncle?"

"The duke. I expected him to have convinced his king by now."

"I think he will," Roderic replied. "The fact that we have driven the Nerans so far north this quickly will be known to him by now."

"Perhaps the Innish will then decide that you don't require their help," she said, then gasped as he drew her between his knees and began to toy with a nipple.

"No more talk," Roderic said huskily. "Unless you wish to whisper your love for me."

It felt to her as though they were making love underwater. She didn't know where such a thought had come from, but there it was. It seemed that she, at least, moved with a slowness that belied her racing heart, and Roderic's words of love and encouragement came to her as though from across a very great distance.

But her body responded, arching to him, reaching for him, and finally enfolding him within her moist heat. And he was still there, joined with her, when she fell asleep.

Maryana dreamed. In the dream, they were back within the standing stones, and this time they were making love with the soft chanting in the background and with the glow of the stones playing over their bodies.

Then they were on the shore, pressed into the soft sand as they made love yet again while the foaming water lapped about them and the great birds flew overhead, shrieking their unbearably mournful cries.

In her dream, she opened her eyes and saw them there, silhouetted against a flaming sky, still crying. And Roderic, a dark shadow as well, loomed over her, his long, hard body pressed against hers, pushing her more deeply into the sand. But even as she stared at him, trying to see him more clearly, he retreated from her and finally vanished.

Chapter Fifteen

It was a sense of wrongness that finally drew her up from sleep. For a long time she drifted back and forth, never quite reaching full consciousness, but not dropping into the dark abyss, either.

When she finally did open her eyes and focus on her surroundings, the first face she saw was that of Ammy, bending close to her, offering her some water. Ammy's expression was neutral, but as Maryana focused on her, she saw that same careful lack of expression she'd seen on Roderic's face a few times.

She drank the water thirstily, then looked around the tiny cottage, wondering why the lighting was so poor. The windows were open, but to little avail. Had the weather changed overnight?

"Where is Roderic?" she asked, her thoughts still too muzzy to accommodate true fear. He was probably outside somewhere.

"He's gone, Maryana," Ammy replied softly. Her expression was still neutral, but there was sympathy in her eyes now.

"Gone?" Maryana leaped from the bed, forcing Ammy to back up quickly. "Gone? What do you mean? Surely they didn't come here and capture him." Images of Miles flitted through her dazed mind.

But Ammy was shaking her head. "No. He left on his own—just after dawn. He came to tell me what he'd done—and then he left."

"What he'd done?" Maryana repeated, swaying a bit as she stood there, then reaching out to grip the table.

"He drugged you—put a sleeping draft in your wine."

Maryana stood staring at Ammy as though she were speaking a different language. Roderic had drugged her? Believing it was beyond her capabilities.

Ammy pushed her gently into a chair, then told her to eat, that she'd feel better once she had food in her stomach. Maryana did as told because she *was* hungry—ravenous, in fact. Ammy sat down opposite her and waited in a patient silence while she tried to work it out.

"The wine," she said. "He put it in the wine. I started to feel very tired, but I thought it was just because I haven't drunk much wine of late. But why?"

She asked the question, but even in her present muzzy state, she knew the answer. "He didn't want me to go with him."

"He wanted you to be safe," Ammy confirmed. "He told me that both he and your uncle, the duke, tried to persuade you to stay there, but you wouldn't. So he thought this was the only safe place for you now. And he's right, you know; this *is* a safe place."

"He's not leaving me here! I'll follow him!"

"You can't, Maryana. We have no horses here. We've no need of them."

But she didn't really hear what Ammy was saying. Instead, she turned to the nearby window. "You said he left at dawn. What time is it now?"

"Nearly dusk. You slept all day. You *can't* follow him, Maryana. You must do as he says and stay here where it is safe."

The food was working its magic—or perhaps it was just that her true situation was just now dawning on her. "I don't take orders from him!" she snapped

Ammy smiled. "If you did, I doubt that he'd be in love with you. My brother loves you for your strength and courage. But in this, he is right. I've already spoken to Mother Superior, and you are most welcome to stay as long as you must."

Once again, Maryana barely heard her. "He must have planned this from the beginning. It's why he brought me here."

"I think he also wanted us to meet—but yes, you must be right. He must have brought the sleeping draft with him."

"Of course he did! The abbot got it for him!" She was remembering something: a small vial the abbot had handed Roderic days ago, before he'd left them. She'd wondered about it at the time, but had forgotten about it quickly.

"No doubt the abbot blames himself for having gotten you into the midst of this," Ammy said, nodding. She'd heard the whole story the evening before.

Maryana pushed away from the table. "How dare he do something like this? He knows that I could be a help to him! My uncle is at Varley Castle and—"

"He feared that you would risk your life trying to get to your uncle," Ammy interrupted softly.

For two days, Maryana lived with her outrage, straining Ammy's patience to its limits. The only concession she made to her kind hostess was to attend all prayers, since she didn't want Ammy to be forced to find excuses for her absence. But if the nuns with their bowed heads could have overheard her thoughts, they would undoubtedly have prayed even harder for her soul.

During the times when she wasn't attending prayers, Maryana searched every corner of the large compound—just in case Ammy had lied when she'd said that they had no horses. But unfortunately, it appeared that she'd told the truth. The convent was completely self-sufficient, with its own gardens and water supply.

She was well and truly trapped. If she'd given in to Roderic's and her uncle's importunings, she could easily have escaped from the ducal palace—but there was no escape from this place, or rather, no place to go if she did escape.

But after a time, she stopped blaming Ammy and the others, who, after all, had played no role in her confinement other than simply being there. And mostly to help Ammy's standing with the Order, she went to the Mother Superior and confirmed that she intended to send them gold for the care of the girls and their babes as soon as possible—though how soon that might be, she couldn't say.

After that, the nuns stopped regarding her as a curiosity and became friendlier, the word having spread quickly that she was a future patroness of the convent.

The possibility of escape came to her quite by accident when she'd been there for nearly two weeks. She was just returning to her cottage when she saw one of the nuns hurrying to the locked gate in the outer wall. And when it was opened, she saw two men with horses.

Hiding in the shadows next to the cottage, Maryana watched as the men handed over some large sacks to the nun. *Of course!* Why hadn't it occurred

317

to her that the convent must have some way of acquiring game? She'd been eating the meat herself.

The nun pressed some coins into the hands of the two men, then closed the gate. Maryana was tempted to run after the hunters, but the nun was having difficulty carrying the sacks, and finally put one down. As she did so, she saw Maryana, and so Maryana was forced to acknowledge her presence and then help carry the sacks to the kitchen.

Maryana then returned to her cottage to take stock of the situation. By now, she knew how many women lived here, so she calculated that the game was probably intended to last a week, since they all ate sparingly, save for the women with unborn babes and those nursing.

The gate itself wasn't locked, but rather was barred from the inside. She could easily get out, but her absence would be noticed, since she wouldn't be able to put the bar back into place.

No, she thought, *I need another way out. Then I can simply wait for the men to return and offer them gold in exchange for one of their horses.* That they would take her up on her offer, she didn't doubt.

So she spent the next few days studying the convent all over again, this time with an eye to finding another means to leave. And she found it!

The forest grew right up to the walls at one corner, and there was a huge oak with a heavy limb that actually extended a bit over the top of the wall. If she could get up there, she could certainly climb down the tree. She'd done that before.

But reaching the top of the high wall was another matter. It took some more clandestine searching to find a solution to that problem—and then still more effort to begin putting her plan into action.

Fortunately, the corner she'd chosen was somewhat isolated, an area used primarily for storage.

And in a nearby building, she found numerous crates, most of which were filled with what appeared to be old convent records.

The crates were too heavy for her to lift, so she began to remove some of their contents and put them instead into empty crates. No doubt she was destroying someone's careful system of record-keeping, but her upcoming gift to the convent would, with any luck, erase any annoyance over that.

Finally, six days after she'd seen the visitors, she had enough crates ready to carry out to the wall. It had taken her that long because she had to be careful to avoid being seen or arousing any suspicions as to why she was spending so much time there.

In the predawn darkness, one week since the men had last visited, Maryana dressed in the clothing she'd been wearing when she arrived at the convent. But in place of her own cloak, she put on the rough but warm cloak all the nuns and other residents wore, which had been given to her by Ammy because it was heavier.

She opened the cottage door and peered out cautiously. She wasn't really expecting to see anyone, but she couldn't be sure what time those who prepared breakfast might arise.

When she saw no one, she hastened through the silent grounds, glad for the pale dusting of snow that provided some light. It was very cold, and she was grateful to Ammy for the warm cloak with its snug-fitting hood and sleeves to her fingertips.

But the cloak proved to be a hindrance when it came to carrying out the crates, so she took it off until she had piled them up by the wall, happy to see that she had calculated correctly how many she would need.

Then she donned the cloak once again and

climbed up her stairway of crates until she had reached the top of the wall. She put out a foot and kicked away the top two crates. They fell with a noisy thud, but it was unlikely anyone could be close enough at this hour to hear it.

The sky was beginning to lighten. Maryana paused for a moment atop the wall and stared at the silent convent. She wished that she'd been able to leave a message for Ammy, but she'd been unable to think of any excuse to ask for precious parchment. She would have to trust that Ammy would understand.

Then she took off the heavy cloak once more, balled it up, and tossed it to the ground, which, she noted, seemed a very long distance indeed.

Climbing down the nearby tree wasn't nearly as easy as climbing down that other tree long before. She didn't have Roderic to guide her this time, and neither did she have his strong grip to assist her the final yards. Twice she slipped and nearly fell to what surely would have been a severe injury.

But then she was there, leaping the last six or seven feet onto her cloak, almost as though she'd planned it that way. She was shivering by now, but soon became warm again as she donned the cloak.

Then she withdrew from her pocket the gold chain and crucifix Ammy had given her. It wasn't quite as elaborate as those worn by the sisters, but rather was a simpler construction worn by the secular inhabitants of the convent. Still, given her cloak and where she was coming from, she thought she could pass for a nun, if one didn't look too closely.

She walked along the outside wall until she reached the gate, then went past it a ways, now traversing the road that led to it. After she had gone some distance, she left the road and found a spot close by, but concealed from view by holly bushes. There she sat down to wait, unconsciously fingering the small bag of coins in her pocket as she huddled inside the warmth of her cloak.

The two men had come fairly early the previous time, so she could only hope that that was their habit. If she was wrong about the intervals between their visits . . .

That didn't bear thinking about, so she dismissed the thought. Instead, she concentrated on perfecting her story. The truth was, though, that she doubted she would have to worry about her story once they saw the gold. After that, it was only a question of buying food—and perhaps acquiring the services of an escort.

Her nun's disguise might be sufficient to carry her safely to Roderic's lands, but it would definitely be better to have a male escort. After all, nuns weren't accustomed to roaming the countryside alone—not even in peacetime, let alone during a war.

Wrapped in the warm cloak, she drifted off into a light doze and her mind filled with images of Roderic. She was still very angry with him for his trickery, but she knew that her anger would dissolve the moment she saw him again.

She was lost in half-waking dreams of the two of them riding through the fertile valleys of Chamoney, when the sound of horses' hooves snapped her eyes open. And by then, the two men were nearly upon her.

They didn't see her there in the bushes, however, and continued past her with their bulging sacks swinging against their horses' rumps. Maryana paid them no attention, but she did study the two horses. They looked healthy enough, though somewhat dirty with their shaggy winter coats.

She got up and moved with them, then hid beside a thick tree trunk and watched as the convent's gate was opened a few moments after they rang the bell. While they were handing over the game and accepting their payment, she hurried back to her original spot and crouched down among the bushes.

As soon as the gate had closed behind them and they had remounted their horses and turned in her direction, she stepped out onto the road, not wanting to frighten the animals by appearing too suddenly. The men drew up sharply when they saw her, then came forward cautiously, their expressions puzzled.

"Do ye need help, Sister?" the older man called.

"Yes, I do," Maryana replied. "Though perhaps not the help you may be thinking." She was careful to mimic the accents of Sakim nobility, which wasn't all that difficult for her. The speech of the Sakim upper classes wasn't very much different from her own. The differences were more apparent among the peasants.

They both stopped before her, and Maryana now saw that they must be father and son. The younger man was in fact little more than a youth, not quite full-grown. She told them her story.

"I must journey north. My mother lies gravely ill, and the Mother Superior has forbidden me to go to her because of the war. But I must see her before she dies." She even managed to squeeze a few tears from her eyes as she looked at them imploringly.

"I wish to purchase one of your fine horses to carry me there—and perhaps an escort as well, if that is possible. I have gold."

She withdrew her little leather bag and held up some coins, which she saw them stare at with interest.

"The Mother Superior is right, Sister. It would be very dangerous. There is fighting all around us now."

They are good men, she thought. *Elsewise, they would take my gold and care little for my safety.*

322

"But surely it would be possible to go around the fighting—even if it takes a bit longer. I'm very desperate."

"Let me take her, Da," the youth said suddenly. "We have a horse to spare, an' ye were goin' to sell it anyway."

The older man looked at his son with what could have been sympathy. "Don't try to trick me, lad. I know ye want to go join Lord Roderic, but yer ma says ye're too young—and the only son we got."

The boy's jaw set firmly. "I was goin' anyway. I want to help Lord Roderic rid this land of Nerans once an' fer all."

The father turned to her, shrugging. "Our pardon, Sister, but ye can see what's happenin' here. Can ye ride? If so, we'll double up on his horse an' give ye this one. It's a better animal than the one I was goin' to sell."

Maryana assured him that she could ride, and they set off. It turned out that their farm wasn't far away; as they reached it, she recalled having passed it on her way to the convent.

The boy's mother was tearful, but she finally gave in, saying that perhaps the company of a holy sister would offer him some protection for a time, at least. Maryana nodded guiltily. She could only hope that she wasn't sending this poor woman's only son to his death.

The youth's name was Ered, and he was barely fifteen, though he looked older. He was obviously well brought up, because he was very respectful of her, and even reminded her gently that they should offer prayers before they ate and when they settled down for the night. Several times, she caught him watching her with a quizzical expression, and she wondered if he suspected that she was not what she pretended. But if so, he kept his suspicions to himself.

It was easy to get him to talk about the war—and about Roderic. On that subject, the normally quiet young man waxed eloquent.

"But these are not Lord Roderic's lands," she protested at one point. "So how is it that you speak of him—and not of your own lord?"

"Lord Roderic's our leader, Sister. He's the one has brought us together to drive out the Nerans. And he's a good man."

He then launched into a much embellished tale of how Lord Roderic had stolen from the tax collectors to help his people, and how he even persuaded a Neran lady to part with some of her gold for them.

But here Ered shook his head. "I can't credit that last part, though. Not even Lord Roderic could manage to get his hands on Neran gold."

Oh, yes, he could, she replied silently—*and more than the lady's gold, too.* She had to bite her tongue to keep from scandalizing the youth.

"So do you think that when this is over, Lord Roderic will become king of the Sakims?" she asked, curious to see what he would say about that.

The boy looked shocked. "Oh, no, Sister. We'd never have a king. And Lord Roderic wouldn't want that himself. He even took a vow against that."

Several times, Maryana was greatly tempted to tell Ered the truth—if only because she knew he must be wondering how a nun had needed reminding about saying her prayers. It was obvious that both he and his parents were quite devout, and she worried over the impression she must be creating for the young man.

But she managed to hold her tongue. He hated the Nerans with all the passion of youth—and with good cause as well, she reminded herself sadly.

That she had clearly not thought through her deception became apparent to her as they drew nearer to Roderic's lands. He asked her just where she was going, and she was forced to spin a tale quickly—and probably ineffectually.

She told him that he could take her to the home of Lord Roderic's gameskeeper because the family was related to people in her own family service, and they would escort her on the final leg of her journey.

Then she waited nervously for him to inquire about her family and where their lands might be. But as it happened, he never asked the question. Instead, he was overjoyed to be going to the home of someone close to his hero, and expressed the hope that he could then join Roderic's forces.

She assured him that should indeed be possible, then prayed that she wouldn't be given away by Gisel and her family before she could make them understand the situation.

Still, she reasoned, even if she were given away, she would no longer have to fear the boy's reaction if he learned the truth. The servant girl and her family would certainly vouch for her.

They were traveling deep in the woods now, and several times she feared that Ered might not know the way. But it seemed that the boy was one of those rare people—perhaps like Roderic himself— who could find their way under the worst of circumstances.

Still, she fretted silently that they might be taking so long to reach her destination that she would be too late. If the brunt of the Neran army had arrived at the gates of Varley Castle before she did, any hopes she had of persuading her uncle to keep them out of the castle would be lost.

On the fourth day of their journey, shortly after midday, Maryana finally saw something familiar— and knew at last where they were. After riding north for nearly three days, Ered had turned east. This she knew from the sun, which had reappeared after several days of clouds and snow flurries.

They rode up a steep hill out of a narrow ravine—and there at the top lay the ruins of the old
abbey, where the guard commander's wife had
been the bait to trap Roderic.

"I know this place," she told Ered as they
reached the crest of the hill.

But the boy's attention had already been caught
by something in the distance, and Maryana followed his gaze, only then remembering that the
great towers of Varley Castle were visible from this
high ground.

"That's Varley Castle!" he cried. "Look yonder,
Sister!"

"It is indeed," she murmured, thinking how
peaceful it all looked. Did that mean that they'd
arrived in time? She could only hope so.

The castle itself sat on a high hill, surrounded by
open land on all sides, with the town at the base of
the hill and a road that led from it to the water's
edge. There were no signs of battle anywhere, but
Maryana knew that could be misleading. Between
the ruined abbey and the castle and town lay several smaller hills, all of them thickly wooded—and
each one capable of concealing a full—fledged battle.

"The house I seek is in that direction," she said,
pointing. "But it's impossible to tell if there could
be any fighting down there."

"I was thinking just that meself, Sister," the
youth said. "Mayhap it would be better if you were
to stay here while I have a look down there."

Maryana decided that it would be best for her to
agree with that plan, which would surely be what
any convent-isolated nun would do. She wished
him godspeed, then dismounted and let her horse
graze while she paced about, staring at the distant
castle.

Now that her goal was within sight, her optimism began to wane. Could she really hope to persuade her uncle to betray his king? He'd never actually spoken out against the king, although he'd given her reason enough to think that he, too, disliked him. But dislike was one thing and treachery was quite another.

Would she herself ever have betrayed her king if she hadn't fallen in love with Roderic? It was a question without an answer, but it made her realize just how much she would be asking of her uncle.

The hours dragged by as she waited for Ered's return. During that time, she concocted, then discarded, numerous plans—each one more outlandish than the last. It began to seem to her that Roderic had been right to drug her and leave her at the convent.

Until her journey across the straits, Maryana had lived solely in a world that she could largely control and shape to her liking. Now, however, she saw that she was in a situation she could not hope to control—and likely could not even influence to any extent.

But beneath all her musings and her growing awareness of her helplessness to manipulate events lay a terrible gnawing fear for Roderic. Now that she had seen violent death, she could not get those images out of her mind—and neither could she prevent the immeasurably more horrible images of Roderic suffering a similar fate.

The sun was low in the western sky by the time Ered returned, and she rushed forward to meet him.

"The fighting's just down there, Sister," he said, pointing to the wooded hills south of the town. "I seen it meself, but I couldn'a tell who's winning. I talked to an old man who told me that the Nerans are trying to make for Varley Castle, and that there's only a few troops there now. If Lord Rod-

eric and his forces can just get through, he'll have
his castle back, all right."

A very big "if," she told herself, but she shared
the boy's hopes, imagining a reunion with Roderic
there.

"Then we should be safe going that way," she
said, gesturing in the direction of Gisel's home.

"Yes'm, we should. With a full moon, we'll be
there tonight with no problem."

So they rode on as the daylight waned and dusk
fell and then gave way swiftly to night. And with
night came a drop in the temperature that made
her shiver even inside her warm cloak. She'd never
felt such bitter cold before. Her feet were numb
inside her boots, and even the woolen mittens
Ered's mother had given her could not keep the
chill from her fingers.

"Can we risk using the road?" she asked Ered.
"I'm not at all sure I can find the house if we can't."

"We can mebbe keep it in sight," the boy suggested, "but I think we should stay in the woods."

And, as it turned out, his suggestion saved their
lives. They were riding along the side of a hill, with
the road some hundred yards below them, when
Ered suddenly grabbed her reins and put a finger
to his lips. They stopped—and then heard the
pounding of horses' hooves below.

"Nerans," he whispered. "They've got a patrol
out."

They moved deeper into the trees and waited
while a dozen or so soldiers in dark green uniforms
passed by, headed north—the same direction they
were going.

"Is the house along the road?" Ered asked.

"No, it's deep in the woods," she replied, struggling to remember her journey that night with the
abbot. "There's a path that leads to it, and I remember that it's just after a sharp bend in the
road."

As soon as the patrol had disappeared, they rode on, taking care to keep the road in sight. And then, just when Maryana had begun to doubt the accuracy of her memory, she saw the road bend sharply around the base of the hill they were following.

"There!" she cried, certain that she could see the path now.

"I see it!"

They rode down the steep hillside and across the road, after pausing to listen for the return of the patrol. And then the forest closed around them once more.

"Stop right there! I've got an arrow aimed between yer eyes!"

They both came to an abrupt halt and peered into the woods, but could see nothing. The voice was definitely young—and, she thought, scared. Could it be one of Gisel's young brothers—maybe even the boy from whom she'd borrowed clothing to outfit herself as a page?

"It's Maryana," she called. "I've come to see Gisel!"

Then she held her breath as she heard a rustling in the woods. When the boy came out onto the path, he was still aiming an arrow at them. She edged forward, putting her horse between the boy and Ered, whose hand was straying to his own bow. She had not come this far to see two boys kill each other for nothing.

"It's Thad, isn't it?" she asked, having just recalled the boy's name. "You lent me some clothes."

"Lady Maryana?" the boy asked warily. "Is't really you?"

The mittens made her clumsy, but she managed to push the snug hood off her head. "It is I. Is Gisel home?"

"But who's that with ye?" the boy asked in confusion.

329

"His name is Ered, and he helped me get here. He wants to join Lord Roderic."

Then she turned to Ered, to find him staring in openmouthed amazement at her hair. She knew that the gold must be very evident by now, though the ends were still dark.

"He . . . he called ye Lady Maryana," Ered stammered. "But that's the name of the Neran lady that Lord—"

"Yes, Ered. I'm sorry to have lied to you, but I didn't think you would be willing to help me if you'd known I was Neran."

"Ye mean that the story was *true?*" he asked. "Ye really *did* give Lord Roderic your gold?"

"And much more," she said, nodding. "He has my heart as well. When this is ended, we will be married."

Gisel was bashful, but Maryana would have none of it as she embraced the girl happily, then asked for news of the castle. They seated her before the fire, and when Gisel knelt to remove her boots for her, Maryana waved her away.

"I've learned to do a few things for myself," she told the girl, then repeated her question about the castle as she luxuriated in the first warmth she'd known in days. "My uncle is still there?"

"Yes'm, but not so many troops. They're all fighting just south of town. I haven't seen Lord Roderic meself, but I know them that has. It's said that he has a great army and will surely win."

"What about the Innish? Do you know if they've joined Lord Roderic?" But even as she said it, she doubted that the Innish could have mobilized so swiftly.

"Not as I know—but the baron is fair worried about that. I overheard him talking to the guard commander about it. He said that you were down

330

there, trying to talk your uncle, the duke, into helping us."

"I wonder how he knew about that," Maryana mused.

"Mayhap from Sir Miles," Gisel suggested as she handed Maryana a mug of steaming hot tea.

"So he's back," Maryana said in disgust, cradling the mug in her cold hands. "Is he at the castle, too?"

"No'm. From what I hear, he's gone back to Neran."

"That sounds like Miles. He'd want to put as much space between himself and any fighting as possible. But I'm surprised that he'd dare to run off, with the king himself close by."

Gisel hesitated before going on. " 'Twas the king who sent him, if what I heard was right. The king sent him to take charge of Chamoney."

Maryana choked on the tea, and Gisel leaped up to pat her on the back. "Mayhap I heard wrong, milady."

"No, I think you probably heard right. Miles told me that the king has declared my lands forfeit, so he probably wants to make certain that I don't reclaim them."

She stared into the fire, blinking away tears as she tried to tell herself that Miles surely couldn't do too much damage in a short time.

"I need to see my uncle as soon as possible, Gisel. Can you get me into the castle?"

The girl frowned. " 'Twon't be easy, milady. With the fighting and all, they've fortified the rear gate and never open it. Everyone has to go in by the main gate, and the guards check us all.

"There're only ten of us working there now—all women. The baron won't trust even the boys who used to work in the kitchens and the stables."

Maryana's hopes plummeted. There had been dozens of Sakims working at the castle when she was there, and she'd hoped she could slip by unnoticed.

She went to bed still determined to find a way to reach her uncle. She'd come so far and was not about to be defeated now. Gisel had offered her own bed, and though Maryana was tempted to say that she'd be just as happy with a few blankets next to the fire, she understood that the girl would not hear of that. So she huddled beneath the blankets in the tiny bedchamber and contemplated her situation.

She could ask Gisel to carry a message for her, but that seemed too risky. Gisel would certainly do it for her, but she might lose her freedom—and even her family's freedom—in the process, depending on the baron's present frame of mind.

Finally she drifted off to sleep, thinking about her uncle and about Roderic: both of them so close, and yet beyond her reach.

Chapter Sixteen

Maryana was freezing by the time they reached the castle's gate. For three days the temperature had been dropping, making even the snug little cottage hard to heat. Gisel's mother kept shaking her head and saying that such cold portended a very bad winter, but Maryana wondered how it could possibly get any worse.

The snow was falling thicker and thicker, until both she and the horse were completely white. But for that, at least, she was grateful. If not for the snow, she wouldn't be here.

When the snow had begun falling shortly after Gisel returned home from her day's work yesterday, she had suggested to Maryana that the snow could be a godsend.

"We'll all be covered with it by the time we get there, milady, and the guards will be hard-pressed to tell one of us from t'other. Mazy Wills, one of t'other maids, has the chilblains very bad, and she said she wouldn'a go tomorrow if it's snowing. I always meet up with her along the way."

So here she was, pretending to be Mazy Wills, who was indeed unwilling to go to work. They had stopped at her home, and Maryana saw with relief that the girl was about her size, though with a face both longer and narrower than hers. But Gisel had dismissed that problem with a wave of her hand.

"We'll all look the same by the time we get to the gate."

And now came the test of Gisel's words as they brought up the rear of the line waiting to enter the castle. Maryana looked at the shadowy figure just ahead of her and let herself hope. She could just barely make out the woman's shape in the blowing snow, so how much more could the guards see?

Gisel had persuaded Mazy to lend Maryana her horse, a dappled gray, saying that by now the guards probably knew the horses as well as they knew the faces of the riders. But the animal's distinct markings were barely visible beneath its blanket of snow.

The line moved forward. Maryana tensed. She was prepared to identify herself if necessary, but she much preferred to let only her uncle know of her presence. If Gisel had heard wrongly and Miles Foulane were still here, she wanted to avoid him and the problems he represented.

Huddled inside his greatcoat, a guard moved along the line now, counting the riders. Maryana kept her head down, but it was no more than anyone else was doing, since it was the only way to keep the snow out of one's eyes.

She forced herself to remain still as she saw the leather boots of the guard come to a halt next to her horse. Then he moved on to Gisel, who was the last in line. With a surge of triumph, Maryana rode through the door that was set into the huge gate, past two more guards who paid her no attention at all as they huddled around a makeshift fire. She felt a moment's sympathy for them. They were Neran, after all, and like her, suffering greatly in this Sakim winter.

After leaving their horses in the stable, Gisel and Maryana made their way through the snow to the kitchen door, trailing somewhat behind the others.

"Don't stop to take off yer cloak," Gisel whispered to her. "No one'll notice if ye just hurry on up the stairs. Can ye find yer uncle's rooms, then?"

"Yes, I think so—but will he be there?"

"If he isn't, then he'll likely be in the room where Lord Roderic always did his accounts. Ye know that room?"

She nodded and thanked Gisel. When they entered the warmth of the kitchen, she wanted to stay there, but she did as Gisel had suggested, and was reasonably certain that in the confusion of servants complaining about the weather and removing their heavy cloaks, she had made it to the narrow back stairs without being noticed.

Despite having told Gisel that she could find her way, Maryana was momentarily confused as she stepped out into a hallway. But fortunately there was no one about, and she finally got her bearings and headed for her uncle's rooms, passing her old room along the way.

She removed her mittens and pounded on the outer door, then pushed it open when her uncle called out to come in.

He was standing at a window, with his back to her as he stared out at the courtyard. When he neither turned nor said anything, she realized that he must assume that she'd brought his breakfast.

"Uncle, it is I, Maryana."

He turned quickly, his face a mask of confusion. "Maryana?"

She let the sodden cloak fall from her shoulders, and his confusion turned to shock. "It *is* you! My dear niece!"

He came to her and seized her chilled hands in both of his, then quickly led her over to the fireplace. "You have been out in this weather? But how did you get here? Why wasn't I told you'd be coming?"

And just who would I tell? she wondered, but didn't ask. She was grateful to see that he didn't appear to be angry with her.

He offered her some brandy, which she declined, since she feared its effects upon her—apart from any warmth it might provide. Then he peered at her closely.

"It would seem that you have much to tell me."

She smiled. "And I must begin by saying that I regret any problems I have caused you, Uncle. I know that you did the best you could for me."

At that point, they were interrupted by Gisel, who came in bearing a heavily laden breakfast tray. She stopped and stared when she saw Maryana there, and Maryana thought that the girl belonged on the stage.

"I'll just fetch another tray, then, m'Lord," Gisel said, though Maryana could see that the tray she'd brought would suffice for three, let alone two.

Maryana began her story as soon as Gisel had departed, and was only partway through it when the girl returned with a second heavy tray. After that, she talked between bites, explaining to her still-shocked uncle that she hadn't eaten a decent meal in many days.

"So now you know all that has happened to me since I left here, Uncle," she concluded, finishing her meal at the same time. "I've left nothing out."

And she hadn't—except for the night she and Roderic had spent within the circle of stones. That wasn't relevant, in any event, though it continued to loom large in her mind.

The baron had said nothing at all as she talked, and now he frowned thoughtfully. "So it is your belief that the Innish will ally themselves with the Sakims."

"Yes. The duke is on our side—Roderic's and mine, I mean. And he is the Innish king's most trusted adviser."

The baron got up and began to pace around the room, his hands clasped behind his back. "Does it not trouble you, niece, that you are betraying your own people?"

"I do not see it that way, Uncle. The Neran people have no quarrel with the Sakims—and never have had. We've traded with them for centuries and intermarried as well. It is only when we have a greedy king as we have now that war happens."

She paused for a moment, then went on. "I was told by Miles that the king has declared my lands to be forfeit, and I also heard that Miles himself has been dispatched to Chamoney to take charge of them. Is that so?"

The baron stopped pacing and heaved a sigh. "Yes, I'm afraid so. I sent a message myself to the king, requesting that *I* be sent to Chamoney instead. But His Majesty chose Miles. I had thought to preserve something for you, you see."

Not to mention that you wanted to get away from the Sakim winter, she thought. No doubt he'd had her interests at heart as well.

She waved a hand in dismissal. "It doesn't matter. He can do little damage in the short time he will be there."

"What do you mean?"

"Roderic will make the return of Chamoney a condition of the king's safe return to Neran—and he is prepared to forswear any claim to Chamoney when we marry."

"You're assuming that he will win," the baron reminded her. "But not even Roderic can hope to recapture Varley Castle. This place is impregnable."

"And that is why I've come to see you. I want you to keep the king and his troops out of here."

The look he gave her was incredulous, and her words hung between them, reminding her of just how foolish her hopes had always been.

"You want me to refuse the *king?*"

"I will pay you whatever you ask. I know that you must have needs at your own estate."

"What you intend to pay me is no longer yours to give, niece. And what you ask is beyond a price."

Maryana refused to allow herself to become despondent, despite her uncle's refusal to help Roderic and his army—and despite the dark, cold weather. She sensed something beneath his quick refusal—perhaps an uncertainty that might be festering there.

Naturally the baron was reluctant to put everything he had at risk, but she knew that he was essentially a fair-minded man, and on one occasion, he had even admitted to her that he found the king's behavior quite unappealing.

It was a matter of time, she thought—or rather, hoped. But time was a luxury she didn't have. The days were growing colder and stormier: exactly the sort of weather Roderic had said would work to the Sakims' advantage. And yet, the victory she'd been hoping for hadn't happened.

On the other hand, the Neran army had dug in more than a day's ride from the castle, with the Sakim army in their way, and she had only to see the misery on the faces of the castle's guards to know the toll the weather must be taking on them. And true winter, according to Gisel, was yet weeks away.

It was Gisel who brought her the news. Her uncle either didn't know, or had decided not to share his information with her. But through the other servants and their kin, and through other sources as well, Gisel kept her apprised of the situation.

At one point, the girl told her that she could get a message to Roderic if Maryana so desired, but she thanked the girl and said that she didn't want him to know she was there. She feared what might happen if he learned of her presence in the castle. Instead of pursuing a largely defensive strategy of keeping the Neran army from reaching the castle and waiting for winter to do its work—which Gisel said was his plan—he might then decide to do something reckless in order to rescue her.

Instead, Maryana roamed the great castle. Once, when the fog that seemed to linger all day in the valleys below had cleared, she climbed all the way up to the top of the tallest tower and, shivering in the cold, watched the men fighting some distance away. She could barely make them out, but since the Sakims wore whatever they had while the Nerans wore their dark green uniforms, it was at least possible to tell one side from the other.

They seemed to be fighting all day long over one small piece of ground: a low hill south of the town. And three days later, when the fog lifted again, she found them still battling over the same territory. How foolish it seemed to her!

When she wasn't climbing to the top of the tower, Maryana was exploring the depths of the castle's cellars. She was curious to see whether her uncle had indeed laid in heavy stores of food to feed the troops if they should succeed in getting to the castle.

What she found did not give her heart. Room after room was well filled with supplies, most of it taken from Roderic's people. Several times she saw rats scurrying about in the dank corridors, but the supplies were safe behind stout doors.

Once the idea came to her, she set it to action quickly. She already knew that there were stores of food in other storerooms upstairs, and that, in all likelihood, no one would be coming down here for some time.

So she set about slitting open the bags of grain and tearing apart the wooden crates of other food-stuffs as best she could. Then she left open every door. When she paused at the bottom of the stairs and looked back down the dimly lit corridor, she could already see dark shapes scurrying about. The rats and mice of Varley Castle were about to become very fat indeed.

Men fight wars in their way—and I fight in my own, she thought with satisfaction. Even if the Neran army didn't succeed in reaching Varley Castle, these stores would be needed to feed them and would be carried out to them. With luck, there wouldn't be much left.

On the other hand, if Roderic's men managed to capture the castle, there would be little for them, either. But she doubted that would happen. As Roderic had said, the castle could be defended with very few men.

Several days later, fighting down her fear of the rodents, she went back to the cellars and found that her scheme was working well. Rats and mice scurried into hiding when she shone her lamp into each room.

That night at dinner, her uncle broke his silence about the war raging around them. "Our army has broken through the Sakim ranks," he announced, though she noted that it was with little pleasure. "I am told that they will reach the castle within a few days. The king will not be pleased to find you here, niece."

"Do you want me to leave?" she asked, wondering if what he told her was the truth. Perhaps it was. The weather had perversely turned almost warm, which would certainly improve the situation for the larger Neran army.

"No, of course not. I tell you this only because

His Majesty might order you back to Chamoney, if the weather permits a safe crossing."

"How can he do that, when he has taken Chamoney away from me?" she asked archly.

The baron actually smiled. "I meant, of course, that he will demand you return to Chamoney and marry Sir Miles."

Maryana was silent for a moment. "In that case, uncle, I am asking only that you give me some warning, so that I can leave the castle on my own."

"But, my dear, where will you go? If what I've heard is correct, the weather will change again—for the worse."

"If necessary, I will return to the convent where I lately stayed." She wasn't about to tell him that she would return to Gisel's home.

The baron heaved a sigh. "You have put me in a most difficult situation, niece. I will confess, for your ears only, that if Lord Roderic had succeeded in defeating our army and then attempted to capture the castle, I would have surrendered it to him. It is his by right, and although I could probably hold the castle with the meager contingent I now have, I would have been able to surrender without risking the king's displeasure, since he would have been beaten himself."

Two more days passed, and now Maryana didn't need to go to the top of the tallest tower to see how the battle was progressing. She could see it from the lower battlements—and she knew that her uncle was right. The Neran army was making slow but steady progress through the valley below the castle, and were now nearing the town.

Once, she thought she might have glimpsed Roderic down there. At least she saw a huge gray stallion that looked much like his, though the man on it was no more than a tiny figure.

It occurred to her then that not once had she

truly feared for his life—even though she accepted that he might be defeated. And so, when that thought struck her now, it was with all the force of a stunning blow. Even if he survived the battle, there was no doubt in her mind that the king would have him killed forthwith.

The chill that settled deep inside her owed nothing to the cold winds blowing around her. If Roderic died . . .

She turned away from the view and went instead to find Gisel.

"I may have to leave the castle," she told the girl. "If the king comes here, he will almost certainly order me back to Chamoney."

"I will find a way," Gisel assured her. "The guards don't bother to check when we leave, and you are always welcome to stay with us."

Maryana saw the grim look in the girl's eyes. "Roderic is going to be defeated, isn't he?" she asked quietly, her heart thudding in her throat.

" 'Tis very bad, milady. We were counting on the weather to be our ally, but my mother and all the others who know such things must have been wrong about this winter."

Maryana stayed away from the battlements for the next two days, although her uncle reported that the Neran army had now taken over the town. She thought about them raiding the meager food stores of the people—and doing even worse things. At least Gisel and her family were safe, since their home lay deep in the woods to the north of the castle.

That she would soon have to leave, Maryana accepted. But what was she to do? If Roderic was defeated and then escaped, she could try to reach the convent, knowing he would likely come there to find her and then flee south to the land of the Innish—perhaps to fight again one day.

Or would he come for her? He'd sworn to get his own lands and hers back, and failing that, he might not want to see her again. He'd know that she would be safe in the convent.

She was still mulling over her poor choices and trying to hold at bay her gnawing fear for Roderic's life when there was a knock at her door, and she opened it to find her uncle there, his expression very somber.

"The king is coming," she said, to spare him the necessity of speaking the words.

"Yes, but it is worse than that, my dear." He reached out to take both her hands in his. "Roderic has been killed."

"No!" Her shouted denial echoed off the stone walls. "No! It can't be!"

"I saw it myself, niece. They are now fighting in the town and on the hill leading to the castle—and I saw him fall. He was riding that handsome gray stallion of his."

"But he might have been only wounded!" she cried, clinging to that hope desperately.

But the baron merely shook his head sadly. "The king sent an emissary through the lines to tell me that Roderic had been killed. Even if he were only wounded, he could not have survived. I myself saw the men put those who were wounded to the knife.

"I am sorry," he went on. "I truly liked the man— and admired him. But he is gone."

Tears stung her eyes and dried on her cheeks as Maryana stared across the water at the low, rounded hills of Neran. How strange her homeland now appeared to her, after the dark, craggy hills and deep valleys of Sakim.

She had left Varley Castle the same day she'd learned of Roderic's death—not waiting for the king to order her home. Instead, Gisel had arranged passage for her on a trading ship that was taking advantage of the unusual weather to make a final crossing. And the ship's captain had agreed to arrange with his kin on the Neran coast to see her safely back to Chamoney.

She had not yet begun to consider what awaited her there. As she'd done once before, when she'd believed marriage to Miles Foulane to be inevitable, she had separated from herself, putting one foot before the other into a future that no longer mattered.

Several times during the crossing, she'd stared down into the heaving waters and thought about throwing herself into them. But it was thoughts of Chamoney that stopped her. She had little chance now of regaining it—but she would try. She owed that to her people—and to her father and his father and all who had come before them. It was all that kept her going—but it was enough.

The ship docked in the busy port, and the captain contacted his relations, and soon she was riding through the Neran countryside, where the land was still green and the air was almost warm.

Her tears spilled forth again as she reached the boundaries of Chamoney, which were marked by ancient cairns, some of them engraved with the seal of her family. Instead of going to the chateau, she went to the home of her estate manager, who lived several miles from the great house. But she saw the house, and was somehow shocked to see that nothing was different.

In fact, Chamoney looked the same everywhere. She guessed that the harvest had been bountiful, to judge from the crop stubble remaining in the fields, and on the hillsides the grapevines were now bare, twisted cords, though probably that had been a bountiful harvest as well.

As they passed granaries that were filled to bursting and the scattered cottages of her people, she saw some of them, but kept the hood of her cloak over her face. She couldn't yet bring herself to face them, though she knew she would have to do so at some point.

It was only now that she felt the heavy weight of her betrayal. If she had obeyed the king and married Miles, she might, at least, have been able to protect her people from the worst of his future depradations. But now . . .

She left off her thoughts as they reached the road that led to her manager's handsome stone house, which was nestled against a hillside of winter-dead grapevines. There, she used the last of her coins to pay her escorts, then rode slowly up the long lane.

Claudia, the manager's wife, answered the door herself, then gasped in shock before her round face became wreathed in a welcoming smile.

"Milady! You have come home! What wonderful news! Come in!" And before Maryana could do more than step through the doorway, she was calling her husband, who appeared a moment later and mimicked his wife's disbelief and then pleasure.

When they had settled her down in the kitchen and piled food before her, Maryana knew that she owed them an explanation. So she told them the whole story, leaving out very little. As she talked, Claudia's tears began to flow, and Louis, her husband, looked grimmer and grimmer.

"So I am a traitor," she finished. "And I would not blame you for turning me out. It would be deserved. I care not that I have betrayed the king—but I have also betrayed all of you."

But both husband and wife shook their heads. "You have not betrayed us, milady," her manager said. "This king is not deserving of loyalty—and as for that fool, Miles Foulane . . ." He stopped and lowered his head, shaking it sadly.

"Is he here?" she asked.

"Aye, he's here. But he's done little as yet except to hold parties at your home: great drunken affairs with his worthless friends from court."

Maryana winced at the thought of Miles and his friends in her lovely home, but said nothing.

" 'Tis not true that he's done nothing, Louis," his wife remonstrated gently. "He is spending your fortune as fast as he can—and claiming that Louis is holding out on him."

"Which is true, of course," the manager said with a brief smile. "Fortunately, the man has no head for figures or he'd know I'm lying, instead of just suspecting it."

"When the king returns, will he force you to marry Miles?" Claudia asked.

"Perhaps not. It may be that Miles has decided he would rather not have me here at all, since the king has given over Chamoney to his oversight. In fact, I think that will be the case."

"And what will you do, milady?"

"I don't know."

She spent that night as their guest, and the following day Louis took her to the small cottage in the hills where her father and his friends had often gone to hunt. Little more was said about her future, and in truth, she herself gave no thought to it. Instead, she retreated to her memories of the great estate, and then let Roderic into her dreams at night.

Louis brought her her favorite mare, and as the weather remained pleasant—warm even for Neran—she began to go for rides. She took care to avoid going near the chateau, but she couldn't help seeing it many times, from distant hilltops. It beckoned to her, reminding her of happy childhood days and of busy but equally happy times when the running of the great estate had been her responsibility.

Her people obviously quickly learned that she'd returned—and where she was living. A few came in the early evenings to see her, but more brought gifts and left them at her doorstep overnight, coming and going in silence. She could easily identify the giver by the gift: fragrant herbal wreaths from one woman, smooth-as-silk sweetcakes from another, a delicious fish stew from her cook. Their kindnesses invariably brought tears to her eyes, as did the young girl who had showed up her first morning there, insisting that she be allowed to take care of the cottage for Maryana.

All in all, though it was a poor substitute for Roderic's love, Maryana accepted it gratefully.

It was probably inevitable that she would encounter Miles at some point, even though she stayed well away from the chateau. And so, on a day that seemed to be signaling a shift in the weather, she rode along a path at the edge of a wide field—and saw him coming toward her.

It was too late to turn around. She knew he'd seen her, so she simply brought the mare to a halt and waited. He rode hard at her, then reined in his mount viciously. Maryana saw flecks of blood around the gelding's mouth.

"How long have you been here?" he demanded.

"Not long," she replied coolly.

"These are not your lands any longer. You must leave."

"These will always be my lands, Miles—as they were my ancestors' lands before me." Her voice was calm, contrasting with his loud, harsh tone.

"I knew you'd come—once I heard about his death. But I no longer wish to marry you. I have what I want already."

"I didn't for one moment think that you would want to marry me, Miles," she said with a smile. "I've always known exactly what you wanted. I even told you that."

"I'm ordering you to leave Chamoney!"

"And I am telling you that I intend to stay. If you want me to leave, you will have to kill me—and the prospect of that no longer frightens me." She spoke the words in a low voice that still carried with it such vehemence that he was obviously taken aback. For a long moment they stared at each other in silence, and then he abruptly wheeled his mount around and rode off.

So she waited. She knew that he would send someone to get rid of her—most likely thugs for hire. She would fight them—and she would force them to kill her, just as she'd told him. Her life had little value now, but she intended to die on her own land, and not in some convent.

But when a visitor came two days after her encounter with Miles, it was not a hired thug, but Louis, her manager. Maryana saw his grim expression as he dismounted in the front yard of the cottage, and she felt sympathy for him. He had undoubtedly been forced to choose between his job and her, and his family had lived on the estate for many generations. Furthermore, he was no longer a young man.

"I have some unpleasant news, milady," he said after greeting her as she stood on the steps of the cottage.

"I know that Miles has sent you to get rid of me, Louis—and I don't blame you for following his orders. But I will not leave. He will have to hire someone to kill me."

He looked shocked, and then his mobile face settled into an expression of grim satisfaction. "Sir Miles will not be giving me or anyone else any orders, milady. I came to tell you that he is dead."

"Dead?" Maryana reached out to grasp the stone porch post. "I don't understand. How did he die?"

For one brief, giddy moment, she thought that

Roderic had come back, and was making good on his promise to restore her lands to her.

"He was riding this morning up near the old quarry, and from the smell of him, I'd say he was drunk. There are dangerous spots up there, as you well know, milady. If he'd been sober, he would have seen that for himself.

"From what I can tell, his horse must have stepped in a hole and he fell off. That wouldn't have killed him—except that he fell into the deepest of the quarries. You know the one."

She did—and she couldn't imagine why Miles would have been riding up there, drunk or sober. It was an ugly place: bare, rocky ground with hidden holes, and the played-out quarries themselves.

"I can only guess that he must have wanted to see for himself that the quarries were played out. I know he didn't believe me when I told him that."

Maryana moved back into her chateau the following day, after Miles's body had been removed to his family home, escorted by Louis, who explained the cause of his death to his sister and her husband.

"They didn't seem to take it too hard," Louis told her when he returned. "What kind of man doesn't even have kin who weep at his death?"

She followed him to the door, where he turned back and smiled at her. "Welcome home, milady. I can speak for all of us when I say that we're mighty pleased to have you back."

Maryana thanked him, then watched as he mounted his horse and rode down the winding road. She'd gotten over the shock of Miles's death and had had time to think about it. And though she doubted that she would ever be truly certain, she suspected that the story Louis had given her was not the truth.

She lifted her hand and looked down at Roderic's ring, thinking that he would have been pleased to know that Miles Foulane was no longer among the living, though in all likelihood, he would regret that *he* hadn't been the instrument of his death.

The maid who had packed up Miles's belongings had brought her the ring, not knowing its significance, of course, but shrewdly guessing that it had originally been hers. He'd likely intended to sell it, but apparently it had become insignificant after he'd gotten his greedy hands on her money.

Winter came late to Chamoney, but it came with a vengeance. No one, not even the oldest of her people, could recall such a winter. Snow, a rarity in this land, blanketed the fields and lay heavily on the trees and roofs, some of which finally collapsed under the unaccustomed weight.

However, before the winter set in, and then again when a false spring briefly teased the land, stories reached her from those few traders who had braved the straits. By the time they reached her ears, they had passed through many lips and ears, so she didn't know how true they were.

One report said that the Nerans had reached Varley Castle and were holed up there for the winter. Another story claimed that the Sakims had not been defeated, after all, because the Innish army had come in on their side.

And then, during the brief false spring, another report came that Varley Castle was about to fall to the Sakims again, because they were without both food and water inside the castle.

Maryana was inclined to believe the part about the lack of food, since she'd played a role in that. But she considered it unlikely that rodents had gotten enough of the food, given that the Nerans were so close to the castle when she left. And the story about the water rang false. Roderic had told her that the castle had a plentiful supply from an underground stream.

Neither did it seem likely that the Innish had come to the aid of the Sakims in time to make any difference.

So she tended to discount the stories, though in her dreams she gave rein to her hopes and even let herself believe that Roderic had somehow survived.

It was the worst winter Sakim had seen in living memory—perhaps the worst ever. The snows fell almost without surcease, and icy winds found every crack and clawed at the people huddling inside.

But on a day when the snows didn't fall and the winds had died down a bit, six men on horses made their way slowly through the forest. They were completely anonymous in their multiple layers of clothing and their knitted masks, though any Neran would have known them instantly for the enemy. While the Nerans froze in great numbers in their woolen uniforms and greatcoats, the Sakims had long ago learned the art of layering their clothing for warmth. And for years they'd been wearing the knitted masks with holes for eyes, nose, and mouth that had so terrified the Nerans when they had first seen them.

Even the horses with their shaggy coats wore warm blankets to cover their flanks and bellies as the group slowly pushed through snow until the animals could go no farther. Then the group left them tethered in the shelter of the pines and went forward on foot, wearing strange contraptions made of pliant willow branches crisscrossed with leather strips attached to their boots.

Each man carried either a pick or a shovel as they made their way single-file through the woods. Several times their leader stopped briefly and pulled the mask from his face. Then, after listening for a moment, he replaced the mask and they continued on their way.

Presently they came to their goal: a thundering waterfall that ran free even in the worst of winters, plunging into a surprisingly small pond at its base. And there they began to dig and to pile up stones, until the waterfall was diverted almost entirely, and began to flood the surrounding land, where it began to turn to ice even as they continued to work.

"I can only hope that you're right," said one man as he rested momentarily, leaning on his shovel. "I'd hate to think that all this work has been for naught."

"I'm right. In a day or two, they're going to be wondering what happened to their water."

"Aye. First not enough food, and now no water. Are ye thinking what I'm thinking: that the lady Maryana had something to do with the rats getting at their food stores?"

"I never doubted it."

Never had a spring been so welcome—and never had it been so lovely, as though nature herself had wanted to remind people that she could also be gentle and lovely.

Maryana felt the warmth seep into her, too, though with spring came a renewal of her fears about her future. She continued to hear tales of Varley Castle falling once again to the Sakims, but she wouldn't let herself believe them. She remained certain that the king would soon come home in victory, and would either order her to a convent or find someone else for her to marry. She'd been given a reprieve from having her lands stripped—and that was all.

And so, on a glorious day when she was on a hillside, riding with Louis and her vineyard master to inspect the damage done to the vines, she cherished the moment, because she knew it couldn't last. The most she could hope for was that the king would choose a husband for her, and that he wouldn't be as terrible as Miles.

"The damage isn't as bad as I'd feared, milady," the vineyard master said as he examined the vines. And she could see that he was right. On nearly all of them, there were tiny green shoots.

She turned to stare down at the fields spread out below them, where green shoots gave color to the land beneath a gentle blue sky. And then she frowned. Someone was riding toward them—riding very fast.

Louis had seen the rider, too. "Someone's in an almighty hurry," he said as he got out his spyglass and trained it on the rider.

"I don't recognize either him or his horse. A fine animal, though."

The rider was coming steadily closer, and then he vanished from sight at the base of the hill. Maryana turned to Louis. "Is it an emissary from the king, perhaps?" she asked, trying to hide her apprehension.

"No, I don't think so. He wasn't wearing the king's green."

So they stood there and waited to see if the rider was coming their way. It seemed likely that he was, but he was still hidden from their view.

Then suddenly he came into sight again, his speed scarcely diminished even as he rode up the hill. Maryana made a small, strangled sound that she tried unsuccessfully to disguise by coughing.

"What is it, milady?" the manager asked in alarm, at the same time reaching for the long knife at his belt.

"That horse! I . . ." She shook her head and looked away as tears filled her eyes. "It can't be! Roderic's dead!"

She didn't want to look up as she heard the horse draw near, but her face came up anyway. Both the horse and the rider were blurred by her tears, and then Louis stepped quickly between her and the visitor.

"State your business, sir! I am the manager of this estate."

"I'm pleased to meet you then, but at the moment, I'm most eager to see the lady who is hiding behind you."

Her blood was roaring in her ears, but even so, there was no mistaking that voice. Still, it took forever for her to accept what she was hearing, and by that time he had dismounted and was standing before her, with Louis hovering nearby uncertainly.

"You're *dead!*" she blurted, then pressed a hand to her mouth and held it there.

"Apparently no one bothered to tell me that," he said in his gently mocking voice. "Perhaps if you read this, you will believe."

He held the parchment out and unrolled it, and the eyes that couldn't seem to meet his fell on it instead. She gasped as she read the words—and then she finally met his eyes.

"I am a man of my word, love—even though it took me longer than I'd intended."

Then, seeing that Louis was trying to read it as well, he handed it over to him. "But give it back, since I want to have the pleasure of shoving it in the face of Miles Foulane."

The estate manager's face creased in a broad smile. "Then I'm afraid that's one pleasure you'll be forced to forgo, Lord Roderic. Miles Foulane is dead and buried."

Roderic turned back to her and used his thumbs to brush away her tears. "Well, that was only a secondary pleasure. Would you like to invite me to your chateau, milady?"

She gave him her hand, and he lifted her into the saddle and leaped up behind her. The gray stallion carried them both easily as they rode back alongside the fields and up the winding road to the chateau.

"I don't understand, Roderic. Were they all lies? Did my uncle lie to me as well?"

Stretched naked on her bed, he reached for the glass of wine on the silver tray between them, which was heaped with cheeses and some dried fruits. He shook his head.

"No, the baron didn't lie. He *did* see someone fall from my horse and then be killed by Neran soldiers—but it wasn't me."

"Someone else was riding your horse?" she asked, still confused.

"Yes. I was on my way south at the time. I'd received a message from the Innish duke that they were willing to send troops, but only if *I* came to lead them.

"I knew that my absence would provoke confusion and fear, so Tom and I found someone to stand in for me. Only he and I knew the truth."

"Then you *did* capture Varley Castle—with the help of the Innish."

"They were of some help, yes—but in the end, we took the castle because its defenders ran out of food and water."

"But how could they have run out of water? You told me—"

"What I'd like to know is how they managed to run out of *food*. We knew they'd laid in great stores. I heard that somehow the rats and mice got at them, and when I returned to the castle, I saw that was the truth."

He stared hard at her. "In all my years there, we never had a problem like that. We always set traps and then closed the doors when we'd gotten rid of them."

"It's possible that someone opened those doors," she said with a grin. "And it's even possible that the same someone slit open the sacks and tore open the crates."

He threw back his head and laughed. "Maryana's war against the Nerans—and a very effective one at that."

"But you haven't explained about the water. I could do nothing about that."

"You couldn't—but I did. Years ago I became curious about the source of the underground stream that feeds the castle's wells, and I managed to find it several miles west of the castle.

"There's a waterfall. I suspected that it was the source because there was too much water pouring down, and only a small pool at its base, with no runoff stream.

"So we went out there and created several runoff streams—and it worked because the flow is somewhat restricted by ice in the winter anyway."

"So the king was forced to surrender. But what about my uncle?"

"The king tried to sneak out of the castle and get back across the straits during a brief letup in the weather. But we'd anticipated that and were waiting for him.

"Then your uncle immediately surrendered the castle to me. He's still there. I asked him to wait so that he can be present for our wedding. He seemed quite pleased—but not exactly surprised—when I told him that I intended to restore your lands to you as a condition of the king's surrender, and to make no claims upon them myself."

"He wasn't surprised because I'd told him you intended to do just that."

He held his crystal wineglass up to a ray of sun and studied the clear, red liquid inside. "I have to say that His Majesty wasn't quite so gracious. I told him he should consider himself fortunate that I had decided to be so magnanimous in victory and not seize any of his lands."

Then he set down the wineglass and picked up her hand to stare at the ring. She'd already explained that it had been found among Miles's belongings.

"I truly wanted to kill him—Miles, I mean. All the way across, I was envisioning the scene. But in a way I'm glad that it was not I who killed him. I've had enough of blood and death to last more than a lifetime."

"I'm not sure, but I don't think Miles's death was an accident."

"It wasn't."

She was so startled by his words—and the certainty behind them—that she choked on her wine, and a few drops dribbled off her chin and ran in a rivulet between her breasts. Roderic leaned over and licked them off.

"What do you mean?" she demanded.

"I like Louis. He's a good man. But I could see it in his eyes when he told me of Miles's death."

She nodded. "I thought as much. He would never tell me, though, would he?"

Roderic laughed. "Probably not. By the way, I took the liberty of telling His Royal Neran Majesty that no more taxes will be coming to him from Chamoney for a while. So that should keep him in unaccustomed poverty for a bit while our countries rebuild."

Maryana, who sat cross-legged and naked on the bed, with the brocaded coverlet pooled about her loins, threw back her head and laughed. "What a fine idea! Now that money can go to Sakim, to help repair the damages from the war."

"My thoughts exactly—though of course the decision is really yours to make. I meant what I said

357

about Chamoney being yours, love. You may do with it as you wish."

"What I wish right now," she said, removing the silver tray from between them, "is for you to make love to me again."

He arched a dark brow. "I suppose you've already guessed that I'm the weak sort of man who would take orders from a woman."

She laughed, but he did as she wished.

Futuristic Romance

Star-Crossed

Saranne Dawson

Bestselling Author Of *Crystal Enchantment*

Rowena is a master artisan, a weaver of enchanted tapestries that whisper of past glories. Yet not even magic can help her foresee that she will be sent to assassinate an enemy leader. Her duty is clear—until the seductive beauty falls under the spell of the man she must kill.

His reputation says that he is a warmongering barbarian. But Zachary MacTavesh prefers conquering damsels' hearts over pillaging fallen cities. One look at Rowena tells him to gird his loins and prepare for the battle of his life. And if he has his way, his stunningly passionate rival will reign victorious as the mistress of his heart.

_51982-8 $4.99 US/$5.99 CAN

BEYOND BETRAYAL

CHRISTINE MICHELS

Disguised as the law, outlaw Samson Towers travels to Red Rock, Montana, where he finds the one woman that can knock down the pillars of his deception and win his heart— a temptress named Delilah Sterne. While the lovely widow finds herself drawn to the town's sheriff, the beautiful gambler suddenly fears she's played the wrong cards—and sentenced the man she loves to death. Her heart in danger, she knows that she must save the handsome Samson and prove that their love can exist beyond betrayal.

___52264-0 $5.50 US/$6.50 CAN

Dorchester Publishing Co., Inc.
P.O. Box 6640
Wayne, PA 19087-8640

Please add $1.75 for shipping and handling for the first book and $.50 for each book thereafter. NY, NYC, and PA residents, please add appropriate sales tax. No cash, stamps, or C.O.D.s. All orders shipped within 6 weeks via postal service book rate. Canadian orders require $2.00 extra postage and must be paid in U.S. dollars through a U.S. banking facility.

Name_____
Address_____
City_____State_____Zip_____
I have enclosed $_____ in payment for the checked book(s).
Payment <u>must</u> accompany all orders. ❏ Please send a free catalog.
    CHECK OUT OUR WEBSITE! www.dorchesterpub.com

Something Wild

Kimberly Raye

Dependent only upon twentieth-century conveniences, Tara Martin seeks to make a name for herself as a top-notch photojournalist. But when a plea from her best friend sends her off into the Smoky Mountains to snap a sasquatch, a twisted ankle leaves her in a precarious position—and when she looks up, she sees the biggest foot she's ever seen. Tara learns that the big foot belongs to an even bigger man—with a colossal heart and a body to die for. And that man, who was raised alone in the wilds of Appalachia, will teach Tara that what she needs is something wild.

___52272-1 $5.50 US/$6.50 CAN

The MASK

DONNA LEE POFF

Sitting in the moonlight at the edge of the forest, she appears to him as a delicate wood elf, but Anne of Thornbury is no spritely illusion. A fresh-faced village girl, Anne has no experience with love, until she meets the brave yet reclusive lord with the hidden face and mysterious history. She soon realizes that only with her love can Galen finally overcome the past and release his heart from the shadow of the mask.

___4416-1 $4.99 US/$5.99 CAN

Janeen O'Kerry
QUEEN of The SUN

Riding along the Irish countryside, Teresa MacEgan is swept into a magical Midsummer's Eve that lands her in ancient Eire. There the dark-haired beauty encounters the quietly seductive King Conaire of Dun Cath. Tall and regal, he kindles a fiery need within her, and she longs to yield to his request to become his queen but can relinquish her independence to no one. But when an enemy endangers Dun Cath's survival, Terri finds herself facing a fearsome choice: desert the only man she'd ever loved, or join her king of the moon and become the queen of the sun.

___52269-1 $4.99 US/$5.99 CAN

Catherine Archibald — HAWK'S LADY

Haughty young Lady Kayln D'Arcy only wants what is best for her little sister, Celia, when she travels to the imposing fortress of Hawkhurst. For the brother of Hawkhurst's dark lord has wooed Celia, and Kayln is determined to make him do the honorable thing. Tall, arrogant and imperious, Hawk has the burning eyes of a bird of prey and a gentle touch that can make Kayln nearly forget why she is there. As for Hawk, never before has he encountered a woman like the proud, fiery Kayln. But can Hawk catch his prey? Can he make her...Hawk's lady?

___4312-2 $4.99 US/$5.99 CAN

SEDUCED

CATHERINE LANIGAN

**"Catherine Lanigan is in a class by herself:
unequaled and simply fabulous!"**
—Affaire de Coeur

Even amid the spectacle and splendor of the carnival in
Venice, the masked rogue is brazen, reckless, and
dangerously risque. As he steals Valentine St. James away
from the costume ball at which her betrothal to a complete
stranger is to be announced, the exquisite beauty revels in
the illicit thrill of his touch, the tender passion in his kiss.
But Valentine learns that illusion rules the festival when, at
the stroke of midnight, her mysterious suitor reveals he is
Lord Hawkeston, the very man she is to wed. Convinced
her intended is an unrepentant scoundrel, Valentine wants
to deny her maddening attraction for him, only to keep
finding herself in his heated embrace. Yet is she truly losing
her heart to the dashing peer—or is she being ruthlessly
seduced?
_3942-7 $5.50 US/$7.50 CAN

THE LION'S BRIDE — CONNIE MASON

Winner of the *Romantic Times* Storyteller Of The Year Award!

Lord Lyon of Normandy has saved William the Conqueror from certain death on the battlefield, yet neither his strength nor his skill can defend him against the defiant beauty the king chooses for his wife.

Ariana of Cragmere has lost her lands and her virtue to the mighty warrior, but the willful beauty swears never to surrender her heart.

Saxon countess and Norman knight, Ariana and Lyon are born enemies. And in a land rent asunder by bloody wars and shifting loyalties, they are doomed to misery unless they can vanquish the hatred that divides them—and unite in glorious love.

_3884-6   **$5.99 US/$7.99 CAN**